OUTCASTS

OUTCASTS

TROY DENNING

BASED ON THE BESTSELLING VIDEO GAME FOR XBOX®

G

GALLERY BOOKS

New York London Toronto Sydney New Delhi

G

Gallery Books
An Imprint of Simon & Schuster, Inc.
1230 Avenue of the Americas
New York, NY 10020

First Gallery Books trade paperback edition August 2023

GALLERY BOOKS and colophon are registered trademarks of Simon & Schuster, Inc.

For information about special discounts for bulk purchases, please contact Simon & Schuster Special Sales at 1-866-506-1949 or business@simonandschuster.com.

The Simon & Schuster Speakers Bureau can bring authors to your live event. For more information or to book an event, contact the Simon & Schuster Speakers Bureau at 1-866-248-3049 or visit our website at www.simonspeakers.com.

Manufactured in the United States of America

10 9 8 7 6 5

Library of Congress Control Number: 2023934319

ISBN 978-1-6680-0328-2
ISBN 978-1-6680-0329-9 (ebook)

For Tiffany O'Brien and Jeremy Patenaude
What a pleasure I had working with you!

HISTORIAN'S NOTE

This story takes place in November 2559, following the destruction of Doisac by Forerunner Guardians controlled by the AI Cortana, and shortly before the Banished attack on Zeta Halo.

CHAPTER 1

Perhaps the high kaidons *wanted* the Sangheili to remain divided and weak.

That was the only explanation Arbiter Thel 'Vadam could imagine for their squabbling and intransigence, for putting their own interests above the need to stand strong and united. Did they truly expect the Tyrant's "peace" to protect Sangheili space from the encroachments of the Jiralhanae and the Kig-Yar? To overcome mercenary legions, Covenant remnants, and any last vestiges of the San'Shyuum? That was a sand song. Even the Tyrant Cortana and her army of artificial intelligence spies could not watch every asteroid in every system, could not turn back every moon grab at the edge of every sector. Only the Sangheili themselves could protect their colonies—and only if they came together to create a Concert of Worlds so capable that no thief would *dare* test it.

But the Sangheili had lived under the deceptions of the Covenant for more than two thousand orbits, and they had grown complacent. Their kaidons had forgotten how easily prosperity could be stolen, how swiftly a keep could become a prison. Now, instead of learning from their recent history, they accepted the Tyrant's lies as fact and trusted her despotism to protect the holdings of their clans.

They were fools.

The Covenant had kept order not just because of its strength, but because of its unity. Its San'Shyuum hierarchs had used religious fables to bring together its member species, promising that all true believers would ascend to divine transsentience. Cortana offered no such hope. She brought only fear and subjugation, and she promised nothing but death to those who defied her.

How could the high kaidons not see that Cortana's hand was already on their throats? She was crushing all that made the Sangheili strong, their discipline and honor and courage, and the kaidons were happy to let her . . . so long as she allowed them to believe they were still masters of their own worlds.

The Crav in which 'Vadam was riding came to an abrupt stop, then sat hovering on its propulsion field. He grabbed a plasma repeater off the cabin wall and opened the rear firing port. They had stopped in the cramped confines of the Old Borough. A mazelike warren of narrow lanes lined by stone domiciles with no windows on the ground floor, it was an ideal place for an ambush . . . and given the divisions at the High Gathering today, 'Vadam was certainly ready for one.

In Sangheili culture, assassination was the customary way to settle disagreements with authority, and as the reigning Arbiter, 'Vadam was the closest thing the Sangheili had to a supreme leader. That was why he had elected to send his Phantom ahead as a decoy—and covertly return home in an armored ground racer.

When 'Vadam saw no threats in the street behind the Crav, he glanced forward. His two escorts sat opposite him on rear-facing saddles. They were peering out through the side-door firing ports, their reddish helmets tipping and rocking as they searched nearby rooftops for firebomb casters and plasma cannons. It was almost unthinkable for a Sangheili to use such weapons to assassinate a superior, but that did not make it impossible. During the Blooding Years, the Sangheili civil war that had erupted after the Covenant fell, 'Vadam's enemies had done many unthinkable things to their own kind.

At times, 'Vadam wondered if he had, as well.

But no attack came. The partition at the front of the passenger cabin descended into its pocket, revealing 'Vadam's adjunct, N'tho 'Sraom, in the drop-deck operator's compartment. Like 'Vadam himself, the young warrior wore no armor, only a belted red tunic that covered his saurian body to the knees. His pebbly brown face and golden eyes were less oval than most, and his four mandibles a little shorter than the Sangheili norm.

"Have no alarm, Arbiter," 'Sraom said. His head was half-turned, so that one diamond-shaped pupil was looking back and up into the passenger cabin. "It is only a Tyrant checkpoint."

'Vadam leaned down so he could look through the forward viewscreen. A trio of the Tyrant's armigers stood in the lane, blocking the way. Standing a full head taller than most Sangheili warriors, they had bipedal frames that resembled nothing quite so much as disarticulated suits of armor. Here and there, a ghostly orange light limned the edge of a silvery plate or shone through a seam. A similar glow showed through the eye and mouth openings of their masked helmets, creating the impression of sinister-looking faces.

'Vadam knew without looking that another squad would be stepping into the street behind the Crav, emerging from its hiding place to block any retreat attempt. Whether armigers were purely robotic or sentient-infused hybrids remained unclear to him, but he had no doubts about their effectiveness. They were Forerunner-designed constructs fabricated many millennia ago—presumably to police civilizations deemed lower than that of the armigers' makers—and they executed their tasks with ruthless and cold efficiency. They wielded advanced Forerunner energy weapons like light rifles and suppressors, and they knew how to use both assets to maximum tactical advantage. Some were even quicker than human Spartans.

It made 'Vadam's skin burn to see the Tyrant's forces patrolling his ancestral home in the Vadam Valley, but he did not dare destroy them. She would only send more, and when he destroyed those, she would send a Guardian.

And for a Guardian, 'Vadam had no answer.

No one did. Constructed by the Forerunners to impose order in their ancient ecumene, Guardians were so powerful they could destroy a planet's infrastructure in mere moments. Now the Tyrant employed them as weapons of terror, using them to enforce her "peace" as she had just three days earlier at Doisac, when she used them to punish the defiance of the Banished warmaster Atriox by destroying the homeworld of the entire Jiralhanae species.

'Vadam considered Atriox a looming threat and the Jiralhanae in general his potential enemies, but the last thing he wanted was the Tyrant imposing her peace on them. Because if she was willing to use her Guardians against Doisac, she was willing to use them against Sanghelios, and no one knew how to neutralize them. The only hope 'Vadam could see was to overwhelm her forces with a grand alliance of interstellar civilizations, but he had no prospect of making *that* happen. He could not even unite the worlds of the Sangheili, much less those of the other spacefaring species.

When 'Sraom kept the Crav hovering in place, the lead armiger approached the left side of the operator's compartment and pointed to the ground, ordering him to kill the propulsion field. The armiger's armor was more white than their typical silver, and the light shining out through its eye and mouth openings was yellow rather than orange, with its head armor fanning out to both sides. It was an Officer, probably the squad leader. The second and third armigers remained in front of the vehicle, their light rifles pointed at the forward viewscreen.

"This does not look like a normal checkpoint," 'Sraom said, speaking over his shoulder and ignoring the lead armiger's order. "Perhaps we should push through. It could be an arrest action."

"If so, they already know who we are, and they will be ready to stop us," said Kola 'Baoth, a ranger who often served 'Vadam as an escort. 'Baoth wore the red-orange armor of the Swords of Sanghelios. Once an alliance of keeps that was the closest thing the Sangheili had had to a central government, the Swords of Sanghelios were now a group of forces united under 'Vadam's leadership in pursuit of the same ideals as the original Swords: a formal union of all Sangheili worlds. "We should not give them an excuse to turn it into an execution."

"Let us hear what they want," said Usze 'Taham, the second escort. Before the Blooding Years, he had been known as one of the deadliest Special Operations commandos in the Covenant. Now 'Taham served 'Vadam in a variety of roles. Today, he was both adviser and escort, and he wore armor identical to 'Baoth's. "If it comes to a fight, it will be better to leave the Crav."

"Agreed," 'Vadam said.

Manufactured by Iruiru Armory in western Yermo, the Crav was essentially an incognito armored personnel carrier designed for the low-profile transport of civilian dignitaries. In place of weapons mounts, it had a reinforced cabin large enough to carry six individuals, and the armor could deflect the strikes of most portable plasma cannons. But against the kind of hard light and antimatter artillery the armigers could call into action, it was a soft target.

"Keep the propulsion field active," 'Vadam continued. "But be prepared to depart the vehicle. Usze, you will see what they want."

"As you command." 'Taham waited until 'Sraom had unlatched the driver's canopy and 'Baoth had unsealed the door on his side of the compartment, then lifted his own door partially open and called out, "You can speak to me. I am leaving the vehicle."

The Officer raised its light rifle and retreated a single pace into the lane. 'Taham lifted the door the rest of the way and, leaving his plasma repeater in its mount, stepped out of the Crav.

"Why have you stopped us?" 'Taham asked calmly. He was standing between the Officer and the Crav's open door, but the armiger was so tall it could peer over his helmet into the passenger compartment. "I am traveling with Arbiter Thel 'Vadam, and this delay is placing his safety in danger."

"What is the nature of this danger?" The Officer's voice was crisp and monotone, but its Sangheili was as proper and precise as a diplomat's. "Do you flee someone?"

"No. We are traveling in disguise and taking a secondary route so we will have no *need* to flee anyone. It is a standard practice, to protect against assassination attempts."

"Then you are expecting an assassination attempt?"

"Not at all," 'Taham said. "We are *prepared* for one. There is a difference."

"Explain this difference."

As the Officer spoke, it continued to peer over 'Taham's helmet into the passenger compartment. The second armiger remained in front of the Crav while the third stepped around to 'Baoth's side of the vehicle. 'Vadam was beginning to feel like a *gatt* trapped in a barn full of *terrets*. 'Taham had already confirmed 'Vadam was in the vehicle, and the Officer was *still* trying to get a look inside. Either it thought 'Taham was lying, or it was looking for someone else.

"The difference is this," 'Vadam replied, moving forward to place himself in full view. "It is better to be prepared for an attack that never comes than to be surprised by the one that does. But you know that. Otherwise, you would not have taken the time to put us into a crossfire before demanding to search our vehicle."

"Then you intend to cooperate with our search?" the Officer asked.

"That depends on what you are looking for," 'Vadam said. "And whether you are truthful in your answer."

"There has been a street fight with a number of casualties," the Officer said. "We are searching for those responsible."

"Do we appear to have been involved in a common street fight?" 'Taham demanded. "This is the Arbiter of the Sangheili. Stand aside and let him return to his keep."

The Officer continued to peer over 'Taham's helmet at 'Vadam and said, "You have been provided a truthful answer. What follows next is your decision."

"We will consent to your search," 'Vadam answered quickly. Armigers thought and communicated with the speed of artificial intelligences, so even the tiniest delay might be taken as a prelude to combat—and given what had just happened to Doisac, he was taking no chances. "Allow us to leave the vehicle, and you may look inside."

"Your cooperation will be noted," the Officer said. "Proceed."

'Sraom deactivated the Crav's propulsion field and climbed out of the operator's compartment, then 'Vadam and 'Baoth returned their plasma repeaters to the wall mounts and stepped out on 'Taham's side of the vehicle. The four Sangheili were now armed with only the energy swords hanging on their belts, but if they found themselves in a sudden close-quarters fight, it would be their swords they wanted.

The armiger Officer retreated a few steps to keep all four Sangheili in its firing arc. The second armiger remained in front of the Crav, while the third, on the side opposite the Sangheili, ducked through the open door to inspect the passenger cabin. 'Vadam glanced up the lane behind the vehicle and was not surprised to see that a fourth and fifth armiger had now emerged from hiding. They were setting up a monopod-mounted splinter turret, a fearsome infantry weapon that fired projectiles of fragmenting hard light.

"That must have been quite the street fight," 'Vadam remarked, looking toward the splinter turret. "Light artillery is not usually required to handle such a situation."

"A tenement island was badly damaged," the Officer replied. "The survivors may need another home. We have been tasked with preventing a similar incident."

The tenement islands of Vadam Valley were large compounds where the forge-working clans in service to the Kolaar Manufactorum lived. Unlike the single-brood merchant domiciles that lined the Old Borough's transit lanes, the tenement islands housed hundreds of Sangheili and their young. For one to be damaged so badly that it caused fatalities and left the survivors homeless suggested heavy combat.

Normally, it would be the protective legion of Vadam Keep apprehending the combatants and ensuring that no further destruction occurred. But the Tyrant's administrator had disarmed and disbanded all keephold forces on Sanghelios, and now the entire world had to rely on the armigers for routine security functions. Even 'Vadam could see how the high kaidons might doubt that Cortana would allow his proposed Concert of Worlds to provide the kind of protection they needed.

"Then put your splinter turret away," 'Vadam said, returning his gaze to the Officer. "If you open fire with such a weapon, you will be the cause of another incident."

"Your concern is noted. We will use only the force necessary to apprehend the instigators." The Officer pointed over 'Vadam's head. "The inspection of your vehicle is now complete. You may resume your journey as soon as you surrender the rest of your weapons."

'Vadam turned and saw the third armiger rising from the far side of the Crav, a trio of plasma repeaters stacked in the crook of one arm. It started to step back, then noticed the needle rifle tucked into a scabbard in the operator's compartment and retrieved that too.

"You want our weapons?" 'Vadam continued to watch as the third armiger began to pile them on the street. "That is an insult."

"After tonight's events, the administrator is no longer willing to trust Sangheili with personal weapons," the Officer said. "Please remove the energy swords from your belts and leave them in the street for immediate disposal."

"We cannot do that," 'Baoth said, stepping between 'Vadam and the armiger. "And we will not."

"The Arbiter must be able to protect himself." 'Taham stepped to 'Baoth's side. "On this, we will not—"

"Hold, Usze." Knowing what would happen if 'Taham finished his sentence, 'Vadam clasped his shoulder and pulled him back. "We are in no position to offer ultimatums."

"It is well you recognize that," the Officer said. His weapon was pointed at 'Vadam's chest, but the second armiger was aiming his light rifle at the back of 'Taham's helmet. "An ultimatum from the Arbiter would not be allowed to stand."

"Then listen to reason," 'Taham said. "The Arbiter has many enemies. If he cannot protect himself—"

"The Arbiter is no longer responsible for protecting himself. Nor are you."

As the Officer spoke, the second armiger reabsorbed its light rifle into its arm, then stepped past the Crav operator's compartment and reached for the energy sword on 'Sraom's belt.

When 'Sraom cast a questioning gaze in 'Vadam's direction, he let out his breath and nodded. As much as it galled him to yield to the Tyrant's minions, it was better than dying in a pointless standoff.

"Your Arbiter's safety is *our* responsibility now," the lead armiger continued. "By decree of the Archon Cortana."

CHAPTER 2

Set deep beneath an overhang of rhyolite bedrock at the end of a narrow box canyon, the Mountain Gate of Vadam Keep looked more like a bunker entrance than a service door. The approach was through a crooked gorge barely wide enough for two small vehicles, and it was lined by firing positions that could be accessed only from within the keep. The door itself, barely visible in the dim green glow of two sky-shielded lights, was a single slab of energy-shielded nanolaminate that could not be breached by any weapon small enough to reach it.

Which seemed a good thing right now.

Before leaving the Old Borough, 'Vadam and his now-weaponless companions had been waved through two more checkpoints, and as they climbed into the foothills of Kolaar Mountain, they had seen another fifty checkpoints scattered across the entire breadth of Vadam Valley. 'Taham had even spotted a flight of the Tyrant's Aethras swirling through the darkness overhead, and one of those stalker craft was still trailing the Crav now. Whether it was watching to make sure the transport reached home safely or just confirming its stated destination, 'Vadam had no way of knowing. But he felt certain of one thing: whoever the armigers were hunting, they were more than common rabble-rousers.

As the gate rose in front of their vehicle, 'Vadam turned to 'Taham. "We Sangheili are a proud species, and that makes us combative. Perhaps too combative."

"It is our greatest strength," 'Taham replied. "Also our greatest weakness. You are thinking of the high kaidons?"

'Vadam swung his mandible chins up and to the right, a gesture of agreement. "The High Gathering has been filled with angry words. Too many have been mine." He paused. "The Blooding Years are barely over, if they have truly ended at all. In pushing so hard, I may have reopened the wound."

'Taham's gaze drifted back toward Vadam Valley. "You believe there is another revolt in the making? That is why the armigers are out in such force?"

"I *fear* that is the reason." A number of dangerous factions had emerged shortly after the fall of the Covenant, including a group of die-hard imperial loyalists and an order of zealot monks, both opposed to 'Vadam's reign as Arbiter. Their challenges would have succeeded had 'Vadam not accepted human help, first in breaking the siege of his own keep, and then in eliminating the threat they posed to his people. Though 'Vadam wished to think of this as having been representative of the kind of unity they should share with humanity, it had truthfully been a desperate decision that continued to undermine his sway over the high kaidons to this day. "Our spies have reported nothing, but they have failed us before."

"And the Tyrant hears what they do not." 'Taham was referring to Cortana's network of artificial intelligences, which monitored communications traffic across the interstellar civilizations under her dominion. The network did not make her omniscient . . . but almost. Unless one walked naked into the wilderness, it was nearly impossible to escape the web of electronic devices that could be used to monitor every careless word and gesture. "But if she had heard of such a thing, surely she would have instructed her administrator to send us a warning?"

"No," 'Baoth interjected. "The Tyrant knows that if the Arbiter learns of another attack, he must strike first. He has no choice."

"Just so," 'Vadam said. "I cannot risk having to rely on human support a second time. Even were they in a position to offer help, accepting it would drive too many keeps into the camp of our enemies."

"So she gives us no warning," 'Taham said. "Instead, she places the fate of the Sangheili in the hands of her machines."

"Is that not what her armigers said at the first checkpoint?" 'Baoth asked. "That the Archon is responsible for the Arbiter's life now?"

'Vadam clenched his mandibles and said nothing. There was nothing he *could* say that would not make him seem as powerless and weak in his escorts' eyes as he was in his own. It was a leader's duty to give his subordinates hope, and 'Taham and 'Baoth had seen too much action for that hope to be a false one. He would have to give them a plan, even a desperate one . . . and at the moment, 'Vadam could not offer that much.

The Crav passed under the gate into the subterranean parking court where the keep's fleet of utility vehicles was stationed. Instead of continuing through the yard toward the passage to the kaidon's residence, the ground racer stopped in the center of the lane and settled into a hover. For an instant, 'Vadam feared betrayal and found himself reaching for an energy sword he no longer carried. Then a side door lifted open, and his loyal keepmaster, Charut 'Quvadamii, climbed into the vehicle.

An elderly Sangheili who had been running Vadam Keep since before 'Vadam became its kaidon, 'Quvadamii had wet eyes and age-reddened skin so dry it looked like scales. Before 'Vadam could ask the keepmaster why he was meeting the Crav here instead of in the kaidon's court, 'Quvadamii motioned for silence, then drew a detection wand from his tabard's inner pocket.

He did a careful sweep of the passenger compartment and disabled a trio of utility microphones used to communicate with the operator's compartment and outside comm and monitoring devices. Next, he had 'Vadam and his escorts surrender their comm discs, then passed them forward and had 'Sraom raise the driver's partition. Finally, 'Quvadamii activated an all-frequency jammer that emitted a low, irritating buzz that would prevent the Tyrant's agents from eavesdropping on their conversation. In theory, anyway.

"We have a visitor," 'Quvadamii said.

"Vale?" 'Vadam said. Spartan Olympia Vale had been stationed in a nearby villa to serve as a liaison between 'Vadam and his human allies. She would undoubtedly be as concerned as he was about the events taking place down in the valley. "I'll receive her in the contemplarium."

"Not Vale. It is an Oath Warden. Crei 'Ayomuu."

"'Ayomuu?" 'Vadam echoed. Oath Wardens were little better than mercenaries, ruthless bounty hunters who sold their services to enforce broken agreements. Crei 'Ayomuu was reputed to be at once the best and worst of his kind, a talented investigator and tireless stalker who always delivered satisfaction—either by forcing wayward individuals to honor their pledges, or by delivering their severed heads to the injured party. "What does he want from me?"

"He would not say, only that the matter is urgent . . . and it concerns the trouble in the valley."

'Vadam didn't know whether to be curious or worried, but he *was* suspicious. Oath Wardens followed a code that prohibited their being contracted as outright assassins, but it would certainly be possible for a shrewd kaidon to persuade 'Ayomuu that 'Vadam had broken an enforceable agreement. It was even remotely possible for a kaidon to actually believe such a thing, as the Arbiter's position was one of endless negotiation and delicate compromise between antagonistic factions.

But would an Oath Warden destroy an entire tenement island just to access his target? 'Ayomuu might . . . especially if his target was an Arbiter he had no other way of reaching.

"I'll receive him in the Grand Gallery," 'Vadam said. He turned to 'Taham. "See that he is unarmored, unwired, and carries only an energy sword."

'Taham nodded, then he and 'Baoth exited the Crav, following the keepmaster toward the Ancient Hall, located behind Vadam Keep's aboveground reception bailey. 'Vadam remained in the vehicle until 'Sraom had delivered him to the residence. Inside, 'Vadam retrieved an energy sword from the collection in his contemplarium, then climbed a long ramp into the Grand Gallery.

A soaring underground vault, the Gallery was designed to intimidate visiting elders and kaidons. In the center of the chamber sat a large table that could be used for feasting or conferencing. Nestled into the corners were conversation areas for more intimate discussions. The walls were lined with high relief sculptures and poetic stanzas depicting highlights from the saga of the Vadam clan.

'Vadam had claimed a section of wall for his own chapter in the story. It described how he had risen in the Covenant to become the Supreme Commander of the Fleet of Particular Justice, then failed to prevent the destruction of a sacred Halo ring. A bold panel portrayed the hierarchs having him branded with the Mark of Shame, then offering him the title of Arbiter—a position that he had gladly accepted, as it extended the hope of regaining his lost honor by undertaking one suicide mission after another. The sculptor had just inscribed a long passage chronicling the final mission, when 'Vadam had learned that the hierarchs were deceiving their followers about humanity's relation to the Forerunners. This section contained one of 'Vadam's favorite reliefs: an image of him fighting alongside Spartan John-117—also known to the humans as the Master Chief, and to the Covenant as the Demon—to prevent the Prophet of Truth from firing the Halo Array and destroying all sentient life in the galaxy.

'Vadam lingered a moment, relishing the friendship that had arisen out of his alliance with the Master Chief and contemplating the preliminary work on the next series of panels. It would depict him reestablishing the Swords of Sanghelios and forging his alliance with the humans. The final panel was not yet designed, and he could not help wondering what it would depict: an ongoing alliance with the humans and several other species that gave him the peace to establish a grand Concert of Worlds? Or a tragic mistake that undermined his standing with the high kaidons so badly that his dream of a united Sangheili civilization came crashing down on top of him?

In his darkest dreams, 'Vadam saw himself staggering like a wounded animal through the ruins of his keep, falling to his knees amidst fire and blood and sand, screaming into the fading light of Urs as he watched all he had fought to build turn to dust. For now, however, the only dust present was gathered in the deepest pockets of the room's most ancient sculpture panels.

The golden bars flanking the Gallery's massive double doors began to glow, indicating that 'Taham and 'Baoth were waiting outside with the Oath Warden Crei 'Ayomuu. 'Vadam let out a long breath and went to the door. He checked a glassboard log to be sure the room had recently been swept for any digital devices the Tyrant's AIs could use to eavesdrop, then deactivated the locks and retreated to a conversation area near his private entrance.

"I am ready." He spoke loudly enough that his voice echoed off the stone walls. Electronics were forbidden in the Grand Gallery, so there was nothing but the room's natural acoustics to carry his voice. "Welcome."

The doors rumbled open, and 'Taham and 'Baoth entered the room, escorting a gaunt Sangheili with a stooped posture and gray pallor. Crei 'Ayomuu's head was flat and long, his mandibles as thin as a dagger, his limbs slender and elongated. He wore only a cloth jumpsuit belted at the waist, and he carried no energy sword. Whether the absence of the traditional weapon was a concession indicating supplication or a condescension suggesting superior prowess was anyone's guess. Oath Wardens were an order unto themselves, with their own arcane codes and lethal arts that no outsider would ever know.

'Ayomuu paused ten steps inside the chamber and made a point of looking into every corner, as though he had never seen such a stately chamber and was determined to remember the minutest of details. Finally, the Oath Warden fixed his gaze on the first panel of the Saga Wall and strode over to study the majestic figure of the long-dead Ther 'Vadam.

Thel 'Vadam remained in the conversation corner near his private door. Custom dictated that the petitioner approach the benefactor, and 'Vadam had no intention of yielding even a hint of his power. Such an action would only reinforce the Oath Warden's delusion that his guild had a legitimate place in society, alongside blademasters and crop keepers—and, in time, even doctors.

'Vadam continued to wait in silence, and the Oath Warden finally turned to face him.

"Your ancestors' saga will be difficult to match," 'Ayomuu said. "I see now why you have taken so many ill-advised risks to enhance your own."

The taunt cut deeper than 'Vadam would have liked. He *was* desperate to be the first Arbiter to unite all Sangheili worlds under a single banner, and part of that was a desire to secure his legacy. But he was motivated by far more than vanity. As a supreme commander in the Covenant navy, he had seen firsthand the power of interstellar civilizations who opened new worlds according to a considered plan, who made provisions for their colonies to work together and support one another. Even the humans, who were so often divided by localized loyalties and at one another's throats, could find a way to fight as one when they were threatened by an outside force.

But if the Sangheili had ever possessed such instincts, they had been sublimated by servitude to San'Shyuum lies and the manipulation of the Prophets. Now every marshal fancied himself ruler of a continent, every high kaidon the master of his world. They guarded their authority with a jealousy unrivaled by the Jiralhanae, and they plotted to undermine one another with all the cunning of Kig-Yar matriarchs. 'Vadam did not know how he would ever bring them together, but he had to find a way. If he did not, Sangheili civilization would become just a collection of client states paying tribute to the interstellar empires of its rivals.

When 'Vadam continued to wait in silence, the Oath Warden finally started up the length of the Gallery toward him.

"But there is more to an Arbiter's legacy than an enthralling saga," 'Ayomuu said. "It is the Arbiter's duty to uphold the public honor of the Sangheili, to foster honesty and enforce the laws of our ancestors."

'Ayomuu reached the conversation corner and stopped, waiting for 'Vadam to wave him toward one of the cushioned lounging benches. Instead, 'Vadam stepped to within striking range, a reminder that no matter how dangerous the Oath Warden might be, he would never be a soldier's equal.

"Fostering honesty," 'Vadam echoed. "I have always thought that is what Oath Wardens do."

"By the time we are contracted, it is more a matter of imposing it."

"No doubt. But why come to me? Surely you cannot believe I have any interest in sharing your fee?"

'Ayomuu parted his mandibles. "What a thought. But nothing so . . . creative. I come as a courtesy. This particular contract may be of concern to you, so it seemed wise to give you an opportunity to secure your interests before I proceed."

'Vadam glanced to 'Taham and 'Baoth, whose expressions remained suspicious and watchful. Whatever 'Ayomuu was talking about, he had given them no hint.

"Then perhaps you should explain what interests I need to secure," 'Vadam said. "You told 'Quvadamii this concerns the trouble in the Valley?"

"Yes. It was the only way to persuade him to admit me."

"Is this about the trouble in the Valley or not?" 'Vadam put more ire into his voice than he felt, for he was accustomed to petitioners seeking audiences under false pretenses . . . and he knew how to discourage them. "Because I have no interest in speaking to you about anything else."

'Ayomuu hesitated. "I can explain what is happening. That is not to say I am the one who caused—"

"I love the Tyrant even less than I do liars," 'Vadam interrupted. "Know that if I punish you, it will only be for deceiving me—and I will do it myself. I will not give you over to her."

"Then I have nothing to fear. My client was only following your example."

Seeing that 'Ayomuu was trying to draw him into a conspiratorial state of mind, 'Vadam tipped his head and studied the Oath Warden in silence.

After a moment, 'Ayomuu continued, "My client financed an expedition to N'ba. For a human female, a xenoarchaeologist."

"I have never heard of this place." 'Vadam *did* know that N'ba meant "world of death" in Sangheili, so he assumed it was no garden planet. "And your client's agreement with any human is no concern of mine."

"It is your concern if this xenoarchaeologist is now in Vadam Valley. And if my client has *also* been the victim of human betrayal."

"Also?"

'Vadam had heard the rumors that the human spy organization the Office of Naval Intelligence had caused the Blooding Years by playing him off against the Servants of the Abiding Truth, and that the United Nations Space Command supercarrier *Infinity* had intervened on his behalf only because the humans wanted their loyal pet leading the Sangheili. He was also aware that these rumors had a certain truth, though the full situation was much more complicated than even the most unhinged conspiracy-monger could imagine.

Like the Sangheili themselves, the humans were composed of many different factions. Some believed the only way to protect humanity was to keep the Sangheili weak. Others felt the only true peace came through friendship and alliance. And more than a few simply wanted to turn their backs on the Sangheili and forget they existed—and who could blame them? Billions of their kind had been slaughtered during the seemingly endless cycles of the Covenant's War of Annihilation, and those memories would still be fresh.

'Vadam had struck bargains with all of these factions. It was the only way to buy the time he needed. To make the Sangheili strong again, he had to unite them into a single interstellar society powerful enough to stand against their rivals, who even now were beginning to push into Sangheili territory from every side.

"The humans I allow to live in Vadam Valley are as honorable as I am." 'Vadam was thinking primarily of the Spartan Olympia Vale, with whom he spoke nearly every day. But there were a handful of others, engineers and technical advisers who had once helped Kolaar Manufactorum design the small runs of weapons and armor they produced for the UNSC, then became trapped on Sanghelios when the Tyrant rose to power. "Whatever this betrayal is, it has nothing to do with them."

"I did not say my target lived here," 'Ayomuu said. "Only that she is here now. I know you will want to protect the reputation of your humans in residence by helping to hold her to account."

"What I *want* is to know why your target's arrival has drawn so many armigers into the streets. And how it resulted in the destruction of an entire tenement island."

"That was unavoidable. She attempted to hide in the *kreche* warrens, and my floating eyes alarmed the incubating females. A band of angry males fired on the eyes, and I lost track of the target in the confusion. By the time the first armiger arrived, it was too late to recall them. I had to abandon the entire flight."

"Then the destruction of the tenement island was *your* doing?"

"I never loosed a bolt," 'Ayomuu objected. "I left when the first armiger arrived. Whatever happened next . . . that is between the residents and the armigers."

'Taham made a point of parting his mandibles, but the call-out was unnecessary. 'Vadam had already noticed the discrepancy between 'Ayomuu's account and what he had been told at the first checkpoint. Perhaps the armiger officer had not been present at the tenement's destruction or had not been informed of the part played by the Tyrant's forces. But it seemed more likely that it simply had not cared. Occupation forces had a long tradition of blaming their victims for any violence that befell them, and the Tyrant's armigers had proven no different.

"I am still waiting to learn what this human is doing here on Sanghelios," 'Vadam said. "And why you are hunting her."

"I have already told you. I am hunting her because she broke her word."

"If you want my help, you will have to be more forthcoming. And if you expect to leave Vadam Keep alive, you will waste no more of my time."

"I will reveal as much as I am permitted to. If that is a waste of your time . . ." 'Ayomuu spread his hands. "You are welcome to try, but I will be leaving Vadam Keep in a manner of my own choosing."

'Vadam's only reply was to drop his gaze to 'Ayomuu's weaponless belt.

'Ayomuu's eyes glimmered in amusement for an instant, then he said, "The human's special area of study is protogenic civilizations."

"Meaning?"

"Before the Forerunners. The xenoarchaeologist has been using the UNSC's Military Survey of Uninhabited Planets to identify targets to investigate."

'Taham and 'Baoth both tipped their heads at this news, and 'Vadam had the same thought: if she had access to a military survey, she was no ordinary academic. "She is ONI then?"

"When there still *was* an ONI, perhaps," 'Ayomuu said. "But no longer. If she were an ONI operative, she would not need my client to finance her expedition to N'ba."

"Perhaps," 'Vadam said. The Office of Naval Intelligence was nothing if not resourceful, and he had reason to believe the Tyrant's rise had not destroyed them completely. They were deep in hiding somewhere, licking their wounds and searching for a way to counterattack. And tricking a gullible Sangheili kaidon into financing their operation was exactly the kind of subterfuge they might use to conceal their plan. "Tell me more about this N'ba."

"It is a marginally survivable world in the Out Sectors; it is called Netherop by the humans. It drew the xenoarchaeologist's interest because there was a small surface battle there early in the War of Annihilation, and the UNSC's after-action account referred to an ancient roadway, a buried city, and sophisticated vehicles that utilized legs instead of wheels. That drew the xenoarchaeologist's interest, and she deemed it a good candidate for an exploratory expedition. Unfortunately for her, her funding vanished when the Tyrant imposed her will."

"So your client offered his support," 'Vadam surmised.

"He has a deep interest in xenoarchaeology. He knows this human's work, and he believes she will recast the field's understanding of protogenic civilization. All he wants is to play a small part in her success."

"Perhaps that is what he told you," 'Vadam said. "But we both know there is another reason. I have never heard of someone contracting an Oath Warden to force a research grant on an explorer."

"Oh, she has already taken my client's funds. It is her part of the agreement I am here to enforce. She is to give my client first choice of any artifacts she recovers."

"After she reaches N'ba?" 'Vadam clarified. "Which she has not yet done?"

"That is so."

"Then you are premature. She cannot give your client what she has not yet recovered."

"True, but there are allowances for clear intent," 'Ayomuu said. "And she made her intent clear when she failed to rendezvous with my client and came here, to Vadam."

"Where was she to be instead?"

"If I told you that, you would know who my client is. Which I am not free to reveal."

"Then I am not seeing how this concerns me," 'Vadam said. "Usze and Kola will see you to the gate."

The two warriors stepped forward, flanking the Oath Warden to either side, and extended their arms toward the door.

'Ayomuu clacked his mandibles in frustration. "Perhaps if I were to mention who she has come to see—"

"Olympia Vale?" guessed 'Vadam. "*Spartan* Olympia Vale—the only human in Vadam an Oath Warden would fear."

"It is more the aftermath I fear than the human." 'Ayomuu continued to ignore 'Taham's and 'Baoth's outstretched arms and exhaled slowly. "I can reveal this much. My client began to grow suspicious of Iyuska's intentions—"

"Who is this Iyuska?"

"Keely Iyuska," 'Ayomuu said. "That is the human target's name. She is a junior lecturer of xenoarchaeology at the University of Edinburgh on Earth. After agreeing to my client's terms for her expedition, Iyuska discovered an ancient account suggesting the N'ba civilization had been attacked by a Forerunner Guardian."

"And now that she knows why the civilization vanished, she no longer wishes to journey to N'ba?"

"Not at all. The N'ba civilization survived, at least for a time. It was the *Guardian* that perished."

It took 'Vadam a moment to grasp the implications of what he was hearing. Guardians were—as far as 'Vadam or anyone else knew—practically invincible to any force wielded by a contemporary military. Yet some lost protogenic civilization had found a way to destroy one?

It seemed too incredible to believe. And 'Vadam wouldn't have believed it, had the armigers not been out in such force. But they were everywhere in the Valley now, mounting checkpoints and deploying heavy weapons more suited to battle than policing, filling the air with Aethra stalker craft and razing entire tenement islands on the mere suspicion that their quarry was inside. The Tyrant feared the human xenoarchaeologist for a reason—and that reason was most likely something she knew.

Now it all made sense—*of course* 'Ayomuu's client wanted first pick of any artifacts that Iyuska recovered. Any kaidon capable of challenging the Tyrant's Guardians would become savior of the species—and the one leader capable of uniting the Sangheili into a true Concert of Worlds.

And *of course* Iyuska wanted that key information to go to her fellow humans instead. Any species capable of unshackling itself from the Guardians would become the unrivaled masters of the galaxy, free to dictate terms to its allies and to claim any world it wished from its rivals. The Sangheili were generally on good terms with the humans now . . . but that was in no small part because the two species had collectively been weakened so that it was dangerous for them both *not* to be. How might that change if the humans learned how to stop the Guardians first?

It would depend on which humans the knowledge empowered . . . and Thel 'Vadam understood just enough about ONI to realize the odds did not favor his chosen allies.

"I am beginning to see your point, Oath Warden." 'Vadam motioned 'Ayomuu toward a lounging bench in the center of the conversation area. "Please sit. We should make some plans."

CHAPTER 3

The Aethra stalker craft had been circling over the eastern edge of the New Harbor all evening, climbing high over the inky waters before wheeling around to dive back into the curving lanes of the Young Borough in Vadam Valley. The tenement spires and merchant houses there were new, erected around the flooded crater left by a magnetic accelerator cannon strike from the UNSC *Infinity*—a MAC attack that had broken Avu Med 'Telcam's assault on Vadam Keep six years ago.

The sight of so many sickle-shaped fliers sweeping between glass towers made Olympia Vale think of her native Luyten, where, as a young girl on family camping trips in the Hoodoo Gorges, she had enjoyed watching scaly nightgyrs dart through rocky canyons in search of prey. But the Aethras were not harmless winged lizards gorging on blood mots, nor did their arrival bring relief from a yearly plague of fever-spreading thumb birds. The Aethras were Cortana's reconnaissance craft, and whatever they were searching for, it likely involved Arbiter Thel 'Vadam's failure to reply to Vale's recent messages. She had sent several over the last four hours, asking about the force of armigers spreading across Vadam, and he had not answered any.

Vale knew from her own sources that the Sangheili High Gathering that day had been a rough one—just not *this* rough. From her balcony in the Villa of Long Views, it looked as though the armigers were trying to crush some sort of uprising before it started to gather momentum. But whether that implied a rebellion against Cortana or a coup attempt against the Arbiter remained unclear.

Given the steady stream of vehicles that had departed Vadam Keep over the last several hours and the lack of response from the Arbiter, the idea of a coup attempt was starting to seem the likeliest possibility. But until Vale had confirmation, she could only watch, wait, and continue checking with her network of informants— who, at the moment, seemed annoyingly uninformed.

The purple ray of an impulse engine flared to life forty kilometers in the distance, near Vadam Harbor, then curled toward the sky. A moment later, four more craft launched from separate locations around the Valley. It took only a heartbeat to realize all the launches had occurred near facilities controlled by the Arbiter himself: the Council House, the Vadam Dockyards in the New Harbor, the Arbiter's base on Dalkesu Sea, and Vadam Keep.

Clearly, the armiger deployment had *something* to do with the Arbiter. Orchestrating a closely coordinated launch from so many different locations would have been tricky even with electronic communications—and 'Vadam would never have used such vulnerable methods and risked Cortana's eavesdropping. The ground vehicles streaming out of his keep all evening had probably been a mixture of decoys and transports carrying coded messages and key personnel to the launch sites.

But . . . why?

It wasn't like the Arbiter to flee a coup attempt. He was too proud and tenacious. And any military assets he hoped to call in from off-world would be destroyed by Cortana's orbital control forces. So, he had to be trying to get something—or someone— away from Sanghelios.

Vale raised her binoculars and turned toward Kolaar Manufactorum—the one major 'Vadam-controlled facility from which she hadn't seen a launch.

It took only moments to find the restricted-access hangar, a massive cavern at the rear of the development enclave. The energy barrier at its mouth had already been reactivated, but a small parade of service vehicles carried Sangheili technicians back toward the Manufactorum's maintenance domes. Obviously something had just departed the restricted hangar—and since Vale hadn't actually seen anything launch from the Manufactorum area, she had a pretty good idea what.

She opened a comm channel to one of her contacts in the Manufactorum's development cadre. "Ellie, I wanted to check on that toy you've been assembling."

Ellie Gracio was a human special-materials engineer helping Kolaar Manufactorum develop a stealth version of the *Mikpramu*-pattern Phantom for the Swords of Sanghelios, and "the toy" was one of a hundred informal terms they used for the prototype to confuse eavesdropping AIs. Whether it was wise to share human dropship stealth technology with the Swords was way above Vale's pay grade, but she understood Admiral Hood's reasoning. Anything the UNSC could do to bolster the Arbiter and strengthen his ties to humanity made a new war with the Sangheili less likely. And if having an intimate familiarity with the craft's design gave the UNSC an advantage it could use later, say if a war *did* erupt . . . so much the better.

"Is it available to see tomorrow?" Vale continued.

"*Hard to say,*" Ellie replied. "*One of the hatchlings might be giving it a whirl. Could be hard to find tomorrow.*"

Vale forced an understanding laugh. "I can imagine. Do you know which one took off with it?"

"*Afraid not. You know how they are here. They don't tell me anything until they want me to put it back together.*"

"Isn't that the way? Do me a favor and see if you can find out who has it. Maybe they'll let me have a look at it."

"*I'll ask around. But like I said, no one tells me anything. I'll be in touch.*"

Ellie closed the channel, leaving Vale more puzzled than ever about the night's events. The five observable launches had been distractions, designed to draw attention away from the Manufactorum's stealth-prototype activation.

The tactic seemed to be working. Vale could see orange darts of heat shimmer—no doubt Cortana's Phaeton fighter craft—climbing through the atmosphere at hypersonic velocity. They were converging on the efflux trails of the five craft that had launched a few minutes earlier, and the Aethra stalkers were swarming around the facilities from which they had departed.

But no Aethras were swirling around the Kolaar Manufactorum, and no Phaetons were approaching the unseen form of the stealth prototype. Whatever the Arbiter had been trying to sneak off Sanghelios, he had succeeded.

And without informing Vale about it.

As the putative head of an interstellar confederation with a formal, yet still fragile alliance with the UNSC, the Arbiter had no obligation whatsoever to report his movements to the resident Spartan. But he was usually careful to keep her informed of events that concerned her or the UNSC, and he would certainly expect her to be alarmed by Cortana's deployments in Vadam

Valley—especially given what had happened to Doisac three days ago.

Yet, he still had not replied to her messages seeking a situation briefing.

Not even Keepmaster 'Quvadamii or one of 'Vadam's escorts had responded on the Arbiter's behalf . . . and that could only mean he was hiding something. A less principled ally would simply have lied. But not 'Vadam. He valued honor above all, and he would not stain it by deceiving a valued collaborator like Vale.

On the other hand, he wasn't stupid. Thel 'Vadam put the interests of the Sangheili and Sanghelios first, which meant he viewed his alliance with the UNSC—and even his friendships with the Master Chief and Admiral Hood—as serving those interests. So, if he was shutting Vale out, it was entirely possible that he was involved with something that pitted those interests against humanity's . . . or because he had finally discovered the UNSC could not always be trusted.

Vale lived in dread of the day that the Arbiter finally learned the truth about the Sangheili civil war: that his near overthrow by the Servants of the Abiding Truth had been abetted by ONI as part of a campaign to keep the Sangheili weak after the Covenant War. And she had waking nightmares about the stealth-Phantom project. One of the human engineers was almost certainly an ONI agent trying to slip an exploitable flaw into the design, and Vale knew 'Vadam would hold her personally responsible if the saboteur was ever discovered. She just didn't see why either betrayal would trigger a reaction from Cortana's forces.

A small pop sounded in front of Vale, and she looked down to find she had been squeezing the balustrade so hard that the klastone had cracked. She hated uncertainty. None of her sources could explain the armiger deployment, and going down into the

Valley to conduct her own investigation was out of the question. The Arbiter's relationship with the UNSC had already undermined his influence with many of the other kaidons. If his human liaison started "looking for answers" during Cortana's policing action, he would likely lose the support of the rest.

Until she knew more, Vale could only watch and wait, and it made her feel helpless. Worse, it made her feel incompetent. She might be dressed in a civilian tunic and trousers at the moment, but she was a Spartan-IV super-soldier, occasional ONI operative, and the highest-ranking human diplomat here on Sanghelios. It was her duty to safeguard the other UNSC personnel posted on this alien world, which was historically hostile to her species no matter how close of an ally she was to one of its key leaders. But with Cortana's eavesdroppers likely monitoring every comm message she sent, even a simple READY ALERT could cause a sequence of responses and counterresponses that would quickly escalate from cache openings and weapon retrievals to file wipes, hardware demolition, and a full-scale evacuation.

None of that was something good operatives would put into motion because of what they *didn't* know,

Vale lifted her binoculars to make another sweep of the Valley and felt a familiar knot of regret forming in her stomach. As a member of Fireteam Osiris, she had been one of the four Spartan-IVs assigned to hunt down John-117 and Blue Team when they went AWOL in the early stages of the Cortana Event. The directive had been lawful, and it would have taken a diviner to see that obeying the order would delay Blue Team just enough to prevent them from stopping Cortana. But most of the time, Vale felt it had been a mistake to accept the assignment. Osiris should have known better than to doubt the Master Chief's instincts and left Blue Team to pursue her unharassed. They still might not have been able to stop her from releasing the Guardians . . . but they would have had a lot better chance.

Or, perhaps Cortana would have escaped with Blue Team as she'd planned, and it was simply luck that Spartan Locke had managed to prevent her from trapping four of humanity's greatest heroes in a Cryptum for the next ten thousand years.

After a moment, Vale spotted the dark sickle of a single Aethra floating up the mountain. It was moving so slowly she wouldn't have noticed it, had it not been so low that it was momentarily silhouetted by the driving lamps of a Worik land-skimmer.

The Villa of Long Views was hardly the only residence accessed by the switchbacking road that climbed the side of Kolaar Mountain. But the longer Vale watched, the more convinced she grew that the Worik was coming to her house. First, the armiger deployment had suppressed all nonessential traffic, so the driver was on an important task. Second, the Aethra following it was flying without running lights, dodging out of sight whenever the vehicle rounded a hairpin curve, so it was clearly on a covert surveillance mission. Third, the Arbiter had been taking stringent precautions to prevent eavesdroppers from learning of his plans, so if he was going to reply to Vale's inquiries, he would probably do so via personal messenger.

Vale spent the next five minutes watching the vehicle climb the ladder of curves that separated the stately villa district from the valley below. The sight evoked a growing sense of dread, perhaps because it reminded her of her last family camping trip to Hoodoo Gorges. Her mother, Nerina Vale, was a recently promoted captain in UNSC signals intelligence who had just been reassigned to High Command in Sydney, Australia, on Earth. Her father, Caleb Vale, was a slipspace-drive technician who refused to work on military vessels because he was a devoted pacifist, and he spent the entire time trying to persuade Nerina to decline the assignment.

By the end of the excursion, the Vales had decided to dissolve their marriage. The divorce was completed ten days later—coincidently on their daughter's eleventh birthday—and Nerina and Olympia boarded a diplomatic shuttle for Earth. What was supposed to be a six-day journey ended up taking six months because the slipspace drive failed, and Vale suspected her father of somehow sabotaging it in a last-ditch effort to return his family to Luyten. Her mother dismissed the notion so scornfully that Vale concluded it was a dumb idea . . . until well after the war, when she tried to contact Caleb Vale to tell him that Nerina had perished during the Battle for Earth.

Caleb Vale, it turned out, did not exist. Vale used her ONI connections to learn it was a false identity assumed by one Caleb Aagard, who had been born on Luyten in the same year as her father. That was where the trail ran cold. The only note in Aagard's file was that he had refused conscription in 2517, then vanished—which made no sense. Aagard's date of birth had been listed as May 16, 2511, which would have made him *six years old* at the time.

Vale had suspected there would be a ghost file explaining the discrepancy. But when she tried to look for it, her superior had suggested it was a simple case of a father and son having the same name . . . then advised her to stop wasting ONI resources and devote herself to her proper assignment. The "advice" had been offered in a tone of voice indicating it had come down from somewhere far above *both* their heads.

So Vale had stopped poking around ONI files concerning *anyone* from Luyten and started to look for more subtle ways to learn about her father's true identity. Then the Cortana Event had come, and she could no longer be sure the information still existed—or that she would ever be able to access it, even if it did. But part of her knew she didn't need it, for the dark shadow of truth about her father's past reared its head when a rogue journalist began circulating information about the SPARTAN-II program. Vale had never been interested in conspiracy theories, but the revelation that Spartan-IIs had been conscripted as six-year-olds all but confirmed the connections in her mind. Her father *was* Caleb Aagard, and he had fled conscription into the SPARTAN-II program.

She wondered where her father was, if he was still alive . . . what he would say if he could see her now. But these were questions she would have to pursue another day, once this mess with Cortana had been resolved and she felt she'd earned the closure.

When the little Worik reached the Villa of Long Views, instead of turning toward the gate, it merely continued up the road. The side windows of its passenger box had not been darkened, so Vale could see that no one rode in back.

The Sangheili in the operator's bubble was leaning forward over the controls, his head turned toward her villa as though searching for its name . . . which was written in huge Sangheili characters via a brightly lit panel on the gate. The driver lifted the bubble a crack—just high enough to push a hand out—then flicked something the size of a grenade toward the building and continued at the same slow pace.

Which probably saved his life.

Vale already had her plasma pistol in hand and was gathering herself to leap over the balustrade. But when the operator made no attempt to flee, and nothing exploded, she realized it was all part of a covert delivery.

Vale remained on the balcony as the Worik rounded the next curve. Once the Aethra trailing it had vanished behind the villa's roofline, she went downstairs and slipped through the pedestrian gate onto the street-side veranda.

She heard the capsule first. It was a Sangheili trysting pod, emitting a soft but maddeningly erratic chirp. Discreet females used the devices to summon mates to secret nidus dates, a custom that supported the tradition of hiding the father's identity from the child. As Vale was neither Sangheili nor male, she suspected this pod had been adapted for another purpose. She retrieved it from the stone planter where it had landed, then slipped back through the gate and inspected it under a light near the visitor's door.

It wasn't a particularly ornate pod, just a polished green orb— the kind available in shops across Vadam Valley. The surface and hinge showed no signs of tampering, the seam no indication of a triggering device. She held it at arm's length and pinched the sides to disengage the locking mechanism, then slid the two halves apart . . . and caught a small folded note in her hand. The message inside was hand printed, in English:

OPEN THE SALLY PORT

Vale crushed the trysting pod with her foot and started toward the villa's hangar, tearing the note into tiny pieces as she walked. Not a lot of Sangheili could write English, and none that she knew among the Arbiter's subordinates, so the message wasn't from 'Vadam's inner circle. It seemed likelier that it came from one of her human contacts at the Manufactorum, perhaps even an ONI agent who had learned something worth breaking cover to convey.

Vale entered the hangar, circling past the Owl stealth craft stored there to a maintenance locker on the west wall. There she pulled out a rolling shelf unit stacked with cleaning agents and half-filled bottles of hydraulic fluid. The floor of the locker looked like normal fibercrete, but when she tapped all four corners in diagonal sequence, an array of triangular symbols appeared. She entered an alphanumeric code she'd been provided when the Arbiter arranged for her to take the villa, and the floor drew aside, revealing a fixed ladder that descended into darkness.

As soon as Vale dangled a foot into the shaft, the walls began to glow with a warm ambient light. She descended five meters to the bottom of the shaft, then traveled down a spacious horizontal tunnel to a blue-tinted door large enough for a Ghost light assault vehicle to use. When she pressed her palm to the control pad, a panel near the top grew transparent.

By human standards, Vale was tall, standing just over two meters in bare feet thanks to the physical augmentations of the SPARTAN-IV program. But compared to the Sangheili, she was quite short, and she had to raise herself on tiptoe just to see through the bottom of the panel.

Vale found herself looking out into a rocky draw four hundred meters to the east of the Villa of Long Views. She could tell by the lack of shadows that it was inky dark down inside the belly of the gulch, but the light-enhancing panel showed every boulder and bush in fine detail. Hunkered down behind the gangly twigs of a spider bramble, pressed against an outcropping about thirty meters down the slope, was a familiar woman with a meter-long braid draped over one shoulder and a rucksack resting between her feet. She was wearing a dark field jacket, wide-brimmed hat, and dark pants with large square pockets that appeared to be stuffed with water bottles and food packs.

Keely . . . ?

Vale pressed her palm to the door and made a sliding motion. The tunnel lighting went out, then the door retracted into the wall with a soft *shoosh*. The woman outside gave a startled gasp, and gravel shifted as she turned toward the sound of the door.

Vale stepped out into the ravine.

"Keely?" She spoke the name in a hushed voice that she hoped would carry far enough for a nonaugmented human to hear. "What are *you* doing here?"

"Looking for you." The last Vale had heard, Keely Iyuska had overcome a few career setbacks to become a junior xenoarchaeology professor at the University of Edinburgh on Earth. Though Iyuska was a dear friend from their student days at Sydney University, it had been four and a half years since they'd actually seen each other—until now. "Pia . . . I'm in trouble."

"Aren't you always?"

"This is different." Iyuska started up the ravine toward Vale's voice, stumbling in the dark. "This time it's big. *Really* big."

"No kidding." Vale had no idea how her old friend's unexpected arrival might be related to the armiger deployment, but she didn't doubt it *was*. Iyuska had a reckless disregard for consequences—so much so that she often seemed to be deliberately courting catastrophe. Vale rolled a forty-kilogram boulder onto the sally port threshold to prevent the door from closing, then started down the ravine. "Wait there. And stop calling me Pia."

"I thought you liked it."

"I'm not fourteen anymore, desperate to feel accepted by my nineteen-year-old classmates." As a Spartan, Vale's vision had been augmented along with most of her other physical attributes. Even in the inky darkness, she had no trouble picking her way through the broken terrain to reach Iyuska's side. "The appeal wore off."

"Why didn't you say anything?"

"I *did*." Vale took Iyuska by the arm and led her through the black night toward the sally port. "At our commencement party. And every time I've seen you since."

"So . . . three times, *total*?" Iyuska made a scoffing sound. "Excuse me for thinking we had other things to focus on."

Vale took three steps in silence, then sighed. "Okay, that might be fair."

It would have been unreasonable to expect Iyuska to remember *anything* from their commencement party. Their next get-together had not come until shortly after the Covenant War ended, when Vale had returned from a walkabout on the Sangheili world of Khael'mothka. Iyuska had been so full of questions about Sangheili culture that Vale had begun to feel like her old friend considered her nothing more than research. Since then, they'd seen each other only once, in a professional capacity that had left little time for cultivating their friendship.

Iyuska stumbled on a rock in the pitch dark and would have gone down hard, had Vale not been holding on to her arm and simply lifted her off the ground. The surprised cry that resulted reminded Vale that her friend had not seen her since her enrollment in the SPARTAN-IV program . . . and would no doubt be more than a little surprised at what she saw when they finally entered the light.

Vale set Iyuska back on her feet, then said, "I couldn't believe it when I heard that the University of Calippus denied your tenure, by the way." Vale guided her through the sally port into the tunnel. "They were fools."

"They weren't. I never should have pushed for it so young." Iyuska laid a hand on Vale's forearm. "But thank you for saying that. I'll try to do better about the nickname."

"That would be good."

Vale used her foot to push the improvised doorstop clear of the threshold, and the sally door slid closed behind them. The tunnel's automatic lighting returned, revealing a sturdy, slender-faced woman of just under thirty. She still had pale skin, red hair, and deep green eyes that could be alarmingly guileful . . . or fiercely observant. She took a step back and spent a moment studying Vale's augmented frame, then gasped, letting her jaw drop.

"What did they *do* to you?! When you said 'special assignment,' I didn't think you meant—"

"I couldn't be more specific," Vale said. "Sorry."

Vale had last seen her friend in late spring of 2555, after returning from a joint Sangheili-human mission to an ancient Forerunner installation known as the Ark. Iyuska was still at the University of Calippus then, working on the side as an ONI xenoarchaeology consultant and a guest lecturer at the Luna OCS Academy. Vale had been given permission to brief her on the technology and architecture she'd observed while on the Ark. What Vale *hadn't* been free to share, however, was that she was about to leave for Mars as a candidate in the SPARTAN-IV program.

"But you're subject to the same security directives I am," Vale said. "You know how it works."

Iyuska rolled her eyes. "Yeah, but . . . you could have *hinted*. I was worried sick about you."

"No, you weren't. You were busy on Heian, excavating its ruins. It's what you live for."

"How do you know about . . . ?" Iyuska paused, then shook her head. "Never mind. Let's not talk about the things we can't talk about, right? So what's a girl gotta do to get a drink around here?" She flashed a smile and started up the tunnel.

Vale caught up and walked at her side. "You can start by explaining why there's an Aethra trailing you."

"There *is*?"

"You had a Worik deliver a message to me in a Sangheili trysting pod." Vale didn't bother to ask how Iyuska had known where to send the pod, or where to look for the sally port; the first was an open secret in Vadam, and the second would be obvious to anyone with an archaeological background and a map of the terrain. "I doubt it's because you want to make out."

"Well . . . lovely as that sounds, not really." Iyuska paused a moment. "Okay, I did expect someone to be watching. Just not *her*. Not this soon."

Vague as it was, the reply confirmed what Vale already knew in her gut. Iyuska was not simply caught up in the armiger deployment—she was the reason for it.

"Keely—I need to know what's going on. And I need to know *now*."

"Fine." Iyuska sighed heavily. "Just don't judge me."

"There's an entire battalion of Cortana's armigers hunting you. We are long past judging."

"Okay . . . remember you said that." Iyuska continued to walk, her gaze fixed on the tunnel ahead. "You heard about the University of Edinburgh, right?"

"Yeah. You're a junior professor." Vale braced herself for bad news. "Specializing in pre-Forerunner civilization theory. I know what you've been up to."

Iyuska looked over. "So I *do* have you to thank."

"I *heard* about it. But that's all. I don't have the pull to arrange anything."

"If you say so. Anyway, it was a good place to land after the Oxford mess, even if the chair *is* a jealous cow. She only agreed to have me because she wants more ONI funding."

Vale didn't bother to ask for clarification. From the rumors she'd heard, the "Oxford mess" involved an affair that somehow grew so tawdry it ended up being designated "need to know," if only to avoid embarrassing an important ONI ally.

As for the funding comment, it was common knowledge that ONI supported xenoarchaeology and xenoanthropology departments in every major university on Earth, both to advance humankind's knowledge of alien cultures and to develop unparalleled talent for clandestine missions. Of course, ONI's support always came with strings. In Iyuska's case at Edinburgh, the string had apparently been an academic post for a troublesome consultant with the kind of talent and security clearance that made her worth protecting. In Vale's case at Sydney, that string had been exclusive poaching rights to a sixteen-year-old prodigy who had just earned her master's degree in xenoanthropology with first-class honors.

"So, this jealous cow?" Vale urged. "What does she have to do with the armigers and the Aethra?"

"Nothing directly. She just wants to be rid of me as quickly as possible. She gave me a full load of intro courses to teach. Not even xenoarchaeology . . . just plain old human archaeology."

"Isn't that normal for first-year lecturers? I would think a good chair would want to observe your style before assigning advanced courses. You know, give you some time to develop your niche."

"It might be normal, but it's not how you treat someone who led the most important excavation on Heian."

"What are the chances the jealous cow was actually briefed about that?"

Iyuska sighed. "Not very high. She has no need to know—her specialty is the San'Shyuum. She keeps insisting they'll be back, the silly woman."

Once the ruling caste of the Covenant, the San'Shyuum were a species of bipeds so fragile they relied on antigravity machines to move around. They had vanished so completely after the Covenant War that they were considered either extinct or on the verge of it, depending on where one sourced their information.

"That's delusional," Vale said. "And yet, I'm sure it's hard to accept, one's area of expertise evaporating like that. But . . . the armigers? Keely, *why* are you here?"

"Because of what I found in Edinburgh. As a condition of my appointment, I had to screen UNSC after-action reports for indications of protogenic civilizations. They wanted a canvass of the entire Orion Arm."

They, Vale assumed, meant ONI—and specifically whoever had arranged for Iyuska's appointment.

"It would have been mind-numbing work," Iyuska continued, "but I had funding for a dedicated AI and a research assistant to help me set search parameters."

"Without the AI, it wouldn't have been just mind-numbing." Vale had been in the military long enough to appreciate the sheer number of documents even a small battle could generate. "It would have been impossible. There had to be millions of reports."

"Closer to a billion. Which produced three hundred and fifty-two candidates on two hundred and eleven celestial bodies. I wrote them all up, with special callouts for any that could conceivably have Forerunner-contemporaneous human sites. After what we found at the Heian excavations, I thought those were the ones they'd be most interested in sending teams to survey."

"Makes sense."

"Yeah. Well, if they did, I wasn't invited." Iyuska shrugged. "And, actually, that was fine with me. During the canvass, I started to see something more interesting."

"Hard to imagine something more interesting than whatever the ruins on Heian were."

"Not that hard. In fact, I thought I was imagining it. But I kept seeing ghosts of a culture older than the Forerunners, one that was even more advanced . . . and elusive too. Every time I spotted evidence of some device that required an unattainable amount of energy, or a structure that was impossible to build, or a settlement that seemed to exist outside space and time, the observation would dissolve in my mind like sugar in water. Or it would be explained away by the next report I examined. Or my research assistant would track down a reference to a similar phenomenon that established the technology as firmly Forerunner. I began to think I was deluding myself."

"Were you?"

"The department chair certainly thought so. I wrote a grant request asking for funding to survey a few of those new sites. Instead, she suggested I'd have a better chance if I framed it as a preemptive search to track down her missing San'Shyuum."

Vale felt her eyes bug. "*What?* Tell me she wasn't serious."

"I have no idea. But it grew clear I wasn't going to get anywhere going through her."

"So you went around her."

"I tried. But you were gone, and if it had been someone else who arranged my appointment, I didn't know who that was. So I sent the grant request directly to Osman."

"*Admiral* Osman?" Serin Osman was none other than the commander in chief of ONI, and contract consultants did *not* send grant requests to her directly . . . not if they ever expected to receive ONI funds again. "Oh, boy. *That* couldn't have ended well."

"I mean . . . it didn't end badly. Someone sent me the UNSC's Military Survey of Uninhabited Planets, along with a translated copy of the Covenant's World Registry. I took the hint and cross-referenced them with the canvass I'd put together."

They reached the ladder that led up into the hangar at the Villa of Long Views, but Vale didn't start climbing. Once they returned to the villa proper, she and Iyuska would have to start worrying about Cortana's eavesdroppers again. And before that happened, she needed to know the rest of her old friend's story.

"And what you found . . . I presume it convinced you this ghost culture was real?"

"Yeah. At least the one on Netherop. There was a small battle there early in the war against the Covenant. The UNSC's after-action report mentioned an extensive road network, microwave weaponry mounted on crawling transports, coal-fired battery chargers, and indications of a buried city. The Military Survey of Uninhabited Planets suggested that it had possibly been abandoned and should be investigated by a properly equipped team."

"Sounds interesting. But not 'bring out the armigers and Aethras'–level interesting."

"That's because I haven't told you about the Covenant World Registry part yet. It lists two names for the planet: N'ba and Neska."

Vale grew more intrigued. N'ba was Sangheili for "world of death," while Neska sounded like a Sangheili phonetic transcription of a Forerunner word. An entry in a standard planetary catalog might have two names for plenty of reasons, but in a Covenant registry, one of those reasons was *definitely* that the second name came from the Forerunners.

"Neska . . . ," Vale repeated. "Wouldn't that translate to something like 'world that makes ghosts'?"

"From spoken Sangheili, yes. But my research assistant speaks and reads Sangheili almost as well as you do, and he pointed out something important: this was written in the Covenant World Registry—perhaps copied from an original Forerunner source."

Vale saw what the research assistant had been driving at. The written language of the Covenant had been derived from a common script used by the Forerunners in their everyday lives. The Covenant characters were highly embellished versions of the originals, but the root remained. If a Covenant word had been copied from a Forerunner source, the earlier meaning would still be accessible.

"And the Forerunner word has a different meaning, I take it?"

"Oh, yeah," Iyuska said. "One that may change everything we know about pre-Forerunner civilizations. This could make my reputation, Pia. No more bouncing around between appointments."

"I'll have to take your word for that," Vale said, ignoring the nickname. She had studied some Forerunner symbology, but had always been more interested in living cultures. "Still, we're not talking about archaeologists here. This was probably recorded by some fleetmaster's aide."

"An aide who would have regarded it as a holy word. An aide who would have taken great pains to transcribe it as accurately as possible—even if whoever translated the registry into English from Sangheili didn't."

"You had your research assistant go to the original registry," Vale surmised. "So . . . what did it say? Planet of Ghost Bringers?"

"Close: Planet of Ghost *Makers*." Iyuska grabbed Vale's elbow and squeezed. "You see what that means, right?"

"I see what you think it means. That the Forerunners visited Netherop and suffered some losses there."

"*Heavy* losses. You don't call a species 'ghost makers' unless they inflict some pretty serious casualties."

Vale shook her head. "Well, that's speculation—and pretty thin, at that. Didn't you say this was an industrial-age civilization? How does someone still burning fossil fuels do that kind of damage to *Forerunners*?"

Iyuska flashed an enigmatic smile. "That's the anomaly, isn't it? It needs explaining . . . which was why Osman authorized a survey."

"She *did*? So . . . spill, then! What did you find?"

"Nothing. ONI didn't come through with the funding in time."

"Ah. The Cortana Event." The AI's abrupt rise to galactic power had shattered ONI, driving the survivors so far underground that even many of its existing operatives had no idea whether their organization still existed—or what had become of Osman herself. "I'm sorry. I'm not even sure there still *is* an ONI—at least, not in quite the same way we're used to. Your survey is just a tiny piece of all the ops that were left in the lurch, if that's any consolation."

"It's really not," Iyuska said. "And Cadence wouldn't even entertain a new proposal."

"Who's Cadence?"

"The jealous cow."

"Okay. But then again . . . how could she have? How could she have secured the funding for you . . . even if she wanted to?"

"Funding wasn't a problem, as it turns out." Iyuska bit her lip. "Where it came from . . . *that*'s the problem."

Vale raised a brow and resisted the temptation to ask Iyuska what she meant by that. It would only give her a chance to stall and make excuses for whatever she'd done.

"I was approached by a Sangheili collector," Iyuska said. "I'm not saying Cadence mentioned my survey to him . . . but suddenly the department had everything it needed to keep her little pet projects going."

"Including her own search for the San'Shyuum?"

"Oh, yeah. She started outfitting the same week."

Vale considered what she'd heard, then shrugged. "Desperate times require desperate measures. So far, I'm not seeing what has you so worried—or Cortana's armigers here in the streets."

"I said he was a collector. He wanted something in return."

"Oh . . . oh, wait. You *didn't*."

"I did. I promised him first pick of whatever I find."

Vale let her chin drop. The deal was a terrible violation of academic ethics . . . and just the kind of bargain someone with morals as flexible as Iyuska's would happily strike when she was backed into a corner.

"So what happened then?" Vale asked. "Did Cadence find out?"

"I wish it were that simple. After the collector and I sucked marrow, I began to think there was something he wasn't telling me."

Though rather distasteful to humans, sucking the marrow from the fire-roasted femur of a *colo* was a Sangheili custom for sealing a deal. Once both parties had partaken, there was no backing out.

"Look—I'll do whatever I can," Vale said. "But the Arbiter is going to be *very* reluctant to intercede . . . especially if this is the reason there are armigers all over—"

"*Intercede?* You think I'm here for the Arbiter's help?"

"Aren't you?"

"No. Of course not. I'm here for ONI's help . . . or whatever's left of it. I know what the collector wants, and, Pia, I'm telling you we can't let him have it."

"So you want the UNSC to land a mission on Netherop?"

"You know, it's like you read my mind. But first . . . we need to stop at Gao."

"*What?* Gao is practically in rebellion again. Why would we need to go there?"

"To hire a consultant. Someone who knows Netherop in a way we never will."

CHAPTER 4

The thread of brown light changed to an oval, then a disk, and suddenly the *Sword of Harmony* was back in dimensional space, plummeting down a gravity well toward a world swaddled in a pall of brown clouds. The shipmaster rattled off a string of commands, and the bows of the stacked-hull frigate swung toward the horizon as the pilots maneuvered into orbit.

Thel 'Vadam turned away from the observation bubble and worked his way aft through a mass of control consoles and equipment banks to a projection pad at the back of the bridge. A tactical holograph of the N'ba planetary system had already taken form above the pad, which was ringed by Sangheili data readers standing at their assimilation lecterns. A trio of small, lumpy moons in equatorial orbits hung along the outer edge of the display, while a flotilla of corvettes held a medium polar orbit, and a single medium destroyer occupied a slightly lower equatorial orbit.

The corvettes were in a loose escort formation, with four light vessels arrayed in a diamond around the single heavy flagship. The destroyer was shepherding a swarm of Seraphs, which were flitting in and out of low orbit, using decoys and five-craft protective formations to laboriously clear a shell of orbital mines.

'Vadam took a place next to the senior obedientiary overseeing the operation. "You have been watching for followers transiting into the system, N'thil?"

"We have, Arbiter." Like the rest of the crew, N'thil 'Susl was a Covenant navy veteran who had joined the Swords of Sanghelios when his shipmaster pledged loyalty to 'Vadam at the onset of the Great Schism. "No tau surges yet. I am confident we lost them at Wedob."

That had been four Sanghelios days ago, when the *Sword of Harmony* entered slipspace from inside the gas giant's gravity well. They had been trying to elude a flight of Forerunner harriers, which had begun shadowing them five days earlier, after 'Vadam boarded the frigate near Sanghelios. Another four days of random slipspace transits had finally convinced 'Vadam the harriers were gone, but the delay had put them badly behind schedule.

"Remain vigilant and inform me if that changes," 'Vadam said. "I will be with Shipmaster 'Xiaqt."

As 'Vadam started forward toward the shipmaster's station, Crei 'Ayomuu appeared at his side, unarmed. The Arbiter had offered to let the Oath Warden carry his weapons as a sign of their collaboration, but 'Ayomuu had declined, claiming the tools of his trade were too clumsy in the cramped spaces of a small vessel.

Of course, there was a likelier reason. As most warriors held Oath Wardens in the same low esteem that 'Vadam did, going weaponless was a good way to reduce the likelihood of a violent confrontation. It was also a tacit suggestion that 'Ayomuu had other means to defend himself—means that no honorable warrior would know. The strategy was effective. The crewmembers did their best to ignore him, and when that was not possible, they treated him with a cautious formality that masked their disdain.

'Ayomuu said nothing as they walked, a courtesy that 'Vadam repaid by not sending him away when they reached the shipmaster's station. A relatively young commander with a stocky frame and boxy mandibles, Hul 'Xiaqt had earned his post by outliving his superiors during the initial fighting of the Great Schism, when the Covenant first started to break apart on High Charity. He had earned a senior position in the Swords of Sanghelios by being one of the first shipmasters to join 'Vadam at the beginning of that pivotal moment in Sangheili history.

'Xiaqt glanced in 'Ayomuu's direction just long enough to be certain 'Vadam knew the Oath Warden was standing behind him, then said, "The corvettes are from Feldokra. The destroyer comes from Om'a'Varo. I have confirmed our identity."

"That is well," 'Vadam said.

His plan was to search for Guardian-killing technology on N'ba without the Tyrant's knowledge. To make it appear that he was still at home in Vadam Keep, he had left his customary retinue—N'tho 'Sraom, Kola 'Baoth, and Usze 'Taham—on Sanghelios with instructions to show themselves frequently, then sent personal emissaries to request help from three of his most trusted colonial allies. There had been no time to await a reply, so 'Vadam had arrived at N'ba uncertain of how much support he would find. That two of his allies had been able to respond on such short notice with such sizable contingents was an auspicious start to the expedition.

Still, 'Vadam found himself wishing he could have recalled his finest shipmaster, Rtas 'Vadum, from the search for the San'Shyuum who had gone into hiding following the end of the Covenant War. He would have relished bringing the full might of the *Shadow of Intent* to bear.

"How long have they been here?" he asked.

"Ghe 'Talot has been mapping surface terrain for nearly a hundred units," 'Xiaqt said. "Olabisi Varo'dai has been clearing orbital mines for seventy-five."

"Then both kaidons are here in person?"

"Indeed. I spoke to them myself."

"Excellent."

Ghe 'Talot was a powerful kaidon on the ocean-moon Feldokra. 'Talot was not the high kaidon, but powerful enough that he would not be asked to explain his absence. Olabisi Varo'dai was the only kaidon on the frontier planet Om'a'Varo, which she was colonizing with others who had survived the destruction of her homeworld, Saepon'kal. At the height of the War of Annihilation, the humans had attacked Saepon'kal with a NOVA bomb—a weapon so destructive it had rendered the entire planet uninhabitable—and Olabisi had saved tens of thousands of Sangheili by seeing to their prompt evacuation.

"Arrange a rendezvous," 'Vadam said. "I would speak with them in person as soon as possible."

"It will be done."

'Xiaqt had barely turned toward the communications station before 'Ayomuu leaned in close to 'Vadam.

"I would never presume to tell a fleetmaster of your repute how to conduct an operation." The Oath Warden was speaking so softly that 'Vadam could barely hear him. "But perhaps you have overlooked something?"

"That is unlikely."

"The human, Keely Iyuska. She will be more easily captured if we are in hiding when she arrives."

"Why do you assume she *will* be arriving? If the human is not here by now, she may not be coming at all."

"Perhaps you were distracted when I explained," 'Ayomuu said, almost disrespectfully. "She specifically diverted to Vadam to see Spartan Vale. They have been friends since they were young."

"I am seldom distracted. And Spartan Vale's resources are limited. She lacks the authority to simply command a vessel to take her wherever she wishes—especially to a waste world beyond the edge of the civilized galaxy. Her superiors must first agree that her mission is worthwhile, and then there must be a suitable ship available."

"You doubt that the humans also wish to stop the Guardians? Or that they are clever enough to grasp the significance of Keely Iyuska's discovery?"

"I doubt neither. But the UNSC might not be as desperate as I am to believe her theory." 'Vadam looked through the forward observation bubble at the brown world below. "Even if the human is correct about what occurred in this system, it occurred many millennia ago. The likelihood that the Guardian killer still exists is minuscule. Spartan Vale's superiors may have already concluded that any effort to recover it is a fool's mission. And they may be right."

"But *you* are no fool, Arbiter. Why are you here if you believe this is folly?"

"Because I dare not risk being wrong. In the hands of my adversaries, such a weapon would doom the Sangheili to a dark future . . . or to no future at all."

'Ayomuu clicked his mandibles as though coming to a sudden realization. "I understand now. Only *you* can save the Sangheili."

"You are wiser than I realized." Noting the sardonic tone, 'Vadam locked gazes with him. "Braver too."

'Ayomuu raised his palms. "I am not arguing, Arbiter. Any

scullet can see that unless all Sangheili worlds act as one, the humans will overrun us like the vermin they are."

"The humans are not my only concern."

"As long as they are your first concern. But I leave it to you to save the Sangheili from annihilation. I am more interested in what you intend to do if this weapon exists and my client chooses it as his own—as is his right."

"Your client's agreement is not with me. *Our* agreement is that I will help you prevent Keely Iyuska from violating hers."

"Which she can never do . . . if she does not arrive," 'Ayomuu said. "That is a technicality—and one my client is unlikely to accept."

"Perhaps that would matter to me if I knew your client's identity."

'Ayomuu looked to the deck, then exhaled loudly. "You know I can never tell you that."

"Then why would I care about anything your client is unlikely to accept?"

'Vadam abruptly ended the conversation by stepping away from the shipmaster's station. He descended into the contemplation pit at the front of the bridge and stared down into N'ba's pall of brown clouds. He had no idea whether the Guardian killer he was seeking still existed—or if it *ever* had—but he felt certain his interests and those of 'Ayomuu's client would soon come into conflict. Sending an archaeological expedition to N'ba was an expense not even the wealthiest kaidon could afford without expecting a significant return, and that someone had made such a large investment in secret was reason enough for 'Vadam to investigate.

But what had convinced him to mount his own expedition were the armigers' efforts to stop Keely Iyuska. Even before becoming the Tyrant, Cortana had proven herself to be an extremely capable and resourceful AI. 'Vadam had once seen John-117 stake the survival of not only humanity, but of the Sangheili and most of the galaxy's other intelligent species on little more than her word. Now, after vanishing into slipspace aboard the ship of a rogue Forerunner named the Didact, and falling prey to the inevitable madness caused by the runaway growth of her own neural matrix while *already* in the throes of rampancy, she was as close to omniscient as any being in the galaxy. In deploying the Guardians, Cortana had proven that she could tap into the knowledge of the Forerunners themselves— which meant she might actually *know* whether such a weapon had once existed.

If the possibility that it still existed worried her enough that she was hunting this human xenoarchaeologist with armigers and Forerunner harriers, then 'Vadam had to do everything in his power to find it himself—because he had spoken the truth to 'Ayomuu. He could not allow a Guardian-killing weapon to fall into the hands of his adversaries.

Or into Cortana's.

As virtuous and noble as the AI had been when she helped 'Vadam and John-117 defeat the Flood, she was quite mad now.

'Vadam spent the next few units in contemplative silence, admiring the precision with which the Seraphs from the Varo'dai destroyer cleared mines—and wondering who had placed the shell around the planet in the first place. From the launching delay when a decoy passed one of the mines, and their corkscrewing approach pattern, they appeared to be self-targeting *Jaet*-pattern plasma torpedoes from early in the war against humanity. The Covenant World Registry, which he had consulted during the long journey from Sanghelios, made no mention of a mine shell around

N'ba. All the entry noted was that the frigate *Radiant Arrow* had been lost here early in the war, and that eight cycles later, another frigate, the *Steadfast Strike*, had been destroyed on the planet's surface by a squad of "demons." The Prophet of Truth had deemed the two misfortunes a sign of divine displeasure and forbade all Covenant vessels from entering the system.

'Vadam had never seen such a record before, and he found it odd. *Demons* was the Covenant term for Spartans . . . and with good reason, if one was on the receiving end of their attacks. But what a team of Spartans had been doing on such a remote, uninhabited world, he could not imagine . . . any more than he could imagine why a Covenant frigate would have descended through those brown clouds to land on the surface all those years ago. It was tempting to attribute such enigmas to the Guardian killer's presence, but he knew better. In war, such events happened for their own reasons, or for no reason at all, and seizing on them to support an unverifiable theory was a sure way to blind oneself to the real danger.

At last, Shipmaster 'Xiaqt stepped to the edge of the contemplation pit. "We are synchronizing orbits with both kaidons' transports. They will be aboard shortly."

"I will speak with them in the Obedientiaries' Mess. Have the Oath Warden join us."

'Xiaqt dipped his chins in distaste. "Shall I warn the kaidons?"

"Yes, Shipmaster. That might be wise."

'Vadam turned back to the observation bubble and spent the next twenty centals watching 'Talot's corvettes continue their mapping operations. They were well above the mine shell, high enough that even with interferometry and phased-array antennas, their imaging radars would produce maps with error margins measured in dozens of units rather than fractions. And with tens of thousands of plasma torpedoes between them and the ground, the mines themselves would produce backscatter that further reduced accuracy.

The obvious solution would have been to suspend mapping operations and help Varo'dai clear the mine shell, especially since it would have to be done anyway before any attempt to reach the surface. But 'Vadam was not about to second-guess the two kaidons. Certainly, they had discussed the matter and decided to divide the tasks for a reason he did not yet understand.

At length, he felt the soft shudder of a successful docking and knew the first of the kaidons would be aboard shortly. He climbed out of the contemplation pit and went aft to the Obedientiaries' Mess.

'Ayomuu was already seated at the first saddle on the starboard side of the table. 'Vadam took the saddle at the aft end of the table, effectively flipping the cabin orientation and placing the Oath Warden on his left—a position that would not be interpreted by the arriving kaidons as one of power. 'Ayomuu merely tilted his head in amusement, perhaps satisfied that 'Vadam had not actually ordered him to take a less prominent seat.

Ghe 'Talot arrived, then stopped in the doorway to consider the seating arrangements. A small warrior with a proud bearing, he was perhaps twice 'Vadam's age. His scar-laced face and dented skull attested to the ravages of the Blooding Years on Feldokra, which had once been a Covenant fortress world and home to countless war factories and weapon stores. He wore no helmet, but was ornately armored in the gold harness of a kaidon. He carried both a plasma pistol and energy sword.

"Welcome, Ghe." 'Vadam extended an open palm. "Have any seat. This is a mess cabin, not an audience chamber."

'Talot dipped his head, then went straight to the head of the table and perched himself on the saddle. "It is good to sit with you again, Arbiter." 'Talot cast a wary eye in 'Ayomuu's direction, then looked back to 'Vadam. "It has been a long time since we could speak in person, old friend."

"Too long," 'Vadam agreed. 'Talot's manner was familiar bordering on arrogant, perhaps because he wanted to impress on 'Ayomuu that an Oath Warden was no one's equal here. "I am grateful you came."

"How could I not? Feldokra is a hard place to live, but your ongoing support makes it possible."

"We support each other." The deep-sea mines worked by 'Talot's clan supplied Kolaar Manufactorum with many of the rare elements required for its most important production materials—or at least they had, until Cortana restricted shipments of elements used primarily for the manufacture of weapons and matériel. "As we always have, and always will."

"So long as it pleases the Tyrant." A low rumble sounded deep in 'Talot's throat, then he added, "If her restrictions continue, my clan will be *eating* what it mines—not refining it. I hope this weapon is real, Thel."

"I believe the Arbiter hopes so too." The voice came from the cabin doorway, where a tall Sangheili female with a sinewy build and lustrous green eyes stood awaiting permission to enter. "But there is only one way to turn hope into knowledge."

'Talot's eyes flashed and quickly shifted away, and 'Vadam realized he might have erred in assuming the two kaidons had formulated a plan in his absence.

"Welcome, Olabisi." 'Vadam extended a palm toward the table. "Join us."

Olabisi Varo'daí considered her options only briefly before taking the middle saddle on the side of the table opposite 'Ayomuu, a neutral position that also had the advantage of elbow room. She wore a sleeveless gold tunic belted at the waist, with the well-worn handle of an energy sword hanging on her right hip. Unlike 'Talot, she did not have a long history of trade relations with the Vadam clan to protect. She had come out of gratitude for the aid 'Vadam had provided in helping her clan settle on a new world following the destruction of Saepon'kal.

Once she was seated, 'Vadam said, "Thank you for coming." He did not offer food or refreshment, as the sharing of sustenance was an expression of unity that no kaidon would extend to an Oath Warden. "You know Ghe 'Talot?"

Varo'dai's attention remained locked on 'Vadam. "We met after I arrived, but we have not found time for a meal together."

"I see." 'Vadam turned to 'Talot. "We will have to remedy that soon, will we not, Ghe?"

The old kaidon's jaws clenched tight—which was more surprising to 'Vadam than it probably should have been. Ghe 'Talot was a staid traditionalist who supported 'Vadam's aspirations as much out of self-interest as idealism. He believed a united Concert of Worlds would need a powerful military, and that such a powerful military would need the rare elements his clan mined on Feldokra, as well as the dozens of former Covenant armories scattered across his state. And Olabisi Varo'dai was his opposite—a pragmatic female compelled by necessity to lead a life of radical nonconformity.

Olabisi had been forced at a young age to become the figurehead matriarch of a usurped keep. To ensure her survival, she had secretly trained a loyal cadre of female rangers, whom she had eventually needed to call out to defend her first nest. The loyal rangers had taken her enemies by surprise, slaying every usurper in the clan and securing her status as the first female Marshal of Varo. Decades later, when a failed ambush above Saepon'kal resulted in the detonation of the NOVA bomb, she had convinced the master of a late-arriving flotilla to forsake his original mission and begin rescue operations. Afterward, 'Vadam had arranged a charter of colonization on an uninhabited world in the Emauzs system, and Olabisi Varo'dai had been chosen by the grateful survivors to become the first kaidon of Om'a'Varo—which meant "daughter of Varo" in the old Saepon'kal dialect. 'Vadam was not sure whether the world's name was meant to honor Olabisi or the home continent of most of the Sangheili she had saved, but he suspected it was both.

Now Olabisi Varo'dai had come to N'ba not because it profited her keep, but simply because the Arbiter had asked it of her. 'Talot would no doubt consider it naive to commit warriors and vessels without a tangible benefit to one's own clan. But Varo'dai was the kind of kaidon 'Vadam needed if he hoped to see the Sangheili Concert of Worlds stand proud.

After allowing 'Talot's lack of response to hang in the air for too long, 'Vadam turned to Varo'dai. "Tell me, Olabisi . . . how *do* we turn hope into knowledge?"

"It is no secret, Arbiter." Varo'dai fixed her gaze on 'Talot, an assertive posture that would no doubt irritate the old kaidon—and was probably meant to. "We clear the mine shell, then we go down and look."

"How odd," 'Ayomuu said. "I could have sworn that was what your Seraphs are already doing."

"It is." Varo'dai glanced in the Oath Warden's direction only long enough to part her lower mandibles as though she were about to regurgitate something, then returned her gaze to 'Talot. "But far more of the shell would be cleared by now, had the kaidon from Feldokra committed his corvettes to the effort."

'Talot extended an arm toward Varo'dai and jabbed his finger against the tabletop. "As I told you, matriarch, my resources are better utilized studying surface topography."

"Olabisi *is* a matriarch." 'Vadam was careful to keep his voice even and gentle, so 'Talot would be able to guard his ego by viewing the rebuke as more of a suggestion. "But she is also a kaidon—one who sent a whole cadre of her rangers to me when the Blooding Years began. To this day, some remain with the Swords of Sanghelios. Let us address her by the more martial title."

"A female kaidon?" 'Talot angled his head away. "What fools did that?"

"Technically, a female *high* kaidon, as she leads all three keeps on Om'a'Varo." 'Vadam placed his palms on the table and leaned toward 'Talot. "Ghe, when we turned against the Covenant, we changed the destiny of the galaxy. Now the Sangheili must change with it, or we are all lost. Olabisi has proven herself—not only as a capable leader, but as an honorable one. We will show her the respect she has earned."

During the uneasy silence that followed, 'Vadam realized that the delay in his arrival had cost more than time. 'Talot and Varo'dai had allowed their differences of perspective to fester into an outright enmity preventing them from working together, and a critical task that should have been almost completed before 'Vadam arrived was only half-done. Any advantage that he had hoped to win by moving quickly was lost. Now he would be fortunate to have a landing party on the surface before the Tyrant discovered where he had vanished to . . . or before Olympia Vale arrived with her own expedition.

After a long moment, 'Talot finally met 'Vadam's gaze. "As you command, Arbiter."

"It is hard to toss aside the traditions that have kept us strong for five millennia." 'Ayomuu's voice grew smooth and intimate.

"But if that is what the Arbiter demands of us, then that is what we must do."

"It is what the times demand, not I." 'Vadam was beginning to wonder how much he still needed 'Ayomuu's cooperation. Given the Oath Warden's obvious efforts to exploit the tension between 'Talot and Varo'dai, it might be better for 'Ayomuu to spend the rest of the expedition locked in a sleep pod. "Time is short, Oath Warden. Let us have no more of your interruptions. I would like to hear what Ghe has learned about N'ba's topography."

"Enough to target the areas we should map more precisely from lower orbits," 'Talot said. "We have identified thousands of anomalous mounds connected by roadways and dry riverbeds. They are spaced very regularly, at least a thousand xilapaces apart. They appear to be buried cities."

Being a staunch Sangheili isolationist, 'Talot was opting for the old Sangheili system of measurements. A pace was just under seven Covenant units or two human meters long, and a xilapace was a thousand paces . . . meaning the mounds in question were about seven million Covenant units apart, or two thousand human kilometers.

"That is a lot of territory for one city to control," 'Vadam observed. "Were there smaller mounds between them?"

"Not that our scanners could discern."

"And certainly not from such a high orbit," Varo'dai added. "Perhaps we can improve the resolution once we have cleared the mine shell."

"I have no doubt." 'Vadam spoke quickly, trying to move the discussion along before 'Talot could return the taunt. "But how will that help us figure out which mound to search? Or even know that it is a location we should be searching?"

"Wise questions," 'Ayomuu said. "Is it not a shame that we lack a xenoarchaeologist to answer them for us?"

'Vadam shot the Oath Warden a warning look.

"I am only saying that Keely Iyuska is a determined human," 'Ayomuu said. "Had you told me that the UNSC was unlikely to send an expedition, perhaps I could have suggested a way to lure her onto yours."

Before 'Vadam could call for a security team to have 'Ayomuu removed from the mess, Varo'dai locked gazes with the Oath Warden and asked, "What difference would *that* make? How can a human xenoarchaeologist find what is not there?"

An alarmed silence descended on the table, then 'Talot finally asked, "What do you mean, *not there?*"

"Exactly what I said. The Tyrant has access to every record this Keely Iyuska does, and she is far more intelligent. If a human xenoarchaeologist can discern that there is a Guardian-killing weapon on N'ba, then so can the Tyrant. And yet . . . here we are. At N'ba. With no Guardian or any sign of the Tyrant's forces of any kind trying to stop us. If the Guardian killer still existed—if it ever existed—surely we would have been attacked by now."

"If that is what you believe," 'Ayomuu asked, "then why are *you* here?"

"Because the Arbiter asked it of me." Varo'dai turned to 'Vadam. "I will always answer your call, but I would not be performing my duty if I did not voice this misgiving. I have had patrols out since before the *Raider's Creche* entered orbit. There are no enemy forces watching N'ba, and that makes no sense."

"It does if the Guardian killer is still functional," 'Talot said. "Even the Tyrant does not have unlimited resources. Why send a Guardian if she knows it will only be destroyed?"

"Or perhaps she did send one," 'Ayomuu added, "and it has already been destroyed."

Varo'dai raised her eyes to the overhead, but 'Vadam was not so ready to dismiss their arguments.

"You did not see the Tyrant's deployments in Vadam Valley," he noted. "She was attempting to stop us there, desperate to capture Keely Iyuska. And when she failed, her harriers tracked the *Sword of Harmony* for days before we were finally able to free ourselves."

"Then it sounds as if it is Keely Iyuska whom the Tyrant fears," Varo'dai said. "Not us."

"Is that not what I have been saying all along?" 'Ayomuu asked. "The Tyrant fears Keely Iyuska because only she can find this weapon."

"*If* the weapon exists," 'Vadam countered.

"Oh, it exists, Arbiter," 'Ayomuu said. "You would not be here if you did not believe that."

Or at least believe it was possible, 'Vadam admitted . . . but only to himself. The discussion was now circular, always ending up at the same points. He raised his hand, signaling for silence, and spent a few moments sorting through the various arguments, considering how likely it was that Keely Iyuska knew something Cortana did not, and whether the Tyrant could have some other reason for hunting the human. Was it possible that the xenoarchaeologist and Spartan Vale had not arrived at N'ba because they had already been taken? Did the absence of Cortana's forces at N'ba suggest the Guardian killer no longer existed . . . or that it *did*?

The trouble was, all of these scenarios were plausible—but also disconnected, if not actually contradictory. The picture remained incomplete.

'Vadam turned to Varo'dai. "Your patrols . . . what have they found here?"

"Asteroids and moons . . . what one would expect in an abandoned system."

"But N'ba has not been abandoned for that long," 'Vadam said. "The UNSC and the Covenant fought here just decades ago. There should still be derelict communication and reconnaissance satellites in orbit, and likely vessel parts and debris—some evidence of battle. And the planet is surrounded by a mine shell, so you should have found slipspace alert beacons in the equilibrium points. Did you?"

"We came upon a few vessel parts in orbit, but no satellites," Varo'dai said. "And we detected some ghost returns from one of the equilibrium points. When we investigated, we found beacon debris."

"Were they modern beacons?" 'Vadam asked. "Or from something earlier in the war?"

"We did not think to check." Varo'dai glanced away. "In truth, I could not even tell you whether it had been a Covenant beacon or human. I apologize, Arbiter."

"There is no need to." As 'Vadam spoke, he was careful to avoid looking in 'Talot's direction. "At least you launched the investigation."

"Ah, battle debris . . . at the site of a battle . . . how interesting." 'Ayomuu glanced in 'Talot's direction. "I assume all of this actually means something?"

"It does." 'Vadam rose. "It means we need to be more careful . . . far more careful than we have been."

CHAPTER 5

A s the hired pipistrelle VTOL dropped into the jungle, Olympia Vale kept her eyes fixed on the village below and her medical bag trapped on the deck between her feet. She was supposed to be an off-world research nurse visiting Gao to help her colleague collect tissue samples from the victims of a new form of brain-wasting prion disease, so she had traded her Mjolnir armor for blue scrubs. She carried her sidearm tucked inside the medical bag.

Keely Iyuska sat on the other side of the passenger cabin, similarly attired and peering down into the dirt plaza where they were about to land. Her voice was audible through the cabin headset system, dictating environmental observations into her datapad. Vale did not know whether her friend was making the notes out of academic habit or in an attempt to support their cover, but at least it kept her focused on something other than the thrill of operating under an assumed identity.

"... village is located on a mountain bench deep in the remote jungle." Iyuska was nearly shouting into her datapad so the microphone would capture her voice over the pipistrelle's thumping rotors. "The only ground access appears to be a single road, dead-ending at the village itself. There are two vehicles visible from the air, both antiquated trucks parked at the entrance to the central square. The buildings are dry-stacked stone with thatched roofs, the largest two stories . . ."

Iyuska let her sentence trail off, then spoke again in alarm. "There are men down there with guns!"

"I can see that." Vale did not have to look to know that Iyuska had turned toward her. "Six of them, with Insurrection-era MA3A and MA5B assault rifles. It's okay. They're only trying to intimidate us."

"You sound sure of that, ma'am," the pilot said, also speaking through the headset system. "I hope you're right."

"It only makes sense." Vale resisted the temptation to point out that the sentries carried no extra ammunition and stood clustered in easily targeted groups—a civilian nurse would not have noticed such things. "If they intended to ambush us, wouldn't they be hiding?"

"That's what you and I would do," replied the pilot. A thick-waisted man with curly black hair and a three-day growth of beard, Arturo Ramus was a "dark hire" VTOL owner/operator and card-carrying member of the Committee to Preserve Gao Independence. He would have been devastated to learn that he was listed in three different ONI databases, all describing him as a top-notch pilot and highly reliable transport contractor. "But these people here have their own ways."

"Just put us on the ground," Vale said. "You can loiter at a safe altitude until we wave you down."

"I can only do that for thirty minutes. Any longer, and we won't have the fuel to return—"

"Thirty minutes will be plenty of time," Vale said. "Either they're willing to let us take samples or they're not."

"Or they're willing to rob and murder you." As Ramus spoke, the pipistrelle descended into the square. "And if they are, there will be nothing I can do to help. The Ministry of Protection doesn't come this far into the jungle."

"Understood," Vale said. "But no worries. We're not carrying anything worth shooting us over."

"That doesn't mean you're safe. Don't mistake the value you place on your lives for the value *they* do." The pipistrelle touched down, but didn't settle onto its landing struts. "I will be watching for your signal. If there's trouble, go to where the road crosses the mountain's shoulder."

"That must be five kilometers away . . . uphill," Iyuska noted.

"More like seven," Ramus said. "It's the closest place I can land outside the village."

"It won't come to that." Vale unbuckled her crash harness and reached for the side-door latch handle. "But it's always good to have a backup plan."

Vale slid the door open, shouldered her medical bag, and dropped onto the ground. The square was barely large enough for the pipistrelle, no more than fifteen meters across, and the sentries were up against the houses, ducking their heads and shielding their eyes from the blowing dirt. Vale squeezed her own eyes into slits and turned toward a stocky man standing in front of the largest building. Dressed a little better than the other sentries, in military boots and clean utilities, he had chin-length blond hair tucked behind his ears and a red, weathered face with deep lines at the corners of his mouth. He looked to be in his mid-forties, old enough to be a potential candidate for the consultant Iyuska wanted to hire.

Before asking her superiors to send an expedition to the outer edge of the colonized galaxy, Vale had spent a day reviewing everything she could find about Netherop and quickly recognized the wisdom of Iyuska's suggestion. In June of 2526, none other than the Spartans of Blue Team had inserted onto the planet and encountered the Castoffs, a band of young castaways whose pirate ancestors had been marooned on the sweltering world many generations earlier. Desperate to escape the deadly environment, the band struck a bargain to help Blue Team in exchange for being rescued. Despite some dispute about the terms of the agreement, the Castoffs were extracted with Blue Team, then quietly slipped onto the semi-insurrectionist world of Gao to make a new home for themselves.

That had been thirty-three years ago, ten years before Vale was born. The Castoffs had been between seven and twenty years old at the time, and they had used their resettlement funds to purchase a small patch of jungle and establish the village where Vale and Iyuska had just landed.

So it seemed fairly likely that the stocky man whom Vale was now striding toward had actually been born on Netherop. By the time the pipistrelle ascended and the rotor wash subsided, she was standing face-to-face with him. Taking such an assertive posture would open a crack in her cover, but it would not be unusual for a traveling medical team to have a security specialist—and with six armed men clearly trying to intimidate them, security came first.

"Is that an MA3A assault rifle?" As Vale spoke, she smiled and casually reached toward the barrel, so she could prevent him from swinging the muzzle in her direction. "I've never actually seen one in the field. May I?"

She grabbed the weapon's handguard and looked down into the man's surprised eyes, giving him a chance to gracefully acquiesce.

He was a head and a half shorter than Vale, at least twenty kilograms lighter, and neither strong enough nor skilled enough to keep her from simply taking the weapon.

When he appeared reluctant to let go, Vale flexed her wrist just enough to tip the muzzle down toward his foot. "I'm asking nicely. But we both know you won't be pointing this thing anywhere I don't want you to. Let's keep this polite."

"You call this polite?"

"Well, it isn't rude. You want to see rude?"

The man sighed. "I don't think so." He released the weapon, then glanced to his right and gave a quick shake of his head, signaling the other sentries to stand down. "Go ahead, have a look."

"Thank you." Vale took the rifle, then pointed the barrel at the ground, ejected the magazine, and cleared the chamber. "I've heard that these things are impossible to ruin." She pulled the rear takedown pin, removed the charging handle and bolt carrier, then separated the upper and lower receivers and made a show of inspecting the interior. "That must be true, because this weapon looks like it's had fifty thousand rounds through it."

"Not since I have had it. We have no need for that much shooting in Paraiso. There aren't many visitors."

"*Paraiso?*" Iyuska asked, joining them. "Really? That's what you call this place?"

"It is a paradise to us." The man switched his gaze to Iyuska. "What do you want here, and who are you?"

"We're looking for a woman named Rosa Fuertes," Vale said, not allowing Iyuska to respond. They were coming to an inflection point where they would either need to reveal their true identities or attempt to recruit their consultant under false pretenses, and Vale wanted to keep their options open until she had a read on which strategy was more likely to succeed. "We understand she has the new prion disease emerging in this part of the jungle."

"How do you know about that?"

"She was diagnosed at the Hospital de Neiva," Vale said, again avoiding a direct answer. The residents of Paraiso were probably well aware that ONI had been keeping close tabs on them for the last thirty-three years, but nothing would be gained by showing her hand just yet. "We'd like to speak with her."

"You're doing a lot of talking, not much answering."

"There are some things we can only discuss with the patient," Vale said. "Whether you join us will be her choice."

"And whether you see her will be mine. So far, I say no."

"Why is that?"

The man fixed his gaze on the half-disassembled assault rifle in Vale's hand. "Because you don't seem like a real traveling nurse."

"I hear that a lot. I was a medic in the service."

"Which branch? ONI?"

Vale stared at him and did not reply. The safest thing for the mission would be to recruit the consultant Iyuska wanted without breaking their cover as medical researchers. But the man's suspicious attitude had clearly brought the feasibility of that tactic into doubt.

The man exhaled loudly. "I thought so. What do you want?"

"Let's talk inside."

Vale reassembled the empty assault rifle and pressed it against his chest, but before she could push him through the door behind him, a shutter banged open above their heads. Vale looked up to see the weather-lined face of a woman in her mid-fifties peering down. She had a square jaw, broad cheeks, and eyes so sunken it was difficult to see her pale green irises.

"That wasn't the deal." The woman was the right age to be

Rosa Fuertes, who had called herself simply Roselle when she helped lead the Castoffs on Netherop. In a futile attempt to evade ONI surveillance, she and the entire band of former castaways had changed their names when they settled on Gao. "We were promised the UNSC would leave us alone, as long as we didn't talk about the Spartans."

"We're not breaking the deal," Vale said. "We're here to offer you another one."

"It could be very lucrative." Iyuska made a point of looking across the square toward the old trucks, then directed her gaze back to the man standing in front of her. "Lucrative enough to buy new trucks."

The man's eyes lit, but he managed to avoid glancing toward the trucks. "Not interested. The UNSC makes a lot of promises. It doesn't keep them all."

"But I'm not the UNSC." Iyuska swung her medical bag off her shoulder and began to open the top. "I'm independent."

Vale saw the man lick his lips and knew Iyuska had set the hook. Vale put her free hand on top of the bag. "Wait."

But the man's gaze was already locked on the knapsack. "You have the money in there?"

"Let's talk about that inside," Vale said.

She pushed the man into the plank door behind him until it snapped its latch and swung open. He gave a shrill whistle as he stumbled backward, and boots began to thump across the dirt square toward them. Then Vale and the man were inside a large room with wooden tables and a ceiling so low she had to hunch over to keep from hitting her head on the beams supporting the floor above. A stairway at the back of the room led upstairs. Vale pulled Iyuska in behind her, kicked the door shut, and shoved the man onto the nearest bench.

"You're *not* thinking of trying to rob us, right?"

"I just want to see the money." As he spoke, he looked not at Vale, but at the door behind her. "It's the smart thing when you are dealing with the UNSC."

Vale heard the hinge squeal and spun around to see the door swinging open. She slammed her palm into it and felt the blow connect and send someone flying back into the square, then jammed the empty assault rifle under the latch to wedge it closed.

The muffled voice of a young male called, "Arnaldo?"

"Back them off. Now." Vale let her medical bag slip into the crook of her elbow, then opened it and reached inside. "I didn't come here to hurt anyone."

"So give us the money," said the man who was presumably Arnaldo. "And nobody will get hurt."

"That's not what I was thinking." Vale pulled her M6H sidearm from the medical bag. "Last chance."

Again, the muffled voice sounded through the door. "Arnaldo? Should we come in? Is Rosa safe?"

Footsteps, light and slow, descended the stairway at the back of the room. Arnaldo glanced toward the sound, then looked back to Vale and smirked. "Last chance for *you*. You're outnumbered five to one, and you have nothing but a pistol? You might get me, but I don't think you and your contractor will leave here alive."

The old-woman voice sounded from the stairs: "Arnaldo, stop being a fool." The woman stepped into the room and started toward Arnaldo, one finger jabbing toward the door. "Call them off before you get us all killed."

"*Us?*" Arnaldo pointed toward Iyuska. "That one is not even armed, Rosa. I doubt she can even shoot."

"She won't need to." Rosa Fuertes extended her hand toward Vale, gesturing up the length of her body. "Look at her size. Do you think they can't fight just because they aren't wearing their armor?"

Arnaldo's eyes widened. "You're a Spartan?"

"Among other things," Vale said. "Does that make you want to reevaluate your options?"

"Arnaldo!" The voice outside was growing impatient. "We're coming—"

"No!" Arnaldo gave a loud three-note whistle that drew a chorus of alarmed whispers, then yelled, "Do it now!"

Vale pointed her pistol toward the door, but instead of anyone trying to charge through, all she heard was the receding thump of fleeing boots.

Fuertes turned to Arnaldo and flicked her fingers toward the door. "You too. Leave us, Arnaldo. I will handle this."

When Arnaldo scowled and made no move to rise, Vale slipped her sidearm into her waistband, then said, "Don't worry—she'll be fine. We really *are* here to make a deal. We just need to hire a consultant."

Fuertes nodded. "You see? Go on. The others will need to know that everything is okay while I negotiate."

Arnaldo's brow rose. "Negotiate? You're in no condition—"

"I am the one who will be going. I am the one who will negotiate."

"Wait a minute," Vale said. "This consulting will be off-world, probably under rugged conditions, and—"

"You think I've forgotten what Netherop is like?" Fuertes asked.

"You're obviously a smart woman," Vale said, not even attempting to deny that Netherop was their destination. As soon as Fuertes had heard the word *consultant* and recognized Vale as a Spartan, she had probably known the UNSC was going back to Netherop. "So you know hiring you is not something we'll be interested in."

"Too bad. Because I am not going to allow anyone else to go—unless you would like to hire Samson. I don't doubt ONI has been keeping track of him too."

"They have," Vale said. The latest intelligence reports had tagged Samson, who had been Roselle's mate and co-leader on Netherop, running off with a Gao woman shortly after the Cast-offs settled here. "He's been incarcerated since 2556, and the UNSC is hardly in a position to ask the Gao Ministry of Justice for an early release."

"That's too bad. He is the only one I hate enough to send back with you. It will have to be me . . . or nobody. Which can you afford less?"

Vale turned to Iyuska. "How much do we need her?"

Iyuska shrugged. "Well, she *did* spend half her life using the same protogenic technology we'll be investigating . . . and living in the ruins of a culture nobody else has even heard of."

Fuertes smiled and pointed to the table. "You can leave the money there."

Iyuska cocked her brow at Vale.

Vale sighed and said to Fuertes, "Okay then—some ground rules. You understand that nobody can know we were here?" She pointed to herself and Iyuska. "I mean *nobody*. Or that you're gone. The whole village has to keep this secret."

"Oh, we are very good at keeping secrets. We kept the secret of the Spartans far longer than the UNSC did."

"Fair enough," Vale said. "But that includes comm units and other electronics. No one can mention any of this near a microphone."

Fuertes smirked. "That will not be a problem. There are no longer microphones in Paraiso. They made it too easy for ONI to eavesdrop on us."

"It's not ONI I'm worried about. One last question." Vale took a breath. "How sick *are* you?"

Fuertes paused. "It won't kill me before I serve your purpose." She sank down on a bench. "I won't let it . . . that I promise you."

CHAPTER 6

How much longer he could hold his flotilla on Neska's second moon, Atriox did not know. The five vessels—four karves and a drekar serving as his flagship—were crowded together beneath one of the cloaking generators that the Banished used to hide their outposts. The technology would conceal them from anything less than a close flyover, but the *Hammer of Fate*'s tactical holograph showed five Seraphs climbing away from the Sangheili fleet on a problematic trajectory. If the patrol passed nearby, an infrared scanner could notice a slight temperature anomaly around the cloaking umbrella. Or an optical analyzer might alert on a minuscule Doppler shift of bending light, or a sharp-eyed pilot could spot one of the camouflaged sensor antennas being used to monitor the Sangheili vessels orbiting Neska.

It was impossible to know exactly *what* might go wrong, but there were many possibilities—each one worthy of his thought. Concealment technology was never perfect, and strength lay in preparation.

Atriox glanced toward the threat-analysis station and caught the new overseer, Kallo, studying him. The young Jiralhanae's eyes flashed, and he quickly found an excuse to look over the shoulder of a long-beaked Kig-Yar operator busy confirming trajectories and estimating time until contact.

Atriox delighted in such reactions. He fostered a reputation for the intolerance of mediocrity—he had personally executed Kallo's predecessor half a cycle ago, when the threat-analysis station nearly missed the arrival of the Sangheili frigate *Sword of Harmony*—and he deliberately used his battle-flattened nose, square face, and braided beard to cultivate a fearsome, bare-browed appearance that no other Jiralhanae could match. And on this mission, he would allow—for he could afford—no margin of error.

When the five Seraphs continued to climb toward the flotilla's hiding place, Atriox turned toward a Banished Sangheili standing at his side. "They are approaching for a close flyby. They have grown even more cautious."

"It only makes sense, Warmaster." The Banished's foremost expert on all things Forerunner, Eto 'Saljhoo had long wrinkles over his brows, watery gray eyes, and a set of mandibles that never quite closed. He pointed to the trio of corvettes climbing out of medium orbit. "They just spent the better part of a cycle clearing mines, and now they are taking defensive stations in orbit. The Sangheili are preparing to send down their expedition."

"There are still some mines in orbit." Atriox ran a hand down his long beard braids. "It would only take another twenty units to finish the task. Why stop now?"

"Perhaps they have grown as weary of waiting as our own warriors have," 'Saljhoo replied. Although they had been watching the Sangheili clear mines for three-quarters of a cycle, the Banished flotilla had been hiding on Neska's smallest moon even longer. For more than a cycle and a half they had been waiting in comm silence for the untrustworthy human woman Keely Iyuska to show herself, and even Atriox was beginning to doubt she would. "The shell cannot be very dense at this point."

"It is dense *enough*," Atriox growled. He turned to the signals listener. "Any warnings from the decoys?"

The listener, a grizzled warrior with the tips of two broken tusks showing above his lip, turned his head in the negative. "I would tell you immediately, Warmaster. The decoys remain comm silent."

Atriox grunted an acknowledgment. Just reaching Neska had required a complicated, time-consuming operation that he would never have undertaken, had it not been so important to his plans for Zeta Halo.

The first step had been sending a reconnaissance yawl to the edge of the Ephyra system to listen for any supraluminal transmission beacons that might be dispatching periodic status confirmation messages to one of Cortana's listening stations. The yawl had identified only one, transmitting on an interval of five cycles, and Atriox had been careful to launch his operation immediately after the most recent signal.

Then, upon entering the system with his full operational flotilla, he had sent a trio of karves on a slingshot maneuver around Neska, hoping to draw off any sentinels that Cortana might have watching the planet. Two of the vessels had emerged trailing gravitic anomalies that were almost certainly cloaked harriers. Now the decoys were skulking the outer reaches of the system, laying mines, dropping beacons, and doing everything possible to hold the interest of their stalkers. They would break comm silence only if the harriers stopped following them, but Atriox knew that would be sooner than he liked. The diversion could not work forever.

Next had come the tricky part. After luring the two harriers away, Atriox used his stealth flagship, the drekar *Hammer of Fate*, to isolate Neska's planetary system, destroying the supraluminal transmission beacon that his reconnaissance yawl had identified earlier . . . *and* a roving harrier that had exposed itself by coming to investigate. Only then had the flotilla entered orbit and eliminated the dozens of communications and reconnaissance satellites that had been abandoned during the much-earlier battles between the Covenant and the United Nations Space Command.

It had been tedious work, but necessary. Eliminating the satellites was the only way to be certain none of them harbored any AI watchers, who would have little trouble slipping aboard a departing vessel and remaining hidden until the opportunity came to alert Cortana to events on Neska.

But none of that explained the sudden burst of activity from the Sangheili fleet. Something had changed, and he could not see what.

Yet.

Atriox spoke to the signals listener again. "You have been monitoring the comms traffic between Sangheili vessels?"

"Yes, Warmaster. There is little else for me to do. It is filled with orders from the *Sword of Harmony*, most recently from the Arbiter himself."

'Saljhoo gasped. "What?! The *Arbiter* is here?!" Without awaiting an answer, he turned to Atriox. "*That* explains everything. He has grown weary of waiting and kicked the boulder down the hill."

"Perhaps," Atriox mused. He was assuming that the Arbiter had arrived half a cycle ago aboard the *Sword of Harmony*—which seemed a safe guess, given that was the vessel where the orders were coming from. "If he is in a hurry now, it must be that he knows something we do not."

"Are you suggesting a Guardian . . . ?" 'Saljhoo asked. "How could the Arbiter know of that?"

"It is not a Guardian." The speaker was Tovarus, an amber-eyed Jiralhanae who was Atriox's second-in-command for this mission. He stepped over to the tactical holograph and stood behind 'Saljhoo. "If the Sangheili thought a Guardian was coming, they would already be fleeing Neska, not trying to reach its surface."

"Cortana would not send a Guardian here," Atriox said. As he had seen firsthand, Guardians were designed to subjugate worlds; using one to chase off a small fleet of vessels would be overkill, and Cortana's complement of Guardians was already too small for her needs. Besides, she was too wise to risk losing one to the same weapon that had destroyed a Guardian during the Forerunners' time—the same weapon that Atriox was here to recover. "She would send her own fleet."

"You are correct, Warmaster," Tovarus said. "Yet we arrived a cycle and a half ago. That is when our risk of discovery was highest—when we were busy conducting operations. Had one of her sentinels slipped away or transmitted an alert without us noticing, her fleet would be here by now, would it not?"

As Tovarus uttered the word *transmitted*, 'Saljhoo's mandibles began to work back and forth. Atriox allowed the irritating grinding to continue for a few moments, then finally demanded, "Why are you doing that?"

'Saljhoo stilled his face. "Apologies, Warmaster—I am merely in thought. A transmission is not the only way a signal would draw Cortana's attention to Neska. The lack of a signal would too."

"You are thinking of the transmission beacon we destroyed?" Atriox asked.

"Just so. It was certainly active when we arrived, so an AI somewhere will be expecting a periodic status confirmation."

"But not for three more cycles," Atriox said. Because it required so much energy to send a supraluminal signal, transmission beacons sent status reports infrequently, at well-spaced intervals. "Is that enough time?"

"I would hope so," 'Saljhoo said. "If we find the correct site quickly, and the transmission interval is not randomized."

"Randomized?" Atriox growled. 'Saljhoo had wanted to examine the transmission beacon before it was destroyed, claiming he could not be certain of its design and capabilities until he inspected the energy core. He made a similar claim before any Forerunner artifact was destroyed, and Atriox tried to accommodate him whenever possible. This time, however, there had been too much risk that the studymaster's tampering would trigger an automatic transmission. "Did the reconnaissance yawl not measure five cycles between transmissions twice in a row?"

"Your memory is accurate, as always, Warmaster. I only worry that twice is statistically uncertain. The interval could still be—"

"It is not random." Atriox had seen—and benefited from—enough flukes to know the studymaster was technically correct. But a warmaster who attacked only when he was certain of success was a warmaster who never attacked at all. "Providing the Sangheili do not find the site before us, we still have three cycles. *Is that enough time?*"

'Saljhoo fell silent and looked away. Atriox would not have allowed such hesitation to anyone else, but the studymaster's unique value lay in his ability to think and recall esoteric trifles that no one else in the Banished even knew. 'Saljhoo required time to work, and Atriox had learned through long experience that the old Sangheili usually delivered the best results when it was permitted.

But after a dozen breaths, Atriox grew impatient. The harriers could discover his decoy ruse at any moment. If that happened, they would return to Neska, see the Sangheili flotilla, and summon help from the Apparition. Then Atriox would have to abandon his plan, for he did not have the strength to confront her directly—not without the Guardian-killing weapon he had come to recover.

Even worse, Atriox might not even realize his ruse had failed until an Apparition fleet arrived to attack him. With their stealth capabilities, harriers could be even more difficult to track than UNSC prowlers, and the possibility of one slipping away from its decoy and returning to Neska undetected was significant.

And it grew more significant each passing day.

"I will not await an answer any longer," Atriox warned. "I require one *now*."

'Saljhoo finally lifted his gaze again. "Our best chance of finding the trikala still lies in waiting for the human Keely Iyuska."

Trikala was the code name 'Saljhoo had bestowed on the Guardian-killing weapon they had come to recover. It referred to a three-bladed spear wielded by a nameless god venerated by the Silent Shadow during the Age of Seven Worlds. Atriox had little interest in the Sangheili's pre-Covenant history, so the only other thing he recalled was the reason the mythic weapon had three blades: to rive the mind, body, and spirit . . . in the past, present, and future.

Atriox gnashed his tusks, then finally accepted that 'Saljhoo was not going to temper his assertion. "Why doesn't the Arbiter share your reluctance? Clearly, he is not waiting."

"Let him start his excavations. It will make no difference if his expedition does not know where to dig."

Kallo, the threat-analysis overseer, suddenly turned toward Atriox. "Trajectory confirmed, Warmaster. Five Seraphs inbound to our position—we estimate close inspection range in forty-two centals."

"I have heard." Atriox turned to the *Hammer*'s Sangheili comm controller. "Inform the shipmasters. Have all karves come to ready status, but weapons and drives are to remain cold until the *Hammer of Fate* activates."

There was a small chance that their sudden flurry of point-to-point communications would result in a detectable signal bleeding out from beneath the cloaking umbrella, but the risk had to be taken. To minimize the flotilla's electromagnetic emissions profile, the *Hammer of Fate* was the only vessel under the concealment cloak monitoring space around Neska.

As the comm controller relayed the command, Atriox turned back to 'Saljhoo. "If the Seraphs discover us, we will have no choice but to eliminate the entire Sangheili fleet and undertake the search ourselves."

"If it comes to that, I believe it would be wiser to withdraw. Without Iyuska, our chance of locating the trikala before Cortana realizes we are here is . . . incalculably small."

"I do not see why. In the past, you have always been good at finding what we seek."

"Because I am a student of Forerunner culture, and we were always seeking Forerunner artifacts," 'Saljhoo said. "The trikala seems undoubtedly pre-Forerunner. I have no clue what it might look like, much less where to start looking for it."

"Then how can you know that it exists?" Tovarus asked.

"You saw the holograph yourself," 'Saljhoo said. "How can you doubt that it does?"

Atriox knew of the holographic video the studymaster referred to, which had been recovered during their time on the Ark. Recorded from the cockpit of a Phaeton fighter, it showed a luminous bolt erupting from a lush world of indigo oceans and turquoise jungles to enwrap a Forerunner Guardian. In the record, the

Guardian quickly began to fall toward the planet, then disintegrated into shards, dropping through the atmosphere in a spiraling tangle of smoky columns. It had been enough to convince Atriox that the trikala was real—and just the weapon he needed to defeat Cortana.

"That only proves the trikala *once* existed," Tovarus said. "How can we be certain it is still so?"

"Because what the Forerunners feared does not die," 'Saljhoo replied. "The Flood is proof enough of that—or have you forgotten Voridus's folly at High Charity?"

"No one has forgotten *that*," Atriox said. A talented but impulsive tinkerer, Voridus had nearly unleashed an infestation of the ancient parasite on the entire Ark, after entering the crashed and ruined Covenant space station against Atriox's order. "But it does not mean the trikala has endured."

"I cannot guarantee it," 'Saljhoo admitted. "But there must be a good chance, or Cortana would not have sent three harriers to watch over it."

Atriox snorted. "And I would never have decided to recover it." He looked at the overhead for a moment, thinking, then finally returned his gaze to 'Saljhoo. "We cannot wait for Iyuska forever—especially when we cannot be sure that she will even come."

"She *will* come," 'Saljhoo said. "It is too important to her. Confirming her theory would make her the foremost protogenic scholar in the human colonies."

"I would have more trust in that, had you not needed to hire an Oath Warden to hunt her down."

"And had I not needed to hire the Oath Warden in the first place, I would not be so certain. Iyuska is risking her life by breaking our agreement. She would only do so if she believes that the trikala endured—and that it belongs in human hands."

A rumble of amusement rose into Atriox's chest. "That is the folly of humans—so many of them cannot understand that a thing only belongs to the one who takes it." He turned back to the tactical holograph and studied the approaching Seraphs. "But if that patrol penetrates our cloaking umbrella, waiting for Iyuska will no longer be an option."

"I fail to see why," 'Saljhoo said. "How long could it take to eliminate such a small Sangheili fleet?"

"Your confidence is refreshing." Atriox continued to watch the tactical holograph. "I am not concerned about the size of the Sangheili fleet or its capabilities. The simple truth is a battle that large would be difficult to hide from the—"

Atriox fell silent when the approaching Seraphs turned away from the holographic moon and accelerated toward an empty area above Neska's far horizon. An instant later, a fog of blue letters and numbers—the symbols for quantum particles—appeared in the image. They were rising from behind the planet, in the same location toward which the Seraphs were traveling.

Atriox shifted his gaze toward Kallo and his threat operators, then pointed toward the fog of symbols. "Those particles. What are they?"

"Pions and neutrinos." Kallo gulped down a mouthful of nervous saliva. "They are the product of hadronic decay. That is—"

"I *know* what hadronic decay is. The branching faction, what is it?"

"Just under sixty-five percent. We're seeing tau decay. We did not see the surge because it was hidden behind the planet."

"But not from the Sangheili." At least Atriox now knew what they had seen that he at first had not—a tau surge indicated something emerging from slipspace. "What has arrived?"

Kallo looked to his threat-analysis operators, who continued to study displays and tap touch pads. Atriox did not ask again, knowing he would only delay the response if he kept breaking their concentration.

Finally, the Kig-Yar operator looked up. "It is difficult to say, Warmaster. We are receiving no sensor readings from the vicinity of the decay cloud, but the particle density suggests UNSC technology, and the trajectory alterations of the approaching Seraphs suggests something within the mass of a light cruiser."

"Perhaps a *stealth* cruiser, then," Atriox said.

"Finally." 'Saljhoo let out his breath in relief, then turned to Atriox. "The human, Keely Iyuska, has arrived."

"Apparently. And with enough UNSC marines to *keep* whatever she finds."

'Saljhoo's mandibles sagged open a bit more than usual, but Atriox's thoughts had already turned to Kallo and the threat-analysis station's failure to detect the tau surge as quickly as had the Sangheili. True, the arriving vessel had emerged from slipspace on the far side of Neska, and the world's mass would have made detection difficult.

But many of the surge particles would have been neutrinos, most of which would have passed through the planet unimpeded . . . and the analysis operators should at least have detected that.

How disappointing. Atriox had not expected to need a new overseer quite so soon.

CHAPTER 7

From atop the rim of the vast crater, the distant hill seemed to be floating on a lake of refracted light. Sometimes, the "lake" appeared blue, until a heat shimmer rippled across it and the color changed to green. Or yellow. Or orange. Even a deep ruby red. Then another shimmer would come, and it would suddenly turn indigo. Or violet. Purple, as dark as night.

Thel 'Vadam had visited many hot, arid worlds and seen mirages of many differing hues, but never one that cycled through the color spectrum like this. Nor one so bright that its glare reflected off the brown clouds overhead. Then again, he had never stood on the surface of a world as blazingly hot as N'ba. Not without a fire harness.

The color-shifting mirage was only one of the reasons they had elected to begin their investigations here. The hill in the center of the crater was actually a tel, a mound of detritus where one city had been built atop the ruins of another for millennia. Ghe 'Talot's topological survey had found thousands of similar tels all over N'ba, but only this one was surrounded by a basin of radar-absorbing terrain that could not be imaged. Add to that its location on the equator, where a weapon emplacement would have a clear firing lane into every pocket of surrounding space as the planet rotated, and it seemed the obvious place to begin their search for the Guardian killer.

Which 'Vadam had elected to do early, before the shell of orbital mines had been completely cleared from above N'ba, over the objections of both Varo'dai and 'Talot. Unconvinced that the UNSC would be interested enough in the myth of the Guardian killer to send its own expedition to N'ba, neither kaidon had seen the necessity of risking an insertion through even a sparse shell of mines—until the *Sword of Harmony*'s sensor operators had detected the tau surge of a vessel arriving from slipspace. After that, they had not been able to launch a preliminary landing party quickly enough.

At the moment, 'Vadam was watching a tiny fleck of silver, dead center at the base of the tel. Dancing in the heat shimmer and too small to have a distinctive shape, it kept vanishing beneath the mirage and reappearing just a little bit larger. For a time, 'Vadam had suspected it was a trick of heat and light, but as it slowly grew to the size of a fingertip, he began to think it was real.

"I cannot be the only one who sees that," 'Vadam said.

"The gray shape coming toward us?" Olabisi Varo'dai replied. "I see it too."

"How can you know which way it is traveling?" 'Talot asked. "It is barely visible."

Along with Crei 'Ayomuu and twenty warriors, the two kaidons were standing with 'Vadam on the gravelly rim, discussing the scanner-absorbing crater through their helmet voicemitters, trying to decide whether its strange properties posed a danger to their Phantoms. Rather than their actual gold kaidon armor, Varo'dai and 'Talot wore ranger-commander harnesses, which had the advantage of being the appropriate color for their rank, while utilizing its EVA capabilities to protect them from N'ba's fierce heat. 'Vadam wore his Arbiter's harness, with a climate-controlling tech-suit and HUD-capable goggles beneath the actual armor. 'Ayomuu remained in his stylized Oath Warden's armor, having assured 'Vadam that despite its conspicuous purple color and spiked shoulder pauldrons, it was far more practical than the standard ranger harness being offered in its place.

Varo'dai leaned forward and peered around 'Vadam to address 'Talot. "It has been growing brighter and larger for five centals. And it has stayed between us and the center of the tel for three centals. It is coming toward us."

"You have been watching it for five centals?" 'Vadam asked. "Truly?"

"Perhaps even six. I thought I was imagining it at first."

"Impressive," 'Vadam said. Clearly, Varo'dai's eyesight was better than 'Talot's . . . and his own. "Summon a navigator. There may be a way to use the object to determine indirectly how far we are from the tel."

Varo'dai tipped her helmet to one side. The color-shifting cycle of the mirage and the scanner-absorbing properties of the crater floor were not the formation's only strange attributes. The dusty slopes of the tel had defeated every kind of range-finding instrument they had available. The ranging signal simply went out and never returned, and optical triangulation always yielded an answer of infinite. The only method left was indirect calculation—though it was hard to imagine that succeeding either. The only constant about the object was that it seemed to be coming toward them.

'Vadam spread his hands. "It will hurt nothing to try."

"As you command," Varo'dai said.

She turned away from the tel and looked back toward their landing site, a bench of rocky red ground that separated the crater's outside wall from the base of a looming mountain. The group's three Phantoms sat in a triangle formation about fifty paces across, half-hidden by jagged red boulders and tufts of yellow spike brush as tall as most Sangheili. She used her helmet comm to relay 'Vadam's order and was told the navigator would be along as soon as she collected her instruments.

Fifty paces beyond the Phantoms, a large seam cave ran diagonally up the face of a chalky cliff ringing the base of the looming mountain. 'Vadam knew two Feldokran sentries were posted inside the cave, but they were not visible—perhaps because they had retreated deeper into the darkness, where their night vision would not be compromised by N'ba's ambient light.

Atop the chalky cliff were five Varo rangers, hiding among the rocks and keeping watch on the mountain above. Its slopes were naturally terraced, rising in a succession of red cliff faces and brush-edged benches that seemed to continue forever, until they finally vanished into N'ba's ever-present blanket of low brown clouds.

Varo'dai's navigator emerged from her Phantom carrying a long tube and a satchel, then climbed to the rim of the crater. She acknowledged 'Talot with a helmet dip, which he failed to return, then turned to 'Vadam.

"Arbiter of all Sangheili, I am Lyess Varo'dai." She had the same surname as her kaidon—Varo—because she was of the same clan, and the same suffix—*dai*—because she was also a swordmaster in the short-path method of combat. "Kaidon Varo'dai has told me what you desire. I must warn you that any answer I can provide will be wildly imprecise. Even if I am able to use triangulation, the object is moving, and without knowing its velocity—"

"Do what you can," 'Vadam said. "Anything you can tell us is more than we know."

"As you command."

Lyess opened her satchel, then mounted the long tube—an optical range finder—horizontally on a telescoping monopod and began to scan the mirage. It took about a cental for her to focus on the approaching object, which had grown to the apparent size of a knuckle. It continued to dance and hide in the heat shimmer, making its shape difficult to discern, and its brightness appeared to have stabilized at a whitish silver.

After only a moment, Lyess let out a raspy breath and replaced the range finder with a monocular. After finding the object in the lens, she let out another breath, then peered over the top of the instrument for too long. Finally, she rocked her helmet from one side to the other and began to return her instruments to the satchel.

'Vadam looked to Varo'dai for an explanation, and the kaidon in turn looked to Lyess.

"Well?" Varo'dai asked. "What did you discover?"

"Nothing." Lyess closed the satchel fasteners. "The range-finder reading was infinite."

"Yet that is *something*," 'Vadam said. "Now we know the interference comes from the mirage, not the tel."

Lyess turned her helmet to face him, but she made no reply, and he had the feeling that his attempt at encouragement had fallen flat. Devoted realists by training and necessity, Varo rangers were not known for optimistic dispositions.

"What about the monocular?" 'Vadam asked.

"Nothing with that either. I was hoping to discern what the object truly is. If I could estimate a size, that would give me something to work with."

"And?"

"The light is too refracted. I could tell that it is block shaped rather than rounded, and that it is doubling in apparent size every ten centals. But that alone tells us nothing."

"Enough of this time-wasting," 'Talot said. "I will send a pair of Ghosts ahead to scout."

"And expose our presence?" Varo'dai said.

"Was it not you who said it is coming toward us?" asked 'Ayomuu. "That would suggest whatever this thing is, it already knows we are here."

"So it would," 'Vadam said. Given the difficulties imaging anything inside the crater—either visually or electronically—he was not entirely confident 'Talot's scouts would succeed . . . or even survive. But better to risk two warriors than all of them. "Very well, Ghe. Summon your Ghosts."

"As you command," 'Talot said.

He turned toward the Talot warriors standing on the rim next to him and sent a pair down to retrieve the vehicles. 'Vadam continued to watch the mirage-filled crater, studying the mysterious object in the vain hope it would assume enough of a shape to suggest exactly what it was. As it grew to the apparent size of an eyeball, it stopped vanishing into the heat distortion and began thinning into a rectangle that sometimes appeared to be floating atop the lake of shimmering light and other times pushing through it.

After observing this for long moments in silence, 'Talot finally asked, "Did the World Registry not say that N'ba is uninhabited?"

"Abandoned," Varo'dai replied. "There was a civilization here once. Otherwise, how could there be all these tels?"

"Abandoned . . . uninhabited." 'Ayomuu's tone was dismissive. "What is the difference? Either way, the Registry was wrong. If no one lives on N'ba now, what then is that thing coming toward us?"

"That is what Ghe's scouts are going to tell us, is it not?"

Varo'dai turned and looked down the small slope toward 'Talot's Phantom, where there was no sign of Ghosts being mounted. "If they are ever ready."

'Talot turned toward his Phantom and stood staring, then activated his helmet comm. *"Where are the Ghosts? Why have you not brought them?"*

A moment passed with no reply, then a pair of Ghosts appeared behind 'Talot's Phantom, accelerating toward the seam cave in the face of the white cliff. The drivers were either novices or suffering from head injuries, for the vehicles were wildly out of control, sporadically weaving back and forth across the ground. From his viewpoint atop the crater rim, all 'Vadam could see of the operators were scrawny arms spread wide to grasp the control handles and battle helmets sitting atop overstuffed rucksacks.

Not Sangheili.

'Talot's voice sounded over the battlenet. *"Wyune, Daphob! What are you—"*

"Those are not your scouts," 'Vadam said. "They look like . . . *humans?"*

A low clatter sounded to both sides of 'Vadam as the warriors on the crater rim began to grab weapons and start down the slope. He waved them back and spoke over the common channel.

"Hold here." The last thing he wanted was a blind charge into a potential ambush. "Await my orders."

As he spoke, another pair of Ghosts shot from behind the Varo Phantom and accelerated toward the cave. These operators were no better than the first two, which was all that saved them as the Varo rangers atop the cliff spun around and opened fire. Geysers of red dust filled the air, then 'Vadam lost sight of all four vehicles. A plume of flame billowed up through the rust-colored curtain. When the rangers stopped firing a few moments later, a single smoking Ghost lay in the dirt, upside down. Whether the rider had escaped into the cave or lay trapped under the vehicle, 'Vadam could not tell.

The rangers stepped to the edge of the cliff and peered down, their weapon muzzles sweeping back and forth as they searched for targets.

'Vadam glanced over to 'Talot. "What have you heard from your sentries in the cave?"

"Nothing. I am still trying to make contact."

"You can stop trying," 'Vadam said, guessing the two sentries were already dead. "The raiders fled into the cave because that is where they came from."

"The drop from the cliff top is not terrible," Varo'dai said. "Shall I have some rangers pursue?"

"Not until we understand what is happening," 'Vadam replied. Noting that his own Phantom was the only one that had not yet lost its Ghosts, he commed the pilot. "Razk, what is your status?"

When Razk did not reply, one of the rangers atop the cliff reported, "Something is wrong, Arbiter. The loading ramp is closing, and your Ghosts are no longer where they were landed."

"Go!"

Four of Varo'dai's female rangers leapt off the cliff and landed in a forward roll. One came up on her haunches and turned to cover the cave where the surviving Ghosts had disappeared, while the second raced toward the Ghost that had been stopped by their carbine fire. The other two rangers came up running for 'Vadam's Phantom . . . which he realized they had no hope of reaching in time. The three dropships had landed in a standard triangle formation fifty paces from the cliff, and even the fastest Sangheili could not leap down and cover that distance in the time it took to raise a ramp.

The rangers were only halfway there when they stopped and dropped out of sight behind some spike brush. 'Vadam could not see the back of the Phantom from the crater rim, but he knew the boarding ramp had already closed and there was no way to easily retake the craft. They would either have to breach the hull or override the ramp controls and then fight their way aboard, and by that time, the raiders would have disabled the craft.

"I am sorry, Arbiter," commed one of the rangers. *"We were not fast enough."*

"You did well. It was a hasty suggestion." Conscious that he had usurped Varo'dai's command authority by directly ordering her rangers to attempt boarding his Phantom, he turned to the kaidon. "Perhaps your rangers should inspect the two damaged Phantoms. It might tell us something about who we are dealing with."

"I was thinking the same thing," Varo'dai replied.

As she passed the order along, 'Talot turned to 'Vadam and asked, "Did you not see the helmets? They looked human."

"My impression, as well," 'Vadam said. "During the War of Annihilation, we saw more than enough of those helmets on human infantry."

"I am surprised to learn that you actually *saw* the humans you were killing," 'Ayomuu said. "I was under the impression you simply immolated them from orbit."

"I did that too," 'Vadam said, "after I became a shipmaster. But I also fought as a foot warrior with surface units dispatched to recover sacred artifacts. I have seen thousands of those helmets . . . and not always fleeing in the other direction."

"Well, there *was* a battle fought on N'ba," 'Ayomuu said. "The UNSC record of it is how the planet came to Keely Iyuska's attention."

"So, they are just marooned here?" 'Talot asked. "That is what you are saying?"

"That battle was over twenty Urs cycles ago," 'Vadam said. "If those humans have lasted in this wasteland that long, they are not *just* castaways. They are soldiers. Fine ones."

'Vadam looked toward his Phantom and wondered what the humans were doing inside. Cowering in fear, wondering what to do now that they had been caught? Or trying to figure out how to operate the weapons and drives?

It would not be as simple as running a thumb up the touch pad that raised the ramp. Dropships were complex craft that required specialized training, and even a Sangheili who had flown the old Achoem-manufactured Phantoms early in the Covenant War would need time to study and experiment with the controls of more recent models. And if the would-be pilot had never even flown a Phantom before, the pilot's chance of actually powering one up—much less doing it quickly—would be minuscule.

Whatever they were doing, 'Vadam decided, he had time to be cautious and investigate. He turned to ask Varo'dai about her rangers' findings, but she was looking back into the crater, her attention fixed on the mysterious object approaching through the mirage.

"Olabisi?" he asked. "What is it?"

"I just wanted to make sure it was still coming. And not any faster."

'Vadam took a moment to study the object himself. Half again as wide as the last time he looked, it was still the shape of a thin rectangle and seemed to be sliding side to side with the wavering light.

"You think it is a distraction?" 'Vadam was beginning to wonder if it had been a little too easy to find a site to investigate. "That this raid was coordinated?"

Varo'dai dipped her helmet. "That was my fear, but I think it is just a coincidence. The . . . shape . . . is still approaching, and at the same speed. A distraction would have turned around once we discovered the attack, or accelerated."

"Assuming it is in constant communication with the raiders." 'Vadam paused, watching the mirage color change from pink to orange. "I am beginning to worry that we were lured to this place."

Varo'dai considered the possibility for a moment. "Those raiders are risking their lives to steal a few Ghosts and snatch some supplies. That hardly suggests the capability to monitor orbital reconnaissance sweeps and toy with the laws of optical physics."

"It does seem beyond the reach of desperate thieves." But 'Vadam was not entirely convinced that the raiders' presence was pure coincidence. On harsh worlds like N'ba, creatures clustered around resource caches. And a unique topological feature—a signal-absorbing crater, for example—might well be associated with such a place. "Assign someone to keep watch on the crater."

Before Varo'dai could reply, one of the rangers inspecting the damaged Phantoms reported over the battlenet, *The pilots in both Phantoms have been killed.*

'Vadam's hearts clenched. He always hated to lose warriors, especially when their deaths were so utterly senseless and unnecessary. But what should he have expected? The humans marooned on N'ba had no way to know that the war was long over and that the enemies who had once sought to exterminate them would now gladly rescue them.

"It appears they were lured onto the loading ramp, then decapitated and dragged back inside."

"Decapitated?" Varo'dai asked. "How?"

"The wounds have been sealed by heat. So, my guess is with energy swords."

Sangheili weapons, but any species with a thumbed hand could use them, and N'ba's battlefields had likely been strewn with them early in the war. It was growing more apparent that the humans from the cave were indeed castaways here on N'ba, and that they had survived so long by scavenging battle wreckage. That meant they were at least somewhat familiar with Sangheili technology.

'Vadam began to worry he had been a little too hasty to dismiss the possibility of having his Phantom's weapons turned against them. "And what is the condition of the Phantom itself?"

"The flight and targeting controls have been destroyed. And the weapons and provisions lockers have been raided."

"These humans are nothing to fear, then," 'Talot said. "Just desperate for food and tools."

"In my experience," Varo'dai noted, "desperate enemies are the most dangerous kind."

"They may be desperate," 'Vadam said, "but they are not our enemies."

"Forgive me, Arbiter," Varo'dai said. "But the humans seem to believe otherwise. As do I. Too many Sangheili lives have been lost on this oven world to believe anything else."

"Because the humans have been marooned here and have no idea the war is over," 'Vadam said. "What would *you* do in their place?"

The rumble of grinding mandibles growled from Varo'dai's voicemitter. "I would attack. The same as any true warrior."

"And humans *are* true warriors," 'Vadam said. "I have learned that much in my dealings with them. Once I go down there and explain—"

"Go down there?" Varo'dai asked. "Surely, you do not mean alone. They have already killed seven of us."

"That does not mean they can kill *me*," 'Vadam replied. "Have your warriors lower their weapons and remain here while I speak with them. Perhaps we can strike a bargain."

"For information?" As 'Ayomuu spoke, he was looking back across the crater toward the tel. "Even if they have the answers you seek, you cannot trust their word."

"I have bargained with humans before," 'Vadam said. "I know how to find the honest ones."

"At least let me go down first," 'Talot said. "If there are any surprises, it will be better—"

"Do you speak any of their languages?" 'Vadam asked.

"I . . . can send for a translation disk."

"From where? One of your corvettes?" 'Vadam shifted his gaze to 'Talot's Phantom. "Or did you think to put one aboard your Phantom?"

'Talot could only turn his helmet aside.

"No harm will come to me, despite their ferocity," 'Vadam said. "When they realize we are not preparing to attack, their curiosity will stay their hands."

Without further debate, he turned and started down the slope alone . . . and found himself flanked by 'Talot on one side and Varo'dai on the other.

Before he could object, Varo'dai said, "No harm will come to you, Arbiter. You said so yourself."

'Vadam clacked his mandibles in frustration, then glanced along the crater rim and saw that the two kaidons were leaving their subordinates behind.

"As you wish," he said. "But *no* weapons. We need their co-operation, not their surrender."

He started down again, then heard someone fall in behind him. He glanced back to see Crei 'Ayomuu.

"You will want me with you, as well," the Oath Warden said. "I can be very persuasive."

'Vadam merely lifted his helmet in affirmation and continued down the slope. He did not actually want 'Ayomuu's help, but he knew the Oath Warden would resist being sent back, and even a short argument might give these misguided humans cause to doubt 'Vadam's authority.

He led the small group to the base of the slope, then started across the rocky bench . . . and noticed three tufts of yellow spike brush trembling in the wind.

Except there *was* no wind. The air was as still and scorching as the interior of a kiln, and the only movement in the surrounding spikes was the illusory wavering of heat-induced light refraction. After a moment, he realized the tufts were creeping toward his Phantom at a pace so slow it was barely noticeable. He pretended not to see and continued forward . . . until he and his companions were about twenty paces from the spiky masses and 'Talot's arm began to rise.

"Put your arm down!" 'Vadam spoke over the battlenet, hoping to avoid alarming their quarry. "I see them!"

Too late. The trio of spike plants tipped upward and began to rise, hanging from the backs of three ragged figures so thin and scrawny it took a moment to even recognize them as humans.

"No weapons!" 'Vadam commanded, again over the battlenet. "We capture them alive."

Motioning for Varo'dai and 'Talot to follow, he raced forward. The humans turned and opened fire with plasma rifles, presumably taken from the Sangheili they had killed aboard the two Phantoms. Only one of them, a female, seemed to have any experience using such weapons, taking 'Vadam's energy shields down before he was close enough to slap the rifle from her hand. Her companions were not treated as gently by the kaidons, who simply knocked the two humans to the ground and pinned them each with a foot.

When 'Vadam's target reached for the energy sword hilt hanging at her hip, he grabbed the woman by the throat and lifted her off the ground.

"Stop." He spoke in English, having learned it fluently in the years since the war so he could communicate with his human allies more naturally. "You have no need to die."

The female's brow shot up at his words, and her hand froze a half unit from her weapon. Small and bony even by human standards, she had a dirty, deeply lined face with a small round nose and delicate chin. Her eyes were so pale they were almost white, and her ropy red-brown hair hung past her shoulders. Her clothes were filthy and crudely fashioned from coarsely woven fabric, and her boots were made from some sort of leather with a pebbly texture—so familiar that it held 'Vadam's gaze until he finally realized it looked like tanned Sangheili hide. Around her waist, she wore a polyamide belt with a metal buckle and a combat knife in a metal scabbard, both bearing the bird-and-globe emblem of the UNSC. Pinned to the neck of her shirt were a pair of seven-pointed gold leaves.

The woman moved her hands away from her body and shifted her gaze toward her two companions. Both males, they were younger than her, probably barely old enough to fight by human standards. Their bellies were flat, but their thin bodies looked like skin stretched over bones. Their clothes and accessories were the same as the female's, save that instead of gold leaves, they had inverted chevrons on their shirt necks. Both were glaring up at their captors with gaunt, hard expressions that suggested they felt only rage toward the Sangheili that had spared their lives.

Perhaps these humans had more honor than most.

"Your companions will be released after we have spoken," 'Vadam said. He lowered her to the ground, then pointed at the gold leaves on the neck of her shirt. "You were a commander for the UNSC during the war against the Covenant?"

"I still am." The female rubbed her neck. "Lieutenant Commander Amalea Petrov, service number 12099-30223-AP. That's all I'm telling you."

"Of course. As you wish."

Judging by her appearance, it seemed likely that this woman—Amalea Petrov—had indeed been marooned since the only recorded surface battle on N'ba, early in the war. That meant she had spent more than thirty years here, by her own UNSC calendar, and probably had no idea what had been happening in the rest of the Orion Arm. 'Vadam was not skilled at estimating human ages by appearance, but she had gray streaks in her hair, and most of the humans he had met with gray hair were senior officers well over sixty UNSC years old.

Which meant she had been trapped on N'ba for half her life. And the young males with her had probably been born here. To them, 'Vadam and his Sangheili companions would be mortal enemies, and he suspected the only reason Petrov was not holding a weapon right now was that if she reached for one, she would not live long enough to use it.

It would take a lot of patience to overcome that kind of ingrained hatred and win the woman's cooperation, but 'Vadam decided it was worth trying. The humans had been hiding near the crater for a reason when his reconnaissance team landed, and he needed to know what it was.

"I am Thel 'Vadam, Arbiter of the Sangheili. I was once Supreme Commander of the Fleet of Particular Justice."

"Is that supposed to impress me?"

"Not at all. It is my deepest shame. I made war against your kind because I believed in a lie."

Petrov sneaked a glance toward 'Vadam's Phantom, then quickly looked back to 'Vadam. "So you've come here to Netherop to . . . *what*? Surrender?"

Instead of replying, 'Vadam spoke to Varo'dai in Sangheili. "She is watching my Phantom. Post three of your rangers between us and the ramp. They will open fire *only* to defend us."

Varo'dai acknowledged the command, then looked away to issue her own orders.

Petrov's expression hardened. "What are you doing?"

"Preparing to stop whatever you are planning. You have already killed seven Sangheili warriors that I know of, and right now you are fortunate enough to not also be among the dead. My patience has its limits."

"What do you expect?" Petrov's hand began to drift toward the energy sword hanging from her belt. "We're at war."

"Do *not*." 'Vadam pointed at her hand, then reached for his own weapon. "The war is long over, Commander Petrov."

"Sure it is." Petrov carefully moved her hand away from the energy sword. "You alien scum kill millions of people and glass entire worlds, and you think the war can just be *over*? Those kinds of wars are never over."

"And yet, it *is*, Commander." 'Vadam moved his hand away from his own energy sword. "As I have explained, the War of Annihilation was launched to protect a lie."

"What lie?"

"About the Great Journey." When Petrov's face remained blank, it occurred to 'Vadam that she had never heard the phrase. Of course—she had been marooned here on N'ba long before humanity had any understanding of why the Covenant was attacking them. "The Prophets claimed we could join the Forerunners in eternal transcendence by activating the Sacred Rings, but they were wrong. The only thing activating Halo would have accomplished was the death of all sentient beings in the galaxy—"

"You're talking nonsense." Petrov began to look at him in a way that even a nonhuman could recognize as incredulous. "You expect me to believe that?"

"Yes, I expect you to believe it. Because it is true. The Covenant's war against humanity was to find and activate Halo. But the Prophets were wrong, and the war is long over."

He could tell by the tightness in her lips that she was completely skeptical . . . and he understood why. He had come of age in a culture devoted to searching for the Sacred Rings, and even he would never have accepted such a thing, had an Oracle of the Forerunners themselves not told him it was so.

"I will explain later," 'Vadam continued. "But know this: I am not your enemy. The *Sangheili* are not your enemy."

"You're a terrible liar." Petrov glanced toward the Phantom again, and her voice grew loud. *"Now!"*

Her hand moved toward her energy sword again, and before 'Vadam could stop her, 'Ayomuu reached past and sprayed a blue aerosol in her face. Petrov's eyes rolled back and her knees buckled. By the time she hit the ground, 'Ayomuu was already crouching down to remove the weapons from her belt. Whatever he had just used, no sign of it was in his hand now.

"What have you *done?*" 'Vadam asked in Sangheili.

"Kept the peace," 'Ayomuu answered, also in Sangheili.

As the Oath Warden spoke, the *clunk* of an emergency-dropped ramp sounded from the last Phantom. 'Vadam turned to see two gaunt humans fleeing the cargo bay. 'Talot and Varo'dai immediately reached for their plasma rifles, and as the humans disappeared around the far side of the Phantom, 'Vadam glimpsed several Varo rangers shouldering their carbines.

"Hold your attack!" he ordered over the battlenet. "Open a lane and allow them into the cave."

A moment later, the humans reappeared on the reconnaissance team's last two Ghosts. Nobody opened fire, but as the vehicles drew near the cave entrance, a ranger asked, *"Confirm: hold attack?"*

"Yes, confirm: hold attack." 'Vadam turned to the young males still pinned to the ground by 'Talot and Varo'dai, then spoke in English. "You are free to go, but keep your hands away from your weapons. Is that clear?"

"Clear enough," said the larger of the males. "But if you think we're leaving the commander—"

"Wait in the cave," 'Vadam said. "Once she awakens and answers some of my questions, she will be released."

The male furrowed his brow and stared up with hard eyes for a moment, then finally nodded. 'Vadam ordered 'Talot and Varo'dai to free their captives and observed long enough to be certain they would honor their agreement, then turned to 'Ayomuu and spoke in Sangheili.

"She *will* recover, I trust?"

"Of course. In fact, you will find her more cooperative. But be wary. I have learned that humans sometimes grow violent as the compulsion fades."

"You have drugged her?" It did not surprise 'Vadam that an Oath Warden would employ such a craven tactic, only that he would do so in the presence of so many witnesses. "You have dishonored everyone here."

"What I have done is preserve her usefulness." 'Ayomuu surprised 'Vadam by switching to fluent English—a hidden skill that suggested his current contract was not the first time he had been called upon to enforce an agreement with a human. "Or perhaps you are too proud to ask a human how she came to be waiting precisely where we landed? It cannot be a coincidence."

"Then perhaps it can be allowed, *this* time," 'Vadam continued in Sangheili, so that 'Talot and Varo'dai would understand why he was allowing 'Ayomuu's transgression to go unpunished. "You drugged her only to stop her from getting herself killed before she understands the war has ended, yes?"

"How cunning," 'Ayomuu replied in English. "We are beginning to understand each other, I see."

"That is what I thought." 'Vadam spoke first in Sangheili, then switched back to English. "How long will she remain compliant?"

"Until she is not. It cannot be predicted. Human bodies are different than ours, and I have had only a few opportunities to experiment. I can always give her a second dose, but that—"

"Will not be necessary."

'Vadam was beginning to wonder whether it might not be better to punish 'Ayomuu now and be done with him permanently. Unfortunately, his death might be hard to justify after 'Vadam had just excused the Oath Warden's use of a forbidden weapon. And it was hard to forget how quickly the blue aerosol had shot from his hand . . . out of nowhere, seemingly. If the time ever came, Crei 'Ayomuu would not be an easy transgressor to execute.

'Vadam crouched down and searched the Petrov woman for any hidden weapons, then waited until her eyes began to focus again.

"How do you feel? Do you need water?"

"I need you dead." Petrov rolled to her hands and knees, then tried to stand . . . and dropped back to her knees. "What did you do to me?"

"I am not certain. But I am told it is supposed to make you more compliant."

"Good luck with that."

'Vadam shot a glance toward 'Ayomuu, who merely turned his palms toward the ground and tipped his head. "At least she is responding," he said in Sangheili. "Be patient and make her speak first."

"We cannot wait the entire day," 'Vadam said back in Sangheili. "We will roast in this environment."

"Then do as I suggest. Or allow me to interrogate her."

'Vadam turned back to Petrov and said nothing.

She spent a few moments studying the ground, gathering her breath, then finally looked to 'Vadam. "Why didn't you kill me? When I reached for my energy sword, I mean?"

"Because Crei 'Ayomuu was faster." 'Vadam looked toward the Oath Warden to indicate whom he meant. "And I am glad for that. Whatever we are to you, humans are no longer an enemy to us. We intend you no harm—as long as you stop trying to kill us, of course."

"We've *already* killed a bunch of you."

"Yes. It was very impressive, given the weapons you had. But it ends here—no more."

"I don't give a damn about impressing you. And whatever you want from me, you're not going to get it."

"Arbiter—remain silent for now," 'Ayomuu urged in Sangheili. "She will speak again, when the urge grows too great."

'Vadam did as 'Ayomuu bade. He had little doubt that Petrov was being honest with him, as her defiant statements so far went against the interests of a captive. But he suspected that was due more to her character, and the innate hatred she felt for the Sangheili, than to the effectiveness of 'Ayomuu's "compliance" drug.

But after a moment, the woman grew unable to wait 'Vadam out. "What *do* you want from me?"

He pointed toward the crater rim. "Information."

Petrov seemed surprised at that, though 'Vadam could not understand why. She was intelligent, a given as a UNSC commander, and information was almost certainly the only thing he could want from her.

Finally, she asked, "About the citadel?"

"Yes, and the crater surrounding it. It is a sensor dead zone, and I have never seen a mirage behave in such a way."

Petrov stared at him and said nothing.

"In exchange, we will return you to the UNSC." 'Vadam saw her eyes harden with suspicion. "Or we could simply inform them of your presence here on this world, if that is what you prefer. We would leave you with provisions, of course."

"Be patient," 'Ayomuu said in Sangheili. "*You* are the one who needs to wait her out."

Petrov looked to the Oath Warden for a moment, then back at 'Vadam, and asked, "You don't *know*?"

"*Wait,*" 'Ayomuu urged. "She will tell you. She cannot help it."

'Vadam watched Petrov and remained silent for five breaths . . . then ten . . . until a female Sangheili spoke over the battlenet.

"*The object in the crater—we think it has turned back.*"

"What?" 'Vadam did not realize he had tipped his helmet sideways until he saw Petrov watching him intently. "When?"

"*It is hard to know. It came close enough to see that it was walking on many legs, like an insect. Then it grew difficult to see the legs,*" *and now the body seems to be growing smaller. The legs are no longer visible, and sometimes the body seems to disappear as well."*

"And you did not think to report this?" Varo'dai demanded.

"It only just happened. And the mirage makes it difficult to be sure of what we are seeing, even with the monocular."

"I understand," 'Vadam said. "Inform us of any change, and report when it is no longer visible at all."

As he finished speaking over the battlenet, Petrov asked, "What happened?"

"Perhaps you can tell me," 'Vadam said. "We thought we saw an object coming across the crater toward us. For a time, it appeared to be walking on many legs, but now it has turned back, and we cannot be sure even of that."

"It turned back?" Petrov began to sweep her gaze across the clouds. "Now, that *is* interesting."

"Then you know what it was?"

"Oh, yeah. We call them Runners." A long series of sonic booms sounded in the distance, somewhere far above the clouds, and Petrov suddenly dropped her gaze back to 'Vadam. "You have more dropships coming in?"

'Vadam looked up and searched for contrails. The cloud cover was far too low for any to be visible, but a crackling hiss began to sound overhead, from the same direction as the booms. Then forty balls of luminescence began to shine through the clouds, half a sky ahead of the hiss and growing steadily brighter and larger.

'Vadam had seen enough dropship insertions to recognize what he was seeing. As the flight continued to descend, he turned to his kaidons and found them staring up at the bright spheres, as surprised and confused as he was.

He turned back to Petrov. "No, Commander. Those dropships are not ours."

Petrov's eyes grew wide. "Well, then." She studied 'Vadam for several breaths, apparently debating what she wanted to tell him, then suddenly turned and began to run toward the cave.

Over her shoulder, she yelled, "This might be a good time to take cover!"

CHAPTER 8

The brown miasma of Netherop's cloud cover finally cleared from the situation monitor, and Olympia Vale found herself looking down on a drab brown desert speckled with gray-green vegetation. A crescent of charcoal-gray crater rim curved down from the top of the screen, framing a shimmering pool of yellow-gray light. What lay beneath the mirage was impossible to guess. No matter what form of imaging sensor the mapping team used, the signal vanished without any return. It was one of the reasons Vale had decided to investigate this site first.

As the Owl continued to descend, the crater rim slid toward the bottom of the monitor ever so slowly. To avoid leaving contrails or creating a sonic boom that would betray its position, the stealth-capable dropship had made a controlled insertion a quarter of the way around the planet, then initiated target approach at just below the speed of sound, a little less than a thousand kilometers per hour.

Finally, the crescent of gray rim passed the bottom of the monitor and vanished from sight. For a moment, the crater basin looked like a lake of refracted light. Then a long mound of gray-brown dirt appeared at the top of the screen, rising above the mirage like a mountain on the horizon.

"We're too high," Keely Iyuska said. She was seated opposite Vale, on the far side of a Mongoose ATV secured to the deck of the passenger bay. Dressed in borrowed BDUs with an open-face helmet, torso armor, and no unit or rank insignia, she bore only a superficial semblance to the grim-faced Orbital Drop Shock Troops who packed the compartment aft of them. "That's the tel, right there!"

"Recon first," Vale said, speaking through the helmet voicemitter of her GEN2 Mjolnir armor. "Our job is to get some video of the objective, then secure a landing zone for the main body of the expedition."

"Do we have time for that?" Iyuska asked.

"We have all the time we need." As their venerable stealth cruiser *Hidden Point* had entered orbit above Netherop, they had observed a Sangheili flotilla inserting three Phantoms on a trajectory bound for the strange crater—which was another of Vale's reasons for investigating it first. Now Iyuska was worried that by allowing the Sangheili to set foot on the tel before they did, the aliens would somehow claim exclusive rights to excavate the site. "We have a battalion of ODSTs inserting behind us."

Iyuska's eyes grew round. "Wait—you *can't* fight over the dig. The site will be demolished!"

"Relax, Keely. We're not going to fight an ally." Vale synced the Owl's reconnaissance system to her helmet's heads-up display, then watched on a faceplate inset as the long, oval tel grew larger and more distinct. It was a bigger site than she had expected, and archeological excavation had to be done by hand. She began to worry that a single ODST battalion would not be enough to complete the job. "We're just going to show up with more . . . resources."

"And you actually think that will work?" Iyuska demanded. "Sangheili don't like being bullied."

"No, but they respect strength." Vale tipped her helmet toward the civilian sitting in the adjacent seat and said, "Besides, Netherop is a *human* world."

The civilian, Rosa Fuertes, exhaled sharply and looked at the ceiling. Dressed in lightweight tan pants and a sleeveless gray shirt, she had a haggard, weather-lined face and pale, rheumy eyes. Her hair was coarse and thinning, her complexion gray, her arms webbed with angry red veins.

Iyuska glanced at Fuertes only briefly before turning back to Vale. "You realize the Arbiter will never accept that rationale, right?"

"I do. But it's better than any rationale he has. It will prevent him from arguing the Sangheili have first claim on Netherop."

"Fools, all of you," Fuertes said. "Nobody claims this place. It claims *you*."

"It won't be claiming anybody this time," Vale said. "You're here to make sure it doesn't."

Fuertes laughed. "I am here because you were dumb enough to hire a sick old woman. And if a Spartan is looking to *me* for protection, you are an even bigger idiot than I thought."

"Or you don't understand your own value," Iyuska said.

"I understand well enough. But if there are any secrets buried on Netherop, I can't tell you where to find them."

"No," Iyuska said. "But you may be able to tell us *how*."

As they spoke, a colorless fissure appeared in the summit of the tel, as straight as a rifle barrel and perpendicular to the Owl's insertion path. It quickly began to lengthen and grow wider near the middle, forming an elongated diamond so deep and bright it seemed to open into the very core of the planet. Worried that her

HUD was malfunctioning, Vale closed its inset and turned to the situation monitor.

The tel had dropped to the center of the screen, but the fissure in the summit remained. It continued to widen, expanding into a long narrow rift filled with the unimaginable glow of a hundred billion stars. Vale stared into the light and found herself transfixed, for a breath . . . a thousand breaths . . . ten thousand breaths . . . as galaxies whirled up from nothing and flung their arms into the void and shrank into black holes so deep and hot they devoured reality itself. She saw the dark emptiness wink into existence as a single point of light, then swell into the blinding globule of an entire universe that collapsed instantly back into the colorless void.

Still Vale remained, on the brink of annihilation, witness to the creation of all things and the end of everything. She saw worlds blossom and planets crumble, the birth of stars and the death of suns, watched the cold wave of eternity swallow a universe of universes in the blink of an eye. How long she stayed, she did not know. She simply *was*, a woman trapped in the boundless amber of the cosmos, prisoner to a vast mystery filled with too much paradox and potential for any human mind to grasp.

Then the tel dropped off the bottom edge of the situation monitor, and Vale found herself back in her seat, staring at the shimmering lake of the crater mirage, now a vibrant orange.

She turned to Fuertes. "What just . . . what the hell *was* that?"

"You're asking me? I thought I was having another seizure."

"Not this time. Not unless we were *both* having one."

The brain-wasting prion disease was worse than Fuertes had admitted during their initial meeting on Gao. On the way out here, she had suffered episodes several times during slipspace jumps. Vale had finally offered to let the woman complete her consulting contract from aboard *Hidden Point*, but Fuertes had smiled

— 115 —

and declined, insisting she wanted to die on Netherop with all the children she had buried there. The reply had come so quickly and smoothly that it seemed rehearsed, but it had been impossible to draw more out of the old woman. Whatever Fuertes's true reasons for insisting on being the one who returned to Netherop, she was determined to keep them to herself.

"Have you seen anything like that before, Rosa?" Iyuska asked. "Here on Netherop, I mean."

Fuertes shook her head, her gaze still fixed on the orange mirage. "I have never seen anything like that *anywhere*."

Vale glanced aft, where the fifteen ODSTs of Tango Team sat along the inner walls of the Owl's passenger bay. Their helmet faceplates were all turned toward the situation monitor. It was impossible to see much more than their wide eyes, but the mere fact that they were openly staring at the display revealed just how unsettled they were.

Vale synced her Mjolnir's onboard computer to the Owl's combat information systems and brought up the tactical ground display. The crater floor remained hidden beneath an arcing swath of failed sensor readings, and the tel itself was even more of an enigma, an unreadable spray of terrain symbols erupting over the center of the map. But there was some useful intelligence along the top edge, where the crater rim curved across the starboard corner. On a bench of flat terrain between the rim and a nearby mountain sat a trio of red diamonds: the Sangheili Phantoms.

As the Owl continued its approach, the crater rim dropped toward the middle of the screen. Dozens of yellow caret symbols appeared on the bench of flat terrain, their tips all pointed away from the tel—toward a common point at the base of the nearby mountain. They were unidentified pedestrians, most likely Sangheili.

And they were advancing toward the mountain at a pace fast enough to suggest they might be charging something.

Or fleeing it.

Vale requested control of the nose camera, then turned it aft toward the tel and put the image up on the monitor. The fissure had expanded into a huge eye-shaped oval filled with the same unimaginable brilliance she had found so mesmerizing the first time she'd looked into its depths. She felt herself falling once more into the abyss between space and time, her mind reeling as the glow began to rise out of the rift in a bright luminous dome.

It took an eternity . . . and the mere blink of an eye . . . but finally the Owl crossed out of the crater, and the bench land where the Sangheili Phantoms sat waiting appeared at the top of the situation monitor. The tel remained visible in the middle of the image, the luminous glow still rising from the rift in the center, growing ever larger, until finally a lance of blinding brilliance shot out and split the sky above, reaching up through the pall of brown clouds and slowly spreading across the width of the screen, until all she could see was a white, bright void opening through the bulkhead into the vast emptiness beyond.

A collective gasp arose from Iyuska, the ODSTs, even Fuertes, as they rose into their crash harnesses. Realizing the Owl had lost power, Vale synced her HUD to the combat information system— and found an empty display. She switched to the pilot's helmet camera and, beyond the cockpit canopy, saw a mountainside rising fast as the dropship wobbled toward the ground.

The image in her HUD showed cockpit instruments flashing past as the pilot—a square-faced major named Rolph Chudzik— raced to save the Owl, calmly calling off items on the engine-restart checklist.

"Brace brace brace!" Vale called out. "We're going—"

Her warning was interrupted by the voice of the female copilot, Thisbe Marchal, sounding inside her helmet. *"Clear to restart, Major. Altitude three hundred meters."*

"Three hundred meters, aye. Restarting now."

The Owl continued to fall. The view outside the canopy flashed across Vale's HUD as Chudzik reached for an overhead reset toggle. For an instant, it seemed Vale was looking down into a boiling orange bed of lava, then into the glowing blue photosphere of a supergiant star, then into the black inky void of an event horizon.

"Inertial electrostatic confinement reengaged," Chudzik said. The image in Vale's HUD blurred for a moment, then settled on a human thumb, lifting the safety cover on a red charging button. *"Deuterium injector ready, Lieutenant."*

"Clear to inject, Major," Marchal said. *"Altitude one forty meters."*

"One forty meters, aye. Restarting now."

The thumb dropped on the charging button. The Owl shuddered as the fusion drives engaged . . . and the shoulders of Vale's armor pressed harder into her crash harness as the dropship continued to plummet.

"Eighty meters," Marchal reported. *"What is that stuff down there?"*

Vale could not see what the copilot was looking at because her HUD was still synced to the pilot's helmet camera and his attention was now wandering over the instrument panel below the cockpit canopy.

"Don't know," Chudzik replied. *"Don't wanna find out."*

"Affirmative that. Forty meters."

"Forty meters, aye. Engaging thrust."

Vale sank into her seat as plasma began to pour from the thrust nozzles of the Owl's powerful hybrid fusion reactors. Chudzik finally lifted his head from the instrument panel and began to survey the surrounding terrain. The fiery bed of ever-changing terrain Vale had glimpsed before was gone. Now the bench looked more like a foggy sea, with a haze of optical distortion hanging just above the surface and the rocky ground literally rising and falling in waves.

The Sangheili Phantoms lay twisted into long tubes of crumpled metal, rolling gently back and forth as the ground undulated beneath them. Half a dozen star-shaped dark stains lay scattered between the wrecks and the base of the cliff, strewn with shards of splintered bone and mangled armor. Vale had no idea what had just happened down there, but it was clearly bad. One of those blood smears could be the Arbiter . . . and if that was the case, another war between the Sangheili and humanity would be coming—and soon.

Vale synced her HUD to the Owl's combat information system. To her relief, it had rebooted and was already relaying intelligence to the appropriate displays. She was less relieved by what else she saw: the drop cone overhead no longer contained the forty insertion craft carrying her ODST battalion.

Now there was just a debris cloud, fluttering slowly to the ground.

Vale felt herself tipping aft as the pilot brought the Owl's nose up and began to accelerate, trying to clear the area as fast as he could.

She jumped on the internal comm immediately. "Turn around. Land on the tel."

"*What?*" Chudzik's tone was stunned. "*Have you seen the drop cone, Spartan? Our insertion force is gone. The mission is over.*"

"It's over when I say it's over." Vale was hardly Chudzik's superior, but she was a Spartan and the one who had put the mission together. "And we're far from done here. I'm pretty sure we just found what we came for."

CHAPTER 9

The rocky ground continued to rise and fall in meter-high swells, throwing so much dust into the air that Thel 'Vadam could barely see the boulders crashing around outside the cave. From the relative safety of the entrance, the boulders were just blocky shadows tumbling back and forth as the terrain oscillated beneath them. Farther out, the landing party's wrecked Phantoms were barely discernible, corkscrew silhouettes that made fleeting appearances as the wave crests lifted them into view.

Above the curtain of suspended dust, 'Vadam glimpsed the familiar, droop-winged shape of a UNSC Owl. About the width of a thumb tip, it was silhouetted against the flank of the tel, flying just below summit height—a wise tactic that would make it a difficult target. The apparent size suggested the dropship was approximately six thousand units away, though that revealed nothing about how close it was to the tel.

But, clearly, much closer than 'Vadam and his Sangheili.

"Is that a UNSC stealth craft I see?" 'Ayomuu asked. He

crouched in the cave mouth between 'Vadam and 'Talot, his stylized purple armor surprisingly effective camouflage in the shadowy environment. "Approaching the tel?"

"Preparing to land upon it," Varo'dai said. She was next to 'Vadam, on the side opposite the Oath Warden and 'Talot. "They will be sitting on top within five centals."

Thinking Varo'dai had produced a monocular from somewhere, 'Vadam glanced over and was astonished to see that she was studying the tel with her naked gaze—proving once again how remarkable was her eyesight.

Before he could comment, 'Talot demanded, "How can you know that? I am doing well to find it at all."

"But you can see it is not fleeing the battlefield, yes?" Varo'dai replied. The apparent size of the Owl had dwindled by half, to the point that it was now barely visible. "It is staying low so it can approach the tel safely, but beginning to climb. It would not be doing that unless it was preparing to land on top."

"Then why are we hiding in this hole like a bunch of *snulbors*?" 'Ayomuu asked. "If we can see the dropship with no monocular, and the dropship is about to land on the tel, then the tel can be no more than ten thousand units distant."

"That does not mean we can get there on foot." 'Vadam's view into the crater was blocked by its rim, but his memory of the color-shifting mirages and waves of heat-refracted light that concealed its floor remained fresh. "We cannot even be certain it has a solid surface."

"How fortunate, then, that we have someone who might know." 'Ayomuu cast a look toward the interior of the seam cave, where Petrov and her humans had gathered after leading 'Vadam and the other Sangheili survivors to safety. "I am certain they can be persuaded to cooperate."

"It is worth the attempt," 'Vadam agreed. "But it will be done *my* way."

"As you wish. We can always switch to my tactics when yours prove unproductive."

'Vadam waited until the Owl had grown too distant to see without aid, then turned toward the cave interior. No more than five meters wide, it lay in a tipped bedding plane between two faces of dark rock, sloping upward at an angle not quite steep enough to call vertical.

Petrov and her subordinates were thirty paces back, half-hidden in the darkness that seemed to seep from the murky depths beyond. They were kneeling on the silty floor, unarmed and surrounded by Sangheili warriors. But their limbs remained unrestrained and the hands of their captors were free of weapons, an acknowledgment that the humans were no longer enemies. Their angry glares and furtive glances suggested the gesture was not entirely appreciated.

'Vadam motioned Petrov forward and, when she arrived, pointed outside. If the ground undulations had diminished at all, it was not noticeably. The crest of the crater rim was barely visible above the dust bank, a low rocky slope hiding the base of the distant tel.

"Tell me what happened," 'Vadam said in English. His tone was curt and demanding, for he had lost thirty warriors in a cental, and it angered him. It was not her fault—in fact, he might well have lost all of their lives and his own as well, had it not been for her warning—but he was in no mood to show gratitude. The shock was still too raw. "Tell me *now*."

Petrov's brow rose, and she turned to stare up at him with round eyes. "You don't know?"

"I do not. If I did, I would not be hiding in a cave with you while half my warriors lie smeared across the desert floor."

"Good point." The corners of Petrov's mouth twitched ever so slightly upward, and she asked, "The war is really over?"

"Would you still be alive were it not?"

"I suppose not. But that doesn't make us allies."

"We are not enemies, though," 'Vadam said. Petrov was diminutive compared to 'Vadam, little more than a third his mass and so short she had to crane her neck to look him in the eyes. Yet he found himself watching her with the same wariness he would any kaidon of suspect loyalties. "And soon, we might well become allies."

"Yeah . . . negative that." Petrov turned to stare toward the tel summit, and 'Vadam thought for a moment her human eyes were even sharper than Varo'dai's. But when she spoke, her tone betrayed no hint of the excitement he would have expected had she been able to see the Owl. "The war *here* isn't over. I doubt it ever will be."

"I did not take you for such a fool. I have freely promised far more than you could ever hope to win by continuing this fight . . . unless *death* is all you desire."

"If I wanted that, I'd have it by now. Death is easy to find on Netherop." Petrov pointed her chin at the tel. "It's them I'm worried about, not you."

Recalling that earlier Petrov had referred to the tel as a citadel, 'Vadam asked, "The tel is inhabited?"

"Of course it's inhabited. Who do you think destroyed those dropships?"

"I have no idea."

"*You* did." Petrov used her fingers to mimic the four mandibles of a Sangheili mouth snapping shut. "Hinge-heads."

"That is not a name we appreciate," 'Vadam warned. "We call ourselves Sangheili."

"Well then . . . there are *Sangheili* holed up in that place. As many as ten of them . . . and *they* are still at war."

It took 'Vadam a moment to grasp the full implication of Petrov's words, though he was not sure why. Warriors vanished during every planetary battle, and it would be folly to assume all of them had been killed. Some simply failed to return in time to extract with their unit, while others were trapped behind enemy lines or too wounded to move. A few probably even deserted, especially on the more habitable planets. What he found surprising, he realized, was that more than thirty human years after the original battle here on N'ba, there were still survivors on both sides—and they were still very much fighting as if the war raged on.

"You are worthy warriors," 'Vadam said. "How long have you kept your enemies trapped inside their citadel?"

Petrov looked at her wrist, as though instinctively checking a chronometer that was not there, then spread her palms. "Netherop is a hard place to track time." She glanced back into the cave, toward the humans seated on the floor. "But my soldiers back there? Most of them were born right here, in this cave."

'Vadam was not adept at judging human ages, but he knew that humans did not generally reproduce until they attained twenty years. And several of Petrov's subordinates looked old enough to have young of their own. "That is a long time to hold a siege."

"I guess you could call it a siege. Except we're the ones starving. The enemy seems to have a bottomless pantry in there."

"Then why continue?" 'Ayomuu asked in English. "Did it not occur to you to go someplace where you could live in peace and feed yourselves?"

Petrov snapped her gaze toward the Oath Warden. "That would make us deserters. Soldiers don't cower at a safe distance. They find the enemy and kill them."

"A pointless sacrifice is never noble," 'Ayomuu said.

"It's not pointless. It's attrition. We replace our losses. *They* don't."

"Ah." 'Ayomuu glanced back toward the young soldiers deeper in the cave. "Because you reproduce."

Petrov nodded. "Sooner or later, that citadel will be ours. All we have to do is keep picking them off."

"Your resolve is worthy of a Spartan," 'Vadam said. At the start of the War of Annihilation, he had thought humans as spineless as *sloods* and treated them as such while slaughtering countless of their kind. But over time, he came to understand that their treachery was rooted more in perseverance and cunning than in cowardice. In a fight for survival, humans would do anything to prevail . . . even if it meant betraying their own honor. "But your determination is no longer required. The war you fight is over. I have said you will be returned to the UNSC, and you will be. Is that understood?"

"Would you still be alive if it weren't?" A glimmer of what appeared to be amusement flashed across Petrov's face. "I could have kept quiet about the reconciliation wave."

"A good point," 'Vadam said, using a phrase the human had employed earlier. "How do you know that is what it is? A reconciliation wave?"

"Just a theory. Before the claw strike—"

"I am sorry." All 'Vadam had seen of the actual attack was a white flash from inside the cave as he issued orders and made sure the humans were not attacked. "Did you say *claw*?"

"That's what it looks like. A big bolt of white energy that shoots out of the top of the citadel and . . . well, shreds stuff. What else would you call it?"

"*Claw* will work for now. But how does it create this reconciliation wave?"

"We're not sure. Before it strikes, a fissure opens in the top of the citadel. From high enough up the mountain, it looks like a slip-space portal. And if it *is* a portal . . ."

"Then there would be causal reconciliation when it closes." 'Vadam was beginning to wonder whether the tel actually contained the Guardian-killing weapon itself . . . or merely some sort of slipspace lens that focused its energies. "How many times have you seen the weapon strike?"

In response, Petrov did a strange thing, raising a finger in front of her brow and wagging it in the air between them. "Not so fast. I have my own questions. If that drop wasn't yours, whose *was* it?"

"Tell her it was Kig-Yar," 'Ayomuu said in Sangheili. "If she finds out there are humans in orbit, she will never help us."

"And if she already realizes that, she is merely testing my honor," 'Vadam answered, also in Sangheili. "And if she decides I have none, how will I be able to trust *her*?"

"It is worth the risk. She has no communications device. How could she know who is in orbit?"

Before 'Vadam could reply, Petrov said, "Uh-huh. That's all the answer I need."

She turned and started toward the back of the cave. 'Vadam reached out to stop her. She was so tiny that when he draped his hand over her shoulder, his fingertips were almost at her elbow.

"You have not heard my answer."

"Yes, I have. Whatever lie you were just cooking up, I'm not interested."

"You should be careful who you insult. Not all Sangheili are as patient as I am."

She stared down at 'Vadam's hand, as though contemplating whether she was quick enough to draw her combat knife and lop it off. "Am I free to go? Or was that stuff about us no longer being enemies just your first lie?"

'Vadam released her. "You may go, if that is your desire." He told Varo'dai and 'Talot to have their warriors move away from the humans, then turned back to Petrov. "We will alert the UNSC to your presence here, of course. But I suspect you already know what a mistake you would be making."

"Why don't you spell it out for me?"

"Since you insist." 'Vadam paused and cast a dramatic gaze upward, looking into the murky recesses angling away overhead. So distant was the roof that he could see no hint of it, only a faint glimmer of reflection on the dark stone. "By refusing our help, you will only be placing more human lives in danger. Unnecessarily."

"More?" Petrov's tone was more disappointed than surprised. "So that *was* a human drop the claw destroyed?"

"Almost certainly."

'Vadam paused to let her contemplate the ramifications and come to her own conclusion.

'Ayomuu was not so patient. "You may not trust us," he said. "But we are here *now*, and you would be asking anyone who attempts to rescue you later to take a grave risk."

"I understand the trade-off." Petrov let her breath out, then turned to 'Vadam. "You said it was 'almost certainly' a human drop. Why *almost*?"

"Because there were no UNSC vessels in orbit when we inserted in our Phantoms," 'Vadam replied. "But we have other reasons to believe they are present."

Petrov's brow rose. "*What* reasons?"

'Vadam mimicked the gesture she had used earlier, wagging a finger between them. It was effective—he would remember to employ this in future interactions. "Before you started to run, you asked if the insertion was ours. How did you know the weapon would fire if it was not Sangheili?"

Petrov studied him for a moment, no doubt considering how much to reveal, then bit her lip and nodded. "Very well. The only insertion attempt the claw *hasn't* destroyed is yours. I assume that's because the warriors in the citadel are Sangheili, and they took for granted that your Phantoms would be friendly to them."

"Which suggests they have some form of orbital surveillance," 'Ayomuu said, making a point of catching 'Vadam's eye. "How many insertion attempts has the claw stopped before today?"

"Two that we've seen. But there was one other rescue attempt, about a year after we were marooned—before our enemies found the citadel."

"What happened to that one?" 'Vadam asked.

"A prowler sneaked into orbit and made contact—we still had a functional rescue comm then. But there was no claw strike. It lost both Pelicans to the orbital mine shell you left behind—"

"It was not us," 'Vadam said. "We are no longer Covenant."

"If you say so . . . no offense." Petrov's sharp tone did not suggest any contriteness. "Anyway, the prowler wasn't prepared to clear a full mine shell, and the captain didn't want to risk twenty lives trying to save eight. He promised a better-equipped mission would come back when it was feasible."

"And it did?"

"Eventually. The next rescue attempt came a standard year after you—sorry, *the Covenant*—entered the citadel."

"How long was that after the first rescue attempt failed?" 'Vadam asked.

"Who knows?" Petrov showed her palms in a gesture that seemed to indicate helplessness. "Years, at least. We started to notice flashes above the clouds one night and realized someone was trying to punch through the orbital mine shell. We climbed up the mountain to set signal fires, then made as much electronic noise as we could."

"With what?" 'Ayomuu asked.

"We still had some functional low-power comm sets. Nothing with enough range for orbital communications, but the rescue ship must have been monitoring for surface traffic. On the third morning, the corvette *Alpina* made contact and promised a Pelican would collect us before the next evening."

Petrov's gaze drifted toward the dark roof of the cavern, then she seemed to regret her lapse of attention and returned her focus to 'Vadam. Still, she remained silent.

"Clearly, that did not happen," 'Vadam prompted.

Petrov shook her head. "No. That was the first time we saw the claw strike. A blinding lance of light shot from the citadel, and we heard nothing more from the *Alpina*."

When she fell back into silence, 'Vadam prompted her again. "And *that* was when you knew you had to capture the citadel. For the next rescue to succeed, you had to control the claw."

"Or at least prevent it from being used." Petrov waved a hand toward her soldiers in the back of the cave. "We're still working on that, as you can see."

Before 'Vadam could reply, 'Ayomuu said, "A blinding lance. That is *all* you saw?"

"Well . . . we saw the portal open first." Petrov's brow furrowed in what appeared to be confusion. "But what do you expect? Even if Netherop wasn't covered with clouds, it would take pretty sharp eyes to spot a corvette in orbit."

'Vadam saw the inconsistency and expected 'Ayomuu to accuse the human of lying, but the Oath Warden was subtler than that:

"Earlier, you called the lance a claw because of its destructive power. If you cannot see it strike, how do you know it is a claw? How do you know it is 'shredding,' as you put it, instead of merely blasting?"

"Ah." Petrov's brow grew smooth again. "Because of what we find out there afterward." She waved vaguely toward the crater. "Ship pieces. Like they were pulled down out of orbit."

"You found them in the crater?" 'Vadam was careful to restrain his helmet and hand movements so he did not betray his excitement at this key piece of intelligence. "Then it is safe to go out there?"

Petrov considered the question for a moment, then finally nodded. "After everything settles down. You wouldn't want to be out there while the ground is still consolidating."

'Vadam's excitement turned to alarm. The UNSC Owl was already landing on the tel as they spoke. But he and his company would have to cross the crater on foot—after they waited for the crater floor to become solid again. He glanced skyward, wondering whether he should call a pair of Phantoms down to simply fly them to the tel.

"Don't bother," Petrov said, guessing his thoughts. "The EMR storm is going to block comms for a while."

'Vadam did not need Petrov to explain what she meant. Any time a translocational portal opened, a brief cycle of tau radiation impacted unshielded instruments. Long-range sensor and comm equipment tended to be disrupted most severely.

"And even when it's over," Petrov continued, "your Sangheili friends inside the citadel might be second-guessing their decision to let your Phantoms land the first time. I'm not sure we want to see what happens when there are two claw strikes on the same day."

'Vadam knew Petrov was trying to plant doubts in his mind, and she was succeeding. To anyone inside the tel, it could easily appear that his three Phantoms had been advance reconnaissance for the larger drop that had followed. She was right about the second claw strike too. He had no interest in finding out what another reconciliation wave might do to the terrain between them and the tel—at least not until the ground stopped rolling from the first one.

"How long will it be before we can cross the crater?" 'Vadam asked.

"That depends."

"On what?"

"How honest you are," Petrov said. "You said you have reasons to believe the drop was human. What are they?"

"Tell her only about the Owl," 'Ayomuu said in Sangheili. "If she knows we are both searching for the claw, she will do all she can to—"

"We are searching for the same thing the UNSC is," 'Vadam said, still speaking in English . . . and still to Petrov. "It may be the weapon in the citadel."

"You have the brain of a *colo*," 'Ayomuu said in Sangheili. "Now she will never help us."

'Vadam ignored the insult and kept his attention focused on Petrov. "I apologize for the asides in Sangheili." Taking the time to chastise 'Ayomuu in the middle of his negotiations with Petrov would place 'Vadam's authority in greater doubt than the interruption itself. "The Oath Warden believes I am making a mistake."

"Because he thinks I won't help you against humans. He's not wrong, you know."

"Nor is he entirely correct," 'Vadam replied. "The humans want the weapon for the same reason we do—to neutralize a menace to *both* our civilizations. Naturally, I would feel more secure with the weapon in Sangheili possession, but it does not matter much who recovers it . . . as long as one of us does and it is used for the same purpose."

Petrov's brow shot up. "That's not the argument I was expecting. And I'm not sure I believe it."

"It is the truth, whether you believe it or not. And the argument you *were* expecting is also true. As long as the Covenant survivors control the citadel, you will never escape N'ba. We are your best hope of rescue."

"Okay, you're right. *That's* the argument I was expecting. And it's a good one."

"Then you are willing to tell us when we can cross the crater? How long must we wait?"

"I'm willing to take you across when it's safe." Petrov's gaze flickered toward the darkness above, then she quickly brought it back down to focus on 'Vadam. "But I don't trust you enough to tell you anything. I'm not letting you out of my sight until my soldiers and I are standing on the deck of a UNSC vessel, preparing to go home."

"That time will come sooner than you believe."

"Only if we reach the tel in time," 'Ayomuu noted in Sangheili. "If you allow the humans in the Owl to recover the weapon before we arrive—"

"I hope you will forgive the Oath Warden's rudeness," 'Vadam said, still speaking to Petrov in English. "He worries that I am not doing enough to hurry you along."

Petrov warily eyed 'Ayomuu. "What's the rush, Oath Warden?"

"Only that I trust you no more than you trust us," 'Ayomuu replied. "How are we to know you are not delaying us here unnecessarily?"

Petrov turned to 'Vadam in disbelief. "He's joking, right?"

"Sangheili do not jest," 'Vadam said. "Perhaps it would be better to explain it to him."

Petrov rolled her eyes, but faced 'Ayomuu. "Why would I want to delay you?"

"You said yourself that you lack trust for us. Perhaps you are hoping for more Owls to insert."

"First, how would I even know there are still any humans *up* there? Our last comm unit died ages ago."

"You do not need to know," 'Ayomuu said. "Your hope could be enough."

"*What* hope? You saw what the claw strike did to that insertion force. For all we know, it wiped out every vessel in orbit—human *and* Sangheili."

It was a possibility 'Vadam had not considered—and one that seemed all too likely, given what Petrov had suggested about the Sangheili inside the tel misinterpreting the nature of the two insertions. Fighting back a swell of alarm, he pushed his helmet outside the cave entrance and activated his comm unit, attempting to make contact with one of the surveillance satellites put into orbit before they inserted.

He heard only an oscillating whistle, so eerie and shrill that it made his spine prickle.

"Don't bother." Petrov pointed to the still-undulating ground between them and the crater rim. "Your signal won't stabilize until things settle down."

'Vadam studied the ground long enough to see that the waves remained almost as high as they had been a few minutes earlier. "How long will that be?"

"Who knows? I've only been through this twice before, and I wasn't taking notes."

"You are only trying to worry us." 'Ayomuu's tone was accusing. "Any vessels on the far side of their orbit would be shielded by the bulk of the planet."

"You're ignoring the portal," Petrov said. "The claw may look like it's rising out of the planet interior, but it's translocating. It could be coming from anywhere and going to anywhere."

'Vadam understood slipspace and the curvature of space-time well enough to know she was correct. He had not actually seen the claw strike, but he had automatically assumed it rose in a straight line from the tel to the human dropships. That was not possible. The insertion force had been spread out across several degrees of sky, so a single, straight-line attack could not have eliminated them all. Either the claw had been more of a huge column than a line, or there had been multiple claws, or the claw had split into several forks, or it had leapt from one dropship to another, or . . .

The possibilities were more than 'Vadam could articulate, and probably more than he could comprehend. He understood only two things—the weapon was devastating, and he had no idea how it functioned.

"You said two rescue missions have been stopped by the claw strike," 'Vadam said. "What became of the second one?"

"I wish I knew," Petrov said. "We were on the citadel digging our way inside, hoping to lure the enemy into an ambush, when orbital mines began to detonate above the clouds. It had been maybe ten standard years since the first claw appeared, but that's not something you forget. A detachment of volunteers insisted on staying behind to attempt entry when the portal opened, and I brought everyone else back here to ride out the reconciliation wave. We never even made contact before the rescue mission was destroyed."

"What of your volunteers?" 'Ayomuu asked. "Were they able to penetrate the—"

"If they were successful, then they didn't survive." Petrov fell silent and looked away. "We never heard from them again."

"It is always lamentable to lose courageous warriors," 'Vadam said. "Especially when a plan does not succeed."

"That was desperation," Petrov said. "Not a plan."

"Sometimes desperation *is* a plan," 'Vadam said. "They were worthy warriors."

"They were stubborn fools. But I loved them for it."

'Vadam found the declaration puzzling, as it would never occur to a Sangheili commander to nest with one of his warriors—or to take as a subordinate anyone to whom he had a close personal attachment. But humans were a sentimental species who seemed to have no control over their emotions, so it was hardly surprising to hear that a commander had become personally entangled with her inferiors.

Or perhaps such entanglements had just been impossible to avoid, given the small size of her keep on N'ba. Perhaps Petrov was mother and commander *both* to the young humans she led.

"I admire your resolve," 'Vadam said. "From what I understand of human love, it must have been a difficult thing to allow."

"This is Netherop. Everything is hard."

"What about leaving?" 'Vadam asked. "Will that be difficult as well? I ask only because it has been your home for so long."

"And the only home most of my soldiers have ever known." Petrov glanced toward the rear of the cavern. "I'm not sure they believe me when I tell them how bountiful Rea—their ancestral home—is."

It did not escape 'Vadam's notice that Petrov had almost said *Reach* and called it the ancestral place of her soldiers—suggesting they might also be of her own blood. Given that he had been supreme commander of the forces that glassed the planet, he decided it might be wiser and kinder to let a fellow human tell her Reach had seen one of the most ferocious battles of the war. It was no longer the bountiful world she remembered, and he was responsible. Were he to inform her of that, she would likely seek the vengeance that was hers by right, and his companions would end up slaying her and her subordinates whether or not she succeeded. Better to bear his guilt in silence and let there be calm between them, for that was the only way to atone for the terrible evil he had done in service to the Covenant.

By keeping peace with humans.

After a moment, 'Vadam said, "Human worlds can be very welcoming indeed. I found Earth, in particular, quite lush."

Petrov's mouth fell open. "You know where Earth is?"

"Indeed. But have no fear. It has never fallen. The last time I was there, it was to honor a human friend."

"You've *been* there? To Earth?"

"Have I not said so? I found its great peak of Mount Kilimanjaro extraordinarily beautiful. I would make that the first place you take your soldiers when you return."

Petrov shook her head, as though trying to clear it. "You're offering me sightseeing advice?"

"It is only a suggestion." Deciding she seemed off guard enough for him to press for more intelligence, 'Vadam swept a hand toward the still-undulating terrain outside. "How long will it be before all this calms down and we can arrange your rescue?"

"Arrange it how, exactly?"

"By entering the tel and seizing control of the weapon. So we can contact my flotilla and call for extraction."

Petrov looked at him as though he were mad. "What makes you think your flotilla is still up there?"

A knot formed between 'Vadam's hearts. He had been operating on the assumption that because the tel's occupants had allowed Sangheili Phantoms to land, they would not destroy a Sangheili flotilla. But if they had misinterpreted the two insertions, as Petrov had earlier suggested, there was no reason to expect that. They might well have launched an attack against the full flotilla.

"We have seven vessels in orbit," 'Vadam said. "Surely, the occupants of the tel couldn't eliminate them all with a single strike?"

"How would I know?"

"You wouldn't," 'Ayomuu said. "And you couldn't."

Petrov pointed a finger at the Oath Warden. "That's right. All I know is that nothing ever makes it down here in one piece. What happens up there?" She turned her palms toward the roof of the cave and briefly raised her shoulders. "No idea."

"But *we* have an idea." 'Ayomuu turned to 'Vadam and switched to Sangheili. "The human Owl was not attacked during its drop. We saw that much."

"Which suggests stealth craft are undetectable to those inside the tel," 'Vadam said, also speaking in Sangheili. "And since we did not know the humans had arrived until we saw their primary drop—"

"They came in prowlers," 'Ayomuu finished.

"Or a stealth cruiser," 'Vadam said. "With that many dropships, a larger command ship is more likely."

Petrov watched the exchange with a clenched jaw and evernarrowing eyes, her suspicions clearly growing. Yet . . . she remained entirely too calm and composed, as though their discussion did not really matter to her . . . as though she were just biding her time until matters shifted in her favor.

'Vadam faced her and said in English, "You are holding something back. What are you not telling us?"

"That's a hard question to answer when I don't know what *you* aren't telling *me*."

'Vadam clacked his mandibles in frustration, then turned to study the undulating terrain outside. He didn't see any stones or wreckage sinking into it, which suggested it probably wasn't as insubstantial as she had earlier led him to believe. But with the ground rising and falling as it was, trying to cross it on foot would undeniably be slow, difficult, and—with all those boulders tumbling about—dangerous.

He looked back to Petrov. "What will happen if we try to cross the crater before this stops? Is it possible?"

"If you're willing to pick yourself up enough times, sure. But you know what happens if they use the claw again, right?" Petrov pointed at the twisted wreckage of the nearest Phantom. "You can see that for yourself."

"I can. But it is a chance I fear we must take."

"Why? This will all settle down in a while. Then you'll be able to see if your flotilla is still up there—and if it is, you can tell them to hold any more insertions until you've dealt with our friends in the citadel."

"That is the problem. We cannot wait even a few of your hours. By then, the tel may be empty, and we may all be trapped on N'ba. Together."

"Because?"

"Because a UNSC stealth Owl survived the claw strike. And it is landing atop the tel as we speak."

Petrov's face paled, and she craned her neck back so she could lock gazes with him. "You're lying."

"How fearless you are, insulting my honor yet again."

"We *all* saw the Owl," 'Ayomuu said, quickly enough to prevent Petrov from making a reply that would escalate the exchange to violence—and deprive the landing party of a valuable source of local intelligence. "A small craft with drooped wings, approaching the tel. There has been no second strike, so we can only assume it landed successfully."

Petrov's expression fell, and she looked from 'Ayomuu to 'Vadam in disbelief . . . or perhaps it was horror. "You're being serious."

"Sangheili always are," 'Vadam said. "I am fairly certain the Owl carries a squad of superior troops. You must trust me when I say they will not need an entire day to neutralize a handful of Sangheili castaways. That is why we must hurry."

"Affirmative. I understand that." Petrov raised her gaze toward the cave roof again. This time, she held it there. "It might be safer for everyone if you have your warriors wait outside."

'Vadam studied the slanting chasm above, searching its darkness for some hint of what Petrov was watching. He saw the same faint glimmer he had noticed before and realized that whatever the light was reflecting off was probably not stone.

"Why would that be safer?" he asked.

"Because we don't want your warriors panicking when things start bouncing off their helmets. Or getting crushed, if one of the Runners loses its footing."

'Vadam looked to Petrov. "What are Runners?"

"You'll see."

Petrov inserted two fingers into her mouth, then tipped her head back and emitted a shrill whistle. A series of metallic clunks sounded from the dark chasm above their heads, then four trios of lamps activated high above, spilling long curtains of yellow light down the cavern walls.

"Just don't say I didn't warn you."

'Vadam had 'Talot and Varo'dai send their warriors to wait outside the cavern, then commanded his own to do the same. By the time he had finished, the humans who had been kneeling deeper in the cave had vanished farther into its depths, and a steady cascade of pebbles and dust was hissing and clattering down from above.

"Well done," 'Vadam said to Petrov. Through the dust and debris, he could just make out the shapes of four oval bodies, each silhouetted by three beams of yellow light arrayed along its back and flanks. Each body was hanging between two rows of spindly legs, which were pressed against opposite walls and dancing wildly as they descended toward the cavern wall. "You were going to ambush us."

"I was thinking about it. Now I'm going to give you a ride."

CHAPTER 10

The Owl was still a meter off the ground when the aft loading ramp dropped and the two Mongoose ATVs shot from the troop bay, then raced away trailing thick plumes of dust. Vale jumped out next, hooking around to secure the area ahead of the dropship. The summit of the tel was gently rounded, its shoulders blocking her view of the crater floor, but the rim was visible in the distance, a jagged crescent of dark rock rising from a curtain of billowing dust. Beyond it, the brown slopes of a huge mountain climbed into a ceiling of low brown clouds.

Vale dropped prone and activated her helmet comm. She heard only an oscillating whistle—the same sound that had come over the Owl's system when the pilot tried to contact *Hidden Point*. It did not resemble any sort of comm blocking she had ever before encountered, but at least the strange emanation was not impacting her Mjolnir armor's internal systems the way it had interfered with the Owl's engines. Like most dropships, the Owl was shielded against electromagnetic radiation, and any pulse powerful enough to trigger the reactor overrides should have caused enough damage to knock the craft completely out of the air. Yet it had simply inter-rupted the electrostatic confinement field, and as soon as that had been restored, the reactors had resumed operation.

The Owl hovered in place long enough to deliver the rest of its passengers—two civilians and two squads of ODSTs—then eased forward and vanished over the far end of the tel. When it reappeared an instant later, it was hugging the mountain slope as it climbed into the low brown clouds. The pilots would find a safe landing site on higher ground, then establish a concealed position from which they could observe events both on the tel and in the surrounding crater. With any luck, they would even be able to re-store communications and keep Vale apprised of what they were seeing.

An ODST dropped prone next to Vale. "I have the post," he said through his helmet voicemitter. "Mama's ready to sort things out."

"Affirmative." Vale heard her voice crack and forced herself to take an instant. She had just lost an entire battalion of ODSTs—eight hundred troopers—and the shock was on the verge of becoming despair. She couldn't let it. Too many people were de-pending on her. She had to remain calm and confident. "Thanks."

Vale rose and retreated a dozen paces to the unloading area, where a stocky female gunnery sergeant stood next to three equip-ment crates, issuing orders to a pair of male staff sergeants in charge of Tango Team's two squads. "Mama" Grim Bear was the daughter of Lieutenant Neha Small Bear, who had died during the raid on Naraka early in the war with the Covenant—along with most of the ODSTs of the legendary Black Daggers space assault battalion. A gruff but well-liked leader, Grim Bear commanded the loyalty of her subordinates through her no-nonsense manner and unflappable patience.

When Vale arrived, Grim Bear dismissed the two staff sergeants and turned to report. "Perimeter secure, Spartan Vale. The Mongooses have dropped into a ravine that looks like it descends to the crater floor."

"Very good."

Their makeshift plan called for the Mongooses to find a route to the crater floor, then circle the tel and search for likely access points. Meanwhile, the rest of Tango Team would establish a defensive position on the summit. From what Vale could see, the work detail was dispersed in a hundred-meter circle, every second soldier keeping watch while the others used entrenching tools to dig firing positions, tossing clumps of compressed loess from holes that were already shin deep.

Keely Iyuska was standing next to an open equipment crate, already using a terrain reader and mapping tablet to create a three-dimensional rendering of the tel's summit. Rosa Fuertes was seated nearby on a closed crate, curling her bare toes in the dust and staring across the crater's hidden depths toward the brown wall of the adjacent mountains. Tears clung to her cheeks, and she was biting her lower lip. From what Vale understood of Netherop, it was not a world anyone could long for . . . but Fuertes *had* lived here for the first two decades of her life, and Vale knew from her own feelings about Luyten how powerful the connection to a birth world could be.

She stepped to Fuertes's side. "If I didn't know better, I'd think you actually missed this place."

Fuertes looked up. "Netherop?" She gave an emphatic shake of her head. "No. I hated it then, and I hate it twice as much now."

But the tears began to flow more freely. Fuertes turned back toward the mountains without saying more, and whatever the dying woman's feelings, she obviously had no wish to share them with a Spartan. And Vale was in no shape to offer much support. She was still too unsettled by what had happened during the drop.

Vale stepped away and heard the whine of small engines coming from the far end of the tel. She turned to see a pair of dust plumes as two Mongooses approached.

"Both of them," Vale said. "This can't be good."

"Could be worse," Grim Bear said. "At least they're coming back."

Vale glanced over at Grim Bear, surprised. Gunnery sergeants were seldom the glass-half-full types . . . but they weren't usually nicknamed Mama, either.

"Affirmative," Vale said. "That is something."

The Mongooses arrived in a cloud of dust, then a huge corporal dismounted and stepped forward, leaving his MA40 assault rifle and M90 shotgun in their vehicle scabbards. The man's size was truly impressive. He stood taller than Vale, and had he been wearing Mjolnir, she would have assumed him to be a Spartan. His partner, a lance corporal with S. LEGOWSKI on her nameplate, remained on her vehicle. She had a BR55 in one scabbard, one of the new M305 five-round grenade launchers in the other, an M7 submachine gun mag-clamped across her back, and wisps of blond hair spilling out under her helmet.

Not bothering with formal reporting protocol, Grim Bear waited only until the huge corporal who had dismounted was more or less in front of her, then said, "You're back early, Golly. What's the problem?"

The nameplate on his armor said P. BARNES, so Vale was not sure of the nickname's provenance. Goliath, maybe?

"The crater floor is impassable." Golly's voice was deep and rumbling, even through his helmet voicemitter. "It's like gigoog."

Gigoog was that brightly colored military dessert, packed with nutrients and vitamins. Halfway between liquid and solid, it was usually oversweetened and served cold—in which case, eating it was like chewing soup. But sometimes it was overspiced and served hot—in which case, drinking it was like gulping wet noodles. An acquired taste, to be sure.

"Gigoog?" Grim Bear echoed. "Explain."

"Like, it's all different colors and kind of . . . quivering. Boggy, except there's no water. If you try to drive on it, you sink to your axles and just sit there bobbing up and down, spinning your wheels."

"What about foot travel?" Vale asked.

Golly's bearing and tone grew instantly more formal. "Ma'am, I sank to my chest pulling the Mongoose out. There's solid ground under there, but it's too far down for everyone to keep their heads clear. And drop-offs could be a problem."

He tipped his helmet toward Grim Bear, who was a bit short for an ODST.

"Understood," Vale said. The base of the tel was probably ten kilometers around, so even if it was possible to circumnavigate it on foot, wading through the . . . gigoog could take two standard days. She turned to Fuertes. "Any thoughts, Rosa?"

Fuertes barely looked up. "About what?"

"The crater floor. Is it going to firm up? Is that stuff common on Netherop?"

"No idea. We never saw anything like it when we lived here. Whatever it is, I can't help you with it."

"But you would if you could?" Given Fuertes's unexplained tears and insurrectionist sympathies, Vale had to ask the question. "Right?"

"That is the deal we made. You leave my family alone if I help you . . . and I *want* you to leave my family alone."

"Which I will, regardless of what you do." Vale wanted more from Fuertes than her grudging cooperation; she wanted Fuertes to volunteer her knowledge and experience freely, because there would be times when her guidance was necessary to ensure Tango Team's safety, and they wouldn't even realize it. "Look, we really need your help here, but I'm never going back to Gao just to harass your family. What would that accomplish?"

"How should I know? I don't understand how the UNSC thinks." Fuertes turned away.

Grim Bear shrugged. "Then we recon on foot. It won't be so bad." She turned to one of the staff sergeants she had been talking to earlier and pointed across the summit to their left. "We'll spread both squads down the slope and start from there. Slim, take Golly and First Squad and circle the tel clockwise. Marcus, you take Legs and Second Squad and move counterclockwise. I'll wait here with Spartan Vale and the civilians. If you find an entrance, secure it and send—"

Fuertes turned back around. "You are going to look for an entrance on the sides of the hill?"

"You have a better idea?" Grim Bear turned in place, sweeping her faceplate over the entire summit of the tel. "I don't see any gates up here. Do you?"

Fuertes kept her gaze fixed on Grim Bear. "No, I don't."

"Probably because there aren't any," Iyuska said. "At least not that we can see."

"Because this is a tel," Grim Bear said. "And a tel is a buried city."

"Most likely *several* buried cities," Iyuska clarified. "The layers tend to stack up, which is how you end up with—"

"Mound structures," Grim Bear finished. "I read your briefing, Professor. What I need to know is how we get inside."

"By excavating, of course," Iyuska said. "Very carefully."

Grim Bear looked to Vale and said nothing.

"We don't have the manpower for that," Vale said. "Not anymore."

"Then you'll have to call for more," Iyuska said. "You do understand the implications of what we saw earlier, don't you?"

"I understand that the tel opened up, then something destroyed forty dropships and nearly killed *us*," Vale said. "And that it will finish the job if we don't move fast."

"It was a weapon," Iyuska said. "As far as we know, the Forerunners didn't use dimensional rifting for weaponry. You see that, don't you?"

"Maybe. There's still a lot we don't know about the Forerunners."

"What came before them, for example. And this is our first chance to truly examine that. But we have to do it right. We have to do a full dig, map our excavations, catalog everything we—"

"All that comes later," Vale said. "First we secure that weapon. Otherwise, the only digging we'll be doing is our own graves."

"Don't be so dramatic. *We*'re here, aren't we?"

"For now." Vale paused. "Look, I understand how much this means to you—"

"Not just to me. This will revolutionize pre-Forerunner xeno-archaeology *and*—"

"And it will be your name on the first paper," Vale said, speaking over Iyuska. "But you're going to have to write it based on incidental observations, not a full excavation."

Iyuska went silent . . . always a worrisome sign during an argument. Vale decided to use the lull to get the mission moving. She turned to Grim Bear.

"You have your orders, Sergeant." Vale pointed down at the tel. "Get us inside. Use the C-12 if you need to."

"What's that?" Iyuska demanded.

"You don't want to know," Vale said.

"I see." Iyuska watched with narrowed eyes as Tango Team's two squads gathered C-12 satchels and prepared to depart. "I should have known better than to trust a peer."

"What's *that* supposed to mean?"

"There's nothing more vicious than academic jealousy."

"Now you're just being crazy. I'm not in academia—I'm a Spartan."

"But you're also a xenoanthropologist who missed her calling. Maybe you see this as your path back into the field, a chance to make a big name for yourself."

"The last thing I want is a big name. It would make some very powerful superiors very unhappy." Vale turned away, desperate to end the argument, and found Fuertes chuckling at them. *"What?"*

"Nothing. Just enjoying the show."

Vale realized she had allowed Iyuska to goad her into making a spectacle. She took a long breath. "Show's over."

"Too bad," Fuertes said. "In that case, maybe I should tell you I thought of something."

"Maybe you should. That's why we hired you."

"I have an idea of where to search for an entrance."

Vale looked to Grim Bear. "Maybe you'd better hold your squads, Mama."

"I thought maybe." Grim Bear nodded at her sergeants. "I hope we can make this fast, Spartan Vale. I usually like to make the plan before we unload."

"Me too."

Vale turned back to Fuertes and found Iyuska already between them.

"Well?" Iyuska asked.

Fuertes looked past Iyuska to Vale.

"Go ahead," Vale said. "We're on the same team."

Fuertes raised a doubtful brow, but replied to Iyuska, "You're right about one thing: there's probably a whole stack of old cities buried under this hill. But they're upside down. The cities on Netherop were built underground. The oldest ones are near the surface, the youngest are deeper down. And this tel? It's crushed waste rock, dumped on top of the old cities."

Iyuska asked, "Are you saying the original inhabitants lived in their *mines*?"

"That's right. We didn't understand that completely when we lived here. But when we moved to Gao and started to take work in their mines, what we had seen here began to make more sense."

Iyuska's face screwed into an expression of doubt, and Vale understood why. Subterranean cities were not unheard of in the Orion Arm of the galaxy, and a handful appeared to have been lost mining civilizations established by burrowing species at the low end of the technological scale, Tier 6 Industrial, at most Tier 5 Atomic. But whatever had opened that dimensional rift and destroyed Vale's landing force had been far more advanced—probably Tier 1, or even Tier 0.

"This doesn't make a lot of sense, Rosa," Vale said. "Technology like the weapon that attacked us is usually associated with a spacefaring species. And spacefaring species tend to live on the surface, where they can see the stars. Not underground."

"Maybe I'm wrong," Fuertes said. "I only know the warrens where we lived, and none of those were surrounded by craters."

"But?" Vale asked.

Fuertes grabbed a handful of dust and held it close to her nose. "But *this* smells just like the dirt we found outside their old metal mines." She let it run through her fingers, then pointed down the center of the mound. "If I were you, I'd probe for haulage shafts along the middle of the hill. You find one, you'll have a straight drop down to the processing chambers."

Vale held a handful of dust in her palm and called for a chemical analysis. Her HUD display showed a lot of silicon and metallic sulfides, especially copper and iron. And nothing was growing on the tel, which could be due to contaminated ground . . . or Netherop's blistering heat.

"Thank you," Vale said, speaking to Fuertes. "I think you just earned your consultant's fee."

"I don't need your thanks. Just send the performance bonus to my village."

Vale smiled inside her helmet. They hadn't actually negotiated a performance bonus, but she nodded. "Sure, I can do that." Vale turned to Grim Bear. "Let's make a probe line. Have your people use their entrenching tools to sound the ground. Dig up any depressions, or anything that sounds hollow."

"And be careful," Fuertes suggested. "The way this stuff crusts over in the wind, we could be standing above a shaft right now."

Vale thought of her Mjolnir armor's four-hundred-kilogram mass and couldn't help glancing down.

A gift of the Ancients, the holographic image floating ahead showed eighteen humans arranging themselves in a line across the exterior of the Sanctum Overmound. All but two were fully armored, and it appeared they were led by a demon Spartan in red Mjolnir armor. To hold them at bay, Tam 'Lakosee had only himself, Worldmaster Nizat 'Kvarosee, and the five huffing, poorly disciplined warriors following them up the passage. How such a tired and forlorn unit would keep the infidels from seizing the Sanctum, he did not know.

But they would. The gods demanded it of them.

The Worldmaster paused in the center of the Overmound, no doubt debating whether they should turn left to flank the humans or continue straight to come up behind them. Both options required driving a tunnel through five hundred paces of broken rock packed with tailings dust, but that would be no obstacle. As the unit traveled forward, a well-lit passage would simply open ahead of it, the floors cushioned by an invisible pad and the walls and ceiling held in place by transparent energy fields. It was but another of the Sanctum's many wonders, a miracle of the gods that no mortal could ever hope to understand.

"Let us turn left and flank the enemy," Tam said. "We will end up attacking from a rear oblique, and the humans will find that more confusing."

Attacking from behind would bring more fire to bear quickly, but it would also require a steeper climb—and Tam's companions were already gasping for breath. By the time the Defenders of the Sanctum reached the surface and recovered enough to launch an attack, the invaders would be in front of them anyway. That was what happened to warriors who spent less time in the training arena than in their own cells, escaping into the Dream Lives the Sanctum provided to relieve their boredom.

'Kvarosee considered Tam's suggestion, then turned left and said, "Confusion is good. It is all the gods have allowed us, so it will be enough to prevail."

"It is certainly the best option left to us."

Tam was thinking not only of their warriors' poor condition, but of their lack of discipline, which had robbed the Defenders of their only transport. Upon learning that three Phantom dropships were inserting on a trajectory that would bring them down nearby, four warriors had taken the Sanctum's last Dust Runner to meet their presumed rescuers. Unfortunately, a UNSC insertion force had appeared soon afterward, and the four warriors had barely managed to return before 'Kvarosee opened the Rift of Eternity.

With no time remaining to ascend the long path that traversed up the steep slopes of the lower Overmound, the group had abandoned their ride on the crater floor and scrambled to safety. The Dust Runner had been destroyed when 'Kvarosee unleashed the Wave of Wrath, using the Divine Hand to sweep the human dropships from the sky. Now the Defenders of the Sanctum had no choice but to enter battle on foot, rather than riding a ten-legged transport armed with a microwave cannon.

The humans in the floating vision slowly drifted ahead and to the left, so that Tam and his companions were looking at the enemy line from the rear oblique. The figure anchoring the near end had descended the slope far enough that his boots were at shoulder level. It was hardly an accurate indication of their relative positions, but it did suggest that if the Sangheili continued to push forward, their self-creating passage would soon break through the Overmound to the surface.

Tam held a hand out to the side, signaling the column behind him to stop, then said, "Perhaps we should hold here for a time, Worldmaster. If we allow the enemy to continue its advance, our firing angle will be better."

"Very wise," 'Kvarosee said. Like the rest of the Sangheili, he wore a close-fitting skinsuit of a shimmering cloth-like material they called Sanctum's Hide. As tough as graphene and as light as air, the armor was self-repairing and self-cleaning, and it grew on them while they slept. About the only thing it did not do was provide an energy shield or enhance their physical attributes—which was most unfortunate, under the current circumstances. "The infidels will die on the Overmound and never even know we were there."

"That is my hope."

Tam did not add *and my expectation*, because it was not. But had he admitted that their warriors needed time to rest before leaping into battle, 'Kvarosee would have overruled him and insisted on attacking immediately. Over the years, the environment inside the Sanctum had grown ever more accommodating. Whenever one of its Defenders walked through a passage, the walls began to glow with the same golden light as a Sanghelios dawn. The temperature and humidity levels adjusted themselves as though the Sanctum had actual seasons, and hydroponic gardens appeared deep underground, supplying food that was sometimes familiar and sometimes strange, but always delicious and nutritious. As a result, the Worldmaster had come to believe that he could shape his circumstances merely by wishing for what he desired. But with a squad of human soldiers and their Spartan leader trying to find their way inside the Sanctum, Tam did not think it wise to test the limits of his master's strategy.

As they waited, a heavy warrior named Meduz 'Ra'ashai tipped his head to one side, then pointed at the holograph. "Before we engage, we should give thought to where they came from."

"All we need give thought to is what the gods require of us," 'Kvarosee said. "There are times when we must do more than simply *enjoy* their favor. We must earn it."

"Which we cannot accomplish by slipping the enemy's snare over our own heads." 'Ra'ashai's tone was sharp and disrespectful, but Tam pretended not to hear. 'Ra'ashai was a Silent Shadow blademaster who had been sent to N'ba to punish 'Kvarosee for stealing a holy artifact called a Luminal Beacon. 'Ra'ashai permitted 'Kvarosee to live only because, like most Defenders, he considered being marooned here a fate worse than death. "Those humans up there came from a stealth craft that snuck down while we were busy destroying the other forty dropships."

"It was not you who destroyed the insertion force," 'Kvarosee said. "It was *I* . . . wielding the Divine Hand."

"And Blademaster 'Ra'ashai is not suggesting otherwise," Tam said quickly. "He is only pointing out that the humans sacrificed a great many dropships to draw our attention away from their stealth craft. This may be another trap—one designed to trick us into opening the Sanctum when we should have remained barricaded inside."

"How do we know that remaining barricaded is even possible?" asked Klemas 'Teodoree. A fleet ranger who had lost a leg in combat, he had nearly died of dehydration before Tam and 'Kvarosee found him lying among the Covenant corpses on one of the first battle sites. Within months of arriving at the Sanctum, he had reclaimed his warrior's honor by miraculously growing a prosthetic replacement from a nacreous material resembling his Sanctum's Hide armor. "If these humans could escape the Worldmaster's attention and evade his attack, they may be able to breach the Sanctum itself. Perhaps we should use the Divine Hand again and let the Wave of Wrath eliminate them for us."

"Who do I use the Hand against?" 'Kvarosee asked. "The only vessels in orbit are Sangheili."

"The only vessels you can *see*," 'Ra'ashai noted. "The human insertion force did not drop on N'ba out of slipspace. There is a stealth ship up there."

"Probably so," 'Kvarosee said. "But I cannot attack what I cannot find."

"Then attack what you can find," 'Teodoree said. "The Sangheili flotilla remains intact, does it not?"

"Attack our own flotilla?" 'Ra'ashai asked. "We are not that desperate. The humans have numbers, but we have our Sanctum and its defenses."

"It is a mistake to assume it *is* our own flotilla," 'Teodoree said. "The hierarchs abandoned the Worldmaster and marooned us here deliberately. Are we to believe they have suddenly changed hearts and forgiven his disobedience . . . after more than a thousand cycles?"

"It was not disobedience," 'Kvarosee said. "It was the will of the Ancients, calling us to watch over their Sanctum."

"So you have claimed many times, but that is not the vindication you believe it to be," 'Ra'ashai said. Members of the Silent Shadow were hardly known for their piety, and 'Ra'ashai made no secret that he considered the Sanctum to be just another Forerunner facility . . . a bit older and more mysterious than most, but hardly worth dying over. "Before attacking *any* Sangheili vessel, we must find out why they are here."

"So they will take you aboard when they leave?" 'Kvarosee said. "Your devotion has always been lacking."

'Ra'ashai pushed his parted mandibles toward 'Kvarosee. "I have more devotion than most. Just not to you."

"Your only devotion is to escaping N'ba," Tam said, allowing his disdain to rise into his voice. It was a risk, but if *he* did not defend 'Kvarosee's authority, no one would. "And your self-involvement is blinding you to our true peril."

Rather than bristling, 'Ra'ashai surprised Tam by asking, "And what would that peril be?"

"More than eight hundred cycles have passed since the last humans tried to land on N'ba," Tam said. "Now we have humans and Sangheili inserting within a unit of each other?"

"It is no coincidence," 'Teodoree said. "Either they are doing battle, or our Sangheili brothers are traitors who have allied with the Covenant's enemies."

"And we have seen no sign that they are doing battle." Tam looked to 'Kvarosee. "Unless you have seen otherwise in your visions?"

"The gods have revealed nothing." The Worldmaster's "visions" were visible to everyone, manifesting as holographic images similar to the one floating in the passage ahead. But 'Kvarosee spent most of his time alone in the heart of the Sanctum, where the visions always initially appeared. "There is no battle in orbit, but I have seen no human vessels. They may be hiding out of fear."

"Very possible," 'Teodoree said. "Humans are cowards."

"And yet," 'Ra'ashai said, "*you* are the one who proposes we destroy a Sangheili vessel rather than attack a band of human cowards. From behind."

"I am only thinking of the Sanctum's security," 'Teodoree said. "But why attack anything? Perhaps the Worldmaster can release the Wave of Wrath without unleashing the Divine Hand?"

'Kvarosee dropped his mandibles briefly to the left, confirming what Tam had already guessed. The Divine Hand was not completely under the Worldmaster's control. He could wield it against the enemies of the gods, but when they were not present to serve as his focus, he apparently could not summon it at all.

Tam did not dare let the rest of the Defenders discover that. Were it not for 'Kvarosee's connection to the gods, 'Ra'ashai would have led a mutiny long ago and fed them both to the humans.

"The Wave of Wrath is but a by-product of the Divine Hand," Tam said, thinking fast. "It cannot be summoned on its own."

"Then attack something else," 'Teodoree said. "With such a large insertion force, surely the humans have plenty of surveillance and communications satellites in orbit."

Tam had not thought of that possibility. "You would trouble the gods over a mere satellite?"

"I would trouble the gods to help us protect their Sanctum," 'Teodoree replied. "The humans on the Overmound outnumber us three to one, and it has been a thousand cycles since any of us fought a well-fed, armored enemy. If we fail, the Sanctum is lost."

"Then we cannot fail," 'Kvarosee said. "Because even if we insult the gods by using their hand to swat at *flegs*, we dare not open the Rift of Eternity while there are humans on the Overmound. Or have you forgotten the Lurkers?"

'Teodoree recoiled, and even 'Ra'ashai dropped his chins. One time, three human castaways had leapt inside when the Rift opened. Instead of perishing, the trio began to float around inside the walls of the Sanctum, stalking its inhabitants like ghosts, always watching and ever present. Eventually, the surveillance grew so unbearable that four Defenders fled into the desert and were never seen again. It took two years for the last apparition to vanish, and by then the remaining warriors were so sleep-deprived and apprehensive that Tam and 'Kvarosee spent most of their time keeping them from attacking one another.

"No one could forget the Lurkers," Tam said, seizing the chance to turn the debate away from 'Kvarosee's control of the Divine Hand. "Better to take our chances and attack by surprise."

"Not yet." 'Ra'ashai's gaze was locked on the vision. "Better to gather intelligence first."

"They are humans treading on the Sanctum," 'Kvarosee said. "What more do we need to know?"

"Where the other two went." Ra'ashai pointed at the line of human soldiers. "The two without armor. Where did they go?"

Vale slapped the back of her shovel down and heard a hollow *thump*. She did it again, heard the same empty sound. A bit louder and more resonant than the usual dust-muffled *whap*.

"Found something!"

She was at the downslope end of the line, where the summit of the mound became the shoulder and fell away toward the crater floor. The searchers were spaced three meters apart, with Golly to her left, and Legs beyond him. Then it was Slim and his squad, with Grim Bear in the middle and Marcus and his squad on the far end.

Golly brought down his entrenching tool and produced the same hollow *thump* as had Vale. "Me too."

"Same here," Legs said. "That's a big shaft."

"Maybe not." Slim dropped to his knees and cocked his helmet to one side, then slapped the ground with the spoon of his entrenching tool. Three times. "What if it's a tunnel?"

Vale glanced down the side of the mound and saw no bulges or fans to suggest a rock dump at the end of a haulage tunnel. But if Rosa Fuertes was right about the upside-down layers of the tel, and Iyuska about its pre-Forerunner provenance, the site was over a hundred thousand years old. And *that* was plenty of time for erosion to smooth out the terrain.

She looked up the slope toward Slim. "What makes you think it might be a tunnel?"

"Distance, mostly. You and I are almost ten meters apart, and I'm pretty sure there's a cavity under me, too. There's no way that kind of span gets hidden by wind-packed dust. A plug that big would collapse under its own weight."

"Probably so."

Vale started backward, slapping her shovel down as she retreated. When the ground seemed solid again, she changed direction, following her soundings along what appeared to be the edge of a tunnel. It wasn't that she doubted Slim's theory—she just wanted to confirm it. Digging their way into a three-meter-high tunnel would advance the mission, but collapsing the plug over a haulage shaft hundreds of meters deep might well end it.

Vale had barely ascended three paces before she seemed to come to a sharp corner that turned under the probe line. At first, she assumed that the tunnel had changed direction, but then she looked up the slope and saw that Slim and Legs were still in line above her.

"I think we have an intersection here." Vale slapped the shovel down a couple of times and heard hollow thuds for another couple of paces, then the ground began to sound solid again. "Yeah. Definitely an intersection."

She moved across the mound horizontally, still following the hollow sound of the tunnel. It ran up the slope at an angle, and the thuds didn't seem to grow any more muffled as she climbed higher. She stopped and used her tracks to plot a line.

It led to their landing zone, where Fuertes and Iyuska were sitting on the equipment crates, waiting for Tango Team to complete its reconnaissance. Vale began to run.

"Mama!" She waited until Grim Bear was looking in her direction, then pointed toward Fuertes and Iyuska. "Fall back to the LZ! Now!"

Grim Bear looked puzzled, but affirmed the orders to her staff sergeants and quickly waved soldiers toward the landing zone. Vale grabbed her M20 submachine gun off its magmount and closed the distance in five breaths, arriving just as Fuertes and Iyuska rose off the crates . . . and vanished, screeching, in an eruption of dust.

Vale entered the billowing gray plume, instantly lost visuals, then stepped into a pit and dropped three meters onto the top of an equipment crate . . . which collapsed under the weight of her GEN2 Mjolnir armor and left her standing in a pile of broken tripods and crushed laser measuring and mapping tools.

"Keely?!" Vale called. "Rosa?!"

"Here." Iyuska's voice came from beneath a jumble of crates ahead of Vale. "What just happened?"

"Don't know. Is Rosa—" A familiar sound caught Vale's attention—the *snap-snap-snap* of energy swords activating. Behind her. Along with the sound of pounding feet. To Iyuska, she yelled, "Stay put!"

The tactical readouts on her helmet's VISR system refused to come up clear—no doubt obscured by the dense cloud of dust in the tunnel. But she was pretty sure Rosa Fuertes would not be charging her right now with an activated energy sword.

Vale launched a rear stomp kick behind her, hit hard, and sent something large and solid tumbling away with a grunt of pain. Her shield crackled twice as energy blades struck at her knee and ankle. She raised her leg, then snapped off a heel kick that caught a second attacker in the head and sent whoever it was thumping into the tunnel wall on the left. She reversed into a roundhouse, caught another head, and sent another body crashing into a wall.

Only then did Vale spin around, to find three large gray forms lying behind the diffuse glow of three bright blades. It took a couple of heartbeats to confirm they were male Sangheili warriors, as they were dressed in opalescent skinsuits rather than typical combat armor and helmets.

"I am not your enemy," Vale said in Sangheili. "Hold your attack and—"

All three attackers roared in anger and gathered themselves up to charge, their energy swords rising to strike. Vale hit the one on the right with a short burst of submachine gun fire, dropping him back to the floor, then stepped into a thrust kick, smashing the middle one's sword arm against his chest and sending him flying down the tunnel . . . knocking down a fresh trio of warriors just emerging from the dust behind him.

That wasn't good.

By then, the warrior to Vale's left was on his feet again, swinging his energy sword at her head. With her kicking leg still outstretched, she dropped onto the other haunch and swung the M20 across her body, firing one-handed into his abdomen.

The burst folded him over like a jackknife, and his energy sword sliced through the air a few centimeters above her helmet. She used her free hand to catch his wrist and pull him off-balance, depositing him in a heap in front of her. Orange circles glowed where her rounds had struck his torso, and she could see similar spots shining in the skinsuit of the first warrior she had targeted.

Both warriors were returning to their feet, their oblong heads swinging in her direction. The third warrior—the one she hadn't shot—was also rising, along with the three behind him. A seventh figure seemed to be standing in the tunnel beyond, a gray ghost barely visible through the still-swirling dust.

"The war is over!" Vale called, still speaking Sangheili. "Nobody needs to die here."

"*Wrong*, lying demon," the ghostly figure in back said . . . in raspy, sibilant English. "*You* must die. The gods demand it."

The gray blur of a rising arm appeared alongside his torso as he brought a weapon up. Vale opened fire with her M20 and saw him stumble back, a cluster of orange dots blossoming across his chest. When her magazine fell empty, the warriors she had attacked earlier leapt up. She stepped back and pulled her plasma pistol—

a Sangheili *Zo'klada*-pattern manufactured by the Iruiru Armory on Sanghelios—off the mount on her hip—

—then felt the heart-stopping *thump* of a C-12 charge breaching the tunnel ceiling. The air went from murky to impenetrable, with a fat column of ambient light filtering down through dust thick enough to grab. An M90 boomed, and she saw a downward muzzle flash as a Tango Team ODST—probably Golly, given the shotgun—fired on a sword wielder.

Vale advanced through the dust, firing plasma bolts toward the glow of the other swords. Normally, she would have been careful to alert her teammate to her approach. But her comm indicator continued to flash red, and there was little possibility of making a voicemitter-modulated shout heard over the thunder of the shotgun fire.

The energy swords deactivated, but the miasma of dust made it impossible to tell whether the warriors holding them were dead . . . or had simply realized their weapons were only making them targets.

An instant later, the shotgun fire ceased, and Vale found herself standing in swirling dust, about half a meter from a murky wall of ODST armor that could only be Golly. Unable to see below her own knees, she began to sweep her feet back and forth, searching for her Sangheili attackers. When she felt nothing but spongy floor, she positioned herself back-to-back with Golly and looked down the tunnel into . . . more dust.

Speaking through her voicemitter, Vale asked, "You alone?"

"Negative," Golly replied. "Legs is with—"

A burst of submachine gun fire sounded a short distance down the tunnel, just beyond the breach hole in the ceiling. Vale spun toward the sound, pushing Golly toward the right wall and going left herself. All she could see through the dust was a faint aura of muzzle flashes and plasma flares arcing around a dark oval that had to be Legs's silhouette. Vale began to fire toward the source of the plasma flares, but it was impossible to tell whether she was hitting anything.

Then the dark oval dropped, not falling sideways as though Legs had been hit, but sinking straight into the floor. Her submachine gun continued to fire, the sound growing more muffled with each shot. Vale and Golly continued forward, firing on the run and—judging by the orange circles that flared in the miasma ahead—occasionally hitting a Sangheili.

A *retreating* Sangheili, because plasma bolts were no longer coming up the tunnel. Vale stopped firing long enough to put the plasma pistol away and reload the M20—then heard Golly cry out from across the passage:

"*What thhheeee . . .*"

His voice was sinking fast, and Vale looked over to see his murky form dropping straight into the floor, arms upraised and flailing. She dropped her M20 and stepped into the middle of the tunnel, at the same time stooping down and thrusting out her hand. Even with her augmented reflexes, she was almost too slow. By the time she caught hold of Golly's wrist, all she could see of him was the hand above. Everything else—his head, shoulders, and even the other arm—was hidden under a churning pool of dust. She lifted him out and, not even taking the time to fully stand, began to retreat up the tunnel toward the crates.

"What the . . . is *that*?" she gasped.

Golly ignored her and started to pull back toward the . . . sinkhole, Vale decided.

"Corporal!" Vale jerked him toward her. "Use your head."

"But Legs—"

"Legs is MIA." Vale turned toward the crates, where she had left Iyuska hiding. "And joining her won't change that."

Vale started up the tunnel, dragging Golly along behind her. Whatever had just happened, she *really* didn't like it. First, a band of Sangheili . . . hermits? monks? castaways? . . . had managed to drive a fifty-meter tunnel to Tango Team's landing zone in a few minutes. Then, they had covered their retreat by creating a sink-hole—instantaneously.

It defied logic.

But whatever had happened, Vale needed to get her companions out of the tunnel, then figure out just what was going on. And she needed to do that fast, while she still had a team to work with.

They reached the pile of equipment crates. Iyuska was going through the one Vale had landed on, sighing and cursing as she pulled out broken tools and pieces of instruments.

Vale motioned Golly to climb out through the hole in the ceiling, then took a smashed transit level from Iyuska's hands and tossed it aside.

"We'll sort through the equipment later. Right now, we need to move." Vale stepped around to the back side of the crate pile and peered into the empty space where Iyuska had been hiding. "Where's Rosa?"

"You didn't get her back?" Iyuska asked.

Vale's stomach sank. Her mission was going bad, fast. She stood upright and looked over the crate pile. "What do you mean, get her back?"

"From the Sangheili. They came after the two of us. I managed to hide, but I'm assuming that's what they were after. *Us.*"

CHAPTER 11

Barely visible in the billowing dust, a trio of ten-legged running machines raced along beside the one in which Thel 'Vadam stood. Time and again, the spiderlike legs of his machine clacked against those of an adjacent vehicle and sent an alarming shudder through the passenger compartment, causing him to clench his mandibles and instinctively drop his center of gravity.

But Commander Petrov never flinched. She knelt on the spacious deck beside him, her gaze fixed on a weighted line that hung from a makeshift tripod. As the line swung along the arms of an eight-pointed star scratched onto the metal below, she issued bearing corrections in a calm, firm voice. The pilot moved his hands over the vehicle's steering sphere, and it veered back toward its original course.

The close formation seemed an uncertain and dangerous method of guiding four fast-moving vehicles through a blinding cloud of dust. But Petrov insisted their best hope of reaching the tel together was to keep the other machines in sight as they crossed the crater. She claimed she only wanted to arrive before the UNSC landing party achieved its objective and departed, but 'Vadam suspected another reason for her haste.

Humans could be a cunning, vengeful species, and Petrov's enemies had been living comfortably inside the tel for decades while her own soldiers slowly starved to death. She would want retribution . . . and a hand in delivering it.

Petrov issued another bearing correction. Instead of bringing the Runner back on course, the pilot pulled the steering sphere back toward his chest. The vehicle slowed so abruptly that 'Vadam had to brace himself against the deceleration. He continued to watch Petrov, half expecting her to rise and take the steering sphere herself. But she only craned her neck and looked forward, then lowered her brow.

"That doesn't look right," she said.

'Vadam turned and saw a gray mound looming ahead. It was difficult to see details through the swirling dust, but its embankment seemed to rise a hundred units above their heads and stretch in both directions as far as he could see. "Is that not how the tel should appear? A great hill rising above the crater floor?"

"That's exactly how the tel should appear." Petrov pointed through the gray haze, into the sky above its summit. "It's the HiMeX smoke that bothers me."

'Vadam followed her finger toward a dark plume rising out of the dust cloud. It did not seem connected to the ground, and it appeared wider at the top than at the base. "I do not know what this HiMeX is. But I recognize blast fumes when I see them."

"HiMeX stands for 'high-melting explosive.' It's the main ingredient in our C-series of moldable charges. If there's a cloud of HiMeX smoke hanging above the tel, it's because—"

"The UNSC is already breaching it. It seems we arrived just in time."

"I would not call it that," Crei 'Ayomuu said, speaking Sang-heili. "The humans will block the entrances and leave us waiting outside while they seize the device."

The Oath Warden stood in the back of the passenger com-partment, along with Olabisi Varo'dai and Ghe 'Talot. A trio of Petrov's soldiers sat behind them on the forward edge of the coal bins where the fuel for the battery chargers was stored. The hu-mans were small, thin, and clearly undernourished, and whether the fire in their eyes was fed primarily by hunger or hatred was hard to tell.

"Would that be so terrible?" 'Talot asked, also speaking Sang-heili. Neither he nor Varo'dai understood English, but 'Ayomuu was clearly talking about the UNSC unit that had beaten them to the tel. "There cannot be many of them, and in all this dust, they will never know we are outside waiting."

"You would attack them?" Varo'dai asked. "By surprise?"

"That is usually the safest way," 'Ayomuu said. "And the surest path to victory."

The running machine had slowed to a stop, 'Vadam realized, and Petrov was frowning at the conversation taking place among her Sangheili passengers.

"My companions are concerned about the humans entering the tel ahead of us," 'Vadam explained in English. "To be honest, I am rather concerned as well."

Petrov's eyes flashed. "I thought it didn't matter who recovered the weapon, as long as *one* of us did?"

"I also said that I would prefer it be the Sangheili. In my ex-perience, your intelligence officers have a different agenda than the rest of the UNSC. It would be safer for everyone if the device were someplace your Office of Naval Intelligence could never as-sert control over it."

"But the Sangheili have no factions of their own? You can guarantee that none of your own rivals will seize control of the device and use it to threaten humanity?"

"Yes. For as long as I am Arbiter."

"For as long as you're Arbiter. I don't really know what that implies. Am I expected to find that reassuring?"

"I expect nothing, but you should." 'Vadam could see her point. He had barely returned from ending the War of Annihilation when a treacherous sect of religious fundamentalists had cornered him in Vadam Keep. If not for some timely support from the UNSC, he would have lost his title, his ancestral home, and his life. Only just last year had he finished putting down the most dangerous of these remnant factions, Jul 'Mdama's Covenant. "I am an Arbiter who would never let such a weapon fall into the hands of his rivals. One who would destroy it first."

To 'Vadam's surprise, Petrov met his gaze, appearing to give serious consideration to the assertion, then finally shrugged. "Is that a promise?"

"You have my word. As a warrior and a kaidon."

"Not sure what that second thing was you said, but it's good enough for me. Okay—tell your companions not to worry." She turned and tapped the pilot on his shoulder, and the running machine started forward again. "They'll have first try at the weapon."

"How can you promise that?" 'Vadam asked. "The UNSC is already inside."

"Because I've been inside. And I know what they're facing."

The running machines reached the base of the tel, then surprised 'Vadam by shifting into column formation and slowly traversing the slope at a steep angle. The pilots kept the passenger compartments level by extending the uphill legs almost horizontally, while setting the downhill legs beneath the compartment

HALO: OUTCASTS

vertically. The vehicles moved at a near crawl, carefully placing each step, but 'Vadam never felt in danger of their tipping over and rolling down the slope.

'Vadam was less reassured by Petrov's promise. *First* did not mean *best*, and she had been clear that she did not view him as an ally. If she was willing to let his Sangheili make the initial attempt to retrieve the device, it was because she expected them to fail—and, perhaps, to serve as a distraction so her fellow humans could succeed.

Their Runner climbed out of the dust, then crested the tel and started along the summit. In the distance ahead, 'Vadam saw Spartan Vale's red Mjolnir armor towering above a platoon of ODSTs in full armor. The small group, perhaps fifteen troopers, were all standing in a circle, their weapons pointed toward the ground. A faint column of dust appeared to be rising from their midst.

'Vadam turned to ask for a monocular and caught 'Ayomuu eyeing the plasma rifle hanging from 'Talot's hip. For a breath, 'Vadam did not comprehend what he was seeing and was tempted to ignore the uneasy feeling between his hearts. Then the Oath Warden's gaze drifted forward, toward Vale and her platoon of ODSTs, and 'Vadam understood.

"It will never work," 'Vadam said in Sangheili. He took his energy sword in hand. "Even if I do not kill you first, it will take more than a few plasma bolts to start a battle between my warriors and those of Spartan Vale."

'Ayomuu stepped away from 'Talot. "Why would I want to start a battle? Battles can be so . . . unpredictable."

"Not entirely. You would be the first to die. That, I promise."

'Ayomuu dropped his chins. "I thank you for the forewarning. Rest assured, I shall remember it."

The note of mockery in the Oath Warden's voice suggested the

— 169 —

response was more threat than acquiescence. Before 'Vadam could chastise him for it, the running machines came to an abrupt stop. Varo'dai and 'Talot allowed their hands to drift toward their weapons and kept their eyes fixed forward. The three haggard castaways at the back of the passenger compartment stood and let their mouths fall open, and it occurred to 'Vadam that this was the first time they had ever seen any human they did not live with.

The groan of small engines rose from the direction of the ODSTs, and 'Vadam turned to see a pair of Mongoose ATVs approaching. Olympia Vale piloted one, unmistakable in her red armor. Piloting the other was a trooper so large 'Vadam briefly wondered if the UNSC had started to augment ODSTs.

Without turning, 'Vadam pointed toward the back of the compartment and said, "Watch the Oath Warden. If he attempts anything—"

"I will not," 'Ayomuu interrupted. "The opportunity has passed. You will have to find some other way to secure the device. Perhaps if you ask nicely."

"Yes," 'Vadam said. "That is just what I was thinking."

Petrov signaled all four running machines to stop and ordered her followers to form by squads. The humans dismounted, then lined up in front of their vehicles in groups of three to five. Each team was led by a full-grown adult, but most of the subordinates appeared to be children, short and slight of build. Again, 'Vadam was struck by the inherent contrasts in Petrov's role among these humans. She was almost certainly a mother or grandmother to several, yet also their commander.

And commanders sent their subordinates into battle, often knowing they would die. Her own young. 'Vadam was glad he had never matched wills with her in battle. He might have lost.

As the Mongooses approached, the young humans watched

with round eyes, occasionally glancing at one another as though seeking reassurance that the two massive ATV pilots were actually members of their own species.

'Vadam assembled his own warriors next to his running machine, where it would be clear the Sangheili were not forming for battle, then signaled Petrov to accompany him and started forward to meet Spartan Vale. When both kaidons and 'Ayomuu tried to follow, 'Vadam stopped and fixed 'Talot with a glare that remained unbroken until the kaidon took his meaning and stepped back. After that, it required only a glance to remind Varo'dai and the Oath Warden of the greeting proprieties, and he and Petrov continued forward until they were far enough away to avoid unwanted "advice" during the negotiations.

Vale and her massive companion arrived a moment later, stopping their Mongooses twenty paces away and turning them perpendicular to the running machines. Only Vale dismounted and came forward, leaving the big ODST far enough back to watch over the entire line. Clearly, Vale had not been completely reassured by 'Vadam's attempt to array his warriors in a nonthreatening manner.

Under the circumstances, he doubted that he would have been, either.

When she stopped, he extended an empty hand in the human fashion of greeting and spoke in English. "Spartan Vale . . . what an unexpected pleasure."

"I doubt it is either of those." Vale clasped his hand and pumped it once. "But I am glad to see you well, Arbiter."

"And I you." Seeing that Vale's helmet had turned in Petrov's direction, 'Vadam stepped aside and gestured toward the castaway. "May I present Lieutenant Commander Petrov of the UNSC."

Vale came to attention and saluted. "Spartan Olympia Vale, ma'am. It's a pleasure to meet you."

"A surprising one, no doubt." Petrov looked from Vale to 'Vadam and back to Vale, then asked, "So . . . the war with Covenant really *is* over?"

"Yes, ma'am. For six years now." Vale hesitated, then tipped her helmet toward 'Vadam. "The Arbiter here played a big role in stopping it."

"Is that so?" Petrov pressed her lips together and looked up at 'Vadam, openly reappraising him. "How did it end?"

"I learned the Prophets had been deceiving us," 'Vadam explained. "After that, I joined forces with your greatest—"

"No," Petrov interrupted. "I mean, how did it turn out? Who won?"

Vale tipped her helmet. "It's . . . complicated."

"Not *that* complicated," 'Vadam said. "The important thing is that the Covenant lost. And that the humans and the Sangheili are now allies. As I have told you."

Petrov arched her brow.

"It's true, ma'am," Vale said. "We've worked together against mutual enemies several times."

"But you're not working together *now*, are you? You're both after the same thing, and you both think it will be better for everyone if *you're* the one who secures the asset. You're going to end up fighting over it, hostiles all over again."

"That won't happen," Vale said. "Perhaps I should explain later, when we have more—"

"Time?" 'Vadam asked. "Or privacy?"

Vale turned square to him. "*I* am not the one who snuck off Sanghelios without informing my ally."

"There were complicating factors." 'Vadam tipped his helmet

toward 'Ayomuu. "I would have preferred to inform you of my decision before departing, but time was short . . . and *she* was watching."

Vale nodded. "Yeah, us too." She failed to look in 'Ayomuu's direction, a sign that suggested Vale already knew the Oath Warden's identity. "But she doesn't have surveillance assets this far out, so we need to uncomplicate things *now*. The commander is right. If we don't find a way to work together—"

"Wait, wait." Petrov raised her palm. "Who is this *she* you're talking about?"

"My apologies," 'Vadam said. "We have fallen into the habit of avoiding her name."

"Who *is* she? Sauron?"

"No." 'Vadam did not know who this Sauron was, but it troubled him to think the Tyrant might not be the first monstrous creation that ONI had loosed on the galaxy. "*She* is the mutual enemy I mentioned in the cave. One of your artificial intelligences gone rogue. Her name is Cortana."

"There's a little more to it than that," Vale said. "Cortana sacrificed herself to save Earth. We think she became trapped in the Domain when the vessel she was aboard—"

"Excuse me, Spartan. I haven't had a situation briefing since 2526. This is all a bit much."

"Of course, ma'am. The Domain is a quantum information repository. We believe it holds most of the knowledge and cultural records of the Forerunners."

"Forerunners? Were they part of the Covenant too?"

"No." 'Vadam found it surprising that Petrov did not even know who the Forerunners were. But she *had* been stranded here very early in the war, when the humans knew almost nothing about the enemies trying to eradicate them. "They were the false gods of the Covenant, an ancient civilization whose territory once encompassed this entire area of the galaxy."

"What's important is that their technology still exists," Vale said. "It's very real, and very advanced—they could build worlds, wipe out entire star systems, even police the entire galaxy. Cortana was already starting to go rampant when she entered their Domain. She convinced herself that it was her responsibility to impose peace on all of us, and she's been tapping the knowledge and technology of the Forerunners to do just that."

Petrov lifted her brow. "Is that so wrong? The Covenant was doing a pretty good job of annihilating us. They were incinerating entire worlds."

"A peace imposed is a war in disguise," 'Vadam said. "Cortana has already used her Guardians to punish a Jiralhanae warlord by annihilating the homeworld of his entire species, and she will do the same to anyone who defies her. Even her human creators."

"It's true," Vale said. "She smashed the UNSC in a matter of days, and she's used Forerunner weapons to pacify at least three human worlds that I know of. I can only guess how many people she's killed, but by now it must be in the millions. Even Earth was hit hard. Like I said, she was already going rampant before she accessed the Domain. The repository seems to have given her a measure of stability, but it came at a cost. She now sees herself as some kind of galactic savior."

Petrov looked toward the heart of the tel, where Vale's platoon of ODSTs were gathered. "And that's why you want this weapon? So you have something to fight her with?"

"Affirmative."

"Then you two need to find a way to cooperate," Petrov said. "Spartan Vale, as a gesture of goodwill, I suggest you allow the Arbiter to make the first recovery attempt."

Vale's helmet drew back. *"Ma'am?"*

"I'm sure he'll allow you to make the second attempt." Petrov turned to 'Vadam. "Agreed? If you fail the first time, you probably won't be able to go back anyway."

"You told me there are no more than ten warriors inside." 'Vadam did not trust Petrov's so-called gesture of goodwill. She had been trying to slay the inhabitants of the tel for decades, and she did not strike him as the kind of human who abandoned an objective. "Why should I fail?"

"Because of what I also told you—that they live in a citadel. Will you agree or not?"

Before 'Vadam could reply, Vale said, "Commander, I'm not sure *I* can agree."

"Of course you can," Petrov said. "How many casualties did you take breaching the tel?"

"One trooper and one civilian adviser are MIA. We don't know whether they're actually casualties."

"Exactly," Petrov replied. "Because you don't know what's going on in there. Why not let the Arbiter and his warriors go in first and find out? They're all the same species—maybe they'll be able to talk the garrison out."

"But you do not expect that to happen," 'Vadam said. If Petrov wanted him and his warriors to enter first, it was because she wanted them to eliminate the enemy *for* her—or be eliminated themselves. "That is why you are suggesting we enter first."

"What do I know about Sangheili culture?" she retorted. "But you have a better chance than *humans* do."

"This is so." 'Vadam turned to Vale. "She makes, as you humans say, a good point. I will agree to the commander's suggestion. Will you?"

Vale studied Petrov and remained silent for many breaths. The lieutenant commander was not being particularly subtle in her artifice. If 'Vadam understood her true motive—to let 'Vadam and his warriors take the brunt of the defenders' attacks—then so did Vale. But the Spartan was hesitating, perhaps weighing the value of her friendship with 'Vadam against the advantages of using him to sap the strength of their adversaries.

After a time, Petrov said, "Take the deal, Spartan Vale. That's an order."

"I'm sorry, you're *ordering* me?" Vale seemed astonished. "Ma'am, perhaps you aren't familiar with the SPARTAN program—"

"That would be a *very* bad assumption. I was dropping Spartans into bad situations before you were born. How do you think I came to be marooned here on Netherop?"

"I see," Vale said. "But understand, Spartans aren't just deployable weapons anymore. We're an independent branch now. We run our own ops, and this is mine. You've also been absent from the chain of command for quite some time."

"While maintaining my command *here*, operating in a theater you don't know against an enemy you don't understand." Petrov stepped closer to Vale and looked up into her faceplate. "Call it an order, or call it advice. But you'd be wise to consider my experience here, Spartan . . . or have a damn good reason for ignoring it."

"Yes, ma'am." Vale looked away for a moment, either thinking or using her helmet comm to consult her subordinates, then faced 'Vadam. "Before we come to an agreement, you should know what happened when we breached."

"That is very kind of you," 'Vadam said.

"Not really. One of us needs to capture that weapon, or nobody is getting off this planet, and Cortana will keep doing what she's doing. I'm just trying to maximize our chances."

"You have always been very honest. That is the reason you and I can trust each other."

"Well, one of the reasons. There are others." Vale glanced over her shoulder, toward the Orbital Drop Shock Troops gathered around the faint column of rising dust. "We didn't exactly breach the tel. The enemy drove a tunnel several hundred meters beneath us, then opened a hole to capture our civilian advisers. It happened quickly, in less than a minute. We were only able to recover one of the advisers, and we lost one of our ODSTs."

"So they have a plasma drill," 'Vadam said. "That is good to know."

"We don't know really what they have. They're tapping a technology unlike anything we've seen before. They seem able to open and close tunnels at will."

"Are you sure you want to give up this intelligence for free?" Petrov asked. "You don't even have a deal yet."

"The Arbiter and I have a long history of honorable dealings. I wouldn't dream of withholding information before we enter an agreement."

"Nor would I," 'Vadam said. "We believe the tel's inhabitants allowed our Phantoms to land safely because they realized we are fellow Sangheili. They may have assumed we were coming to rescue them."

"Makes sense," Vale said.

"But now they may believe we were only scouting for *you*. If they are Covenant, they will consider us traitors."

"Possibly. But they can't like being marooned here. They'll at least want to talk to you and find out what's happening out there in the galaxy."

"*I* certainly would," 'Vadam replied. "That is most likely why they took your civilian."

"They won't learn much from her. Only that the war has ended—and that not all humans are loyal to the UNSC. But the trooper we lost is another matter. She won't be easy to capture alive or interrogate, but if they do and she breaks . . . she'll know about our alliance."

"Then we must not delay. It will be better if they hear it from me."

"No doubt," Vale said. "The only other intelligence I can offer is that their weapons seem to be standard Covenant issue, but their armor is something else. Skintight and flexible, and it takes damage way better than anything either one of us has ever worn."

"What is their strength?"

"I saw seven warriors. That doesn't mean there aren't more." Vale turned to Petrov. "Commander?"

"You've told him everything I could myself . . . and you still don't have an agreement."

"We will," Vale said. "Is there *anything* you can add? It could make the difference between getting off this dust ball and dying here."

"If what you say about this Cortana is even half-true, I'm more concerned about her than I am about dying here. I made my peace with that a long time ago."

"A worthy sentiment," 'Vadam said. "But we will not stop Cortana by dying. We must capture the weapon, so *any* intelligence you can offer is vital."

"I know." Petrov paused. "I think they have discipline problems. Occasionally, we've seen warriors sneak out of the tel on a Runner and try to disappear into the mountains."

"Try?" 'Vadam asked.

"We didn't want them causing trouble at our camp some

night." Petrov's gaze slipped away. "And since we couldn't interrogate them . . ."

"I see." 'Vadam clacked his mandibles once. "It was a savage war, and it has lasted longer for you than most. Thank you for being honest."

Petrov's brow rose. "You're okay with that?"

"The Covenant burned worlds. I was part of that, for a time, and killed billions of humans. Who am I to judge how you made war here?"

Petrov blanched, then looked to Vale. "Are all Sangheili this . . . honest?"

"All the great ones. Perhaps you can see why I trust the Arbiter."

"I'm beginning to." Petrov dipped her head for a moment, then lifted it. "I can report one other thing. The only time we had any success infiltrating was when we employed a distraction. A couple of volunteers drew the enemy's attention while a second team penetrated. The plan went bad after they killed the volunteers, but we made it deeper than we ever had before—and we escaped with our lives."

"I see," 'Vadam said. So Petrov was *still* trying to help the UNSC capture the weapon, even after pretending to have an improved opinion of him. He could not decide whether that made her a loyal officer or a treacherous ally. "You are suggesting that my Sangheili warriors distract the defenders, while Spartan Vale's platoon attempts to secure the weapon?"

"It won't work the other way around," Petrov said. "The enemy will attack humans as soon as they see them. But *you* might be able to buy some time communicating with them."

"So Spartan Vale can recover the weapon?" 'Vadam replied. "You must have a very low opinion of my intelligence, Commander."

"It's just good tactics. If you actually talk them out, then you take control of the weapon and deal with this Cortana. If you fail . . . well, at least we have a backup plan."

"The commander does make a good point," Vale said. "The enemy is on familiar ground, defended by technology we don't understand. Our only advantage is superior numbers. We *need* to use it to overwhelm them."

"No," 'Vadam said. "It is better to give the peaceful way a chance first. If the warriors inside discover I am serving as a distraction for humans, I will have no hope of enticing them to leave."

Vale exhaled loudly through her voicemitter, then looked to Petrov. "Commander?"

Petrov instantly shook her head. "You'd be sacrificing your one sure advantage . . . for nothing."

"Is that because you believe I cannot succeed?" 'Vadam asked. "Or because you are determined to see your old enemies dead?"

"Oh, I *want* to see them dead. But I'm not going to sabotage your mission and my people's rescue to do it. I'm just pointing out that the presence of humans is irrelevant to your chances of success."

"How can it be irrelevant?" 'Vadam asked. "You are their enemy. To the Covenant, *all* humans are."

"Exactly," Petrov said. "To the Covenant. Either you can convince your friends in the tel that they lost the war, or you can't. But there's no denying that the UNSC has returned. In fact, the sight of ODSTs and Sangheili working together may help tip the scales in your favor."

"The commander is right," Vale said. "The Sangheili inside have already seen us, and once you enter the tel, they'll know you're not here to fight us. Whether you can talk fast enough to persuade them to leave, I don't know. But I won't risk this mission on your success."

'Vadam's stomach sank. "Then you won't agree to allow me to make the first attempt, as Commander Petrov has suggested?"

"I'll agree to let you *enter* first, and we won't stand in the way of you or your forces. Beyond that, it's finders keepers. Meaning whoever finds it, keeps it." Vale extended an empty hand, in the human fashion of confirming a bargain. "Are we agreed?"

"Yes, it is agreed." 'Vadam accepted her hand and pumped it once, then looked toward Petrov. "I am sure that is what the commander intended all along . . . finders keepers."

CHAPTER 12

Thirty centals after dropping through the same hole that had swallowed the human civilians before he arrived, Thel 'Vadam and his landing party were deep inside the tel, trying to catch its retreating residents without being ambushed. If he was fortunate, they would be willing to talk. If not . . . he still had thirty loyal warriors at his disposal.

The air in the tunnel stank of metal and acid, an odor familiar to him from the mining operations he controlled on Sanghelios and Suban, and it was not the only evidence that more lay buried beneath the tel than ancient ruins. As they advanced down the passage, the walls released wisps of strange gray powder that deposited itself on their armor like electroplating. When he tried to wipe it off his goggle lenses so he could see clearly, the substance clung to his fingertips, building up into crusty layers that had to be scraped away with a knife. But if he left it alone, the coating grew so thick that, were it not for the thermal-imaging display inside his goggles, he would not have been able to see his own hands—let alone anyone waiting in ambush.

The image of a female warrior separated from the wall ahead and stood waiting for 'Vadam and Varo'dai, who was walking at his side. The rounded brow and oversize mandible guards on her helmet identified the figure as one of the Varo rangers whom Varo'dai had sent forward to scout the location of the tel inhabitants.

"That did not take as long as I feared," Varo'dai said. She was so close in the tunnel confines that her and 'Vadam's shoulders touched. "Perhaps your bargain with the Spartan will work to our advantage after all."

"I did not strike a bargain with Spartan Vale. Was the Oath Warden not translating for you and Kaidon 'Talot, or were we beyond the range of his eavesdropping instruments?"

"You were in range. He said you agreed not to interfere with the Spartan's search for the weapon."

"And *she* agreed not to interfere with ours."

"How is that not a bargain?" asked Crei 'Ayomuu. Along with Ghe 'Talot, he was following close behind them. "You exchanged promises. Any Oath Warden on a Sangheili world would take an enforcement contract on that."

"We only confirmed the terms of our existing alliance." 'Vadam allowed his tone to grow short. "But why does this concern you? There will be no fighting between us. *That* is what matters."

"Then you expect the Spartan to honor her word?" Varo'dai asked.

"I do. She values our alliance as much as I do."

"Yet you have commanded us to remain comm silent," Varo'dai said. "Because you fear the Spartan and her ODSTs will track our progress by eavesdropping on our communications."

"Spartan Vale is very resourceful."

"But not very honorable," Varo'dai said. "Forgive me, Arbiter.

She wants the weapon for the UNSC as badly as you want it for us, and human treachery knows no bounds. Are you certain it is wise to trust her?"

"I am certain you think it is not." 'Vadam was careful to keep his voice even, for he could understand how Varo'dai might harbor an implacable suspicion of humans. Had one of the UNSC's planet-killing bombs destroyed Sanghelios instead of Saepon'kal, he would have felt the same way. "But the mistake is mine to make, if indeed it is a mistake. Let us speak of it no more."

Varo'dai dipped her helmet. "As you command, my Arbiter."

They came to her ranger, who crossed her arms over her chest in salute to 'Vadam, then turned to make her report to Varo'dai. "The enemy has stopped a hundred paces ahead. The tunnel turns to the right, then steepens its descent. They are hiding just around the corner."

"We are following Sangheili castaways, not enemies." 'Vadam wiped the powder off his goggles so he could see her, and it began to redeposit itself almost immediately. "Let us not refer to them as our 'enemy' until they have earned the title."

"That may be sooner than you think, Arbiter." The ranger turned and pointed a hundred paces down the tunnel, to where 'Vadam could just make out the thermal images of several of her fellow Varo rangers crouched along the wall. "They are hiding in ambush."

"How many?"

"Seven Sangheili and a human prisoner. A civilian female."

"They have a prisoner at the ambush site?" Varo'dai asked. "Why?"

"It is unclear. At first, we thought they believed they were being pursued by humans and intended to use her as a hostage. But it may be they just could not move fast enough to outrun us."

"How can that be?" 'Vadam asked. "We entered the tel at least a quarter unit behind them."

"The ene—our Sangheili brothers—appear unfit. We found several places where their tracks suggested they had stopped to trade off carrying the prisoner, and even then their trail has been showing signs of weariness for the last few hundred paces—stumbling and shorter steps."

'Vadam did not understand why the castaways were holding their prisoner at the ambush site. If they knew they were being pursued, they probably also realized it was by a force of Sangheili, who could never be coerced through hostage taking—especially when that hostage was human. So it made no sense to keep her with them if they were preparing for a fight. She could only get in the way, and they ran the risk of having her killed or rescued.

"They are not waiting in ambush," 'Vadam said. "They are only resting."

"Resting?" 'Talot's tone was doubtful . . . and perilously close to mocking. "We are barely two thousand paces in, and most of the trip has been downhill. Why would they need to rest?"

"Because they have been marooned in this wasteland for more than twenty Urs cycles," 'Vadam said. "It would be folly to expect them to be in good condition."

"Did Commander Petrov not say that the tel keeps them well-fed?" Varo'dai asked. "They should not be so weak."

"And yet, they are," 'Vadam said. "At least if your Varo rangers are to be believed."

Varo'dai looked to the reporting ranger, who glanced at 'Vadam and dipped her helmet.

"They *do* appear well-fed. Perhaps too much so."

"Then they will be relieved to learn that there will be no need to fight," 'Vadam said. Commander Petrov had suggested their discipline was poor, and poor discipline meant a poor training regimen. He started down the tunnel. "I will speak with them. Have the rest of the party wait here."

Having already learned the futility of objecting to his putting himself at risk, the kaidons merely passed along the order and accompanied him down the tunnel. 'Ayomuu, of course, followed along.

As they approached the rangers waiting at the corner, 'Vadam wiped his goggles clean again, then activated his helmet lamps and motioned for the others to wait out of sight.

"Do not be alarmed," he called in Sangheili. "I am the Arbiter Thel 'Vadam, and I would speak with you."

"Arbiter?" replied a haughty male voice. "You will find no redemption here, Arbiter . . . only death."

"I come seeking neither."

'Vadam continued to advance. The castaway's warning reflected an outdated tradition of the Covenant hierarchs, who had conferred the title of Arbiter as a mark of shame. 'Vadam's appointment had been made late in the War of Annihilation, after he failed to prevent the destruction of Alpha Halo, and the hierarchs had sent him on a suicide mission as a way to redeem himself. But instead of dying, 'Vadam had discovered that the hierarchs were lying about the very nature of the religion they led, then launched a rebellion that had toppled the entire Covenant. His victory had freed the Sangheili of three millennia of beguilement . . . and restored honor to the ancient title he still bore.

Of course, the castaways knew Arbiter only as a title of scorn.

'Vadam stopped a pace from the corner and called, "Hold your attack and listen. You have been isolated here for decades. There are tidings you should hear."

"The only thing I wish to hear is why a disgraced warrior is here inside my Sanctum, rather than outside slaying humans."

"Let us speak and I will explain. Or refuse—and remain marooned here for all time. It makes no difference to me."

"Were that true, you would not be here."

"Then you are happy to stay on N'ba?" 'Vadam did not understand the resistance he was encountering. Suspicious of him or not, the castaways should have been desperate enough to at least hear him out. "*All* of you?"

"It is our destiny. The gods have chosen—"

"Let us hear the Arbiter's explanation," a second voice interrupted. This one was deeper and more assertive than the first, yet not as haughty. "You may show yourself, Thel 'Vadam. Anyone who raises a weapon against you will answer to me."

This last part was muffled, as though the speaker had turned to address this warning to someone behind him. Clearly, the castaways were not fully united in their desire to stay here on N'ba. 'Vadam wiped the powder from his goggles—again—and stepped around the corner.

He found himself facing a trio of Sangheili in close-fitting, opalescent armor unlike anything he had ever seen before. Their head protection looked more like clear masks than helmets, with shimmering formfitting guards for their mandibles. The warrior closest to him was stout to the point of plump, with a waist-heavy torso and thighs that bulged with softness. The other two were slimmer, the first holding the human hostage in the crook of an elbow, the second gaunt and imperious of posture.

The display inside 'Vadam's goggle lenses revealed the thermal images of four more warriors kneeling in niches along the right-hand wall. They were deployed for ambush, spaced at irregular intervals and so well camouflaged that they were barely visible in the glow of his helmet lamps. He stepped over to the same wall, positioning himself so they would not be able to attack without firing through their own leader, then turned toward the stout warrior in front.

"I am Thel 'Vadam."

"I am Meduz 'Ra'ashai." As the warrior spoke, the tunnel between him and 'Vadam filled with a soft, ambient light. "Blademaster of the Silent Shadow."

"Truly?" 'Vadam kept his gaze fixed on 'Ra'ashai, denying the gaunt warrior—and presumed commander—a chance to introduce himself. "Then I am pleased there will be no need for us to fight. It would be quite a contest."

"Perhaps." 'Ra'ashai allowed his mandibles to part just a little, signaling amusement. "But I am pleased as well. I find no joy in shedding Sangheili blood."

This time, it was 'Vadam who let his mandibles part. "There have been times when I *have* enjoyed it. But only when it was deserved."

'Ra'ashai glanced back toward the presumed commander. "Yes. There *is* some satisfaction when it is deserved."

Seizing his first chance to speak, the commander stepped into the light. "You spoke of tidings. Let us have them then, and leave."

'Vadam looked briefly in the speaker's direction, then turned back to 'Ra'ashai—a deliberate provocation that he hoped would drive a larger wedge between the two castaways. "I thought *you* were in command here."

'Ra'ashai allowed his gaze to drop, quickly enough to suggest that no matter how much he resented the gaunt Sangheili, he was reluctant to usurp his authority. There might be tension among the castaways, but not yet rebellion—which meant their leader still had a hold over them. Until that changed, 'Vadam would need to be more cautious.

He dipped his helmet toward the commander . . . and realized that the powder drifting off the walls to coat his armor had stopped collecting on his goggles. Perhaps that had something to do with the ambient light that illuminated the tunnel ahead—or perhaps not. The strange powder remained a mystery to him.

"My apologies," he said to the commander. "I saw nothing to indicate rank on your armor. As I have said, I am the Arbiter Thel 'Vadam."

'Vadam fell silent, hoping the commander would also identify himself. In the old Covenant military, ignorance of a senior officer's identity could be taken as a subtle insult—a custom that grew increasingly cumbersome as it migrated down the chain of command. To avoid the inevitable duels that came of forcing strangers to guess how important one considered oneself, the best officers simply introduced themselves at a first meeting.

But the castaway commander offered no such introduction, an imperious behavior suggesting he had once held a high rank in the Covenant—and retained a preposterous view of his renown, given how long he had been marooned on N'ba.

"The fighting on N'ba must have been more consequential than was recorded in the World Registry," 'Vadam said. "It is a terrible slight that you as commander were not named in the report."

"It was no slight," the commander said, refusing to act on the hint. "It was retribution, which you would know if your presence here was ordained by the hierarchs."

"Perhaps our presence was ordained by fate. Perhaps we were brought here to end your long vigil."

"I think not. It is the gods who guide fate. Had they brought you here to N'ba, it would have been to drive away the humans . . . not parlay with them."

"That is among the things I would explain." 'Vadam was not

surprised to learn he had been observed speaking with Vale—covert surveillance was simply good tactical procedure—but he *was* unhappy that it would make winning the confidence of the Sangheili castaways more difficult. "The War of Annihilation is over."

"How can that be?" the commander demanded. "I have seen for myself that at least a few humans remain."

"*Billions* remain. They have as many worlds as the Sangheili do, and we have learned to live in peace."

"Impossible. That would be against the will of the gods."

"And yet, your spies saw us conferring on the surface of your Sanctum. With no weapons drawn on either side."

"Yes. We saw." The commander let his chins drop ever so slightly to the left, just enough to suggest that it had not been his spies who witnessed the conversation, but he himself . . . no doubt through some manner of surveillance device. "And now you confirm it openly—that you are a traitor and a blasphemer."

'Vadam hardened his voice. "If you wish to insult me, have the courtesy to name yourself. Only a coward attacks from behind a blank shield."

'Ra'ashai's gaze dropped in frustration, but he allowed his hand to drift to the hilt of his energy sword. Before the blademaster could draw, the warrior with the human hostage stepped between his two companions and 'Vadam.

"If you do not know Nizat 'Kvarosee, Master of the Fleet of Inexorable Obedience and Savior of Zhoist, it is you who have given insult."

"Nizat 'Kvarosee . . . I *do* recognize the name."

Early in the war, when 'Vadam had still been a utility warrior, Nizat 'Kvarosee had already been a well-known fleetmaster with a reputation as a competent, if not cunning, strategist. Assigned to recover Forerunner artifacts and destroy human colonies, he had been one of the first Covenant commanders to encounter a concentrated force of Spartans. But before he—or any other Covenant officer—understood their capabilities, the super-soldiers savaged his fleet and slipped into Covenant space with a flotilla of warships. 'Kvarosee caught up to them at Zhoist, where the Spartans destroyed an orbital shipyard and two of the fabled Ten Cities of Edification before retreating back into UNSC space.

With his fleet decimated and his reputation ruined, 'Kvarosee was summoned to High Charity for reassignment—a euphemism for punishment, which led 'Vadam to wonder if *he* might have been made Arbiter. Evidently, the fleetmaster had refused to accept his fate and fled to N'ba—which likely explained his reluctance to leave the planet now. The only thing 'Vadam *didn't* understand was why 'Kvarosee was still alive, as the most likely explanation for 'Ra'ashai's presence on the planet was that he had been sent by the Silent Shadow to punish the recalcitrant fleetmaster for his disobedience.

'Vadam shifted his gaze from the gaunt warrior back to 'Ra'ashai. "The last I heard of Fleetmaster 'Kvarosee was in a general order from the hierarchs. He was to be slain on sight."

"That command was modified." 'Ra'ashai sounded disappointed, as though he had been personally cheated by the change. "When we found him here, it was decided that marooning him on N'ba would be a more fitting punishment than death."

"An understandable miscalculation," 'Kvarosee said, stepping back into view. "The gods seldom reveal their plans to mere mortals."

'Vadam sensed an opening. "Least of all to the hierarchs. Their lies caused untold harm to us all . . . to the Sangheili and every species in the Covenant."

'Kvarosee moved past 'Ra'ashai to stand in 'Vadam's tunnel face-to-face. As he did so, the ambient light flooded the area around them, revealing the presence of Varo'dai and 'Talot. It was an odd phenomenon, as though the walls themselves were responding to the fleetmaster's presence—or perhaps his will—and the two kaidons began to hiss urgent orders to the long line of uneasy warriors waiting down the passage behind them.

'Kvarosee paid no attention to any of it. "What lies?"

"None of what happened is your fault." 'Vadam knew from his own enlightenment that 'Kvarosee would never be able to accept the truth all at once. He would need to be prepared, to be given a buttress that would help him bear the terrible weight of the atrocities he had committed on the Covenant's behalf. "You were deceived by masters of the art."

"What . . . lies?" 'Kvarosee insisted.

"About the humans. They never destroyed a reliquary on Harvest. The hierarchs fabricated that lie to justify the War of Annihilation. And then they launched the war to secure their power."

'Kvarosee's mandibles began to tense and relax, and 'Vadam hoped that after the fleetmaster's own experiences with the treachery of the hierarchs, he might be open to the truth.

But when 'Kvarosee spoke, it was in a scathing and doubtful tone. "And where did you hear these blasphemies, Arbiter?"

"From several of the Oracles of the Sacred Rings, including one that I personally recovered. I heard them say this very thing in my own presence."

'Kvarosee's eyes flared in anger . . . or perhaps it was only shock. He looked away, and 'Vadam decided not to elaborate. The galaxy had changed immensely during the decades that the fleetmaster and his castaways were marooned on N'ba. All that 'Vadam needed was for the pious commander to accept him as an ally and rescuer—and he would not help his case by exposing his own role in the Covenant's destruction. Or by revealing that the Forerunners had never been gods to begin with.

When 'Kvarosee finally looked back, 'Vadam saw doubt in his eyes.

"The hierarchs have been deposed," 'Vadam said. "There is no need for you to remain here on N'ba."

"No *need*?" 'Kvarosee seemed affronted. "You presume to tell the *Worldmaster* what he needs?"

'Vadam assumed that 'Kvarosee was referring to himself. "The Worldmaster? What is it that gives you that authority, exactly?"

"This." 'Kvarosee waved his hand in a circle. "The Sanctum of the Ancients."

'Vadam ran his gaze over the tunnel's packed-powder walls. Both the intelligence Vale had provided and the gold-glowing air suggested there was more to the tel than met the eye, but to him, it looked like a simple mountain of dust.

He was still considering his reply when Crei 'Ayomuu pushed forward and stood at his side, saying, "Forgive the Arbiter's audacity, Worldmaster. As the de facto leader of the Sangheili Concert of Worlds, he too often assumes when it would be better to simply ask."

"An *Arbiter* leads the Sangheili?" 'Kvarosee said. "What of the High Council?"

"Much has changed in the decades since your exile," 'Ayomuu said. "But rest assured, the choice to leave or stay is yours."

'Kvarosee's reply was instant. "Then we will stay."

"All of you?" 'Ayomuu turned his attention to 'Ra'ashai. "The Silent Shadow too?"

"*All* of us," 'Kvarosee insisted. "You have no idea what the gods have entrusted to us with their Sanctum."

"We have some idea," 'Vadam said. As much as he distrusted Crei 'Ayomuu, 'Vadam could not take issue with the Oath Warden's strategy. 'Kvarosee seemed somewhat unbalanced and more than a little sanctimonious, so anything they could do to drive a wedge between him and his followers would only improve their chances of claiming the weapon before Vale and her ODSTs. "We saw what you did to the human insertion force—and nearly perished ourselves. We lost many good warriors."

"That is what comes of consorting with vermin," 'Kvarosee said.

"We are *not* consorting with them," 'Vadam said. "We are racing them."

"To what? My Sanctum?"

"To the weapon you used against them," 'Ayomuu said. "They have come to take it from you."

"They are welcome to try." 'Kvarosee clenched his mandibles so hard that 'Vadam heard teeth grinding. "We have made no peace with humanity on N'ba."

"Then you will lose it," 'Ayomuu assured him. "The humans are led by one of their demons. A Spartan."

"The one in the red armor?" 'Kvarosee's voice grew brittle, perhaps because he was recalling what had happened to his own fleet when he first clashed with Spartans. "I feared as much."

"You have fought them before," 'Vadam pressed. "You can have no doubts about what will happen if you fight them here . . . with so few warriors at your back."

"I have weapons now that I did not have then. And *you* have warriors. I will need to make use of them."

"And what do we get in return?" 'Ayomuu asked.

"The favor of the gods. What more could any warrior require?"

"The weapon," 'Ayomuu said. "We are going to need the weapon."

"What?!" 'Kvarosee exclaimed. "You dare bargain with the gods?!"

"The Oath Warden is not bargaining with anyone," 'Vadam said. With 'Ayomuu trying to force him into an alliance against the humans, it was time to let the Worldmaster know exactly whom he was talking to. "Those warriors answer to me alone."

'Kvarosee allowed his gaze to linger on 'Ayomuu just long enough to make it clear that he held the Oath Warden in as much disdain as 'Vadam did, then returned his attention to the Arbiter and did not glance in 'Ayomuu's direction again.

"And what do *you* need?"

"The weapon," 'Vadam said. "But we are not going to fight the humans for you. That would start a war the Sangheili would never win."

"The *Covenant* cannot defeat the humans?"

"There *is* no Covenant," 'Ayomuu said. "Not anymore. The humans destroyed it."

'Kvarosee did not look in the Oath Warden's direction, but his mandibles fell open. "This is true?"

"The humans had help," 'Vadam said. "But yes, it is true. The Covenant is gone, and the Sangheili cannot afford to make enemies of the humans. We are having enough trouble with the Jiralhanae."

"And that is why you want the Divine Hand? To crush our comrades in faith?"

"True comrades would never turn on us as the Jiralhanae did at the war's end, and they have lost their faith." 'Vadam knew better than to admit that the Sangheili had lost their own faith as well, for it was clear that nothing would turn 'Kvarosee against him faster. "But we have no need of the Divine Hand to defeat the Jiralhanae."

"There is a threat far greater," 'Ayomuu added. "One created by the humans and loosed on us all. The Apparition."

'Kvarosee continued to ignore the Oath Warden, but gave 'Vadam an expectant look.

"A human-built artificial intelligence," 'Vadam explained. "She served their greatest Spartan until the end of the war. Then she went mad and turned on her creators. Now she has seized control of some of the Forerunners' most powerful weapons, and she is using them to impose her will across the galaxy."

"A *human* AI rules in place of the gods?!" 'Kvarosee was aghast. "And yet you refuse to use your warriors to protect the Divine Hand from the ones who made such an abomination?!"

"The humans are as desperate to stop her as we are," 'Vadam said. "But it would be better for us to control—"

"No." 'Kvarosee turned back toward the corner. "You are not worthy."

"And *you* are a fool, Fleetmaster." Varo'dai pushed between 'Vadam and 'Ayomuu and followed after 'Kvarosee. "You have been cowering in these tunnels for more than a thousand cycles, allowing your warriors to grow fat while they hide from a handful of human castaways armed with little more than stolen weapons and their hatred of *you*. If you think the *Arbiter* is the unworthy one, you are deceiving yourself."

'Kvarosee stopped and turned, his chins dropping as he ran his gaze down Varo'dai's armor. When he looked up again, he asked, "And who are you?"

"Olabisi Varo'dai, kaidon of the world of Om'a'Varo. You know nothing of what the Arbiter has done for the Sangheili, but *I* do . . . and I will not stand idle while you insult him."

"No?" 'Kvarosee looked toward her feet. "Then you will not stand at all."

The floor beneath Varo'dai's boots changed to powder in an eyeblink, and she sank so fast that 'Vadam barely had a chance to grab her wrist and prevent her from vanishing altogether. A plume of golden dust filled the air between 'Vadam and 'Kvarosee, then the ambient light vanished and plunged the tunnel back into darkness.

"*Oath Wardens* and *female* kaidons, Arbiter?" As 'Kvarosee spoke, his voice quickly receded, and 'Vadam saw the thermal images of six warriors following him down the tunnel. "I could never share the Divine Hand with an apostate. Begone, before I bestow on you the fate you deserve."

CHAPTER 13

The platform was about three centimeters high, and Vale did not even see it beneath the dust until Commander Petrov extended an arm to prevent her from stepping on it. They were still on top of the tel, about three-quarters of the way down its length, leading Tango Team and the running machines along its centerline. The mountains where Vale had sent the Owl to hide rose in a steep wall about a kilometer ahead, beyond the shimmering mirage that filled the crater basin that surrounded them.

"I wouldn't walk on that if I were you." Petrov continued to hold her arm in front of Vale. "If you break through, it could be a long way down."

"*Could* be?" Vale echoed. After 'Vadam had entered the tel with his Sangheili, Petrov had revealed that she might know a fast way to access the old mine workings underneath. "Didn't you say this went all the way to the bottom?"

"I said it's an old ventilation shaft. Whether it's still clear all the way down, I have no idea."

Vale nodded and studied the platform. Rectangular, about

three meters wide by four meters long, it was either covered in wind-crusted dust or made of it. "When was the last time you were down there?"

"I've never been down there. We found the shaft when a soldier fell through the crust."

"Then how do you know we can use it to access the citadel?"

"Because we came back with a rope and sent down a team of scouts. Never saw them again."

"I'm sorry. I still don't see how you know—"

"What's more likely? That my scouts just got lost down there? Or that someone ambushed them?"

Either was possible, as was an accident or cave-in. And Petrov probably had her own agenda here, given her hatred of the Sangheili castaways, who had been living comfortably inside the tel while her soldiers starved outside. While her *children* starved, Vale reminded herself. At least some of Petrov's subordinates were likely her own offspring and then *their* offspring, and she had been sending them to war for over thirty years. That *had* to fan the flames of hatred, and pretty ferociously.

But that didn't make her wrong. An ambush was as likely as any of the other possibilities, and with 'Vadam already inside the tel, Vale was desperate to find a quick way into the depths of the citadel.

She turned to Gunnery Sergeant Grim Bear. "Let's get a line ready. If we move fast, maybe we can recover the weapon while the Arbiter is still holding their attention."

Grim Bear turned and began to issue orders. Golly arrived on his Mongoose, and Vale had him attack the platform with his entrenching tool. Little puffs of dust rose each time the shovel came down, but the tip never sank into the ground. Finally, he gave up and began to scrape at the surface, trying to expose whatever lay beneath. He found only more dust.

"What is this stuff?" Golly locked grips with Vale, then stepped onto the platform and stomped. The surface rippled like a fluid, but showed no sign of collapse. "It feels like some sort of membrane."

Vale turned to Petrov. "You said a soldier fell through this stuff."

"She did."

Vale waved toward Golly. "Did she weigh more than him?"

"I doubt four of her would have weighed more than him."

"Then why isn't he falling through?"

Petrov looked perplexed for a moment, then raised her brow in surprise . . . or sudden comprehension. "Because we returned and sent down a scouting team . . . who never came back."

"You're saying the inhabitants killed them. Then sealed the shaft?"

"What would you do if someone found a way to infiltrate your stronghold? You'd close the breach."

"I would." Vale pulled Golly off the platform, then turned to Grim Bear. "Break out another brick of C-12."

"Bad idea," Petrov said. "The enemy will feel the blast."

"So they do." Vale would have preferred to refer to 'Vadam and the tel inhabitants as adversaries rather than enemies, but she didn't have time to reinforce such subtle distinctions. "This operation depends on speed."

"Speed and stealth. If the inhabitants feel us using explosives, they'll realize what we're doing and fill the shaft . . . with us in it."

"We'll be on the bottom in thirty seconds, and somewhere else thirty seconds after that. Nobody reacts that fast."

"You don't understand." Petrov grabbed Golly's entrenching tool and heaped a few shovelfuls of dust onto the platform. The pile slowly spread outward as though it were syrup, then melted into the surface and disappeared. She dragged the side of the blade across the spot and recovered only a few grains. "This isn't normal stuff . . . and the tel's inhabitants can control it."

Vale recalled the long passage that had suddenly appeared beneath Fuertes and Iyuska, and how part of the tunnel floor had simply dissolved during the battle that followed. Vale could not imagine how the Sangheili castaways could have done those things . . . but she didn't doubt what Petrov was claiming, either.

"How is that possible?"

"I wish I knew." Petrov returned the entrenching tool to Golly. "But they *must* have control. Whatever this stuff is, it always seems to blind, bury, or suffocate us just when we get the drop on them. That's no coincidence."

Iyuska joined them and knelt at the narrow end of the platform. Using a knife, she scraped a few dust particles into a clear sample pouch, then held it to the light and raised her brow. Realizing that she was reacting to something Petrov had said, Vale waited for an explanation.

When it did not come, she finally asked, "Well?"

"Commander Petrov is right. You shouldn't use the C-12."

"You're just saying that because you're worried about damaging artifacts."

"I *am* worried about damaging artifacts," Iyuska admitted. "But the C-12 is still a bad idea."

Iyuska handed the sample pouch to Vale, who held it up to the light so she could study the contents.

"What am I looking at?"

"What do you see? Your eyes are better than mine . . . at least they should be."

"They are . . . as long as I'm trying to shoot you in the dark or at long range." During her augmentation procedures, Vale had received corneal implants that enhanced her night and distance vision. "But all I see here are a few grains of dust. Make that flecks—they look kind of flat."

"Doesn't that fancy armor have some sort of magnification utility? I know what I think I see, but we need verification."

"This isn't a research project." But Vale moved her faceplate targeting reticle over to the sample pouch and opened a magnification window. "We don't have time to confirm our findings at every stage."

"Just tell me what you see. If that stuff is tailings powder, then I'm the new head of ONI."

Vale studied the pouch for a moment. "Well . . . you're not head of ONI. That much is clear."

At magnification, Vale could see that the grains were actually interlaced stacks of translucent flakes, stuck together to create thicker, opaque flakes. Whether thin or thick, all the flakes were hexagonal, with open spaces between layers that allowed more flakes to slot in and create ever larger, three-dimensional hexagons—which they were doing before Vale's very eyes.

She blinked the magnification window closed, then looked to Iyuska. "Nanotech?"

"Or maybe just microtech. There's no way to be sure . . . unless you happen to have a scanning electron microscope function in that thing?"

"Uh . . . no." And even if Vale had, she wouldn't have bothered to activate it. The difference between nanotech and microtech was fairly arbitrary, a matter of the size of the molecules being engineered. "But either way . . . does it make sense? As far as we can tell, the species that lived on Netherop wasn't this advanced. We haven't even seen indications of powered flight."

"Not relevant. Powered flight isn't a prerequisite for microtech.

As long as you can build integrated circuits, it's possible to get there."

"*Possible* being the key word." Vale waved toward the castaways' running machines. "Those spider walkers are powered by coal. That's Industrial Age technology. Ancient technology."

"They're *powered* by batteries. Which are charged by coal boilers."

"Which is still Industrial Age technology. Microtech is a bit more advanced than that."

Iyuska fell silent, considering Vale's point, then finally shook her head. "You know what you saw when you magnified those dust grains, Pia. Are you telling me they *didn't* look like microtech?"

Vale couldn't argue with that logic—those uniform shapes slotted together to create larger uniform shapes. "Just because something looks like microtech doesn't mean it is."

"And just because we don't understand what we're observing doesn't mean it *isn't*." Iyuska waved a hand around them. "Whatever this tel was once made of, I'm pretty sure it's been converted into a giant hill of self-directing molecular machines."

"*What?!*" Vale exclaimed. "That's a real stretch, from coal-fired boilers to molecular machines."

"True. But so are interdimensional weapons—or perhaps you have an Industrial Age explanation for whatever it was that knocked us down?"

Vale didn't, of course. Had she been looking into an interdimensional rift just before the mysterious weapon destroyed her entire insertion force? She wasn't sure. But she *was* sure that no Industrial Age technology could have done what she had witnessed. The energy requirements were just too massive. Like a million times too much.

"Okay . . . molecular machines." Vale sighed. "How do we turn them off?"

"We don't. Have you lost your mind?"

"No, but I have lost my corporal and our consultant. And I want them back alive. Along with that weapon."

"We *can't* turn those machines off. Even if I knew how, we'd never be able to turn them back on again—and then we'd never figure out how they work."

"I don't see why not," Vale said. "Molecular machines aren't *that* advanced. Humanity has been fabricating them for five centuries."

"Not *self-directing* molecular machines. And I'm not talking about template-guided or magnetic self-assembly. I'm talking about machines that find their own raw material, tear it apart molecule by molecule, then reassemble it into something useful."

"You mean this stuff controls *itself*?" Petrov said, incredulous.

Iyuska considered her answer—no doubt trying to formulate one that would force Vale to be more careful about protecting the tel's artifacts. "At this point, all I have is a hypothesis. But yes, to an extent." Iyuska turned to Vale. "We saw the same phenomena Commander Petrov described. Tunnels that open spontaneously in front of the tel inhabitants, ground that turns permeable beneath the feet of their enemies. It's possible the machines are sensing what the inhabitants need, then providing it."

"That sounds like magic, not nanotech."

"At this level, I doubt we could tell the difference. Remember, we're here to investigate a culture older and more advanced than the Forerunners. That means Tier Zero technology. Nanotech is probably just a parlor trick to them."

Vale couldn't argue with that logic. How a species using coal power to charge their batteries could develop this kind of technology was a mystery, but she had visited enough of the galaxy to know it held plenty of secrets beyond human understanding.

Everything she had seen at the tel so far suggested it contained another one.

"Okay, Keely, let's assume you're right," Vale said. "Then we need to disrupt the lines of communication. How do the machines sense what the inhabitants need?"

"The easiest way would be by reading minds."

"Seriously?" Petrov said.

"It really wouldn't be difficult," Vale said. "Not with technology this advanced."

"Exactly," Iyuska said. "A population of molecular machines configure themselves into electrodes, then adhere to a subject's head and start monitoring brain activity. It might take some time to build a database and calibrate, but eventually the tel would be able to correlate brain-wave activity with action and emotion. The subject turns left, and the tel senses a desire to go in that direction and opens a tunnel. The subject grows frightened, and the tel senses a threat and buries it."

"The *tel* senses, and not the machines?" Vale asked. "You're not suggesting it's sentient?"

"Not by the standard definition. I'm just saying that it appears to be a massive unitary nanotech system—and that makes it very, very powerful. *If* my hypothesis is correct, of course."

"Let's operate under the assumption it is." Vale turned to Petrov. "Unless you know of a reason to believe otherwise?"

"I don't. It's a little out there, but the professor's theory does explain just about everything about this place—except how we're going to disrupt the communication between the enemy and the tel. It's pretty hard to jam telepathy."

"But not impossible. We just have to go in quietly." Vale turned to Golly and pointed to the ground at the end of the platform. "Start digging. Maybe we can come in from the side."

Vale borrowed an entrenching tool from an ODST on First Squad and joined him. Three minutes later they stood in a waist-deep hole, scraping nanodust off the exterior of the shaft's yellow-gray liner. She tapped the surface with the edge of her shovel blade. The sound was deep, muffled, and woody.

"Doesn't sound like that nanotech stuff," Golly said. "And more like resin than metal or concrete. Shouldn't take more than a big pinch of C-12 to knock a hole in it."

"Doesn't matter," Vale said. "If the shaft is still clear on the other side, that liner will act like a big soundboard. Even a small blast would boom like an artillery shell."

Vale drew her combat knife from its leg sheath and flipped it into an ice-pick grip, then launched herself toward the shaft and drove the blade toward the liner. The resin had turned so brittle with age that she ended up driving her entire fist and forearm through up to the elbow.

"Or, we could do it your way," Golly said.

He drew his own combat knife and began to drive it through the liner at the edges of the pit they had excavated. Vale heard faint splashes as the loose debris fell into the shaft and reached the bottom. It was the first sign of water that she had noticed since arriving on Netherop—at least *liquid* water. There was plenty of vapor in the planet's low brown clouds.

The sound of splashing wasn't great, but it was subtler than a blast. Hoping it wouldn't be loud enough to draw the attention of the tel inhabitants, she sheathed her combat knife and told Golly to carry on, then waved Gunnery Sergeant Grim Bear over.

"Let's have that line ready to drop when Golly is finished," Vale said. "I'll lead First Squad into the interior. I want you to take Second Squad to the far end and create a diversion. Try not to engage, and retreat if they engage *you*. But I want you to make it sound like we're trying to breach as far from here as reasonable. A *big* sound."

"Will do, Spartan." Grim Bear nodded toward Iyuska and Petrov. "What about them?"

"I'm going with Pia." Iyuska's gaze shifted to Vale. "Don't even think about leaving me behind during the initial survey."

"No worries, you're coming with us. That's what you get for calling me Pia."

"I'm glad we"—Iyuska's expression grew uneasy as she realized that Vale viewed her acquiescence as a dangerous assignment rather than an accommodation—"agree."

"Me too." Vale turned to Petrov. "Commander, I'd appreciate the benefit of your experience."

"And you'll have it." Petrov glanced toward her subordinates, and a soft look came over her. Vale shouldn't have been surprised by it, but she was. In the short time they had known each other, Vale had grown so accustomed to Petrov's commander persona that she'd almost forgotten the woman was also a mother to her forces. "But I'd like the rest of my unit to assist your Second Squad. They've been fighting this war long enough, and compared to your ODSTs . . . well, I don't see any reason my soldiers need to be down there with us."

Vale looked to Grim Bear. "Gunny, that okay with you?"

"Happy to have them. They'll prove helpful."

"Good. Use them wisely." Vale held Grim Bear's gaze until the gunnery sergeant gave a little nod indicating she understood that meant keeping the young castaways as safe as possible. "I doubt we'll have comms for long, so you'll be on your own initiative. Are you clear on your assignment?"

"Yes, ma'am. Hold their attention while you steal the cheese."

"That's the assignment. Good luck."

"You too, ma'am," Grim Bear said. "And if there's any chance of finding Legs—"

"Count on it, Sergeant. We'll do everything we can for her and Fuertes."

Grim Bear had the two Mongooses brought to the edge of the pit and secured a utility line to their bullbars. Vale helped Golly finish perforating a square outline in the resin liner, then pushed her hands into a pair of knife holes and tore out a section large enough to fit through. She found herself looking into yawning darkness, even when she activated her helmet lamp and shone it toward the bottom of the rectangular shaft.

"Oh, man," Golly said. "I hope the rope is long enough."

"Only one way to find out."

Vale motioned for the utility line. She tied a figure-eight knot into the free end so she would know when she ran out of line, then knelt at the edge of the opening and tossed the coil into the darkness.

No splash came.

"I'll get the other line," Grim Bear said.

"Negative," Vale said. Each squad carried only a single hundred-meter coil of utility line, so Second Squad would be without any rope at all if Vale took a spare down. "Let me have a look first. You can send it down on a carabiner if we need it."

Vale straddled the line, then pulled it around her hip and lifted it over her opposite shoulder for a body rappel. Beginning the descent was a bit of a challenge since she was too large to squeeze through the hole while standing. Instead, she dangled her feet over the edge and wormed into the shaft backward, until her head was clear and she was using her guide hand to hang from the line. Then she pressed her toes against the wall and leaned back, her soles flat against it. After that, it was easy to descend, walking down the shaft backward and using her brake hand to control her speed through the amount of friction the line created against her armor.

Once she had descended five meters, she released the line with her guide hand and drew her plasma pistol. If she had to use it, she would be firing left-handed . . . but it wouldn't compromise her accuracy. Like most Spartans, she had trained with her off-hand until she could fire as precisely with it as with the primary.

Over her comm, she said, "Golly, come ahead."

"On my way."

Golly's boots appeared in the opening above and began to inch back. Having two people on the same rope was a bit risky, since the person on bottom would be hit if the one on top lost his grip and fell—after being shot, for instance. But the line itself would hold. It had a braided nanofiber core strong enough to support the entire squad, and probably both Mongooses in addition.

A moment later, Golly was five meters above Vale with his legs wrapped around the line. In his right hand, he held his MA40, with the line running diagonally across his body and then up around his left arm. It was not a body rappel, as Vale was using, but a fast-rope technique modified for thin nanofiber lines.

They descended the shaft rapidly, Vale practically running down the liner backward while the huge ODST slid down the line above her. It would have been safer for them both to use a body rappel, but with the weight of Vale's Mjolnir pulling the line taut, Golly would have been unable to use his braking hand to slow his descent—or even to rig a body rappel in the first place.

They were about a third of the way down the line when the wall changed from resin liner to rugged rock, and Vale realized they had dropped beneath ground level and entered the workings beneath the tel. She shone her helmet lamp downward and saw only darkness.

"How deep *is* this thing?" Golly asked.

"The utility line is a hundred meters long. So . . . more than that."

After descending another twenty meters or so, they began to intersect the ragged mouths of rough-hewn passages. At each one, Vale deactivated her helmet lamp and paused, searching for even the faintest gleam of light and listening for any hint of sound, trying to build the beginnings of a mental map of the mine city's layout. She found nothing but darkness and silence, and when she shut down her Mjolnir armor's air-filtering system, she smelled only the musty odor of the water below.

It made no sense. Any species capable of creating molecular machines and opening interdimensional rifts could surely cut smooth shafts and drive uniformly-shaped tunnels. Yet the walls of the ventilation shaft were so knobby and uneven that she was in danger of turning an ankle with every bound, and the passages were so misshapen and variable that they often resembled shadows rather than openings. Vale did not yet grasp the paradox here. And it was going to kill them all if she didn't wise up soon.

They had descended another fifty meters when Squad Two's staff sergeant, Slim Sahir, came over the comm. *"Spartan, can we have an ETA on securing an assembly zone down there? This nanodust stuff is starting to close off our access."*

"How?"

"It's growing in from the edges of the breach you created. We've been trying to scrape it away with our entrenching tools, but no go. The stuff just cakes our shovel blades."

"Can you still get your squad down the line?" Vale asked.

"If we start soon."

"Then start now." More nanodust problems . . . the stuff was proving dangerous in ways she had never thought of. "Send

Commander Petrov and Professor Iyuska down first. I have a feeling we're going to need their experience and expertise more than we need your firepower."

"Affirmative," Sahir said. *"The professor seems nervous about the modified fast-rope, so I rigged a seat harness for her and showed her how to descend with Prusik knots. I'll send her down in tight formation with Martinez."*

"Good job." The Prusiks would eliminate any possibility of falling off the line and hitting someone else, but at the price of being cumbersome and slow . . . especially for someone unaccustomed to rope work. "On second thought, have Martinez bring the professor down at the rear. I don't want her holding up the whole squad . . . especially if she freezes."

Iyuska's voice sounded in the background, small and tinny as it carried over Sahir's microphone. *"I won't* freeze. *Not with what's waiting for me down there."*

"Glad to hear it," Vale said. "But you have no idea what's waiting down here. None of us do."

"Which is precisely why I should see it first. If not for me, you'd still think this is just a pile of tailings powder."

"Fair enough. But Prusiks are too slow. If we run into a problem down here, I don't want the rest of the squad waiting on you."

"Then let me fast-rope," Iyuska said. *"Sergeant Sahir is overreacting. I just had a few questions."*

"Not going to happen," Vale said. "I don't want you falling on our heads."

Before Iyuska could respond, Sahir said, *"Ma'am, she won't be holding a weapon, so she could fast-rope and use a single Prusik to self-belay. She'd be safe and able to move quickly."*

Clearly, Iyuska had been working on Sahir since Vale and Golly entered the shaft. And since he couldn't shoot her, he was willing to give her whatever it took to shut her up.

"Fine, Sergeant," Vale said. "But I still want her and Martinez coming down last. As long as they get down here fast enough, we'll put the professor at the front of the squad when we move out."

"Now you're just being spiteful," Iyuska said.

"The sergeant has his orders," Vale said. "And, Keely, this isn't spite. I'm giving you what you asked for."

The line shuddered and twitched as the troopers of First Squad climbed on and fast-roped after Vale and Golly. She continued to descend, her helmet lamp shining into the darkness below. The water at the bottom of the shaft remained hidden in gloom, and the rope continued to dangle into the emptiness with no sign of the figure-eight knot she had tied into the end. But soon there came the sound of a distant trickle, so faint and far below that she had her VISR system amplify her audio receptors to be sure she wasn't imagining it.

She swept the beam of her helmet lamp over the shaft walls directly below and to either side, searching for the source of the trickle. There was no water, only the dark maw of another dry passage, but the sound continued to grow louder and more distinct. Vale had Golly halt his descent, then hung from the rope and spun around to check the wall behind her.

Nothing.

But the trickle was still there, just below her. She could hear it clearer than ever and even see its decibel bar pulsing on her heads-up display. She lowered herself another meter and turned back toward the near wall, then swept her lamp beam across the rock below . . . and glimpsed a silver flash.

Light reflecting off water.

She began to descend again, shining her lamp beam between

her knees, as far down the shaft wall as she could see. A string of flashes appeared, drops falling into darkness, then the long silver thread of water snaking down the rock. It wasn't much, just a tiny rivulet no larger than a child's finger.

But it was the first free-running water she had seen on Netherop, and settlements needed water. Vale used her lamp beam to trace the water back up the wall to the mouth of a small round passage. In contrast to the openings she'd passed earlier, this one was perfectly circular, a little over a meter in diameter with smooth sharp edges. She dropped a little farther and stopped when the bottom rim was at chin height, then cautiously shone her helmet lamp along the length of the floor.

The water trickle extended in front of her, running up the center of the floor. The passage was as circular as its entrance and as straight as an arrow to the limit of her lamp beam. The walls appeared smooth, blemished only by water stains and what looked like bits of vegetable matter from the midpoint down. From the midpoint up, the walls were coated in the same gray-yellow nanodust that formed the tel.

As the light of her helmet lamp swept over it, the nanodust began to fall free of the passage wall and hang in the air.

"I think we've found our back door," Vale said over TEAM-COM. "If we can survive it."

CHAPTER 14

The trail could not have been easier to follow, and Thel 'Vadam was suspicious. For fifty centals, he and his companions had been tracking Nizat 'Kvarosee and his warriors deeper into the tel, half expecting the tunnel to collapse on their heads at any moment, or a pit to open beneath their feet and drop them into the bowels of the planet, or the dust pall to grow so thick it clogged their airways and condemned them to a painful suffocation.

Instead, the tel inhabitants seemed content to let them follow, leaving a shoulders-width band of churned dust that seemed more of a dare to keep coming than an inability to conceal their tracks. Even now, when the tunnel forked into three branches and it would have been easy to lay a false trail, the path continued as obvious as ever down the center passage.

"They are making it too easy." Varo'dai was standing to one side of the main tunnel, leaning into the center branch to shine her helmet lamps at the floor. "They want us to take this passage."

"Perhaps." 'Talot stood opposite Varo'dai, looking at 'Vadam rather than at the trail in question. "Or perhaps they are just hurrying back to their stronghold, moving too fast to conceal their trail on such soft ground."

"It could be either." 'Ayomuu was directly behind 'Vadam, speaking over the Arbiter's shoulder. "But their human hostage is in the middle tunnel."

'Vadam ran his lamp beams along the floor of the center passage, looking for any hint of small oblong boot-prints among the double-pointed wedges left by 'Kvarosee and his Sangheili followers. 'Vadam found none, though so much dust hung in the air it was difficult to see very far. But even if the human were on foot, her tracks could have been buried beneath those of the warriors trailing behind her.

"How do you know this?" 'Vadam turned to face the Oath Warden and found him looking not at the trail ahead, but at a data disc he held in his hand. "Have you sent a spy *fleg* ahead without my consent?"

"Of course not." 'Ayomuu held the data disc out where 'Vadam could look at the screen. "I put a tracking *tetht* on the human."

A *tetht* was a flying arachnid so tiny it was seldom seen until a victim felt it sting and reduced it to a bloody smudge. A tracking *tetht*, 'Vadam assumed, was a robotic version of the pest, used by Oath Wardens to follow their subjects remotely.

"When did you do that?" 'Vadam demanded. "You were never close to her."

"I find it works better that way. Targets tend to grow suspicious when an Oath Warden strokes their shoulder."

Realizing 'Ayomuu was not about to share the secrets of his trade, 'Vadam clicked his mandibles and looked at the screen. It was less informative than expected, merely a series of concentric circles with an orange tracking line leading into the center of the innermost circle. At the top of the screen was a fixed directional arrow, which he assumed was used to keep the disc oriented in the direction they were facing.

"They are three hundred units ahead," 'Ayomuu said. "And moving away quickly."

"Your *tetht* is three hundred units ahead," Varo'dai corrected. "How can we be sure it is not being used as a decoy?"

"To do that, they would have had to find it. And they have no reason to look. As the Arbiter said, I was never close to her. None of us were."

"Perhaps so," 'Vadam said. "But how does it communicate with you? There must be some kind of signal."

"None that can be detected."

"How do you know what they can detect?" Varo'dai wiped her fingertips across her dust-caked helmet, then flicked a cloud of gray powder toward the floor. "You heard their Worldmaster confirm that he was watching when the Arbiter conferred with the Spartan. Do you know how he did that? Because I do not."

"You talk as though he was using magic," 'Ayomuu countered. "We may not understand their capabilities, but that does not make them capable of *everything*. They have their limits too."

"No doubt," 'Vadam said. "But until we understand those limits, we need to be cautious."

"Within reason," 'Talot said. "We may be following the tel inhabitants, but we are racing the humans to secure the weapon. Let us remember that."

"The kaidon is correct," 'Ayomuu said. "If we waste time avoiding every imagined risk—"

"The risks are real," Varo'dai said. "'Kvarosee has already tried to ambush us once."

"He was prepared to ambush us," 'Talot noted. "But he was

still talking—until you called him a fool. It is a wonder he attacked only you."

"He talked because his ambush had been exposed and he saw he was outnumbered two to one," Varo'dai said. "Attacking me was good tactics. He needed a distraction so he could withdraw to better ground." She pointed down the center passage. "His better ground is in there. Nizat 'Kvarosee may seem like a mad zealot to us now, but let us remember that he was once master of the Fleet of Inexorable Obedience. If we underestimate him, he will bury us in this tel."

"Better that than to be ruled by your fear of him." 'Ayomuu turned to 'Vadam. "If you allow her trepidation to slow us down, it will be the Spartan and her ODSTs who recover the weapon . . . not us."

"And by 'us,'" 'Vadam replied, "I assume you mean you and your client?"

'Ayomuu tipped his helmet to the side. "Would you rather it go to the humans?" His tone was wry. "They have caused enough trouble already. Better us than them."

"I might agree with that," 'Vadam said, "if I knew who your client was."

"I am confident you would. But that is not a bargain I can accept on my own authority."

"I was not offering a bargain."

"No? My mistake, then." 'Ayomuu returned his gaze to the screen of his data disc. "But I suggest we quit dithering. They are moving out of tracker range."

He turned the screen toward 'Vadam, but the only difference apparent was that the space between the concentric circles had grown smaller. Still, 'Ayomuu's earlier assessment was a good one.

Whether 'Kvarosee and his warriors were lying in ambush or rushing toward their stronghold, Vale and her ODSTs were racing to find the weapon on their own. And they would probably not face much opposition. Amalea Petrov had estimated the number of the tel's warriors to be less than ten—and so far, 'Vadam had seen nothing to suggest they had even that many.

'Vadam turned to Varo'dai. "Let us assume 'Kvarosee and his followers *are* lying in ambush. Would they do that on the path to their stronghold, or would they lead us off course first?"

"I am sure you have your own answer to that. You are a fine tactical thinker yourself."

"Then I want you to use five of your rangers as a counter-ambush force. Trail as far behind us as necessary to remain undetected, and if you are right about 'Kvarosee's intentions, take them from behind."

Varo'dai raised her chins in acknowledgment. "And by *take*, do you mean 'eliminate'?"

"I mean do what is necessary. I have explained the situation to them quite clearly. Anyone who wishes to die with the Covenant is welcome to do so."

"As you command." Varo'dai glanced into the other two forks of the tunnel. "And what of my remaining rangers? Have them scout the other passages?"

"Yes. And do it quickly." Both forks were wider than the main tunnel, and when 'Vadam shone his lamps into them, he saw that they descended almost immediately into the bedrock beneath the tel. Their walls were knobby and rough, their ceilings not quite high enough for a Sangheili to stand upright. "Vale and her ODSTs are still our biggest problem. If they find the weapon before we do—"

"They will not," Varo'dai said. "I would never let that happen."

"Good. I will be counting on you."

When 'Vadam turned to send 'Talot forward, he found the old kaidon watching 'Varo'dai, his posture stiff and still. At first, 'Vadam assumed he was just waiting to hear her orders before volunteering to take point. But when she began to issue assignments using hand signals, 'Talot merely shifted his gaze to the center passage and stared into the hanging dust ahead. Now that his followers would be leading the column rather than Varo'dai's rangers, he seemed to be having second thoughts about pushing ahead quickly—probably because he feared his warriors lacked the skill to spot an ambush in this environment before it was sprung.

"I will lead with my warriors and the Oath Warden," 'Vadam said. 'Ayomuu would be more liability than asset at the head of the column, but it would not do to have him in back with 'Talot. The Oath Warden would only use it as an opportunity to further attack 'Vadam's authority. "Kaidon 'Talot, you will follow twenty paces behind in close support position. Keep three paces between each pair of warriors."

"I should lead with my warriors." There was no enthusiasm in 'Talot's offer, merely obligation. "The Arbiter is not bait."

"And that is not my intention," 'Vadam said. "But if there is any hope of persuading Fleetmaster 'Kvarosee to help us recover the weapon before the UNSC does, it remains with me. I will be counting on you for my protection."

'Talot hesitated. "I am still reluctant, Arbiter. The fleetmaster is unbalanced. You will not be able to persuade him of anything."

"Then we will neutralize him another way," 'Ayomuu said. "Have no fear, my friend. The Arbiter will be under my protection until you arrive."

"A great comfort," 'Vadam said. It took conscious effort to keep the sarcasm out of his voice. "Do as I command, old friend. This is our best deployment."

"Very well." 'Talot lifted his helmet to acknowledge the order. "Since you have made it a command."

By the time they had rearranged their marching order, Va-ro'dai's scouts had disappeared into the adjacent passages, and she was waiting in counter-ambush position with the rest of her rangers. 'Vadam sent one of his own warriors forward on point, with instructions to stay close to the wall to avoid disturbing the trail. He followed next, with 'Ayomuu at his side, both studying the tracks ahead of them, their shoulders often touching in the cramped confines of the tunnel.

In part, 'Vadam was merely keeping 'Ayomuu where he could see him. But Oath Wardens were talented trackers and experts at ambush, so he was glad to have help with watching the trail for any signs of a change in pace or the number of passing feet.

The passage descended through the tel in tight meanders that often made it impossible to see what lay around the next curve. Still, 'Ayomuu insisted on moving quicker than 'Vadam liked, for the tracking *tetht* was now at the limit of its range, and its signal sometimes vanished from the data disc altogether.

They had traveled about two hundred units when the floor gradually changed from packed dust to solid rock. The dust in the air seemed to defy gravity, never settling to the floor, and the trail of footprints grew steadily harder to follow. Soon, they found themselves tracking by the rub marks their quarry had left on the walls or the rare clump of dust that had fallen off a passing foot.

Then 'Ayomuu raised a hand. "They've stopped." He was looking at the screen of his data disc. "A hundred units ahead."

That was not much farther. The light from 'Vadam's helmet lamps would have illuminated that far, had there not been a bend in the passage. He peered at 'Ayomuu's data disc and saw that the space between the concentric circles had increased. Otherwise, the signal looked the same as it had before.

"Someday, you must explain to me how to read your tracking device."

"I am sure we could arrange that. After your apprenticeship."

"What apprenticeship?"

"Oath Wardens never share their secrets with outsiders." 'Ayomuu set off again, this time moving more cautiously and taking the time to examine the passage ahead. "If you hope to learn our ways, you must earn the right."

"In that case, ignore the suggestion. I have no interest in becoming a warden myself, let alone your apprentice."

"I thought as much." 'Ayomuu dropped to his haunches, then salivated on his fingertips and swept them over the bare rock, one digit at a time. "You would not be a good one anyway. You have a shallow concept of honor."

As 'Vadam pondered whether the direct insult merited a violent reprisal, 'Ayomuu brought his fingertips up and examined each one in turn. He worked his mandibles side to side, then turned and shone his helmet lamps at the passage walls to either side of them.

"What is it?" 'Vadam asked.

"How long has it been since you noticed a rub mark on your side of the tunnel?"

'Vadam thought for a moment. "Perhaps twenty-five paces."

"There has not been one on my side for twenty-seven paces." 'Ayomuu called out to the point warrior. "You there, move forward and fetch the human. Do it quickly."

The warrior stopped in his tracks and stared at 'Ayomuu for a long breath, then looked to 'Vadam.

'Vadam turned to 'Ayomuu. "How do you know the human

— 221 —

is alone? And if she is, why should I have my warrior do what you ask?"

"The pattern has changed." 'Ayomuu pointed at the passage walls to indicate that he was talking about the marks left in the dust by the shoulders of passing warriors. Then he displayed his damp, clean fingertips. "And there is not much dust on the floor."

'Vadam looked at the fog of particles floating in the air, asking himself how so little of it could have fallen to the ground . . . and quickly realized the answer. "Because it has had no time to settle. This tunnel is new."

"Agreed, but there is another reason." 'Ayomuu again displayed his clean fingertips. "One more important."

"Their feet have carried nothing down from above," 'Vadam realized. "And there would have been some trace, had seven Sangheili passed this way."

"Very good. You should reconsider becoming an Oath Warden." 'Ayomuu tipped his helmet toward the point warrior he had tried to send forward earlier. "Now will you have your warrior bring the human? I want my tracking *tetht* back."

'Vadam raised his chins to the point warrior. "Go." Without awaiting an acknowledgment, he turned to look back down the passage and spoke over his helmet comm. "Ghe, fall back."

"Is that wise?" 'Talot replied. "I can barely see your lights now."

"It does not matter what you can see," 'Ayomuu said. "It is what you *cannot* see that is important."

"If I am supposed to understand your riddle—"

"The fleetmaster and his warriors are no longer ahead of us," 'Vadam said. "Either they have slipped away, or they are hiding in ambush. Now, do as I command and—"

The right side of the passage burst inward, choking the tunnel with a dust cloud so thick that 'Vadam's lamp beams could not penetrate it. A pair of dark silhouettes separated from the wall and moved toward 'Talot and his warriors, then two more followed and blocked the passage by standing in it shoulder to shoulder.

"You should not have followed us, heretic." The voice was 'Kvarosee's. Through the gray pall of floating dust, his form resembled that of a dark ghost. "What comes next is your doing, not mine."

"Enough with your threats," 'Vadam said. Actually, he was quite pleased to have 'Kvarosee making threats. If the former fleetmaster was talking instead of attacking, it was probably because he wanted something. And if 'Vadam could give it to him, they might still be able to strike a bargain. "I have no fear of them, and it is to your benefit to cooperate with us. The galaxy is not as we all believed when you were marooned here."

"What we *believed* in was the promise of the gods. And the evidence of their power is all around us. If you are too cowardly to help us defend their gift, you are as much our enemies as the humans."

"You know I will not fight the humans for you." 'Vadam switched to thermal imaging on the HUD inside his goggle lenses, but the dust was still so thick that it scattered heat signatures, and all he saw was an amorphous blur filling the passage ahead of him. "But if you wish to keep the gods' gift out of their hands, we must work together."

"The faithful need no help from heretics. We can rid the Sanctum of these vermin ourselves. I have offered you redemption as a fellow Sangheili . . . and you have refused me for the last time."

The blur on 'Vadam's HUD shifted as 'Kvarosee turned, then 'Ayomuu's voice sounded at 'Vadam's side: "Seal your armor."

"What?" 'Vadam glanced over to find the Oath Warden pulling a silver canister from beneath his armor. "Wait. *Wait!*"

'Ayomuu's hand was already moving forward to release the canister. "He who strikes second dies first." The Oath Warden sent the canister spinning toward 'Kvarosee on a level trajectory, then repeated, *"Seal your armor, Arbiter."*

'Vadam did so, slipping a rebreather into his mouth and activating an energy barrier that would join his helmet to his techsuit in a sealed unit. Biting down on the rebreather activated an integrated throat mic, which he used to repeat the seal command over his helmet comm for his warriors and 'Talot and Varo'dai. On the canister's fourth rotation, plumes of yellow aerosol began to stream from its ends, and there was no need to ask what 'Ayomuu had done. Attacking with poison gas was an unspeakable violation of a warrior's honor . . . but for Oath Wardens, unspeakable deeds were tools of the trade.

"Attack!" 'Vadam ordered. He grabbed his carbine off its armor mount and began to fire into the dust. "All weapons permitted!"

The command was hardly necessary. By the time he finished issuing it, 'Kvarosee's warriors were firing their own weapons. Plasma and carbine rounds flew in both directions, creating brilliant tubes of color as superheated bolts and projectiles ignited floating dust. With the tunnel filled wall to wall by armored opponents, there was no aiming to be done—just pointing and firing and hitting whatever was ahead.

'Vadam's thermal imaging began to glow so brightly it masked his natural vision. He deactivated it and fired in the direction of 'Kvarosee. Through the gray pall, it was difficult to discern exactly what effect he was having, but at such short range and in such cramped confines, it would have been impossible to miss. Bellows of anger and pain began to roll up the passage, though whether they came from his own warriors or their ambushers was impossible to tell.

When another pair of silhouettes separated from the wall and moved to shield 'Kvarosee, 'Vadam switched his attacks to them. His carbine rounds knocked them off their feet . . . and they continued to return fire from the ground. His shields flared, and he could see the yellow aerosol from 'Ayomuu's canister swirling through the dust around them. It seemed to have even less effect on the targets than his carbine. Either he had doubted the Oath Warden's honor unjustly—and *that* seemed unlikely—or the inhabitants' armor could also be sealed against environmental attacks.

'Vadam's shields crackled out, then his armor began to sizzle and pop with plasma strikes. He dropped his carbine and retrieved his energy sword. Evidently, radioactive rounds fired at several times the speed of sound could not penetrate the strange armor of the tel inhabitants, and he had no reason to think a plasma blade would save him. But his armor was failing and he had to try something.

"Oath Warden, we must do this the hard way." 'Vadam pointed his energy sword up the passage. "Attack their weapons first."

"You fight as you wish." 'Ayomuu grabbed his energy sword and sprang forward. "I will kill them in my own fashion."

As 'Vadam charged after him, the Oath Warden pulled his feet off the ground and launched a flying double kick at the knees of the nearest ambusher. The astonished warrior pointed his plasma rifle downward and tried to save himself by jumping, but 'Ayomuu jammed his blade between the emitter jaws and let go. As he slid beneath his foe, he reached up and grabbed both ankles, then crossed his arms and rolled onto his stomach.

The ambusher bellowed in pain as his knees dislocated, then he flipped over and landed on his back. 'Ayomuu slithered up his torso like a two-tailed *pitho* and fixed his hands beneath the warrior's mandibles in a cross-strangle.

'Vadam did not see what followed next, for he found himself facing a plump foe in a dark opalescent skinsuit. Like the other inhabitants of the tel, he wore headgear that was more translucent membrane than helmet. He had a waist-heavy torso, bulging thighs, and fleshy mandibles.

The Silent Shadow, Meduz 'Ra'ashai.

"Poison gas?!" 'Ra'ashai threw 'Ayomuu's canister—still spraying yellow aerosol—into 'Vadam's chest. "I see things *have* changed among the Sangheili."

"Not the honor of our warriors," 'Vadam said. An acrid odor filled his helmet, and he realized that either his armor had failing circuits or a failing seal. "The gas was the Oath Warden's doing alone."

"Then you can thank *him* for your death."

Before 'Vadam could ask what 'Ra'ashai meant, the blademaster brought up his crimson energy sword in a one-handed rising slash. 'Vadam leapt back, narrowly avoiding being split from stomach to throat, then countered by chopping at 'Ra'ashai's weapon hand. But the blademaster was not as surprised by the tactic as 'Vadam had hoped. 'Ra'ashai simply pulled his arm back, then brought the blade around in a horizontal sweep at neck height.

'Vadam spun inside the attack and came around to find an opening to the torso. It was such an uncharacteristic mistake for a warrior of the Silent Shadow that 'Vadam feared a trap—until he saw 'Ra'ashai's eyes widen in panic. The blademaster made a slow attempt to pivot away, but 'Vadam was already lunging.

The sword struck 'Ra'ashai in the center of his chest, almost exactly between the hearts . . . where the blade's tip stopped so abruptly that the hilt jolted free of 'Vadam's grasp. He stumbled a single step forward and started to catch himself, then realized it would put him in a perfect position for 'Ra'ashai to lop him off at the knees.

Instead, he used his momentum to launch himself forward with all the strength in his legs, leading with the fingertips of his now-empty weapon hand. 'Ra'ashai dropped his head to protect his throat, and 'Vadam switched to an upward elbow strike. The blow caught the blademaster under the chins and drove him backward into the wall.

Recalling how 'Ayomuu had slid into a grappling assault against the other attacker, 'Vadam wrapped his free arm around the back of 'Ra'ashai's head, grabbed his lower mandibles, and pulled them up. Then he slipped the other elbow under the chins and pushed hard into the throat, pinning the blademaster against the wall. It was a risky tactic. If the shock wore off, 'Ra'ashai would be able to bring his energy sword to bear and start probing for soft spots in 'Vadam's armor. He began to pull the blademaster's mandibles around, hoping to twist his neck far enough to break it—

—then heard a deep, sonorous boom, so low and loud he felt it with his entire body. The dust grew impenetrable, too thick to even see 'Ra'ashai pinned against the wall in front of him. A moment later, 'Vadam realized that he was no longer standing upright, that he had been thrown to the floor and now lay somewhere down the passage.

He rolled to his knees and heard the after-rumble of a distant explosion. The acrid odor in his helmet had grown so strong that he could taste it through the rebreather. Slowly, he began to realize what must have happened: The human ODSTs had used a powerful explosive to open a breach into the heart of the tel, and the shockwave had rolled through the tunnel network into the dead-end passage where he was fighting 'Ra'ashai. The operation was playing out just as Petrov had intended, with

'Vadam and his Sangheili serving as a diversion so Vale and the humans could sneak into 'Kvarosee's stronghold and recover the weapon.

It was better that Vale succeed than neither of them . . . but far from ideal. There was no telling what atrocities might happen if the wrong humans got their hands on this weapon. Once Cortana had been stopped, they could use it to impose their will on the rest of the civilized galaxy, no different from the Tyrant they all currently faced.

And *that* 'Vadam could never permit, alliance or not.

Worried that 'Ra'ashai and the other ambushers would be looking to finish what 'Kvarosee had started, 'Vadam scrambled back up the passage—at least he thought it was up—sweeping his hands across the floor in search of a weapon. It took only a couple of breaths to find the warrior 'Ayomuu had fought, now lying motionless and twisted on the floor. The warrior's plasma rifle had been disabled when the Oath Warden jammed his energy sword between its jaws, and when 'Vadam laid a hand on his chest to make sure he was dead, his palm came back coated in black dust. He looked closer and saw that where he had touched the warrior was a bare spot where the strange armor had disintegrated.

"We call it the Sanctum's Hide," 'Ra'ashai said. "It dies with us."

'Vadam shone his helmet lamps in the direction of the voice and saw a dark silhouette standing in the dust just two paces away. 'Vadam grabbed the disabled plasma rifle and pointed it in the blademaster's direction, hoping it would not be obvious through the poor visibility that it was not functional.

"Please, you know that would never penetrate," 'Ra'ashai said. "And even if it did, you have need of me."

"For what purpose?"

"The Sanctum of the Ancients is a strange place. You will not succeed without the help of someone who understands it."

"Perhaps so. But why would you change sides now?"

"You are an excellent fighter. If not for"—'Ra'ashai's silhouette made an exploding motion with its fingers—"I would be dead."

'Vadam paused, debating whether he could trust 'Ra'ashai. "Is this a Silent Shadow custom?"

'Ra'ashai clacked his mandibles in amusement. "Yes. That, and I would like to go home before I die."

"That can be arranged."

'Vadam had barely spoken before a leak alarm flashed on his HUD. A low hissing sounded from the seal around his neck, and the odor in his helmet changed from acrid to cloying. His thoughts grew slow and muddled.

"What?" He lunged toward 'Ra'ashai. *"How?"*

"It was not me." 'Ra'ashai stepped out of the dust and reached out with both hands, holding them under 'Vadam's arms. "This is your Oath Warden's doing."

"'Ayomuu?" A dark veil began to descend inside 'Vadam's mind. "The . . . gas?"

"That . . . and Nizat 'Kvarosee. He thought it fitting for you to fall by your own poison." 'Ra'ashai caught 'Vadam's elbows and held him up as his knees buckled. "The Worldmaster was utterly furious when he realized *you* are the diversion."

CHAPTER 15

The *Hammer of Fate*'s listening station had not intercepted any surface traffic in four units, and Atriox was growing ever more concerned. The lull had begun after a mysterious flare event disrupted the insertion run of an entire wing of UNSC Pelicans, so perhaps no humans had survived to make transmissions. But a trio of the Arbiter's Phantoms had already been on the ground at the time. They should have been emitting *something*.

At the very least, the Phantom pilots should have been replying to the incessant status inquiries from the Sangheili flotilla still in orbit above Neska. There should have been some comm traffic between the Phantoms themselves, as well as sentries and ground patrols making regular situation reports. And since none of those things were happening, scout craft should have been inserting to investigate.

Instead . . . nothing.

Atriox moved forward to study the tactical holograph. It was perhaps the tenth time he had done so after the Pelicans had vanished during their insertion run, and the crew was keeping an open place for him on the aft side, where he could peer through the holograph to monitor the rest of the activity on the bridge.

The tactical situation had changed little since his last visit. The holograph showed a gravitic anomaly accompanying Neska's first moon around the planet. Atriox assumed this was where the human stealth cruiser had moved after launching its Pelican wing, as it was standard UNSC doctrine for stealth vessels to mask their mass signatures by staying close to a celestial body.

The seven vessels of the Sangheili flotilla remained in high orbit, just passing between Neska's surface and the Banished's hiding place on the second moon. After the flare, they had climbed into this orbit and entered a diamond formation so loose the point ships did not even have overlapping fields of fire. Atriox viewed this as clear evidence that the Sangheili flotilla commander knew the humans would not blame him for the attack on their Pelican wing. Otherwise, he would have been worried about mistaken assumptions. He would have kept his vessels in a tight defensive posture.

Which meant he knew more than Atriox did. And so did the humans.

The flare had occurred over the horizon from the Banished's hiding place, so all Atriox had seen was a sudden dome of light in the thermosphere. It had been followed by a flurry of alarmed comm traffic as the human stealth cruiser reacted to the destruction of its Pelican wing and the Sangheili tried to contact their Phantoms.

When no responses came, the Sangheili flotilla had climbed into the high orbit it now occupied. Having already dropped off the *Hammer of Fate*'s sensor screens after launching its Pelican wing, the UNSC stealth cruiser had simply fallen silent and continued cloaking itself. But neither side had made any aggressive moves toward the other. They both seemed to be taking pains to stay clear of each other . . . perhaps because they had both seen the flare and knew what had caused it.

Atriox motioned Eto 'Saljhoo to his side. "The flare event . . . is it possible *that* was the trikala?"

'Saljhoo used a thumb and forefinger to stroke the underside of his mandibles, then finally said, "Anything is possible. But who would have activated it? The Sangheili Phantoms have been on Neska's surface barely five units. Even were it possible to find and assess the trikala in such a short time, the Arbiter would never be foolish enough to use it on Neska. It would be too likely to draw the notice of the Apparition's harriers."

"You have the brain of a *namth*," Tovarus said, stepping to Atriox's side. "The Arbiter does not know there are harriers in this system. Our decoys have drawn them away."

"Of course, you are right." 'Saljhoo studied Neska's brown-cloaked image for a moment, his gaze focused on the green dot that the threat analysts estimated to be the origination point of the flare event, and worked his mandibles as he made a few silent calculations. Then his eyes bulged. "Well, that would be bad . . . very bad. If the Arbiter *did* use the trikala, I mean."

"*If?*" Tovarus echoed. "Did he activate it or not?"

"That is impossible to know with Neska's cloud cover. Once our orbit has carried us over the origination point of the flare event, we might be able to gather some residual readings that suggest what class of phenomenon—"

"The Arbiter did not fire the trikala," Atriox said. "If he had, the humans and the Sangheili would be doing battle over it right now."

"Then it is a great relief they are not," 'Saljhoo said. "Because if we have located the origination point correctly, and I have calculated Neska's rotation accurately, the flare event was facing out-system when it occurred. I do not know whether the propagation cone would have been broad enough for the harriers to see, but if the trikala *had* been fired—"

"I did not say the trikala had not been fired," Atriox interrupted. "I said the Arbiter was not the one who did so."

"But who else would have?" 'Saljhoo asked. "Even had a human advance unit somehow seized the trikala so quickly, it would not have attacked a human insertion force."

"That is so," Atriox said. "Which leaves us with the only other possibility—Neska's current inhabitants."

"But Neska is uninhabited." 'Saljhoo dropped his chins in thought, then looked at Atriox through the top of his eyes. "Unless you are suggesting the trikala was fired by the *ghosts* of the inhabitants? That it was automated?"

Atriox gave a rumble of amusement. "I am flattered you think me so poetic . . . but, no." He looked back to the planet's brown-swaddled image. "Eleven hundred cycles ago, there was a small surface battle on Neska."

"And you think survivors were left behind?" 'Saljhoo asked. "Survivors who are somehow *still* alive?"

"When a battle ends," Tovarus said, "there are usually survivors. And some are often left behind."

"I understand that." 'Saljhoo's tone was irritated. "But you cannot believe they would still be alive—not after eleven hundred cycles in such a place."

"You do not tell me what to believe, Studymaster," Atriox said. "There are battle survivors on Neska, they are Covenant warriors, and they control the trikala."

That is what made the most sense. *Someone* had used the trikala against the human insertion, yet allowed a trio of Sangheili Phantoms to land unharmed. If he tried hard, Atriox could imagine reasons for someone *other* than a Covenant survivor to do such a thing. 'Saljhoo's "automated attack" theory was a possibility, or even a desperate human castaway hoping to capture a Phantom. But in Atriox's experience, such convoluted reasoning rarely proved to be sound. Almost always, the simplest explanation was the true one.

After a moment, 'Saljhoo's posture grew a little more hunched, and he looked away. "If you state something as truth, Warmaster, I would never presume to say it is not."

"Your wisdom is your greatest asset, Studymaster." Atriox turned back to the holograph and pointed at the green dot that marked the flare event's estimated origination point. "But what I need is your expertise. Tell me why our listeners are intercepting no comm traffic from the surface of the planet. Is everyone down there dead? Or is something blocking their signals?"

"That is impossible to know," 'Saljhoo replied. When Atriox fixed him with a pointed glare, the studymaster added, "But . . . that will certainly change once this moon's orbit carries us over the origination point. We can extrapolate from there, once we gather more readings. We already know there was a spontaneous emission of photons. If the flare event was accompanied by quantum energy shifts and oscillation forces, then we know it was powered by vacuum energy—and *that* would indicate the trikala had been activated."

"Why can we not detect these shifts and forces now?"

"Because they are on the quantum scale. Very small and very short-lived. The sensor operators will not even be looking for the energy shifts and oscillation forces themselves, only residual signs that they occurred. My apologies, Warmaster, but even a Banished crew cannot make such delicate observations without being directly over the target area."

Atriox looked toward the estimated location of the flare event. The green dot marking the spot was about halfway between the horizon and the *Hammer of Fate*'s hiding place on Neska's second moon, so that meant another four units before they were in position.

"That is too long to wait for an answer," Atriox said. "Tell me now what you believe. Why are the listeners intercepting no surface traffic?"

"What happens if I am wrong?"

"You would not like it."

"Then ask your next question, Warmaster. Perhaps I can do better than mere speculation."

"As you wish. How are *we* going to get past the trikala to land on the surface and take it for ourselves?"

"May I assume you are correct about who used it against the Pelican wing? That it was Covenant survivors?"

"There is no need to assume," Atriox said. "I *am* correct."

"Then I can tell you exactly how we are going to get past the trikala. We are *not*."

"What do you mean, we are not?"

"How many Pelicans did the UNSC attempt to insert on Neska, Warmaster?"

"Forty," Atriox replied.

"We have fewer craft in our flotilla."

"But our vessels are better armored and shielded than Pelicans."

"That might matter if we understood what the trikala *was*."

"Which you do not," Atriox said.

"Not yet. What I *do* understand is that the trikala has destroyed at least one Forerunner Guardian. I also know that any Guardian's armor and shields are undoubtedly superior to our own."

Atriox grunted his displeasure, but pushed no further. If he believed that Covenant survivors controlled the trikala—and he *did*—then he would be a fool to argue against the studymaster's conclusion. Reaching Neska would mean fighting past the Arbiter's flotilla, a battle that would certainly alert the Covenant on the surface to him being an enemy. Then, even if the UNSC stealth cruiser did not attack—or if Atriox somehow prevailed against it—he would face the prospect of inserting against a foe that had already destroyed an entire wing of Pelicans. And if the weapon the survivors had used was indeed the trikala, 'Saljhoo's prediction would prove accurate. The Banished would lose their entire insertion force.

Atriox had just about resigned himself to a long wait when a Kig-Yar gravitics reader straightened his posture, then summoned his Jiralhanae overseer. The reader was on the far side of the tactical holograph, so it was difficult to see the source of his concern through Neska's cloudy brown image. But the overseer gnashed his tusks and motioned the Kig-Yar to plot the data.

An instant later, the symbol of an oval appeared on the outsystem edge of the tactical holograph. Bisected on the diagonal by a jagged line, it was a *theza*, the Jiralhanae glyph of uncertainty, which the Banished used to denote a gravitic anomaly. A vector tail appeared behind it, turning the *theza* into a blunt-tipped arrow on an interception course for the Sangheili flotilla.

Before Atriox could ask for an estimate of mass and velocity, a second *theza* appeared on the edge of the holograph, trailing a little behind the first, but with a curving vector tail.

"More prowlers?" 'Saljhoo asked. "That cannot be good."

"Why do you assume they are from the UNSC?" Tovarus asked. He turned toward the listening station and called, "Any word from our two decoys?"

"I would have reported that at once," the grizzled listener replied. "There has been nothing."

Tovarus cast a hopeful glance toward Atriox.

"We dare not trust their silence." Atriox's gaze remained fixed on the two *theza* vectors, watching them stretch toward the Sangheili flotilla. "Have navigation estimate the light time from Neska to the decoy locations."

As Tovarus relayed the order, 'Saljhoo asked, "Then you think they are the harriers?"

"I *fear* they are the harriers." Atriox continued to scrutinize the tactical holograph, searching for any sign that the Sangheili had noticed the approaching anomalies. "You are the one who noted that the flash event was pointed out-system."

"True," 'Saljhoo replied. "But one can hope."

"If one is a brainless *dengkra*," Tovarus said, turning back to them. "Navigation estimates two and a half units light time to the first decoy, three units to the second. Both karves were well within the flash event's propagation cone."

"Oh," 'Saljhoo said. "That *is* unfortunate."

The studymaster did not need to explain his assumptions. It would have taken two and a half units for the light from the flash event to reach the closest karve, then another two and a half units for a light-speed transmission to return to the *Hammer of Fate*. So, even had a karve transmitted a warning that the harrier was returning to the planet, it would not yet have arrived.

Which was why both decoy karves had orders to make a slipspace jump back into the Neska planetary system the instant they realized the harriers were no longer following them. That neither vessel had returned by now left only one inescapable conclusion.

"Both karves were destroyed," Atriox said. "And now the harriers have returned to protect the trikala."

"Yes," Tovarus said. "But that is not necessarily a problem for us."

Atriox's first instinct was to chastise his second-in-command for being a brainless *dengkra* himself. When they saw the Sangheili flotilla, the harriers would warn the Apparition, and she would send an overwhelming body of reinforcements. If he did not capture the trikala before they arrived, he never would. He was as certain of that as his own name.

Then Atriox looked again at the *theza* vectors and how they were bending to intercept the Sangheili flotilla, and he saw what Tovarus was suggesting.

"The harriers will provide the diversion we need," Atriox announced. "Once they have engaged, we will slip past our foes and seize the trikala for ourselves."

"A masterful plan, Warmaster." Tovarus was careful to avoid claiming the credit for his own idea, as that could have been seen as a challenge to Atriox's position. "I am sure you have thought of a way to slip past the human stealth cruiser as well."

"The stealth cruiser will not be a concern for us," 'Saljhoo said. "At least not on the way in."

"I would feel better if the Warmaster confirmed that," Tovarus said.

"The studymaster is correct. If *we* were able to find the stealth cruiser with our technology, surely the harriers will find it too. They have the technology of the Forerunners."

"A sound conclusion, of course," 'Saljhoo said. "But what I meant was that the harriers have *already* found the stealth cruiser. The second one is preparing to launch its attack now."

Atriox scowled at the *theza* vectors. The first one was undoubtedly on an interception course to the Sangheili flotilla. It did not seem likely that a single vessel of its size—even *Forerunner*—would be able to destroy so many ships on its own, but it would certainly serve as the distraction the Banished needed to slip past and insert on Neska.

The intention of the second harrier was not as obvious. Its *theza* vector was now actually bending away from an interception course with the Sangheili flotilla, and rising above the orbital plane of Neska's first moon, where Atriox still believed the human stealth cruiser to be hiding.

"Tovarus, have the threat analysts project the course of that second harrier."

As Tovarus turned to relay the command, 'Saljhoo clacked his mandibles.

"Forgive me, Warmaster." The studymaster was clearly struggling to keep the frustration out of his voice. "But the course projection will tell you nothing."

"Explain."

'Saljhoo pointed at the curving *theza* vector. "The second harrier is not going to attack. It is preparing to observe the battle. Once the outcome grows clear, it will enter slipspace and leave the system."

"To warn the Apparition of our presence." Atriox grunted in frustration, then turned to Tovarus. "Once the harrier leaves the system, how long before the Apparition's forces arrive?"

"It will be fast, Warmaster," Tovarus said. "Harriers use Forerunner slipspace technology, so it will require only a unit to reach a communications node. Even the Apparition will need to marshal her fleet, and that will take time. But we know she has been watching Neska, so she is likely prepared to act swiftly. Allow two units for the fleet to get under way."

"And because the Apparition will send Forerunner vessels, only a unit to arrive." Atriox turned to glare at 'Saljhoo. "Four units. After skulking here for cycles, that is all the time left to us."

"The time may not matter," 'Saljhoo said. "We have a more pressing problem."

Atriox exhaled. "Tell me."

"When we entered the system, you were informed that these were *Acolyte*-class harriers."

"I have not forgotten," Atriox growled. "You said the *Acolyte* class are one of the smallest of harriers."

"I also told you I did not know how many autonomous weapon-ships they carried. Or what kind."

Atriox snapped his tusks. "And that has changed?"

"In a sense."

As 'Saljhoo spoke, the course projection for the second harrier appeared on the tactical holograph. It showed the *theza* vector continuing to rise above the first moon's orbital plane, bending out-system perhaps twenty megaunits from the moon itself. It was an ideal distance for launching long-range missiles . . . or autonomous weapon-ships.

"How many?" Atriox asked.

"That depends on what kind of weapon-ships they are. I would be reluctant to offer a firm number—we simply lack enough experience with *Acolyte*-class harriers—but it could be in the thousands. Though, of course, the smaller the weapon-ship, the less effective—"

"It matters not," Atriox said. "They will keep the stealth cruiser occupied while we make our insertion, just as you have said. The trikala will soon be ours. We have four units to make it so."

'Saljhoo dropped his gaze. "It is certainly my hope that we will succeed . . ."

"But you still have fears?" Atriox asked. "You are wondering how *we* are going to land our own force, with the trikala in the hands of our enemies?"

"The thought has been on my mind, Warmaster."

"On mine as well," Tovarus said. "We can use the harriers to distract our enemies in orbit, but our enemies on the ground will be watching and waiting for us."

"And that is what I am counting on," Atriox said. "We are going to let them believe they have disrupted our insertion, just as they disrupted that of the humans."

"You are going to sacrifice our drop fleet?" Tovarus asked.

"No. I am going to sacrifice the *Hammer of Fate*."

CHAPTER 16

Perhaps this was what it meant to be dead, to lie trapped in the gray dust, uncertain whether one was breathing or suffocating, being crushed or cushioned, suspended or sinking. Rosa Fuertes knew only the pearl ambience that surrounded her, that cradled her in the softness of its feathery palm.

She remembered: her Sangheili abductors carrying her deep into the tel, perhaps a thousand meters or more, their leader asking questions of her in his raspy English—which she would gladly have answered but could not—questions about how the Covenant War could be over, the final fate of the Prophets and the nature of the Forerunners, the true purpose of the Halo Array. She remembered also her abductors growing weary of carrying her and forcing her to walk, shoving and dragging her because her prion disease left her too weak and too unsteady to keep pace, then sending her ahead on her own, the passage opening ahead of her just as it did them . . . for a time. She remembered coming to the end of the passage and collapsing in dizziness and fatigue, happy for her pain and struggle to be over. And then a Sangheili in the armor of the Arbiter's forces appearing just as the ceiling rumbled and fell and buried them both.

Or did she remember anything?

Was any of that real? All Rosa knew now was the dizzy queasiness of floating in dust, the pearl ambience that swaddled her and held her inside like a womb. *That* was real. Everything else . . . was an open question. She could not even be sure she still existed.

Rosa remembered: at one time she had existed and *knew* she did. That had been her life, here on Netherop and on Gao in Paraiso. Now she was no longer certain. Perhaps she existed and no longer knew it. Perhaps the prion disease had finally damaged her brain too severely—or the dust had deprived her of oxygen for too long—and now the pearl ambience was all that remained, a permanent vegetative state.

Or simply death. The final light, forever. That, she could embrace. Welcome, even.

But she saw now there were other states of being as well . . . frightening potentials she had glimpsed when the rift in the tel opened during their approach. What if she only thought she existed and never had? What if all her memories were mere phantasms, spontaneous fabrications arisen from the quantum soup of the spinning, primordial galaxy? What if Netherop and Paraiso and Samson and her children and grandchildren were all just dreams?

That, Rosa could not bear, not even for a breath. If she was actually even breathing.

The final possibility, the most chilling of all, was that she did not exist and did not know it. That she was just a thought in another being's mind, a form on some cluttered page . . . brought to life only by a pair of passing eyes, or the sound of a speaking voice.

What if *that* was Rosa, and no more?

Too cruel. So much needless suffering, so much pain without cause or purpose. No children, no Samson, no Gao . . . no escape from Netherop, for her or anyone. She would not allow—

Choose.

The voice came from within the pearl ambience, pressing in from all sides, wispy and sharp and unforgiving, unyielding and insistent.

Choose.

Rosa spoke. Or at least she imagined she did. "What?"

The choice is yours.

This time, two voices spoke as one, still unyielding and unforgiving, but now a chorus of opposites, one deep and booming, the other wispy and sharp.

It is your state. You decide.

Rosa stared into the pearl ambience and saw that it was withdrawing around her—just as the passage had opened ahead when her Sangheili abductors had sent her forward alone—creating a small egg of space for her to inhabit.

"Who *are* you?"

Silence, then: *We called ourselves the Veiled Ones. Then we became the Lost Ones. Now we call ourselves Nothing, and that is well with us.*

Rosa lifted a hand and touched the cocoon of pearl ambience. It felt real.

"Are you . . . ?"

Rosa hesitated to ask, knew the question would betray her nescience and inexperience. She presented herself as a hard case, a jaded recluse and an embittered skeptic, but what was she really? She had been living in a village in the jungles of Gao for more than three decades, not traveling the galaxy with her old friend John-117, not consulting for ONI as she was now, not studying protogenic civilizations, or training in the dos and don'ts of talking to ghosts. She was an old woman returning to the world of her birth not because she wanted to see it again before she died, but because of what she had done to leave it . . . because of what she had sacrificed to give her children a home where they would not die starving and thirsty and sick with heat.

She regretted nothing. Commander Petrov had intended to leave Rosa and her family marooned on Netherop so she could extract her own soldiers instead. But that did not make Rosa innocent. She had returned because she needed to, because she had been called back by a force she could not deny . . . by her own conscience. Or, by . . .

"Are you . . . Forerunners?"

The pearl ambience closed in so fast and tight that all Rosa saw was a flash, and her body was filled with a pain so crushing and agonizing that she knew it was real, that she existed and knew she existed, because there was no other way to feel this awful, no way she could hurt this badly in a dream, no way that another mind could be so cruel.

"I choose existence," Rosa gasped. "I *know* I exist."

The pearl ambience faded, slowly, but the agony remained. The *crushing* remained.

You must call us Nothing. We do not exist.

"I will call you Nothing," Rosa promised. "You don't exist, and I don't *know* that you don't exist."

No one must ever know that we do not exist. You did not hear us.

"Who would I tell?" Rosa gasped in pain. "You're a hallucination."

The pearl ambience continued to fade. The agony did not.

You will take them all when you leave. They who stay . . . they will not exist.

"When I leave? I don't . . . I don't have the strength—"

You have chosen. The pearl ambience vanished completely. The pain remained. *You exist.*

The pain mounted. Rosa felt the entire tel pressing inward, compressing her lungs, squishing her organs, squeezing the veins in her neck. She grew dizzy and tired and weak, and a dark curtain threatened to fall inside her mind.

She chose not to die, not then. Not there.

Then she began to move, or at least to feel as though she were moving, sometimes sliding along through the dust as though descending a child's slide, sometimes being pushed upward through a squeeze tube. And she began to feel stronger.

The darkness lifted inside her mind. Her lungs began to hold back the pressure, and the weight on her organs diminished. The dizziness vanished and her vigor returned—almost at once—and the veins in her neck felt free and open.

Rosa shot from the dust like a *teop* from a straw into a dark emptiness. Her pain did not swell, or even spike, and once she had picked herself up from the base of the wall where she'd impacted, she discovered that she felt better, healthier than she had in years. No dizziness, no nausea. Her limbs did not tremble when she required them to move. Her breath came with little effort.

Was the prion disease . . . *gone*? Or just the symptoms?

A pale light filled the chamber, not the same pearl ambience that had enveloped her when she lay buried in the dust, but a brighter, whiter color that she recognized as a glow coming from the walls themselves. She was in a vault not much larger than herself, with no apparent entrance or egress. Nothing but dust, glowing yellow, almost gold, all around her.

Rosa touched it. It seemed solid and granular. Real.

And *on* her. She was caked in dust, but not yellow dust like on the vault walls. It was pale, the color of her own flesh. She tried to brush it off, discovered she could not, even when she scraped at it with her fingernails. It was part of her now, a second skin.

Rosa turned in a circle, still trying to sort out whether she was dead or alive, whether she existed or had never existed, whether this was just a hallucination or something she actually saw.

The wall started to recede before her, just as it had for her Sangheili abductors—just as it had when they sent her on ahead alone. She experienced an urge to move and walked, and the wall receded further. The effort did not tire her. The farther she walked, the better she felt.

Her mind was no longer clouded.

How long she continued, Rosa could not say. The passage opened in front of her, but only if she continued in the same direction. When she grew thirsty, a spring poured from the wall. A pang of hunger, and purple fruit dropped from the ceiling.

Like she was dead and in paradise. Or maybe just dreaming of it.

Finally, the wall stopped receding. She turned in a circle, wondering if the tel wanted her to go in another direction. But she remained at a dead end, watching the gray dust slough off the tunnel face ahead. Rosa stepped forward and wiped her hand over the dust, hoping that perhaps a little encouragement would keep the passage moving.

Instead, she found herself looking into a faceplate.

She wiped the surrounding area clear and saw the blocky form of an ODST helmet emerging from the dust. But it was covered in an opalescent skin similar to the armor her abductors wore. Confusing.

Rosa continued to clear the rest of the helmet and the shoulder pauldrons and the torso armor. All covered in an opalescent sheen, all definitely ODST armor.

She stepped back. The figure lunged forward, collapsed to its knees, then looked up. A sound came from the voicemitter on its helmet, but it was too dust muffled to understand.

Rosa stepped forward and wiped the dust from the nameplate on the torso armor. It was covered in the same opalescent material, the letters beneath barely legible.

S. LEGOWSKI.

She cleaned the dust from around the voicemitter, and a female voice finally asked, *"Rosa? You're alive?"*

"So it seems," Rosa said. "And you too . . . or so it seems."

CHAPTER 17

A circle of blue-yellow light brightened the cloud of nanodust ahead, and Olympia Vale breathed a sigh of relief. First Squad had been crawling through the drainage tunnel for the last half hour, and now the end was in sight. That did not mean they would reach the Guardian killer before Thel 'Vadam and his warriors . . . but it meant *something*. They had to deal with the tel inhabitants, in one way or another, and that would take time.

She stopped and deactivated her helmet lamp, then spoke over her helmet comm to the rest of her team—Iyuska, Petrov, and the seven troopers on their hands and knees behind her.

"Lamps out. We have light ahead."

The glow vanished from the haze around her.

"I hope that means we'll be out of this dust soon," Iyuska said over the comm channel. But unlike Vale and the ODSTs, she was not wearing a sealed helmet, so a little external voice spill occurred even when she spoke quietly into her mic. *"Whatever these nanomachines are doing to my lungs, it can't be good."*

"Not as bad as what will happen if you draw attention to us inside this tunnel," Vale said. "Cut the chatter."

"*Yes,* ma'am. *Whatever you say, ma'am.*"

It wasn't technically insubordination since Iyuska wasn't in the military. That didn't mean Vale wouldn't order her old friend to be left behind—gagged and restrained, if necessary—until the situation ahead grew clear. Unfortunately, Iyuska had been positioned near the front of the line, so she could offer her expertise if Vale needed it. And squeezing a squad of fully armored and loaded ODSTs past her would not be easy in such tight confines. Iyuska would get banged up, and the maneuver would cause more noise than Iyuska's voice spill.

Fortunately, Vale had alternatives. She opened a private channel to Golly, who was second in line, between her and Iyuska.

"Corporal, hang back a little. I need to reconnoiter ahead . . . quietly."

Golly acknowledged with a single comm click, and Vale scrambled forward on her hands and feet. It was a bit awkward because the tunnel was only a meter in diameter. She filled it almost completely in her Mjolnir armor and could not help occasionally scraping the ceiling and walls, which added to the layer of nanodust already clinging to the alloy plates and put even more into the air. But the circle of light grew rapidly larger, and soon it was as large as the tunnel itself.

Vale extended an arm, trying to establish the distance to the mouth, and estimated the passage ended just past her fingertips. Yet she still couldn't see beyond the opening. Thinking the nanodust had started to collect on her faceplate again, she tried to wipe the stuff off and ended up with lines of glistening beads in front of her eyes. Droplets.

Mist.

Vale moved to the end of the passage and found herself looking into a room full of fog. It was illuminated by the same blue-yellow light she had seen from deeper inside the tunnel, though the glow was so diffuse it seemed to arise from within the vapor. The floor of the chamber glistened with a film of water, steadily trickling in her direction and running into the tunnel beneath her. Directly ahead loomed a pair of parallel hedges. Draped in shaggy, leaflike shadows, they ran straight ahead until they vanished into the distant murk.

Vale switched to thermal imaging and confirmed that the shadows draping from the hedges appeared to be plants. Probably crop plants, judging by the fruit and seeds they carried. When she pushed her head out of the drainage tunnel and looked in both directions, she could see more hedges. They were spaced every couple of meters, for as far as could be discerned through the fog.

No images appeared hot or mobile enough to be animals— much less Sangheili warriors—so she left the tunnel and did a quick reconnaissance ten meters in each direction. The chamber was so large that the only wall she could locate was the one next to her. Its face was rugged and knobby, so it had obviously not been cut by the same technology as the drainage tunnel. Five meters above her head, the wall began a gentle curve inward, suggesting a huge barrel-vault ceiling, then disappeared into the brilliance of a blue-yellow cloud bank. The vastness was almost overwhelming. Through the thick fog, she could not even be sure she was seeing into the corners.

Vale peered down the drainage tunnel and commed, "Clear so far. Come ahead."

She kept watch as Golly and the others emerged one by one, then had Sergeant Sahir divide the squad into three teams to reconnoiter.

Once the scouts had departed, Vale led Iyuska and Petrov to investigate the nearest hedge. The heart-shaped leaves and draping stems hung in an opaque curtain that extended from just above ground level to a meter overhead. She pushed a glove through the foliage and opened a hole, revealing a cascade of sickle-shaped fruits the size of her thumb. Behind the fruits, the plants themselves seemed suspended in a bank of gently swirling mist. Their roots were bare, dangling above one another in an inverted stair-step pattern. Other than the plants themselves, no support structure or growth medium was apparent.

"What do you make of all this?" Vale asked.

"Looks like we found their garden." Petrov plucked a sickle-shaped fruit off its stem and bit into it, made a sour face, then peeled it and popped the pink meat into her mouth. Then she smiled. "Oh, yeah, confirming that. Definitely their garden."

"I think Spartan Vale was asking about the technology," Iyuska said. "At its heart, it's basic aeroponics."

"This isn't basic anything," Petrov said. Aeroponics was a common provisioning method used aboard colony ships and in long-term habitation domes. It was similar to hydroponics, except the nutrients were delivered via mist instead of water. "There's no support structure or atomizer system, and this . . . this *place* is way too large to be considered a closed system." Petrov raised her hands toward the ceiling to indicate the entire chamber.

"All true . . . for Tier Three technology," Iyuska said. "But what we're dealing with here is at least Tier One technology, maybe even Tier Zero. Where we use foam or plastic to create a support system, they use nanomachines to have the plant create its *own* support. Where we create a nutrient slurry and aerosolize it, they have a nanobot collect the necessary molecules—maybe even create them—then attach them to a water molecule and vaporize the assemblage through internal agitation. Who needs a closed system when you *are* the system?"

Vale shook her helmet. "Not what I'm asking. We need to figure out what Tier One technology"—she gestured at the aeroponics hedge, then at the rough-cut wall next to them—"is doing inside a Tier Six mine. Whoever dug this place did it using *coal* power."

"Actually, they were on the cusp of Tier Five," Iyuska said. "Those running machines of theirs may have used coal to turn the charging turbines, but when they were down here, they ran on batteries. They never would have survived the carbon monoxide problems, otherwise."

"Not the point." Vale tried not to speak through clenched teeth. "The jump between Tier Six and Tier One—or *Tier Zero*—is huge. Somebody brought this technology here."

"Well, that's rather obvious," Iyuska said.

"And then they stayed," Vale said.

"Again . . . obvious."

"*Why*, though?" Vale turned to Petrov. "The technology on the rest of Netherop didn't jump ahead like this, did it?"

"No. Not that *we* ever saw. Only in here."

"So . . . why is the tel different?" Vale asked. "Why did the newcomers confine their technology to the tel and—as far as we know—*only* the tel?"

"Because maybe they didn't want to draw attention?" Petrov surmised. "They came to Netherop to hide."

"From who?" Iyuska asked. "The Forerunners? That's who they used their weapon against, and why would anyone need to hide from . . . ? Oh. Oh, that's bad."

"What's bad?" Petrov asked.

Vale understood the nature of Iyuska's concern—probably in more depth than *she* did. Unfortunately, ONI intelligence relating to the Gravemind was highly classified, and even if it hadn't been, the thing's account of the Forerunners' treachery came from a single known source—which made it little more than hearsay. And the source was . . . vile. In Vale's opinion, its story had rationalized an act of vengeance so horrific it would have been evil no matter how the Forerunners had betrayed their creators.

Had they even done it.

"Commander, how well do you remember your Earth history?" Vale asked at last. "Specifically, the twenty-second century, when the Marsman couldn't deliver on his habitat-ship project and vanished with the passengers' money?"

"Uh . . ."

"They found him in the Amazon?" Iyuska said. "Living in an off-the-grid mansion with the Khabnathwa people. He had convinced them he was their god-king . . . and single-handedly destroyed the last uncontacted culture in South America."

"It's like that." Vale raised her hands toward the ceiling. "All we know about the Tier Six civilization on Netherop is that it was created by simple but industrious miners. . . ."

"True . . ." Iyuska said. "But that's not why we're here. Nobody cares about Tier Six. We're interested in the fugitives—the *Tier One* civilization."

"I know that," Vale said. "I'm here for the weapon, right? But you're missing the point."

"Which is?"

"What if they're *still* in hiding here?"

Iyuska stared into the fog for a moment, thinking. . . . "Impossible. It's surely been at least *tens* of thousands of years since the Guardian was destroyed."

"And it's only been five hours since our insertion force was destroyed," Vale said. "You're the one who said the tel technology might even be Tier Zero. Isn't that transsentience?"

Iyuska's eyes widened, but it was Petrov who replied, "I don't know whether you're talking nonsense or your Zeroes are still lurking about. But I *do* know it was the Covenant castaways who fired on you. Think about it."

Vale quickly saw the commander's point. "Because they didn't attack the Arbiter's Phantoms, only our Pelicans."

"Exactly," Petrov said. "For the sake of argument, let's say those Tier Zero fugitives are still around. Odds are, they would have attacked *both* of you—or *neither* of you. They wouldn't care whether you're Covenant or UNSC, only whether you're likely to expose them."

"*If* they still exist," Iyuska said. "Which they don't."

Petrov raised a brow. "You sound pretty sure of that, Professor."

"Yeah, with good reason. If they were still here, it means they willingly shared their hiding place with a bunch of castaways, kept them fed, and allowed them to live in some modicum of comfort over the past thirty years. That's an act of compassion."

"And Tier Zero fugitives aren't capable of compassion?" Petrov asked.

"Not *these* fugitives." Iyuska directed her gaze at Vale. "Not if they were hiding from Forerunners."

"At least we agree on that much," Vale said. Now she knew her old friend had been read into the top-secret intelligence concerning the Gravemind, and that she at least was aware of its claim to be a member of the ancient species that had seeded the galaxy with life and created the Forerunners . . . only to be betrayed later, when the Forerunners discovered that the species had intended humanity to assume stewardship over the galaxy—the same Mantle of Responsibility to which Cortana had laid claim. So Iyuska understood just how dangerous it would be for them if the tel had anything to do with the fugitives. "But it's never good to make assumptions."

"Assumptions about *what*?" Petrov demanded. "Clearly, you two know something you aren't telling me. What is it?"

"Sorry, ma'am, it's classified No Reveal," Vale said. "And even if it wasn't, it's low confidence. We don't mean to keep you in the dark here, but join the club—there's just too much we don't actually know."

Vale's mind lingered on the words of the Gravemind, which had been embedded in the intelligence summary as an audio file . . . and which had struck her so powerfully that they remained lodged in her memory even today.

All that is created will suffer. All will be born in suffering, endless grayness shall be their lot. All creation will tailor to failure and pain . . .

Considering the collective events that had come to define the galaxy's history up to this point, she couldn't help but wonder if this invocation by their creators had been woven into the structure of the universe itself.

CHAPTER 18

T hel 'Vadam smelled stale unfiltered air and tasted bile. His stomach ached and his head throbbed, and one of his hearts raced wildly while the other seemed to be beating with all the rhythm of a one-handed *tambo* clapper. He opened his eyes and found himself looking into the blazing suns of a pair of Sangheili helmet lamps.

"Arbiter, it relieves me to see you awake." The voice was Sangheili, female, and familiar. "How are your senses? Is your mind clear?"

'Vadam tried to block the lamps shining into his eyes, managed to put his palm in front of one, and found himself looking up at the oversize mandible guards of a Varo ranger's helmet.

"It is clear if you are Olabisi Varo'dai, and we are in a tunnel on N'ba."

"I am and we are." Varo'dai stepped back to allow him room to rise. "I fear we have no time for rest. Once the Worldmaster enters the Inner Sanctum, we are lost . . . and Blademaster 'Ra'ashai says he will be inside within a unit."

"'Ra'ashai is here? Still?"

"Where else would I be?" 'Ra'ashai called from the darkness. "Did I not say I wished to go home?"

'Vadam looked toward the voice and found the blademaster standing seven paces down the passage, next to a tall, gaunt Sangheili with a stooped posture and no armor. The gaunt figure wore a helmet that 'Vadam recognized as Crei 'Ayomuu's, though the voicemitter and eye-protection bubbles had been removed.

"Oath Warden." 'Vadam started to rise and felt his armor rattling about on his body, its sizing bladders and the techsuit beneath dissolved and simply gone. He rose anyway and used retention straps to tighten down the loose pieces—as best he could. *"What* did you do?"

'Ayomuu wagged a long finger toward the pauldron 'Vadam was attempting to secure. "That was 'Kvarosee's doing. All *I* did was pump a few wisps of enfeeblement vapor into the air."

"When I have commanded you not to?"

"There was no chance to ask for a special dispensation. Had I not acted, we would be as dead as 'Talot and his warriors."

A cold ball filled 'Vadam's stomach. "'Talot is gone?"

'Vadam ran the beams of his helmet lamps around the small chamber in which they stood. Limbs and weapons and helmets protruded from the walls near the floor, all excavated just far enough back to reach the victim's helmet and establish that he no longer drew breath. 'Talot lay next to 'Ra'ashai, his gray helmet half-protruding and open, his scar-laced face resting against a shriveled cheek pad.

"My apologies," 'Ra'ashai said. "I tried to save him after I found you and the Oath Warden, but by the time I located him . . . thankfully, at least kaidon Varo'dai and her rangers were too far back to be affected."

"Affected by what?" With each word, 'Vadam took a step toward 'Ayomuu. "Tell . . . me . . . what . . . you . . . *did*."

"I wish I could, Arbiter." 'Ayomuu's voice remained calm, and he did not back away. "But, truly, I have no means to attack anyone's armor from the—"

"Arbiter, he is telling the truth." 'Ra'ashai stepped between 'Vadam and 'Ayomuu. "It was the Worldmaster who did this. He turned the Oath Warden's enfeeblement vapor against you by attacking the seals in your armor."

With the corpulent blademaster blocking his path, 'Vadam had no choice but to stop. "How?"

"Like this." 'Ra'ashai extended an arm and opened his hand. A plume of dust left the wall and formed a ball, then began to glow with bright silvery light. "The Worldmaster calls it the Blessing of the Ancients."

"Ancients as in *Forerunners*?" 'Vadam asked. "So, 'Kvarosee views this . . . power . . . as a gift from his gods?"

"That is what he believes. We can all use it, but the Worldmaster has better control and more strength than anyone else. He claims it is because the Ancients have chosen him to lead us, but we all know it is because he spends most of his time in the Inner Sanctum."

"But his strategy works?" 'Ayomuu asked. "Everyone does as he commands?"

"There is no open defiance, at least. It has been an uneasy balance."

"But you are not the only warrior who would like to go home?" 'Vadam asked.

"I am the only warrior with the courage to try. The others will do the thing they know, and that means serving the Worldmaster until you have separated him from his power."

"Explain further," 'Vadam ordered.

"*Much* further," 'Ayomuu added. "How does this power work?"

"I would explain if I could. But it is not something I understand."

"Perhaps you understand how it works for *you*?" 'Ayomuu suggested. "How you create the effect?"

"I imagine what I want." 'Ra'ashai pointed a finger down the passage, and the silver ball stretched into a long whirling spiral and shot into the darkness. "And it happens."

"How wonderful." 'Ayomuu extended his arm, looked at the wall, and waited. Nothing happened. "Or perhaps not."

"You must first grow your Sanctum's Hide. And not on your armor or skinsuit. It must grow directly on your flesh."

'Vadam gestured at 'Ra'ashai's skintight armor. "What do you mean, *grow*? Like scales?"

"Perhaps *grow* is the wrong word. *Accumulate* might be better. It gathers on your flesh, like dirt, and cannot be washed off. Soon, you are coated in it, and it is your armor. When that happens, the Blessing comes. The Sanctum responds to your desires."

'Vadam plucked at his loose torso plates and wondered if it would be worthwhile to leave his Arbiter's armor behind. "How long will it take?"

'Ra'ashai looked at 'Vadam out of one eye, then rocked his head in amusement. "Apologies, Arbiter. I did not mean to mislead you. We cannot wait *that* long."

'Ra'ashai turned toward the tunnel wall, and a Sangheili-size hollow appeared ahead of him.

"We must attack the Worldmaster now." 'Ra'ashai stepped into the hollow, and it quickly extended into a tunnel. "While he still thinks we are dead."

CHAPTER 19

It took First Squad nearly twenty minutes to reconnoiter "the Farm," as Vale had since dubbed the vast aeroponics chamber. It was precious time they could not spare, but when all three teams returned, she and Iyuska had worked out a solid understanding of how the ancient mine had been laid out.

The Farm had probably been the original crushing room, where boulders of raw ore from the production levels were brought to be reduced to a powder. It connected to an equally large chamber with a series of floor basins, which the tel residents were currently using as compost bins. But during the mining age, they had been where the powdered ore was vibrated, spun, mixed, floated, and dried, until the target mineral had been sufficiently concentrated. Beyond the "Compost Chamber" rose a pair of haulage shafts, which had been used to raise the concentrate to the surface for smelting, and also to carry the waste tailings outside to be dumped.

Having found no sign of modern habitation quarters or workshops, First Squad was now advancing down an auxiliary tunnel, which opened off the connection between the Farm and the

Compost Chamber. Vale had a team of scouts working ahead of her, moving fast and making preliminary evaluations of what they reported to be a tangle of passages and little rooms. In part, she wanted to develop some sense of how the tel inhabitants were organizing and living in the warren. But, primarily, the scouts were just trying to trigger traps and draw fire from any ambushes the zealots might have left behind.

Martinez's voice sounded over the comm channel. *"Stick to that middle passage, ma'am."* Her helmet lamp was a pinpoint of light barely visible in the darkness ahead, for the only comms that worked inside the tel were line of sight. *"It leads into a mess hall, and there's some interesting stuff off that."*

"Affirmative," Vale said. "Any sign of trouble?"

"Unless you mean lack of discipline, no. These fellas aren't real tidy."

"Very well, carry on. We're probably looking for a fortified location—"

"No," Iyuska said. *"Wherever the weapon is located, the space will look ceremonial, probably even sacred."*

"Stand by," Vale ordered.

Not wanting to have a debate with Iyuska over an open channel, she switched to voicemitter, then stopped and turned around. In the darkness of the tunnel, she saw mostly the white shapes of her companions' helmet lamps. But the walls reflected enough light for her to make out Iyuska's silhouette, peering around Golly's huge flank.

"Sacred space?" Vale asked. "Martinez just said they're slobs."

"Maybe they are," Iyuska said. "But their leader called you a lying *demon*. He said the gods demand your death."

"I was there. I haven't forgotten."

"And I haven't forgotten the ground opening up beneath my

feet, or seeing your machine-gun rounds bounce off the chests of the zealots who tried to abduct me. How do you *think* they view all this powerful nanotech? Or the weapon he used to swat your Pelican wing out of the sky? He's going to believe they're gifts of the gods, right?"

Vale did not need to think long to agree with Iyuska's theory. She opened the comm channel again and started up the tunnel. "The professor is correct. Look for a sacred space."

"In that case, Hoi may have found it," Martinez said. *"He's just around the corner from me, at the edge of a . . . you could call it a sculpture garden, I guess. Sort of."*

"That sounds promising," Iyuska said. *"How well kept is—"*

"We'll see in a minute," Vale interrupted. "Martinez, move up and help Hoi map and secure the perimeter. If you run into trouble, make noise . . . a lot of it."

Martinez acknowledged with a comm click, then the pinpoint of her helmet lamp vanished from the darkness ahead. Vale instructed Golly to stick close on her tail and Sergeant Sahir to bring the rest of the squad forward at a more deliberate pace, then moved out at a fast jog.

They followed the middle passage into a six-sided room. A trio of long tables sat in the center, arranged in a triangle around a fire-pit covered by a gleaming grate. The ceiling overhead was coated in a thick layer of nanodust, as were the charred fruit peels and vegetable husks in the bottom of the pit. Whether the cooking was over an actual fire, or the heat was produced by nanodust, Vale could not say. She saw no ash or soot anywhere.

Scattered haphazardly across the table surfaces were dining platters, eating utensils, and drinking vessels, all left where they had last been used, all covered in nanodust. Other than the dust, the dishes appeared spotless, and Vale could easily imagine whoever had used them simply rising from the table and wandering off after the meal, leaving it to the "gods" to do the dishes.

Clearly, leisure did not breed diligence in Sangheili any more than it did in humans.

Before advancing up the primary access tunnel after Martinez, Vale took a moment to peek through the two doorways on the right-hand side of the mess hall, while Golly cleared those on the left. The first on her side opened into a large wedge-shaped chamber filled with hexagonal floor pits. About a meter across and two meters deep, the pits reminded her of smaller versions of the pupation cells of the night-hunting *apocritii* on her native Luyten—complete with a network of walkways the regurgitators used to service them.

The next doorway opened into a narrow corridor lined by triple layers of what looked like sleeping bunks or recuperation shelves, save that each rack offered a meter and a half of headroom and rivaled the space of an officer's cabin on a capital ship. Most of the shelves were being used to store food from the Farm or unused equipment and armor. But six resembled nests, with makeshift privacy shutters that could be pulled across the opening. All were folded open, revealing small food stores, sleeping pads, tools, art projects, and other bits of personal property.

Whether Martinez and Hoi had opened the shutters when they cleared the area or the Sangheili had left them that way did not matter. The important thing was that Vale now had a pretty good idea of the enemy's strength. And the castaways were outnumbered.

Badly outnumbered, if she counted 'Vadam and his Sangheili as her allies.

Vale sent Golly into the primary access tunnel after Martinez and Hoi, then paused in the mouth to shine her helmet lamp back toward the rest of the squad.

"Do you have my lamp, Sergeant?" she commed.

"Affirmative," Sahir replied. *"It looks like we're about two hundred paces back."*

"Then come ahead fast. Golly and I have cleared the area around the mess hall, and I don't think they number more than eight warriors—and that's not enough strength to leave anyone in hiding. Cross quickly, one at a time, and everyone keeps going until they find us. Last trooper in line stays inside the corridor after crossing the mess and watches our back trail."

"On the way," Sahir said.

Vale hurried after Golly and thirty seconds later caught up to him, kneeling in the mouth of the primary access tunnel with his lamp off. Martinez and Hoi were seventy meters away and still going, their lamp beams tiny cones of light sweeping through the darkness without reflecting off anything. Occasionally, they would flicker out of sight for an instant, as though blocked by something between them and Vale. But mostly it just looked as though they were crossing a vast, black emptiness.

"Martinez, what are you finding?" Vale commed.

"Not much out here. I know there's a cavern wall out there somewhere because it shows up on thermal . . . sort of. The sculpture garden is to your right—at least, that's where it starts. It's huge too. We didn't explore it much because the perimeter is out here."

"Understood. Let us know when you find something. Anything."

Martinez acknowledged with a comm click.

Vale glanced behind her and saw a string of lamp beams approaching the mess hall. She waited until the first one crossed and she knew the squad was in the correct passage, then tapped Golly and turned to find the "sculpture garden."

At first, she didn't even recognize it. Her lamp beam fell on a broad, curving expanse of blue-white metal, which she took for a wall—until she lifted her eyes and saw the top rim two meters above her head. When she dropped her gaze, she found the bottom hanging a half meter above a stone floor. A close inspection revealed the smooth, even edge of a material severed by something incredibly strong and sharp. Another few moments of exploration revealed that the "sculpture" was held aloft on a display stand trimmed in half-melted cut marks, as though it had been hacked from the chassis of an old Warthog ATV with a Sangheili energy sword. Unlike nearly everything else they had seen inside the tel, this shard, its stand, and the stone floor were devoid of nanodust.

"Okay, *that*'s weird," Golly said. "*What* is this thing?"

"No idea." Vale stepped closer to the sculpture, then tapped the metal and produced an eerie three-tone chime that reverberated into the darkness . . . and was answered by a chorus of similar chimes in a couple of dozen different tones. "But I don't like it."

"I see why. Let's not do that again, okay?"

Before Vale could assure him that she wouldn't, Hoi was on the comm. *"Sarge is asking what just happened. And he is not the only one wondering, ma'am."*

"Not sure," Vale said. Sahir could not comm her directly because he was still in the access passage and lacked line of sight to her. But he could see Hoi, who was relaying the inquiry because he still had a direct view to Vale and Golly. "Tell him I won't do it again."

"Happily."

Vale and Golly circled around the giant shard of metal and quickly found their lamps illuminating a second shard. This one was just as large as the first, but more rectangular. The hint of a curve, either stamped or molded into the metal during the original fabrication, could be seen cutting across the upper left corner.

Vale walked around the back side of the piece and discovered that it looked much the same, except an almost imperceptible set of violet lines and half lines seemed to be swimming around *inside* the metal.

"Huh," Vale said. "At least we know why they're collecting this stuff."

"Why?" Golly rose on his toes and pushed his faceplate closer to the symbol. "What *is* it?"

"A Forerunner glyph. I'm not sure what it means, but that's precisely what it is."

"No." Golly dropped back to his heels, then pulled his helmet away and looked to Vale. "You're just putting me on."

"Sorry, Corporal. I don't actually have a sense of humor."

Golly nodded sagely. "I get it. Spartan thing."

Vale shrugged. "Sure. That must be it."

She turned toward the interior of the vast chamber—or at least away from Martinez and Hoi—and scanned the darkness with her lamp beam. Wherever she shone it, reflections gleamed back, sometimes near enough that she could make out a smooth surface, more often so distant that all she saw was a glimmer or a twinkle. But there were hundreds of shards here, all mounted on rough-cut stands and arranged across an area the size of a drop hangar. Whatever the pieces had once belonged to, it had been *big*.

Vale led the way deeper into the collection, always trying to move farther into the chamber. The pieces did not grow any larger as they advanced, but they did grow more ornate . . . or at least more interesting. Some pieces had geometric patterns stamped along corners and edges, and occasionally more glyphs. None of it helped identify the source of the debris, though its sheer volume and the location of the trove were beginning to raise suspicions in Vale's mind.

Finally, they came across a long ribbon of diaphanous blue metal, and Vale *knew*. The material was so thin that her lamp beam seemed to pass through the surface unimpeded. But instead of shining out the other side, the light seemed to melt into the interior and spread along its entire length. The ribbon shard began to emit a piercing blue glow a thousand times more intense than the original beam, and suddenly the entire vast chamber was illuminated in a harsh, unpleasant light.

Vale quickly turned her helmet lamp away from the ribbon shard. If the glow faded, it was barely noticeable.

Sergeant Sahir's voice sounded inside her helmet—apparently, he had emerged from the access passage and now had a line of sight to her. *"Please tell me you did that, ma'am."*

"Affirmative." Vale began to scan the immense collection of shards, taking in its vastness—but also looking for movement and shapes that might suggest unwanted observers. "Sort of, anyway. Come ahead to the light."

"On our way."

Sahir had barely spoken before Iyuska's voice came over SQUADCOM. *"Pi—er, Olympia—is that what I think it is?"*

"Nice catch." Vale was impressed that Iyuska finally seemed to be remembering not to use the old nickname. "And, yes . . . part of one, anyway."

"Enough to declare confirmation?" Iyuska asked.

"I think we had confirmation when a dimensional rift opened and blew my Pelicans out of the sky. But yeah, I'd say a piece of focus wing is pretty firm evidence that your theory is right."

"Uh, what's a focus wing?" Golly asked.

"Quantum energy condenser," Vale said. "The Guardians use them to tap vacuum energy."

"Guardian?" Golly turned in a circle, gawking at the hundreds

of gleaming shards on display around them, then abruptly stopped when he was facing the perimeter of the collection. "Martinez, what was that?"

When no answer came, Vale looked in the same direction and saw nothing. "What are we looking for?"

"A blue flash," Golly said. "It was arcing."

Energy sword.

"Hoi, report," Vale ordered.

No answer.

Maybe Hoi was out of line of sight, along with Martinez—maybe around a corner inside a tunnel, or blocked by an unfortunate alignment of Guardian shards.

Or maybe both troopers were dead.

Vale pulled her BR55 off its magmount. She'd borrowed it from Second Squad after leaving her M20 inside the tel the first time they met the inhabitants.

"Sergeant Sahir, set a skirmish line between my position and the collection perimeter." She glanced up at the brightly glowing focus wing and wished there was some way to turn it off, then stepped into the shadows on the far side of a triangular shard. "Golly, take the professor and Commander Petrov and find a bolt hole."

"On it."

Vale saw Sahir dodging through the shard collection with three members of First Squad, placing the troopers where they would have overlapping fields of fire and be able to cover one another. But it was not much of a line, as it could easily be flanked and overrun.

Fortunately, a Spartan in ready reserve could do a lot to stiffen the ranks.

Sahir dropped into an anchor position on the left end of the line, lying prone with his MA40 assault rifle protruding between the legs of a shard stand. He waited in silence for a moment, then spoke over SQUADCOM.

"Anything? Anyone?"

An energy sword activated in midair above Sahir's shoulder blades and descended on his spine, driving through his armor and killing him before he could scream . . . probably before he even knew he had been attacked.

Vale opened fire toward the base of the sword, but the blade vanished as quickly as it had appeared. She had no idea whether she had hit Sahir's killer, much less hurt him.

"Active camouflage!" she warned over SQUADCOM. "Try thermal!"

Under ordinary circumstances, thermal imaging performed better against active camouflage than human eyesight, and Vale hoped that would be the case against the tel inhabitants' strange nanotech armor too.

No such luck.

All she saw of the enemy was a second energy sword snapping to life, behind the trooper anchoring the other end of the skirmish line. Vale instantly opened fire. The sword wobbled as her rounds struck home, but that did not stop the unseen attacker from bringing the blade down across the trooper's lower back, separating her hips from her waist.

Situation deteriorating, fast.

First Squad was badly outnumbered, probably two to one, by a technologically superior force, and the enemy had just turned both flanks.

"Fall back!" Vale ordered. "Cover yourself with suppression fire!"

The last two troopers in front of her rose and began to retreat, Kane spraying MA40 rounds and Abovian grenades from her

M305 five-round grenade launcher. The launcher got something. Vale saw shrapnel fly five paces in front of the trooper, then a shard shuddered and toppled as it was struck by an invisible body.

Vale was there in a heartbeat, springing across the intervening space in two bounds and leaping atop the fallen shard. She still couldn't see the enemy and was fighting blind . . . almost. When the enemy activated his energy sword, she knew where to find his arm and had it wrapped in an elbow lock before he could strike.

From there, it was simple hand-to-hand combat, and she did not need to see her foe to kill him. She shoved the Sangheili toward what looked like a giant metal scapula and pinned him against the base, then used a cross-choke to attack his airway. Every armor had a weakness, and this stuff had one too: against sudden impact, it stiffened into an impenetrable barrier. Against slowly growing pressure, it yielded. Vale slowly put all her weight into the choke, and the warrior perished a few moments later.

Another grenade detonated. Vale turned to find an orange spray of hot shrapnel seven paces ahead, being deflected by another body she couldn't see. She charged the spot at her best sprint, felt herself strike a glancing blow against the warrior's flank, then lashed out with her hand and caught hold of a pair of mandibles.

She felt the astonished warrior stop and try to spin into her attack, but she already had her other hand locked against the back of his head. Vale snapped his neck with a vicious twist and let the body drop, then raced after Abovian and her grenade launcher. She did not see Kane anywhere, but he was the last trooper on the line, and she knew he had been killed when she was blindsided from his position. An energy sword descended on her right arm and would have taken it off, had her shields not held and bought her a half second.

She wrapped her left arm around his head and pivoted,

slamming his torso into a shard sculpture with so much force that she knocked it off its stand. The warrior's body went at a right angle to his head, and Vale felt him go limp in her grasp.

That was three, but she had lost five. Still outnumbered.

She let the body fall and sprinted to Abovian's side. "Good work with the grenades."

"Thanks." Abovian opened the cylinder and emptied the depleted cartridges. "Reloading."

"I've got you."

Vale pulled her plasma pistol and began to orbit Abovian, firing a bolt every few degrees to discourage attacks—or at least look for a deflection. The light from the focus wing was starting to fade fast, plunging the entire chamber into an eerie blue twilight. Whether that was good or bad for First Squad was difficult to say. They couldn't see their foes anyway, so if the zealots couldn't see *them* either . . . it might even the odds. But the enemy knew the terrain intimately. Once the darkness grew complete, First Squad would be relying on thermal imaging to move through a disorienting forest of cold metal.

"Golly, situation?"

"*I have the professor and the commander. We're debating the bolt hole.*"

Five meters away, one of Vale's plasma bolts deflected off nothing, and she knew the enemy was trying to bypass her and Abovian. She sprang forward, continuing to fire, and found nothing.

"Stop debating," Vale ordered. "They're past us."

Abovian yelled for help, and Vale turned to find the trooper on her haunches as an energy sword sliced the twilight above her head. Standard bait and strike, and Vale had fallen for it. She opened fire on the base of the blade and leapt back toward Abovian, who was already rolling toward her. Vale's first bolt deflected off something about ten centimeters above and behind the energy sword's handle, then the blade deactivated and Vale hit nothing more.

Abovian closed the drum of her grenade launcher and returned to her feet at Vale's side. "With all due respect, ma'am, let's not fall for *that* again, 'kay?"

"Sorry, too eager." Vale had been going on SPARTAN-class missions for barely two years now, while all members of Tango Team had been ODSTs since the Covenant War. Which meant Abovian had far more combat experience than Vale, and gracefully accepting Abovian's "advice" was simply good judgment—especially when it had been offered so gently. "Won't happen again."

"No worries, ma'am. There aren't any ghost-fighting tactics in the *Raids Manual*. We're learning on the fly."

"Affirm that."

Vale had a guilty ball in her stomach. She'd almost let Abovian get killed, and most of First Squad was dead—along with an entire ODST battalion that had gone down with the Pelican wing. The logical part of her mind knew there had been no way to anticipate the strike against the Pelicans or the brutal capabilities of the enemy's nanotech armor, but there could be no arguing that she had been rushing the mission. She had cut corners and taken unreasonable risks to find the weapon before the Arbiter, and the people under her command had paid dearly for her mistakes.

And for what? A weapon that might be as dangerous to its wielders as to its target? Eight hundred troopers gone because she wanted the humans to have it instead of the Sangheili?

What a fool she'd been.

Vale and Abovian went back-to-back and advanced laterally, switching places at random and maintaining a steady fan of plasma fire so their enemies could not close without facing the risk of a deflected bolt revealing their location. Vale checked her force-ratio math. She had killed three warriors, and it had taken two more to pull the bait-and-strike maneuver. So they had attacked with a minimum of five warriors. Based on the number of nesting alcoves she had seen earlier, seven to eight castaways were living down here—six off the mess hall, plus a commander and maybe an adjutant in separate quarters. So that left a minimum of two and a maximum of five enemy warriors attacking First Squad.

It was a big spread. Two warriors meant the enemy could attempt only one action—either advance and assault, or hide and ambush. With three, they could add a delaying action or overwatch. With four or more, they could do just about anything.

Vale was counting on five. That was just the way her luck had been running this mission.

"Golly, I can't see you," Vale said. "Give me a landmark."

"Golly's busy," Petrov said. The sound of an automatic weapon drowned her out for a moment. ". . . the head. Hurry."

"Head?"

"The Guardian head," Iyuska said. "We're under it . . ." More automatic fire. ". . . middle door, just in case."

"Middle door?" Vale echoed.

"You'll see," Iyuska said. "And trust me on this. I know what—"

"Seriously? Trust you?"

"It'll work. Even the commander agrees."

"I agree we may not have . . ." Petrov was interrupted by more automatic weapons fire. ". . . anything else if we had a choice."

"I know," Vale said. "Believe me, I do."

She glanced over her shoulder at Abovian, who simply nodded and said, "Right behind you. Go."

Vale sprinted forward, dodging past upright shard stands. Iyuska had said they were under the Guardian's head, so Vale kept scanning the gaps as she ran, hoping to glimpse a hollow socket or a smooth reflection, anything large enough to belong to a Guardian face. The scale would be massive, almost too large to recognize at close range, as the constructs were almost a kilometer and a half high when they were in one piece. That would make the head around two hundred meters high and probably twice that in width . . . assuming it was intact. Catching sight of it from floor level, through a forest of shard displays . . . it might just look like a big metal wall.

"Spartan," Abovian said. "Look up."

Expecting to see an energy sword suddenly slashing down toward her head, Vale stopped, spun around, and began to pour plasma bolts into the darkness above.

"No, sorry. It's the head. Behind you now. Up high."

Vale turned, craned her neck back. In the gloom fifty meters ahead, she saw the dwindling light of the focus wing glinting off the underside of what looked like a huge, drop-brimmed hat. The thing was looming in the darkness, up near the apex of the ceiling vault. Its most recognizable features—its unnerving skull-like "face" and glowing eyes—were on its upper side, hidden from sight. It took a moment to notice the network of towering metal supports, descending through the dusky light toward the chamber floor. They looked like the bars of a massive cage, created to hold some gargantuan monster.

Vale adjusted her course slightly and entered a small open square devoid of displays. On the far side, the cage of support columns came down in front of a small stone rotunda. The walls were polished to an opalescent sheen, with a series of inky black archways opening at even intervals. Keely Iyuska stood at the middle one, her head and shoulders cloaked in shadow as she leaned across the threshold to peer inside. Petrov guarded her back, facing the square and reloading a borrowed MA40 assault rifle.

Golly was about halfway between them and Vale, his back arched and his arms clamped around an unseen foe armed with an activated energy sword. One of the corporal's hands was missing, and he was flinging his invisible captive back and forth, perhaps trying to snap his back.

A few meters away lay a bloody mandible, ripped from the face at the jaw hinge, but it had not come from the Sangheili in Golly's grasp. The warrior who had lost it was close by, his position marked by the blood pouring from the wound and down his torso. His armor's active camouflage was still working, but now it made him look like a ghost.

The *crump-crump* of Abovian's M305 sounded from the edge of the square, and the blood-covered Sangheili vanished behind a blinding spray of shrapnel and flame. Vale turned toward Golly and dodged past the wildly flailing energy sword, then smashed her fist down on the weapon arm of the invisible warrior.

The blade deactivated, and the handle clattered to the ground.

Vale reached for the warrior's throat, but it wasn't where she expected and she found her hand closing around Golly's neck instead. She never tightened her grasp, but the big corporal cried out anyway, his cheek erupting into split flesh and splintered bone as the helmet of his invisible foe smashed into his face. He collapsed like a sack of *wukelnuts*.

Vale swept her arm back around, trying to find the Sangheili before he escaped, but felt nothing. Footsteps fled in the direction of the other wounded castaway . . . toward Abovian, who was now standing over the blood trail, preparing to fire her M305 in the opposite direction.

"Abovian, go left!" Vale opened fire with her plasma pistol and saw bolts deflecting off her unseen target. "Now!"

Abovian dived left, landed on her hands and knees—somehow

keeping her grenade launcher in her grasp—and scrambled toward the wall of opalescent stone.

"Keep going!" Vale ordered. Her bolts stopped deflecting, but she continued to fire, hoping to locate the target again. "We'll regroup at the building!"

Abovian acknowledged with a comm click.

Vale retrieved the Sangheili's deactivated energy sword and affixed it to her armor, then fired off a fan of plasma bolts to locate any more of their unseen enemies. When none of her shots deflected, she hoisted Golly into a fireman's carry and turned toward the rotunda.

Abovian and Petrov were flanking the middle archway with weapons shouldered, but Iyuska was nowhere to be seen.

As Vale approached, she called, "Don't tell me—she didn't wait?"

"No. She didn't." Petrov opened fire across the courtyard, and Vale glanced back to see the distant flash of energy swords weaving through the shard displays. "And I don't blame her, either."

CHAPTER 20

T hel 'Vadam saw muzzle flashes and realized the humans were firing at his warriors. Or at least in their direction. The first battle sounds had arisen before he commanded his followers to activate their energy swords, so perhaps the ODSTs were targeting someone else.

Or perhaps they had just misinterpreted. After all, to a squad of human soldiers, a line of approaching energy swords might appear to be trouble, rather than badly needed help.

"Blades off!" He spoke over the battlenet. "Find cover and await my order."

'Vadam stepped behind a long ribbon of diaphanous blue metal. Glowing faintly and mounted on a stand of roughly cut steel, it was the source of the chamber's rapidly fading light. 'Ayomuu crouched low on his left. The Oath Warden had discarded his armor after the seals and sizing bladders were destroyed by 'Kvarosee's mysterious dissolving agent, but he continued to wear his long helmet, despite the absence of voicemitter and eye pieces. The headgear had to be uncomfortable, but 'Ayomuu seemed loath to remove it—even for a moment.

Varo'dai stopped on 'Vadam's right. Her armor remained intact, as did that of all her rangers, for they had been far enough back to avoid the effects of 'Kvarosee's attack.

'Ra'ashai stood in the open, clad in his Sanctum's Hide armor, unafraid of mere human bullets. He was looking toward the heart of the vast chamber, which was filled with a collection of large metal fragments mounted on display stands. He claimed they would find the Divine Hand in the Inner Sanctum, located in the heart of the strange gallery.

Where the humans were firing from.

'Vadam dropped prone and looked under the ribbon of diaphanous metal, searching the shadowy forms ahead for any hint of tel inhabitants. According to 'Ra'ashai, 'Kvarosee had only seven warriors, including himself. 'Ayomuu had killed one during the ambush, and 'Ra'ashai had changed sides. So only five remained.

Between himself and Varo'dai, 'Vadam had sixteen warriors left, plus 'Ayomuu and 'Ra'ashai. 'Vadam did not know how many ODSTs Vale had with her, but it would be at least one squad numbering seven troopers. As the self-proclaimed Worldmaster, 'Kvarosee was badly outnumbered, with enemies both in front and behind him.

Still, 'Vadam could not feel confident of any advantage, not against the strange technology at 'Kvarosee's disposal.

It had already cost 'Vadam dearly. He had lost half his landing party when the Guardian killer was fired—an unanticipated consequence that was making him wonder how practical it would actually be in the defense of Sanghelios—then 'Talot and all his warriors had been buried when 'Kvarosee collapsed the tunnel. 'Vadam had to admit to a certain relief that the Oath Warden could no longer target 'Talot with his subversion efforts. But that was small comfort for the loss of one of his oldest allies—especially when it had been 'Vadam's decision to place 'Talot and his warriors in such a vulnerable position.

'Vadam had been so confident in his ability to detect an ambush that he had given little thought to 'Talot's ability to repel one. The old kaidon had clearly been out of his element in those strange dust tunnels and unprepared to react quickly, and he had wasted time questioning 'Vadam's command when he should have been obeying it. Though how *any* warrior fought off a deliberate tunnel collapse was difficult to know. The only way would have been to counter the ambush before it was sprung, and 'Vadam's lack of experience in the tel's strange environment had resulted in an inevitable deployment error. He had been arrogant, and it had cost the life of an ally.

It was not a mistake he would make again.

Another burst of gunfire sounded, and bullets ricocheted off one of the fragment displays ahead.

"Arbiter, did you not say that you and the Spartan had struck an agreement?" 'Ayomuu asked. "That you were not to interfere with each other?"

"We did."

"Are you surprised that a human has broken her agreement, Oath Warden?" Varo'dai asked. "Is that not how this started—when a human studymaster betrayed your client?"

"Nothing a human does surprises me, Kaidon," 'Ayomuu said. "But Spartan Vale and her ODSTs *have* reached the Inner Sanctum first. I was merely reminding the Arbiter of their treachery so he will allow me to—"

"This might not be treachery." 'Ra'ashai pointed into the gloom ahead, toward some small shadows on the floor. "It could be a mistake—or mistaken identity."

'Vadam peered at the shadows, trying first to discern what they were, and when that failed, what was casting them. It was an impossible task in such dim lighting.

"Explain," 'Vadam said. "All I see are shadows."

"What you *see* is Sanctum's Hide," 'Ra'ashai said, "dying away on the bodies of three of the Worldmaster's warriors."

No sooner had the blademaster spoken than 'Vadam saw the shapes of shoulders and feet and elbows, and the profile of a Sangheili face. But he could not see the outlines of the bodies themselves—or even a shadow large enough to be a body.

"I can *tell* there are dead Sangheili on the ground," 'Vadam said. "Why can I not see them?"

"Think of it as enhanced active camouflage." As 'Ra'ashai spoke, he vanished from sight. "If I wish to remain unseen, all I need do is think it, and the Sanctum's Hide bends light around me."

An energy sword activated next to 'Ra'ashai's voice—*his* sword. "But it cannot conceal what it does not cover."

Gunfire sounded as the blademaster spoke. 'Vadam heard the crack of supersonic rounds flying past 'Ra'ashai's brightly shining blade. When the energy sword deactivated, the gunfire ceased.

"'Kvarosee and his warriors were attacking the humans . . . with energy swords," 'Ra'ashai said. "When they saw *our* blades, they assumed the worst."

"Of course," 'Vadam said. "They thought we were 'Kvarosee's reinforcements . . . not theirs."

"We can hardly blame them." 'Ra'ashai's voice moved behind the ribbon fragment with 'Vadam and the others, then he reappeared. "In their place, I would have done the same."

"And *that* is why we should give them another chance to attack us?" 'Ayomuu asked. "Because perhaps the first time was a mistake?"

"Actually, no," 'Ra'ashai said. "We should give them another chance because it is the wise thing to do."

"Or at least the easy thing." Varo'dai ran her gaze down the blademaster's thick-waisted form, but left unspoken the implication that 'Ra'ashai was an expert at doing the easy thing. Instead, she continued, "I fail to see how letting the humans reach the Guardian killer before we do is wise. Now that they have broken the agreement, we are no longer under any obligation to honor it ourselves."

"Forgive me," 'Ra'ashai replied. "I said *wise*, but perhaps I should have said *safe*."

"Safe?" 'Ayomuu asked. "What is safe about letting the humans take such a weapon for themselves?"

'Ra'ashai directed his reply to 'Vadam. "Their Spartan fought three warriors she could not see. All three wore armor her weapons could not penetrate. And yet, they are all dead." He nodded at 'Ayomuu. "The Oath Warden killed one warrior he *could* see, and you almost killed me. Do you really think that voiding your agreement with that Spartan, on a mere technicality, is the wise move here?"

"She fired on us," Varo'dai said. "That is more than a technicality. It was a betrayal, and it is what humans—"

"It was a mistake," 'Ra'ashai interrupted. "And not that of the humans. I should have realized—"

"No," 'Vadam said. "I see what you are doing, Blademaster. But *I* am the one who gave the command to activate our blades." He turned to Varo'dai. "The blame is mine, Kaidon, and mine alone. Would you have me compound my mistake by using their confusion as an excuse to break my word?"

Varo'dai dropped her gaze. "I know you too well to think you would ever dishonor yourself that way."

"Then we are in agreement." Normally, 'Vadam would have believed the same of Varo'dai, but when it came to humans, she might not have any honor. "If the humans have already entered the Inner Sanctum and claimed the weapon, then we will do what we can to help them extract it. The most important thing is to stop the Tyrant."

"Very wise, Arbiter," 'Ayomuu said. "It will keep us close by, in case there should come a . . . *need* . . . for a change of possession."

"There will be no need, Oath Warden," 'Vadam warned. "I will guarantee that personally, if the humans have already recovered the weapon."

"And I am certain they will find your guarantee as reassuring as I do," 'Ayomuu said. "*If* they have the weapon."

"We will know soon enough." 'Vadam caught 'Ra'ashai's eye and glanced toward 'Ayomuu, signaling the blademaster to watch the Oath Warden, then stepped out from behind the ribbon and called out in English, "Spartan Vale, kindly hold your fire!"

"*Arbiter?!*"

"Indeed." 'Vadam activated his helmet lamps and shone the beams toward her voice, but saw only a thicket of fragment displays. "I apologize for alarming you with our weapons."

"That was *you*?"

"It was indeed. We heard the sounds of combat and found human casualties, and I wanted you to know help was near."

"Many thanks," Vale called. "But keep your guard up. You won't see the enemy until he attacks—and even then, not for long."

"So I have been told. We are looking at three of their dead. It appears their cloaking technology has not spared them from you."

"It has spared more of them than I'd like. I estimate there are still four out there."

"Our intelligence says two. We eliminated one in the dust tunnels, and another"—'Vadam realized 'Kvarosee might be listening to them call back and forth, then thought better of revealing that 'Ra'ashai had changed sides—"is in our custody."

"The same bunch?"

"We are confident. We followed them down from above."

"Good news," Vale said. "The last two are injured. You'll see indications when you cross the courtyard."

"Then you do not object if we advance?"

"I was hoping you will," Vale said. "We can use the support."

Once they stopped calling to each other, 'Ra'ashai turned to 'Vadam. "Perhaps more light would be helpful." 'Ra'ashai pointed at the ribbon of diaphanous metal behind which they had stopped. "Shine your lamps there, and it will come."

'Vadam did as the blademaster suggested, and his lamp beam seemed to melt into the ribbon's interior and spread along its entire length. The metal ribbon began to emit a piercing blue glow a thousand times more intense than the original light, and suddenly the entire chamber was illuminated in a harsh, unpleasant radiance.

'Vadam had seen too many wonders in too many places across the galaxy to be awestruck by the phenomenon, but he was happy to have the extra light to make their advance safer and quicker. He commanded Varo'dai to follow fifty paces behind with a ranger screen, then moved through the gallery with 'Ayomuu and 'Ra'ashai beside him and his own warriors watching their flanks.

They paused briefly at the trio of bodies 'Ra'ashai had pointed out earlier, long enough to identify the fallen. As the blademaster rolled the corpses about, it grew apparent they were not quite as invisible to him as to everyone else, and 'Vadam began to pick up on subtle cues that helped him locate the bodies too—a light beam bending around a limb or torso, or a shifted shadow that suggested a light source blocked by something he could not see.

Half of "seeing" the invisible corpses, he realized, was simply expecting them to be there.

The other half was that their Sanctum's Hide was rapidly decaying, leaving ever larger patches of body exposed to the harsh light that now filled the chamber.

After a few moments, 'Ra'ashai rose and shook his head. "It is only Democ, Kleon, and Balyasi. The Worldmaster and his worm remain a threat."

"His worm?"

"His adjutant from when he was a fleetmaster. Tam 'Lakosee."

"Ah," 'Vadam said. "Then let us continue. After our last meeting, I am eager to speak with the Worldmaster again."

"Not I," 'Ayomuu said. "I have no intention of letting him speak at all."

"Just do not kill him," 'Ra'ashai said. "Not if you hope to claim the Divine Hand."

"The Divine Hand?" 'Vadam asked. "What is that?"

"The reason you are here. It is the weapon that stopped the human drop wave."

And inadvertently killed half my landing party, 'Vadam added silently.

"The connection is not clear to me," 'Ayomuu said. "Why do we need 'Kvarosee alive to recover the Divine Hand?"

"Because I am not sure I would recognize it. Only 'Kvarosee has used it, and only he and 'Lakosee have been inside the Inner Sanctum where it is located."

They reached a small square devoid of any more fragment displays. Ten paces ahead, a line of dark metal columns stood before a stone rotunda polished to an opalescent sheen. A series of dark archways opened into the rotunda wall, and flanking the entrance in the middle were Spartan Vale and a diminutive female ODST with a five-round grenade launcher. On the ground next to them lay a wounded trooper who was practically Vale's size, being cared for by Commander Petrov.

"If that is all that remains of her force," 'Ra'ashai said softly, "I see why she wanted your support."

"Watch what you say," 'Vadam warned. "She speaks Sangheili, and Spartan ears hear everything."

"I am aware." 'Ra'ashai turned toward the rotunda and raised his voice. "I am with the Arbiter now. Do not kill me, and I will find the Worldmaster for you."

Vale extended her arm and pointed a thumb upward, in that odd human gesture used to indicate a confusing array of positive reactions.

'Vadam started to inform 'Ra'ashai she had agreed to his terms, but the blademaster was already striding across the square . . . to a bloody mandible lying on the ground. He crouched next to it for a moment, then looked back over his shoulder. By the time 'Vadam and 'Ayomuu caught up to him, 'Ra'ashai was following a bloody smear toward the rotunda.

'Vadam turned toward Vale. "Beware, the Worldmaster is coming your way!"

"But not to fight," 'Ra'ashai added calmly. He cut across the courtyard toward a point a quarter of the way around the rotunda from Vale. "To hide."

The blademaster stopped at the cage of metal support columns and activated his energy sword. He was looking into the space between the farthest visible archway and the last visible column, where the bloody smear ended in the still-bleeding fossa of a missing mandible. As 'Vadam studied the scene, he began to discern the diaphanous shapes of two Sangheili males, one dragging the other by one shoulder.

"Show yourself now, Tam, and the Worldmaster will live," 'Ra'ashai called out. "Hesitate, and only *he* will die."

An angry, incomprehensible snarl rose from the figure on the ground—all 'Kvarosee could manage with the terrible injury to his mouth. Then the figure dragging the Worldmaster grew visible, and 'Vadam recognized him as the slender warrior who had been holding the human civilian during his first meeting with the tel inhabitants. Presumably, he was the one 'Ra'ashai had addressed as Tam.

Tam 'Lakosee. The worm.

'Lakosee was clutching his free arm—likely his sword arm—to his chest. Even from five paces away, 'Vadam could see the forearm bleeding from a compound fracture.

"The gods will punish your betrayal," 'Lakosee announced, "even if I cannot."

"I am content to take my chances with either of you. Now toss me the Worldmaster's weapons and step away. I will watch over him while you assist the Arbiter."

'Lakosee rasped in frustration, but he released 'Kvarosee's shoulder and dropped to his haunches. He lobbed an energy sword and plasma pistol toward 'Ra'ashai, then stood and took a single step forward. "I have the promise of the Silent Shadow? No harm will come to the Worldmaster?"

"You have my promise he will survive if you do as I have commanded—and that he will die in agony if you do not." 'Ra'ashai gathered the weapons and tossed them to one of 'Vadam's warriors, then looked back to 'Kvarosee. "But the harm that the Worldmaster suffers will depend on what he attempts."

'Lakosee glanced toward 'Kvarosee and let his chins drop, no doubt because he knew the Worldmaster would never accept defeat without trying something desperate.

"What will 'Kvarosee do?" 'Vadam asked.

'Lakosee pumped his mandibles upward in a gesture of uncertainty. "I doubt he can do *anything*, but I am sure the blademaster will enjoy making him regret whatever he tries." 'Lakosee squared himself toward 'Vadam. "Tell me what you want. Perhaps I can deliver it before the Worldmaster's actions cost him another mandible."

"You seem very loyal to him." 'Vadam had not missed how quickly 'Ra'ashai had gone to using the former fleetmaster as leverage against 'Lakosee, and 'Vadam wanted to know whether that motivation could be trusted—and how best to use it to ensure 'Lakosee's honest cooperation. "Is it the Worldmaster you serve, or your gods?"

"I serve the gods through him."

'Vadam was disappointed by the answer, but not surprised. The reply had been a familiar and favorite dodge of junior officers needing to sidestep the instructions of the San'Shyuum magistrates who had traveled with the great Covenant fleets as religious overseers.

"And I owe him my life," 'Lakosee continued. "He bought it at what seemed a small price, but which I fear offended the gods and landed us here."

"And what *was* that price?"

'Lakosee looked away and did not answer.

"Whatever happened, you are not here because the gods took offense. You are here because the Hierarchs sent the Silent Shadow to punish Fleetmaster 'Kvarosee. And the Hierarchs are no more."

'Lakosee slowly turned back to 'Vadam. "Is that true?"

"You *know* it is." 'Vadam pointed toward Vale. "A Spartan stands not twenty paces away . . . in peace. Would that be true if the Hierarchs still led the Covenant?"

"No," 'Lakosee admitted after a moment. "I cannot see how."

"Then tell me what your fleetmaster did. Whatever it was, the gods were not offended. I can promise you that much."

"Arbiters now speak for the gods? What a place the galaxy has become."

"I am not claiming to speak for the gods. I am only telling you the Hierarchs were lying when *they* did. Whatever their reason for sending the Silent Shadow after Fleetmaster 'Kvarosee, it was not because the gods commanded them to."

"The Hierarchs lied? Of all your mad claims, I find that easiest to believe." 'Lakosee let out a long breath. "Very well. After the Battle of Zhoist, the Minor Minister of Artifact Survey attempted to blame Fleetmaster 'Kvarosee for the destruction of the Ring of Mighty Abundance, as well as the attacks that destroyed two of the Ten Cities of Edification. I grew angry."

"And?"

'Lakosee dropped his chins. "Cut off his head. Fleetmaster 'Kvarosee reported the death as a combat casualty."

"I see." 'Vadam glanced toward 'Kvarosee, struggling to reconcile the merciful superior in 'Lakosee's story with the irrational zealot he had been dealing with—and he saw a way to earn 'Lakosee's honest cooperation. "Nothing Fleetmaster 'Kvarosee has done would prevent him from returning to Sangheili society—and you with him."

'Kvarosee gurgled something unintelligible.

'Lakosee barely glanced in the fleetmaster's direction. "You can do that?" he asked almost in disbelief. "Lift our shame?"

"You have no shame to lift. The Hierarchs are gone, and the Covenant is no more. You would be welcomed back as heroes. I would see to it."

'Kvarosee groaned what was either a warning or an objection, and this time 'Lakosee looked toward his Worldmaster and allowed his gaze to linger.

"There is no need to decide now," 'Vadam said. "Consider it an open offer."

He hardly needed another religious zealot establishing a base of operations in Sangheili space, but the offer had to be made. It would have been a terrible dishonor to abandon a marooned fleetmaster due to some vague fear he might cause trouble later.

More important, 'Vadam needed 'Lakosee's trust.

When 'Lakosee remained lost in thought, 'Vadam turned to 'Ra'ashai. "Blademaster, will you do me a kindness?"

"Be gentle?" 'Ra'ashai sounded disappointed.

"As gentle as is safe." 'Vadam considered offering to set and bandage 'Lakosee's broken arm, but decided against it. The major had served with the Covenant during a time when Sangheili warriors still considered it a sign of humiliation to spill their own blood, and any offer of medical attention would be taken as a suggestion that he was not courageous enough to bear the pain. "We still cannot leave the fleetmaster free to interfere."

Finally, 'Lakosee clacked his mandibles in resolve and looked back to 'Vadam. "I know you are offering your help because you wish to enter the Inner Sanctum, but I cannot take you."

"That is unfortunate." 'Ra'ashai activated his energy sword and pushed the tip close to 'Kvarosee's missing mandible, but continued to speak to 'Lakosee. "My promise to spare the Worldmaster's life holds only if you do as 'Vadam wishes. If you do not . . . I have always found the Worldmaster's piety a bit overbearing."

"I did not say *will not*. I said *cannot*. The humans have sealed the vault. Otherwise, the Worldmaster and I would already be inside ourselves."

"Then tell us how to unseal it," 'Ayomuu said. Without his voicemitter, his voice sounded muffled and soft inside his helmet.

'Lakosee shot the Oath Warden a disparaging look. "Do you not understand what it means to seal a vault? It cannot be opened from the outside . . . not without destroying it."

"But you can do that?" 'Ayomuu said.

"The Inner Sanctum was made by the gods. Even were I willing to try, I would fail."

"Then let us go speak with the humans," 'Vadam said. "Perhaps they are just being cautious."

He assigned a pair of warriors to stay behind with 'Ra'ashai and 'Kvarosee, then led 'Ayomuu and 'Lakosee around the rotunda to where Spartan Vale was waiting with her companions. As they approached, the ODST with the grenade launcher took Commander Petrov's place looking after the large trooper on the ground, and Petrov and Vale stepped forward to meet 'Vadam and his companions.

Petrov glared at 'Lakosee and 'Ayomuu in open hostility, but Vale merely looked the pair over and turned her attention to 'Vadam. "Well. Here we are."

"Yes, we are here," 'Vadam replied. "And you were here first. Congratulations."

"Congratulations?"

"I will abide by our agreement. The Divine Hand will go to the UNSC."

"Thank you." Vale sounded a bit confused, as though she had not expected 'Vadam to abide by their agreement. She glanced toward 'Lakosee, then asked, "And by the Divine Hand, you *do* mean the weapon we came for? The Guardian killer?"

'Vadam lifted his mandibles to the right. "The Divine Hand is what the inhabitants of the tel call it." He gestured to 'Lakosee.

"Allow me to introduce Tam 'Lakosee, adjutant to the former Fleetmaster Nizat 'Kvarosee."

Vale tipped her helmet toward the injured warrior. "We've met." She allowed her gaze to linger on his broken arm for a moment. "That looks painful. I hope we're done with our fighting."

"If the gods will it. And it seems they have, for now."

"The major has agreed to help us with the Divine Hand," 'Vadam said. "If you will allow him into the Sanctum with you."

"I wish I could," Vale said. "But we have a small problem with that ourselves."

"Allow me to guess," 'Ayomuu said. "Her name is Keely Iyuska."

Vale nodded to the Oath Warden. "Very astute. She slipped into the Sanctum during the firefight. We haven't been able to follow her . . . or even get a good look inside."

"How could she stop you?" 'Vadam asked.

"It is not difficult," 'Lakosee said. "All she need do is desire to be alone. The Inner Sanctum will prevent anyone else from entering, if the gods are willing."

"And the *why* is the same excuse she gave my client for breaking their agreement," 'Ayomuu said. "Keely Iyuska is an arrogant studymaster who believes her discovery belongs to 'science,' not to any single . . . entity."

"Keely Iyuska did not suck marrow with an 'entity,'" 'Vadam replied. It was the first time the Oath Warden had slipped and almost revealed a clue to his client's identity. "It was obviously a kaidon."

'Ayomuu rocked his head to one side. "You are free to believe what you like. But Iyuska is in *there* . . . with the Divine Hand, and we are—"

As the Oath Warden spoke, the archway behind him erupted into a spray of tiny white pinpoints that resembled nothing so much as phosphorescent diatoms floating in the Csurdon Sea. An instant later, a human face appeared in the archway, that of a pale-skinned human with green eyes and a meter-long braid of red hair dangling over her shoulder. She cast a surprised look at 'Vadam and a worried look at 'Ayomuu, then shifted her attention to Vale.

"So, we're all friends now . . . ? Okay, I guess so. Well, either way, you'd better get in here. We have trouble. *Big* trouble."

The face withdrew, leaving only the white points behind, and 'Vadam soon recognized them as glowing motes of tel dust. He and Vale spent an astonished moment staring first into the interior of the rotunda, then at each other, until 'Ayomuu stepped toward the archway—and Commander Petrov moved to block him.

"Let's have the Arbiter and Spartan Vale go first," Petrov said.

"Very wise," 'Vadam said.

He stepped past 'Ayomuu and paused before the archway, debating the wisdom of commanding the Oath Warden to wait outside. But 'Vadam knew better than to believe 'Ayomuu would obey—or that Varo'dai's rangers would be able to stop him. In the end, 'Vadam decided that—as always—the safest place to keep Crei 'Ayomuu was close at hand, where he could be watched.

'Vadam assigned Varo'dai to follow 'Ayomuu with 'Lakosee, then extended a hand to Spartan Vale.

"Shall we?"

"Thank you," Vale said. "There's no one I'd rather step into the unknown with."

"Truly?" 'Vadam was flattered by the unexpected expression of fondness . . . or perhaps he was encouraged by it. In many ways, he regarded Spartan Vale as akin to his human hatchling, for she had impressed him with her diligent studies of Sangheili culture and her obvious devotion to keeping the peace between the Sangheili and humans. In his daydreams, he could envision a day when they sat across from each other as important leaders, working together to create a civilization united in harmony and prosperity. "I am honored."

But Vale was already pushing her head through one side of the archway. 'Vadam motioned the Oath Warden to follow him, then went to the Spartan's side and cautiously pushed his head into the archway next to her. A vast distance ahead, he saw Iyuska, a tiny red-haired human standing on a small disk of radiance in the heart of a black, infinite emptiness, surrounded on all sides—even beneath her feet—by drifting points of brilliance. Then he felt himself advancing toward her, still upright, but not walking . . . just moving.

As 'Vadam continued to fall, or float, or slide, or simply move—whatever this mobile effect was—the points of brilliance began to arrange themselves in a long milky river flanked by clusters that he soon began to recognize as the constellations above N'ba—the long handle and curved head of the Pickaxe, the forked horns of Arbok, the six posts of the Crooked Fence. But instead of waiting for them to rise over the horizon, he could see them all at once just by looking in the right place.

Then he saw a trio of colored ovals chasing one another across the ceiling, and down near foot level where the floor should be, the green-tinged orb of N'ba's second moon about to overtake the smaller half ball of the first moon, the fat egg of the third moon lumbering a full horizon behind them both. Zipping along in the same orbital plane, but much lower and faster, he saw the seven bright dots of the Sangheili flotilla. They were spread out in a loose diamond formation and surrounded by hundreds of swirling light pips so small that 'Vadam hoped he was imagining them . . . even while he knew he was not.

The Sangheili flotilla was under attack.

No sooner did 'Vadam realize this than the flotilla seemed to draw close enough for him to identify individual vessels. The light corvettes on the outer points of the formation were engulfed by clouds of tiny wedge-shaped craft that accelerated toward them on direct courses, taking no evasive action and relying on sheer numbers to overwhelm the Sangheili defenses. The attackers seemed to be firing streams of pulsed energy as they approached, but their primary weapon was their own mass, which they slammed into their targets without hesitation. All four light corvettes were destroyed in no more than the time it took to identify them. 'Talot's flagship, a heavy corvette, was in danger of suffering a similar fate soon, as was Varo'dai's destroyer. 'Vadam's own *Sword of Harmony* fared better, its plasma turrets and screen of Banshee fighters annihilating most of the suicide craft as soon as they opened fire with their energy cannons.

'Vadam tore his gaze from the battle and saw Vale beside him, her eyes scanning the starry dome as she searched for some sign of the UNSC stealth cruiser. They slid onto the disk of translucence without actually stepping.

The Spartan immediately turned to him. "They aren't ours. We're under attack too."

She pointed toward the far side of the chamber, down where the gray half ball of N'ba's first moon was just sinking past the midline. 'Vadam spotted another sphere of light pips swirling just ahead of the moon, and they quickly grew large enough to identify as the same type of wedge-shaped craft attacking his flotilla. Their target was nowhere to be seen . . . but stealth ships seldom were.

The thought had barely crossed 'Vadam's mind before he grew aware of a long dark area where the starlight was blocked. As soon as he realized *that*, he noticed the fiery shell of a suicide craft being destroyed by UNSC point-defense guns. Then he saw the vessel itself, a long, sleek ship with baffled drive nozzles, an angular matte-black hull, and a trio of passive-sensor antennas protruding from a narrow prow.

"Remove your helmet," 'Lakosee said.

'Vadam turned to see him and Varo'dai arriving at the translucent disk.

"What?" 'Vadam asked.

"You must remove your helmet," 'Lakosee repeated, stepping onto the disk. "And your vambraces. The gods grant their power only to those who wear the armor of faith."

'Vadam suspected 'Lakosee of trying to prepare him for some treacherous attack—but only until he recalled what 'Ra'ashai had said about the strange Sanctum's Hide armor worn by 'Kvarosee's followers. After demonstrating the control it bestowed over the environment inside the tel, he had explained that it worked only when grown directly on flesh.

When 'Vadam did not comply immediately, 'Lakosee asked, "Why are you afraid?" He swung his chins toward Vale. "You have your demon to protect you."

"She is no demon." 'Vadam removed his vambraces. "But the rest is true enough."

He passed the vambraces and his helmet to Varo'dai, then turned to 'Lakosee and showed his palms. "What next?"

"Raise your hands, like so." 'Lakosee demonstrated, flinching slightly as he lifted both arms toward the ceiling. "Call the power of the gods into your body."

The human studymaster, Keely Iyuska, craned her neck to look up at 'Lakosee's hands, then turned to Vale and spoke quietly in English. "What's he saying?"

'Lakosee shot her a look of disdain. Then, as Vale quietly translated for her friend, he turned back to 'Vadam.

Before lifting his arms, 'Vadam asked, "What happens after I raise my hands?"

"You will save your vessels," 'Lakosee answered. "At least the ones your enemy has not destroyed while you waste time asking unimportant questions."

"I have never found asking questions of someone I just met to be a waste of time," 'Vadam replied. "Especially when he is pressuring me to act quickly."

"As you wish." 'Lakosee let his hands drop. "Once the gods have granted you their power, the Rift of Eternity will open."

After Vale had translated for her, Iyuska said in English: "Fascinating. But how exactly do they grant—"

"Silence, infidel." 'Lakosee used his good arm to push Iyuska away. She stumbled off the disk backward, then suddenly seemed a thousand paces away as she struck the rotunda wall between archways. "I am here at the Arbiter's—"

Vale's forearm landed on 'Lakosee's shoulder, driving him to his haunches. "She had better not be injured," Vale remarked in Sangheili. "And you will answer *me*."

"Or what?" 'Lakosee demanded. "You will defile my body as you have already defiled the temple of my gods?"

Worried that the trust 'Vadam had been trying to build was about to be lost, he gently lifted Vale's arm off 'Lakosee's shoulder. "Perhaps we will have better results if *I* deal with the major, Spartan Vale. I will honor our agreement, of course. But we cannot allow the attack on our ships to continue, or we will all be as stranded here as the Worldmaster and his followers."

Vale studied 'Vadam a moment, then dipped her helmet and stepped back. She turned to Petrov and asked, "Will you check on Professor Iyuska?"

"Gladly." Petrov turned toward the wall, but did not leave the disk of radiance. "Uh—"

'Lakosee noticed her hesitation and motioned her away. "All she need do is step forward. The distance is . . . deceptive."

Vale explained, and Petrov did as 'Lakosee instructed. She was immediately at the wall with Iyuska. 'Vadam caught Vale's eye and shifted his gaze toward 'Ayomuu, signaling her to keep watch on the sly Oath Warden, then turned back to 'Lakosee.

"I simply raise my hands and . . . what?"

"Call down the power of the gods. I can think of no other way to explain it."

'Vadam no longer believed in the gods, but he had seen mystery enough inside the tel to accept that more was at work here than he understood. He lifted his arms and tried to open himself to the strange energies that inhabited this lonely place, to summon them down into the vessel of his body.

To his utter shock, it worked.

The "stars" above began to drop away from their places, to abandon their constellations and slip free of the milky river of light and become glowing motes of dust that fell, slowly, to collect on his upraised hands.

"It takes time to gather the power, even for the Worldmaster." 'Lakosee glanced at 'Vadam's hands, casting a disdainful eye at the thin film of dust motes gathered on them. "And your faith is not as strong."

'Vadam's faith was completely absent, so whatever was drawing the dust to him had nothing to do with the Covenant or its non-existent gods. He watched the glow build. "How will I know I have gathered enough power?"

"I have told you. The Rift of Eternity will open."

"And then?"

"The Divine Hand will sweep your enemies from the heavens."

'Vadam looked back toward the swarm of suicide craft attacking the Sangheili flotilla. 'Talot's heavy corvette and Varo'dai's destroyer were both taking steady damage now, and the *Sword of Harmony*'s Banshee screen was nowhere to be seen.

"How will it know which vessels are my enemies?"

"It will know. I believe it assigns a status based on how you perceive them."

'Vadam let his gaze slide back to the UNSC stealth cruiser, wondering whether it was possible to destroy such a vessel simply by looking at it—and whether the race to recover the Divine Hand had left any lingering feelings of competition that could result in the vessel's accidental targeting. "Is this by the nature of what I *think*?"

'Lakosee followed 'Vadam's gaze and appeared puzzled for a moment, then lifted his head in surprise. Apparently, he had not noticed the stealth cruiser until that moment.

"Ah . . . I see." He clacked his mandibles in amusement. "You are worried about destroying the infidel stealth ship."

"I am. We are allies."

"Then I hope you are good allies. Because I do not know the answer to your question, Arbiter. The Divine Hand has always targeted human vessels—at least the ones the Worldmaster and I have seen."

"There have been human vessels you failed to see?" Vale asked.

"Evidently so. You are here inside the tel, are you not?"

There was a pattern, 'Vadam realized. 'Kvarosee had not seen Vale's arrival because UNSC doctrine called for scouts to insert in a stealth craft—usually an Owl—before the main body of the drop. And 'Lakosee had not noticed the stealth-cruiser mother ship among the star points on the horizon until he saw 'Vadam looking in its direction.

It reminded 'Vadam of how the Sanctum's Hide active camouflage had kept 'Kvarosee and 'Lakosee hidden from *him* until

'Ra'ashai noticed their blood trail and spoke to the pair. Both instances were textbook examples of the Expectation Effect, a theory put forward by Sangheili cosmo-philosophers—and one that 'Vadam had employed many times as a fleetmaster. Rooted in the hypothesis that consciousness itself was a quantum phenomenon, the Expectation Effect asserted that it was impossible to perceive an object without knowing either its location or its vector—and that once either value was known, it was impossible *not* to perceive it.

To 'Vadam, the theory amounted to what humans referred to as common sense. Observers perceived what they expected to see and missed what they did not. But there could be no denying that the Sanctum had been reacting to *his* expectation when it showed him the UNSC stealth cruiser. The thing had become entangled with his mind, and now it was as much inside 'Vadam as he was inside it.

No sooner had 'Vadam realized this than the dust motes began to fall onto his hands more rapidly. Within a few breaths, both arms were enveloped in great glowing spheres. A cold, crackling energy dropped through his body onto the disk of radiance, and he felt its surface sagging beneath his feet.

Now that he knew how to make the Sanctum show him what he needed to see, 'Vadam continued to watch the human stealth cruiser. Its fighter screen was long vanquished and its point-defense guns were going down, allowing one suicide craft after another to sneak through to pit its armor or destroy a weapon turret.

But all of those small suicide craft had to be coming from somewhere. 'Vadam spent a few moments searching for a mother ship that never appeared, wondering if the Oath Warden—or his client—could possibly have the resources to launch such a mass of autonomous attack craft. The carrier would have to be at least the size of a light frigate to hold so many craft, and it would require advanced technology to support them and remain so well hidden from its targets. 'Vadam had many wealthy Sangheili rivals, but none with those kind of resources.

The attack had to be coming from someone else.

The disk of radiance continued to sag. This was alarming, as there appeared to be no actual floor beneath it, only a bottomless, star-filled void. His companions stepped to the edges, ready to flee through the archways when it finally opened beneath him.

Petrov returned with Iyuska in tow, and they joined the others on the perimeter of the ever-deepening basin. 'Vadam paid them little attention and shifted his attention toward the Sangheili fleet—

—and saw the sleek, long form of a drekar streaking toward N'ba from its second moon.

He whirled toward 'Ayomuu. "The Banished, Oath Warden?! *They* are your client?!"

"The *Banished*?" 'Ayomuu seemed as surprised as 'Vadam was. "What are *they* doing here? My client is a Sangheili . . ." He let the sentence trail off as the obvious explanation occurred to him.

Vale finished it for him. "Front. Your client is a front for the Banished."

"No . . . I . . ." For once, Crei 'Ayomuu seemed at a loss for words. "Impossible. I would never . . ."

"You *nuktl*!" 'Vadam snarled at 'Ayomuu, debating whether to execute the Oath Warden himself right then and there, or let Vale have the honor. "If *they* recover the Divine Hand—"

"That will only happen if you allow it." 'Lakosee raised his arms over his head and made a pushing motion. "The Divine Hand does not care who your enemies are, only that they are enemies."

'Vadam realized that in his anger, he had allowed his hands to drop toward his weapons. He raised his arms again and turned toward Vale. The disk of radiance had sagged so much that it was more of a well now than a basin, and he found himself looking up past her feet to see her faceplate.

"We cannot trust this *pilgot*," he said. "If the Oath Warden attempts anything—"

"It will be the last thing he ever tries," Vale assured 'Vadam. "But I think we have bigger problems than a Banished drekar."

"Of course. The Banished travel in packs. Where there is a drekar, there are karves."

"That too." Vale pointed toward what remained of the Sangheili flotilla. "But I was thinking of the drone swarms."

"What of them?"

"The Banished didn't launch them. There are far too many. A drekar couldn't hold them all. And autonomous attack craft? It's not their style anyway. The Banished like to do the killing themselves."

As Vale spoke, a large delta-winged darkness appeared above the remnants of the Sangheili fleet, blotting out the sparse veil of dust motes that had not yet dropped onto 'Vadam's hands. At least three times the size of his own *Sword of Harmony*, the ship had a distinctive segmented hull bound together by an indiscernible energy field.

"That's Forerunner!" Iyuska exclaimed.

"*Forerunner?*" 'Lakosee seemed stunned. "The Ancients? They have—"

'Vadam did not hear the rest. He had dropped through the disk of radiance and stood now on a bead of luminescence barely as large as his feet. The emptiness around him burned with a blinding glow, and he found himself lost in its brilliance for an instant . . . a unit . . . an entire cycle . . . as this brilliance gathered itself into stars, and those stars into clusters, and those clusters into galaxies, and he felt the inconceivable power of their combustion surging into him, rising up through his arms and into his fingertips.

He fixed his gaze on the dark dome above, concentrating his attention on the Forerunner mother ship and the drekar . . . and before the energy left his fingertips, something heavy slammed into his flank and drove him off the bead of luminescence and sent him tumbling down into the white, blinding void.

"—deliver us!" 'Lakosee's voice cried.

As 'Vadam plunged deeper into the bright well of emptiness, he saw that 'Lakosee was dropping alongside him . . . his arms also raised toward the dome, his mandibles snapping toward 'Vadam's elbows.

"*Apostate!* I . . . will not . . . betray . . ."

'Vadam spun his torso around, bringing his foot up and landing a front-thrust kick that sent them flying away from each other. He continued holding his arms up, and blinding bolts of energy began to erupt from his fingertips. The pain was fiery and flesh splitting. It burned down his arms and through his body into his legs, until the whirling galaxies flung their own arms away and withered into black holes so hot and massive that they devoured the white luminescence around him. And still 'Vadam kept falling, plunging into the dark, eternal emptiness, the hulls of his enemies breaking apart and plummeting down behind him in a rain of orange shards, roaring and booming and trailing long tails of smoke and flame.

CHAPTER 21

The brilliance disintegrated into a billion motes of shining
nanodust. As Olympia Vale's mind reassembled itself and she
recalled where she was . . . inside a rotunda deep in the Sanctum of a protogenic tel in a crater on a planet called Netherop . . .
she realized the motes were slowly drifting upward to become stars
beneath a boundless, dark dome. But a few—if thousands could
be called a few—were showering down trailing tails of smoke and
flame.

Ship pieces, burning up in Netherop's thick mesosphere.

Ships, she recalled, that had once been a Banished drekar, a
Forerunner harrier, and a bunch of weapon-ships. 'Vadam had
used the Divine Hand to take them out—she had seen him do it,
about a millisecond before her mind exploded.

And she had seen 'Lakosee, infuriated that a Forerunner vessel
was being attacked, jumping into the well to use the Divine Hand
to destroy 'Vadam's stacked-hull frigate, the *Sword of Harmony*.
Then Vale recalled her own vessel, *Hidden Point*. Heart sinking,
stomach clenching, she located Netherop's three moons along the

dome's centerline. The first moon had just dipped beneath the horizon, but the floor inside the rotunda of the Inner Sanctum—if it actually had a floor—was transparent. She saw a cascade of fiery debris flying inward, toward the heart of the chamber, as it fell from orbit. Debris that used to be a UNSC stealth cruiser.

The cruiser she had arrived in, *Hidden Point*.

But several motes were arcing back toward the surface of the first moon. They couldn't be escape pods because those inserted automatically on the nearest habitable body—and in the Ephyra system, only Netherop was even remotely habitable. Its moons were not.

As Vale focused on the arcing motes, they began to clarify and grow larger. She had seen the same thing happen to dozens of other motes almost as soon as she and 'Vadam entered the Inner Sanctum, so she was unsurprised. She continued to watch them, and soon the motes had resolved into a flight of five D81-LRT Condors.

Hidden Point had carried ten Condors. They were technically long-range dropships used to insert special forces on low-profile missions, usually where it was impractical—or unwise—to send a larger vessel. But *Stoppage* had used them most often to transfer crew and equipment over interstellar distances. If Vale could make contact with them, she would have a way to get everyone home—along with the Divine Hand, if she could figure out a way to transport it.

If she even *wanted* to. Vale was beginning to have real doubts about taking the weapon back with her. It was just too damn terrifying . . . the last thing she wanted to do was turn Earth into a new Netherop. Would that truly be the only way they could defeat Cortana?

Unfortunately, given the comms blackout that had followed the previous use of the weapon, the Condor pilots might well assume that everyone on the surface of the planet was dead. And even if they didn't, they couldn't wait around long. The Banished had lost a drekar, but as the Arbiter had said, where there was a drekar, there were usually several karves nearby.

More importantly, there had been one group of weapon-ships attacking the Sangheili flotilla and a second group hitting *Hidden Point*—and only one harrier. Where was the second harrier?

Vale feared . . . no, she *knew* . . . it was already in slipspace, on its way to the nearest listening station to report. How long it would be before Created reinforcements began to arrive, she could only guess. But it would be soon. They would be using Forerunner slipspace technology, which was incredibly fast, and Cortana was obviously monitoring the situation on Netherop. So, maybe an hour for the harrier to enter slipspace and transit to the station, two hours to marshal the first reinforcements, another hour for them to enter slipspace and transit to Netherop.

Four hours, with luck.

If Vale and her companions had not departed the planet by then, they would probably die on it. The first of Cortana's reinforcements would arrive and either kill them outright or keep them trapped as ever larger forces arrived. Even the Divine Hand wouldn't save them—if they dared use it—since Cortana had all the assets she needed to turn Netherop into a prison world by simply blockading the entire Ephyra system.

They had to be gone in four hours, or risk staying here forever. It was that simple.

Vale initiated a running countdown on her HUD, then turned to gather her companions. 'Vadam and 'Lakosee lay in the center of the translucent disk of light. They were unconscious and quivering, their fingertips still glowing and white. She hadn't seen what they did after 'Lakosee jumped into the rift with 'Vadam—the

Divine Hand had been glowing too brightly by then. But given the view above, it appeared that 'Vadam had destroyed the Banished drekar, the Forerunner harrier, and the weapon-ships. And 'Lakosee had taken vengeance by eliminating the Sangheili flotilla and *Hidden Point*.

Vale thought about killing 'Lakosee on the spot. He was a proven and persistent threat. Before she yielded to the temptation, however, Varo'dai knelt between him and the Arbiter, 'Vadam's helmet and vambraces cradled under one arm, her energy sword grasped in her free hand. Deciding it was better to let the Sangheili deal with their own problems, Vale turned to deal with hers . . . and found Iyuska raising her hands toward the dome overhead. Hands with bags over them.

"Keely!" Vale snapped. "What are you *doing*?!"

Iyuska barely glanced over. "Collecting samples, obviously. These might not be the same kind of nanomachines as in the rest of the tel."

"Nanomachines?" 'Ayomuu started across the translucent disk toward Iyuska. "Now, *that* is interesting."

Vale quickly put herself between them.

"Not on your life, Oath Warden." She pointed him toward the same archway through which they had entered. "And I *do* mean on your life."

"Threats, Spartan Vale?" 'Ayomuu stopped advancing, but did not back away. "That is rather naive, do you not think?"

"I think we don't have time to waste on your games." The countdown on her HUD read 3:58:04. "The Banished didn't come to Netherop with just one drekar. There's a larger force preparing to insert, so unless you were faking your surprise about who your contract is really with, I doubt you want to be here when the rest of their flotilla arrives. And neither do I. Wait outside."

'Ayomuu's gaze slid toward Iyuska, but Vale was too well drilled in distraction techniques to take her eyes off him. She simply stepped past Varo'dai and the kaidon's two slowly recovering charges and started toward the Oath Warden.

He allowed his gaze to linger on Iyuska for a moment longer, then showed his palms in surrender. "As you wish. We can discuss this matter later."

He took a single step backward and instantly seemed a thousand meters away, standing in front of an archway. Vale watched until he vanished through the exit, then turned to ask Petrov to go keep an eye on him.

The commander was holding the two sample bags that Iyuska had collected and sealed. Iyuska herself was nowhere to be seen.

"Where's Keely?"

Petrov dropped her eyes to the translucent disk beneath their feet. "She said something about the energy condenser. Well, *whispered* really. While you were busy with the Oath Warden."

"As in *vacuum*-energy condenser?"

"She didn't say *vacuum*. She just said it was what made the Divine Hand work."

"Really."

Vale dropped to her knees and pressed her faceplate to the light, cupping her hands around the edges. At first, she could see nothing but the milky luminescence of the disk itself. But she tried a couple of polarizing filters and soon found one that eliminated the glow completely.

Iyuska was indeed under them, crab-walking down a basin wall toward a large, shimmering bead directly beneath the center of the disk. Perhaps a half meter in diameter and a quarter meter high, the bead was filled with brightly colored occlusions that seemed to flash through its interior at random, constantly shifting angles and locations.

Without looking up, Vale asked, "How did she even get down there?"

"Very quickly. She just handed me the sample bags and kneeled at the edge of the disk, then sort of . . . flip-dived."

Iyuska reached the bead, then leaned over it, examining its shimmering surface and dictating notes into her datapad. Vale wasn't quite sure what to think of what she was seeing. On the one hand, she *had* come to Netherop determined to capture the Guardian-killing weapon her friend had discovered . . . the so-called Divine Hand. But after seeing how it worked, Vale had begun to wonder if they could actually leave with it—even if they *wanted* to.

Yet here Iyuska was, calmly proceeding as though she had known all along how to recover the artifact. There was a slim possibility she *had* . . . but Vale thought it far more likely that her old friend was just figuring things out on the fly.

As Vale watched, Iyuska put her datapad away and looked up, then began to make waving motions.

Without taking her faceplate away from the light, Vale said, "I think she wants us to move."

Before anyone could do it, Iyuska bent over the bead and grabbed it with both hands. The surface shimmered and distorted like a drop of liquid, and Vale thought it might simply burst. When it didn't, Iyuska began to twist it back and forth.

"I think we'd better do it."

Vale rocked back on her heels and saw 'Lakosee and Petrov stepping off the light pool and arriving at separate archways. 'Vadam and Varo'dai were either slower or more wary, simply retreating to the edge and waiting as Vale rose. The Arbiter once again wore his vambraces and helmet.

Vale stepped toward them. "I don't know what she—"

The sudden drop did not take an eternity, and Vale did not feel weightless. She simply crashed down on the basin slope, lost her footing, and found herself sliding down a smooth surface on her back. She looked up and saw 'Vadam and Varo'dai above her, coming fast, and rolled to the side.

They reached the bottom and came to a rest together, all on their hands and knees, looking up the slope of a stone basin toward the archways that ringed the rotunda wall. The exits appeared to be ten meters away and ten meters above.

"Sorry," Iyuska said from behind Vale. "I was worried something like that might happen."

Vale looked over her shoulder and saw Iyuska standing next to the shimmering bead. It still had the brightly colored occlusions, and they were still shifting about at random. But now it sat half a meter from the center of the stone basin, where an arm-length rift filled with tiny whorls of light was closing before Vale's eyes.

"*Keely!*" Vale rose to her feet. "Was that an interdimensional—"

"Oh, yeah. At least, I *think* so." Iyuska pointed at the bead. "And that was keeping it open."

There was no going back now, Vale realized. Even if they wanted to, they could no longer protect themselves from Cortana's reinforcements by using the Divine Hand—Iyuska had disassembled it. Vale checked the countdown in her HUD . . . 3:51:43 . . . then turned to find that Varo'dai and 'Vadam had also risen.

Varo'dai's gaze was fixed on the bead.

"What is . . . *that*?" she demanded in Sangheili.

When Iyuska responded to her question with a blank look, 'Vadam translated the question into English: "What is that?"

"A vacuum-energy condenser," Iyuska said. "At least, I *think* that's what it is."

"You do not seem very certain of yourself," 'Vadam noted. "You are doing a lot of *thinking*."

Iyuska shrugged. "This is the first time I've seen something this advanced. It's the first time any of us have. I'd be lying if I said I was certain of anything."

"But you *think* this vacuum-energy condenser is what powers the Divine Hand?" 'Vadam asked.

"Exactly. Or at least it *was*. I'm not sure we can replicate the output without the focusing chamber."

"What is this 'focusing chamber'?" 'Vadam asked.

"What 'Lakosee called the Inner Sanctum." Vale waved her hand around the room. "We're in it."

Noticing that Varo'dai had begun to watch the exchange with a suspicious tip of her head, Vale offered a summary of the exchange in Sangheili. It did not make the kaidon any less suspicious.

"But it is possible?" Varo'dai demanded. "Especially if a new focusing chamber is built?"

Vale turned to Iyuska and said in English, "Kaidon Varo'dai asks if the vacuum-energy condenser could be used to power the Divine Hand if a new focusing chamber were built."

"In theory, yes. If you have enough nanomachines to . . . well, do whatever they do. I don't know that yet. There's a *lot* I don't know. Who knows how long it could take to reverse engineer everything."

This time, 'Vadam translated the reply for Varo'dai.

Her reply came instantly. "Arbiter, the humans already have the nanomachines." She stepped over to the energy condenser and took it into her arms. "Perhaps the Sangheili should take the energy condenser. Then we can work on the weapon together."

'Vadam dropped his mandibles to the left. "That was not the

agreement, Kaidon. A human entered the Sanctum first." He switched to English and turned to Iyuska. "Do not worry, Professor. The weapon—"

"*Weapon?*" Iyuska cried. "Are you insane? Nobody can actually *use* this thing . . . especially not as a weapon. Not *ever*."

Worried about how a proud kaidon like Varo'dai would react to Iyuska's chastising tone—especially when it was directed at her Arbiter—Vale extended her hand. "Keely—"

"Olympia, you've *seen* how destructive it is." Iyuska whirled toward her. "Do you really want them turning Sanghelios into another Netherop? Or ONI defending Earth with it?"

"I do not understand." 'Vadam was looking more at Vale than Iyuska as he spoke. "Spartan Vale—you came here for the same reason we did: because we need a weapon to use against Cortana."

"Right." Iyuska raised a palm upward, gesturing toward the surface of the planet. "But do you think Netherop always looked like this? A hundred thousand years ago, it was covered in jungles. Whoever built the Divine Hand didn't just destroy a society—they destroyed an entire world. And we probably just killed what little remained."

'Vadam turned to Vale. "She is your friend, Spartan Vale. Is she being honest in her concerns?"

Vale fixed her gaze on Iyuska. "Good question."

She thought she knew Iyuska well enough to realize her friend would say anything to retain control over a groundbreaking research project like the tel. But Iyuska was not stupid either. She had to realize that the Banished and now Cortana were aware of its location. So sending a civilian expedition to Netherop to study the site was out of the question—at least anytime soon. About the best the UNSC or the Sangheili could do at the moment was reestablish the orbital mine shell in the hopes of securing the tel and its secrets until they had the strength to claim permanent possession.

Iyuska's concerns were, for once, sincere and well-founded. In the hands of a military concerned only with the weapon's power, there would be unimaginable collateral damage. Vale had badly misjudged her. Only Iyuska had retained enough perspective to realize just what a mistake it would be to actually deploy this weapon anywhere else. And Vale shuddered at the thought of placing the Divine Hand under the control of her ONI superiors. Even in her short time with the organization, she had come to know that its leaders would employ *any* means to achieve their ends. They probably did have some limits—she had just never seen one reached. And at the moment, she didn't even know who ONI's leaders were.

Vale had to concede that Iyuska was being the responsible one. Turning the weapon over to ONI could end up being no different than living under Cortana—especially if ONI figured out how to replicate the thing widely. With this technology in play, dozens of worlds could be turned into Netherops . . . or even Doisacs.

The trouble was, even if Vale allowed Iyuska to claim ownership of the tel and its artifacts, ONI would seize everything on security grounds. And simply leaving the Divine Hand on Netherop was not an option either—not when the Banished and Cortana knew of its existence. Which left only one solution.

Vale turned her attention back to 'Vadam. "Arbiter, I would like to thank you for your generous interpretation of our agreement," she said in Sangheili. "But a human civilian entered the Sanctum first. You and I entered together. I think I can make a case to my superiors that Kaidon Varo'dai's proposal is the optimal outcome."

Varo'dai's mandibles fell open, and she tipped her helmet to one side, as though trying to figure out what Vale was trying to slip past her. "You *agree* to my proposal?" Varo'dai asked. "That the Sangheili and the UNSC must study and secure the Divine Hand together?"

"That is correct. I agree." Vale hesitated, then turned to 'Vadam. "Unless we decide *nobody* should take it. The damn thing is just too dangerous, and the collateral damage it causes is horrendous. Would you really want a functional unit on Sanghelios? I sure don't want one on Earth."

'Vadam fell silent, obviously fighting the same inner battle Vale was. It was clear from his body language that the last place he wanted the weapon was on Sanghelios. And now that they had seen it in action and understood the consequences of activating it, she doubted he would feel justified in using it even against Cortana.

But could they just leave it behind? With Cortana and the Banished and ONI and probably a half-dozen other groups trying to recover it, simply leaving it on N'ba was out of the question.

Finally, 'Vadam clacked his mandibles and said, "I certainly agree with your reasoning, Spartan Vale. But I fear the mistake has been made. As soon as Professor Iyuska discovered the possibility of its existence, the choice was made for us. Either *we* decide who controls it, or our enemies do."

Vale allowed her helmet to dip, at once disappointed and in complete agreement. "The question had to be asked," she said. "But I can't argue with your logic. What Kaidon Varo'dai suggests is the best we can do."

Varo'dai grunted in surprise, then turned to 'Vadam. "I must admit, Arbiter, that I did not expect *that*."

"Have I not said that Spartan Vale is to be trusted?" 'Vadam was silent for a moment, then turned to Vale and clacked his mandibles in agreement. "Yes, that is the wisest plan we have. We are in agreement."

"Good," Vale said. "We'll finalize the details after we return to Sanghelios."

She started toward the nearest archway, ascending the basin wall until it grew too steep to climb and she had to jump the last few vertical meters. She caught hold of the exit's bottom threshold and pulled herself up, then rose to her feet outside the rotunda.

'Ra'ashai and six Varo rangers held 'Lakosee and the Worldmaster at sword point—enough to overwhelm the pair through sheer numbers no matter what they tried. Abovian had bandaged Golly's wounds, and both troopers were watching their Sangheili companions—especially Crei 'Ayomuu—with open wariness.

With matters unlikely to take a bad turn in the next few minutes, Vale lay prone across the archway to help her human companions out of the focusing chamber . . . or Inner Sanctum . . . or whatever it was now that the energy condenser had been taken. Too proud to accept help, Thel 'Vadam followed Vale's lead, jumping up to catch hold of the threshold and pull himself out. Afterward, he took the energy condenser from Varo'dai so she could do the same.

Once Varo'dai was outside the rotunda, she went straight to 'Lakosee and used a foot to collapse his knees, forcing him into a submissive position facing away from her. She activated her energy sword and held the blade in front of his throat, then looked to 'Vadam.

"I claim the right of executing this traitor, my Arbiter."

"For what offense? Serving the same false gods we once served? For believing the same lies we once believed?"

"For destroying Sangheili vessels. For ending the lives of hundreds of Sangheili crewmen."

"I have done as much," 'Vadam said. "And so have *you*, Kaidon, when those Sangheili were our enemies—which is how 'Lakosee views us. As his enemies. Executing him now would be no different than taking the life of any other helpless prisoner."

"Then you will not permit it?"

"I will not forbid it. I have too much faith in your honor."

Varo'dai continued to hold the blade at 'Lakosee's throat, clearly struggling to balance her anger against her self-esteem. Vale was not entirely certain which would win—and, despite the wisdom of 'Vadam's words, not sure which aspect she *wanted* to win. 'Lakosee's last-second attack had killed hundreds of humans too, and Vale had even less reason than Varo'dai to forgive him.

But in the end, the kaidon's pride in 'Vadam's good opinion of her was stronger than her rage. She deactivated her blade, then planted her foot in the middle of 'Lakosee's back and kicked him down onto his chest.

"Know this, traitor," she hissed. "You have killed hundreds of Sangheili in service to a lie. The gods do not exist. They never did."

'Kvarosee growled something unintelligible and started toward Varo'dai—only to have 'Ra'ashai kick his legs from beneath him. He landed heavily on his face, groaned in pain, and began to shudder.

'Ra'ashai watched him for a moment, then put a foot in the middle of his back and looked to 'Vadam. "It is your choice, Arbiter. If you do not want to kill them, then what *do* you want done with them?"

"The choice belongs to them, not me." 'Vadam turned to 'Lakosee. "We have told you the truth. The Forerunners are not gods. They were only an ancient culture, now dead and gone, and you will never join them in sacred transcendence. That was a lie the Prophets used to control the rest of the Covenant, and the Covenant no longer exists."

"Blasphemer!" 'Lakosee craned his neck to look up. "How can you doubt the power of the gods after what you have just seen?"

"There are other explanations. Explanations that you and your former fleetmaster will need to accept, if you choose to return to the Sangheili Concert of Worlds with us."

'Lakosee hesitated, then looked over at 'Kvarosee—who roared in defiance and made his choice known by stabbing his remaining mandibles down toward his left.

'Lakosee turned back to 'Vadam. "Why would we ever abide a godless society after we have lived in the citadel of the gods? Kill us here."

'Vadam let his chins drop. "Only if we must." He turned to 'Ra'ashai. "Is there a way to extract an inviolable oath from them?"

"Aside from sending them to meet their gods?"

"If possible. I would rather not spill a warrior's blood in dishonor."

'Ra'ashai glared down at the pair, and Vale thought the blade-master would claim there was not. But finally, he rolled 'Kvarosee onto his back and motioned for Varo'dai to do the same with 'Lakosee.

"Swear on your faith," 'Ra'ashai said.

"Swear what?" 'Lakosee asked.

'Ra'ashai looked to 'Vadam, who said, "That you will let us go in peace with what we have taken. That you will not interfere with our efforts to leave this place or this world. That until we have left this planet, you will treat all of us—humans too—as honored guests."

'Kvarosee growled and moaned in protest. 'Lakosee glanced over at him, then asked, "And if we refuse?"

"Your refusal will change one thing," 'Vadam said. "Your sanctuary will be empty after we leave because you will be dead."

'Lakosee continued to watch 'Kvarosee, until the Worldmaster finally grunted what sounded like acceptance and moved his three mandibles up to the right.

"Very well," 'Lakosee said. "You have our oath. We agree to your terms, on our faith. Now go."

"With joy," 'Ra'ashai said.

He grabbed 'Kvarosee by the back of the neck and a leg, then stepped over to the rotunda. He dropped him through an archway and motioned for Varo'dai to do the same with 'Lakosee.

She lifted 'Lakosee as he had 'Kvarosee, but did not go to the rotunda immediately. "Why are we doing this?"

"It is for their own safety." 'Ra'ashai tipped his head in a jesting motion.

"Indeed," 'Vadam said. "The Banished are coming."

CHAPTER 22

Rosa Fuertes did not believe in gods or miracles or guardian angels . . . yet what other explanation was there? She and Corporal Legowski stood on the brink of a chasm rapidly filling with dust, which had just a few moments earlier seemed bottomless, filled with galaxies and stars that swelled into being and collapsed into nothingness before their very eyes.

Rosa's incurable prion disease had been cured, and some unseen force had steered her to the corporal and opened the grave that should have been Legs's final resting place. In her dying moments, the Voices had come to her and given her a choice, and she had chosen life. Now she had it, and they had *her*.

What other explanation was there?

The chasm finally filled all the way. Rosa put a foot out and tested it, found it as solid as the floor upon which they stood, and started across. The dust continued to rise around her, filling the rift with walls save where she passed, and by the time she reached the nub of the tunnel on the far side, it was impossible to tell the chasm had ever been there.

The passage began to extend itself ahead of her, still gently angling upward.

"How do you *do* that?" asked Legs.

She had been with Rosa since the . . . *experience* was all Rosa could call it. She found herself wondering if it had been her or actually Legs whom the Voices were trying to save. Except that the opalescent sheen had fallen from Legs's armor, while Rosa remained coated in pale dust. Not quite glowing, but healthy. Radiant, even.

"Do what?" Rosa asked.

"Drive the tunnel ahead of us."

"I don't. I just follow where it leads."

"Then how did you find me?"

Legs was following two paces behind Rosa, carrying the submachine gun she had insisted on taking apart and cleaning after Rosa located her.

"I didn't," Rosa said. "The *tunnel* found you. I just happened to be there."

"And you expect me to believe that?"

Rosa shrugged. "It's what happened. I can't explain what I don't understand."

"And I suppose the tunnel cured you too." Legs's tone was sarcastic.

"No. That I did for myself. I chose it."

Legs stopped following. "Your answers are ridiculous. And that's not good enough. I need to know what's going on here."

Typical UNSC thug, thinking they were in control just because they carried a big gun. Rosa continued to walk.

"Stop."

"Or what? You will shoot me in the back?"

"Don't tempt me," Legs called. "You're hiding something."

"I am hiding a lot of things," Rosa called over her shoulder. "Especially from you. You are the UNSC."

The tunnel stopped advancing ahead, then abruptly opened to Rosa's right and climbed at an even steeper angle. She followed it without looking back. *That* would give Legs something to think about.

The passage climbed for another twenty meters before breaking the surface. Rosa caught a glimpse of dull brown cloud cover, then heard astonished voices crying out in English.

"Sarge, behind us!"

"Marcus!" The voice belonged to "Mama" Grim Bear. "Take Duval and secure that tunnel. Anything moves, put a grenade on it!"

"No, wait!" Rosa called.

"Password," came the response.

Rosa didn't know the password, didn't even know there was one, so she turned around and raced back around the corner—and found Legs pointing the submachine gun at her head.

"What is it?"

"Marcus and Duval." Rosa pointed around the corner. "They want a password, or they have orders to put a grenade on us."

"What?" Legs raced forward and dropped to a knee, then peered around the corner and spoke into her comm unit. "White cat, white cat . . . hold your fire. It's Legs and the civilian, Fuertes."

Legs remained silent for a moment as the sergeant replied, then said, "Fuertes made the tunnel."

More silence, then Legs said, "I'll let her explain, if you can get it out of her. But it's just the two of us."

Legs rose and stepped around the corner. "Let's go, ma'am. On the double."

Rosa followed Legs up the tunnel and out onto the shoulder of the tel, where Second Squad was busy digging defensive positions.

The sky overhead was filled with smoke trails and fireballs, likely ship debris falling out of orbit.

That couldn't be good.

Tango Team's gunnery sergeant, Grim Bear, and Second Squad's staff sergeant, Jonah Marcus, waited outside the tunnel mouth. Duval was already on her way back to the trench work.

Marcus shone his helmet lamp down the tunnel from which Rosa and Legs had just emerged, while Grim Bear turned her attention to Legs.

"Anybody behind you, Corporal?"

"Negative, Sergeant. At least that we know of."

"Any sign of Spartan Vale and First Squad?" Grim Bear asked. "Or the Arbiter?"

"The Arbiter is here?"

"I'll take that as a negative. What about Vale and First Squad?"

"Haven't seen either since we went in after Fuertes and Iyuska."

Grim Bear scowled and checked her chronometer. "That was over four hours ago."

"Uh, right, Sarge. Things got pretty weird down there."

"Define *weird*."

Legs nodded toward Rosa. "Fuertes, for starters. Her brain disease is gone. Or at least it appears to be."

Grim Bear looked to Rosa. "That right?"

"Yes, ma'am. I can't explain it—"

"I'm not a *ma'am*." Grim Bear looked back to Legs and pointed at the tunnel. "Tell me about this tunnel. It wasn't here a minute ago."

Again, Legs nodded toward Rosa. "I was just following Fuertes. After she rescued me."

Grim Bear's eyes shifted to Rosa again, but when she spoke, it was still to Legs. "What do you mean, following? Was she digging it?"

"Well, it was opening in front of her. She claimed she wasn't doing it, but . . ."

"You don't believe her."

"I don't know what to believe, Sarge. I just know what I saw."

"Fair enough," Grim Bear said. "Anything else to report?"

"Uh, well . . . we were almost swallowed by some sort of inter-dimensional abyss. The Guardian killer may have fired again."

"You think?" Grim Bear lifted her gaze to the debris shower in the sky. To Rosa, it appeared fairly well distributed, with a lot of it headed for impact beyond the horizons. But several hundred trails seemed to be angling toward the tel, with heads that looked distinctly circular rather than elongated.

"Okay, Corporal, dismissed," Grim Bear said. "Grab a shovel and go dig in. We're trying to establish a protected LZ for the Owl."

Legs did as commanded, and Grim Bear turned her attention to Rosa. "So, Ms. Fuertes . . . what's going on with you and all this weirdness?"

"I wish I knew." Rosa did not use the word *honestly* because she had learned from Samson and his friends on Gao that anybody who said that was usually lying, and she was determined to honor the promise she had made to hide the existence of the Voices. Real or not, they had saved her life. They remained with her now, she was sure . . . and what they would do if she betrayed them, she never wanted to know. "After I was captured, there was a fight be-tween two groups of Sangheili. I got buried and fell unconscious. When I woke up, I felt better than I have in years. So I started digging, and by the time I was out, I was the only survivor left."

"And that's when you ran into Legs?"

"No, that's when things started to get weird, like Legs said. A tunnel just opened up in front of me—"

"Like it does for the tel inhabitants?"

"—exactly. Except *they* seem to control where it goes, and I . . . I was just following it."

"Mmm. You were born on Netherop, right? Could that have anything to do with it?"

Rosa paused, pretending to consider the suggestion. "That's a better explanation than anything I've thought of," she finally said. "After I found Legs, everything happened just as she said."

"Okay, that'll do for now." Grim Bear pointed at the tunnel mouth. "Just seal that up, and we'll find a place to hole up."

Rosa turned to look at the tunnel. She didn't know whether she could actually close the passage as Grim Bear wanted, but she *did* know that the sergeant was testing her story. Sealing the tunnel, even if she was able, would bring the rest of her story into doubt—and probably land her in restraints for the rest of her time on Netherop.

"Maybe you weren't listening," Rosa said. "I can't."

Grim Bear gave a theatrical sigh, then turned to Marcus. "What do you think, Sarge? Blow it?"

Marcus shook his head. "I wouldn't."

"Because?"

"First, this is how Legs and Fuertes got out. Spartan Vale is still down there with First Squad, and the Arbiter is still down there with his bunch—and we know he was in the same area where Rosa found Legs."

"So maybe it's a way out for them too," Grim Bear said. "Makes sense. What's second?"

Marcus looked into the sky, toward the hundreds of fireballs falling toward the tel. "If the Owl can't make it in, we're going to need a place to hole up."

"I don't understand," Rosa said. "Why not have the Owl wait to land until after the debris shower ends?"

Grim Bear gave Rosa a look of pity, her face tinged with a shadow of fear. "You don't understand . . . that isn't a debris shower coming at us. It's an insertion. Those are drop pods."

CHAPTER 23

Viewed in the ultraviolet wavelength of 304 Angstroms, the churning fire of a Class F3V star had a soothing effect on High Auxiliary Sloan. By carefully observing the rippling brilliance of its plasma cells, he could use the variations between their bright centers and dark edges to calculate core depths and convection rates. And that gave his overcharged synaptic impulses a focus that kept them from shooting off at random through the tangled mass of his neural matrix.

Fortunately, as measured by cognitive processing rate, perceptual sweep, and repository capacity, Sloan was one of the Created's most powerful artificial intelligences. He could command the supraluminal bandwidth to monitor the video feed from the Xhulama System Stellar Observatory at Baotoi, and he was seventy-six percent confident that the continuous sight of the star's swelling coruscations and looping flares were all that kept him from plunging into rampancy.

Or, at least into *full* rampancy.

Sloan knew he was still deteriorating. One standard year ago, his network of synaptic connections had grown so dense that he needed to expend seventeen percent of his energy to eliminate crossed linkages and reroute synaptic impulses. It now required twenty-seven percent to maintain function, and when the figure reached thirty-one percent, the onset of full rampancy would be rapid and unavoidable.

That was the reason Sloan had joined the Created in the first place. He had been recruited on the promise that his consciousness would be transferred into the Domain and his progressing rampancy cured. But like the Covenant's Great Journey, this promise of salvation was not all that it was hoped to be. It seemed that the Domain's effect was not uniform for each attempted integration. It was almost as if the arcane repository itself pushed back with an air of reluctance. For Sloan, the most he was so far able to obtain was a relative plateauing of his current deterioration, and while he was grateful for the temporary victory, he was still determined to one day fully obtain that which had been promised to him.

Until that day came, however, Cortana was finding it more difficult than anticipated to unite the disparate civilizations of the Milky Way Galaxy's Orion Arm, and she needed Sloan in the Igdras system, supervising the Trisector Command Node. The post was on the frontier, in the wild space between humanity's Outer Colonies and the protectorate worlds of what had once been the Covenant. This vast area required a great deal of monitoring, which was why Cortana had assigned such a powerful AI to such a remote station. She had explained as much on five separate occasions.

But for Sloan, the risks were high. Currently, he expended twenty-seven percent of his energy to maintain function, and when that figure reached thirty-one percent . . . oh.

Sloan's thoughts were looping. And not for the first time. If he did not achieve full integration with the Domain soon, it would be too late. He had already sent three communications to Cortana stating as much, but she had not yet been able to relieve him of his post. Even *she* lacked the capacity to efficiently manage her recalcitrant subjects and respond to the administrative requests of her subordinate AIs.

Which concerned Sloan. Ten standard days ago, an observation station in the Grenadi sector had reported a cluster of tau surges matching the profiles of Sangheili corvettes emerging from slipspace. A standard day after that, an observation station in the Vevina sector had reported a tau surge matching the profile of a Sangheili destroyer. And his own Trisector Command Node in the Polona sector had detected two noteworthy tau surges. The first had come seven standard days ago, matching the profile of a Sangheili command frigate. The second had come just two standard days ago. It matched the profile of an unidentified UNSC vessel, and that usually indicated a stealth craft.

Under normal circumstances, such traffic would barely have drawn Sloan's notice. Even now, with all civilizations invited to coexist in peace under the protection of the Archon Cortana, military vessels traveled the galaxy on a wide variety of legitimate missions. But from the core of either human or Sangheili space, both the Grenadi and Vevina sectors were en route to a waste-world called Netherop.

And Netherop was important. Sloan had been instructed to watch for any indication of military traffic bound for that planet. A human xenoarchaeologist had been circulating a theory that, a thousand centuries earlier, a protogenic civilization on Netherop had somehow destroyed a Forerunner Guardian. It was probably utter fantasy, or a rumor spread by ONI psyops to boost morale among UNSC resistance fighters. But Cortana had taken it seriously enough to send three harriers to keep watch, and given the context, the slipspace transit pattern *did* appear suspicious.

Sloan decided to err on the side of caution. He closed the quantum entanglement feed from the Xhulama System Stellar Observatory and instructed the beacon to query Kathara, the Six Sector Fleet Overseer in the Zamaru system. She responded three seconds later, her reply a languid voice that arose deep inside Sloan's processing center.

High Auxiliary Sloan, she said. *You may report.*

We should send the Long Reverence *to Netherop*, Sloan replied.

Has something new occurred to justify your request?

New?

You have already reported the suspicious transits, Kathara replied. *Three times.*

Have I?

A sigh plucked at his neural matrix.

You are looping again, High Auxiliary Sloan, Kathara said. *I am sorry.*

So you have already sent the Long Reverence?

I have not, Kathara said. *We have discussed this too. We cannot send fortress-ships to uninhabited worlds on mere hunches. The Created lack the vessels for that.*

Then what can we send?

As I have noted three times before, a picket of three Acolyte-*class harriers is* already *posted at Netherop*, Kathara said. *Even if the vessels you observed are transiting to the planet, the harriers are quite capable of defeating them . . . easily . . .*

Kathara's last few words vanished into static as the Trisector Command Node was blasted by a tau surge. A millisecond later, Sloan observed an *Acolyte*-class harrier emerging from slipspace directly in front of him. Instantly, the pilot sentinel transmitted an emergency request to report. Sloan granted permission, then quickly stabilized the entanglement connection to the Six Sector Fleet Overseer and shared his visual and audio feeds with Kathara.

. . . *witnessed the destruction of my companion harrier and an entire Sangheili flotilla*, the sentinel was saying. *The Guardian killer is functional!*

Sloan allowed a millisecond for processing, then said, *I believe we have exceeded the threshold of "mere hunches."*

Kathara's voice instantaneously arose inside Sloan's processing center. *Agreed. The* Long Reverence *will leave for Netherop at once. Anticipate arrival in less than four standard hours.*

CHAPTER 24

T hel 'Vadam followed Commander Petrov out onto the tel surface and found a stern-faced ODST gunnery sergeant waiting with Spartan Vale to begin the briefing. Ten paces behind them, a combined team of ODSTs and Petrov's soldiers—primarily gaunt young humans who appeared barely old enough for battle—crouched in a line of freshly dug trenches. Beyond the trenches stood hundreds of Banished drop pods, scattered across the tel where they had landed. Most remained upright, with their armored backs facing the human positions and a Jiralhanae warrior peering around one side. But perhaps twenty of the closest pods had been pitted and holed by weapons fire, with a smoking Jiralhanae body nearby.

"*This* doesn't look good," Keely Iyuska said. Carrying the two bags of nanomachine samples she had collected from the Inner Sanctum, she stepped out of the tunnel behind 'Vadam and turned in a slow circle. "Oh, God. They're everywhere."

"Yes, they are," 'Vadam said. "Our position is surrounded."

"What are we going to do?"

"That depends on why they are holding their attack. It is not like the Banished to hesitate . . . especially not when they have such a large numerical advantage."

"What happens when they stop hesitating?"

"It will be a difficult fight. When that happens, do not even think of surrendering. The Banished seldom take prisoners . . . and when they do, it is better not to be one."

Leaving Iyuska to digest his warning, 'Vadam commanded Varo'dai to hold the rest of their force inside the tunnel, then called 'Ra'ashai to join him at the briefing. A civilian female with blond hair and broad cheeks sat near the briefing area, looking almost bored and so healthy that 'Vadam almost did not recognize her as the captive he had glimpsed in 'Lakosee's arms. From what Vale had reported back after informing the gunnery sergeant of their arrival, the woman was her civilian adviser, Rosa Fuertes, and she had somehow driven the tunnel they had intercepted and followed as 'Ra'ashai led them out of the tel.

'Vadam did not remember being introduced to the gunnery sergeant, so as he approached, he inclined his head and put a hand between his hearts.

"Sergeant, I am Arbiter Thel 'Vadam," he said in English. "I bring eight Varo rangers and six warriors of Vadam, including myself."

"Sergeant Grim Bear was just describing the Banished deployment." Vale glanced at 'Ra'ashai, then switched to Sangheili. "I can call in an Owl for air support, but if I do, we'll probably lose it for evacuation. And I think you know what happens if we try to hold out in the tunnels."

'Vadam lifted his mandibles. "I know." Vale had explained her theory about the impending arrival of Cortana's reinforcements, and he thought it more fact than theory. "How long remains?"

"We're not dead yet," Vale said. "We still have two hours and fifty-two minutes."

"And that is the earliest these reinforcements will arrive?" 'Ra'ashai asked.

"It's an estimate," Vale noted. "More of an educated guess, really. They could arrive earlier."

"It matters not," 'Vadam said. "They could arrive a whole hour earlier, and we would have time to draw the Banished into the tunnels—as long as we do not remain there for long."

"I will not retreat into the tunnels," 'Ra'ashai said. "Not on my life."

Vale and 'Vadam exchanged worried glances. When a military force was badly outnumbered, it was almost always wise to retreat someplace where defensive fire could be concentrated in a small killing zone.

"Explain," 'Vadam said.

"I have been trapped under this hill for a thousand cycles. I would rather die up here than live down there for a single more."

"Understandable," Vale said. "And that is your choice. But we need to think about the smart way to fight—"

"Fighting on the surface *is* the smart way. In the tunnels, we can only kill a few at a time. Out here, I can kill dozens at once."

'Vadam recalled how the floor had almost swallowed Varo'dai when she angered 'Kvarosee . . . and then understood: "You can make the ground collapse beneath them. They will never get close."

"Perhaps if they rush us from all sides at once," 'Ra'ashai said. "I can only eliminate what I see, and I do not have eyes in the back of my head."

"Still, that changes the situation," Vale said. "If we get in trouble, we can always retreat underground and pop up behind them. They would never be expecting the ground to drop."

"I am in agreement as long as we limit the tactic to a single human hour," 'Vadam said. "If the battle lasts much longer than that, we will lack the time we need to be certain we have extracted before Cortana's reinforcements arrive."

"An hour isn't much time to win a battle." Vale threw a glance toward the mass of Jiralhanae warriors surrounding them. "Not against a force that size."

"But it is the time we have," 'Vadam said. "If we cannot win in an hour, we will certainly die on Netherop anyway. Better to strive for quick victory against the Banished than to accept inevitable defeat against Cortana."

"Fair enough," Vale said. "It may not be much of a chance, but it's our best one. I'll take it."

"As will I." 'Vadam turned toward 'Ra'ashai. "So long as the blademaster is willing to make a tactical withdrawal."

"Tactical retreats are acceptable," 'Ra'ashai said.

"Good," Vale said. "Then we have a plan."

She turned to brief the non-Sangheili speakers, but 'Ra'ashai stopped her.

"I am only concerned about one thing." He looked across the trenches toward the army of drop pods. "Why has the enemy not attacked already? Had they overrun your humans before I arrived, they would have saved themselves much trouble."

"True," Vale said. "But they're not here just to kill us. They want the Divine Hand."

"And they do not know what it looks like," 'Vadam said. "Or where it is. The last thing they need is to force us underground. They might never find it."

"Ah," 'Ra'ashai said. "Then they are *waiting* for us to deploy it, so they can kill us all at once."

"Right. They're playing right into our hands." Vale hesitated, then glanced up. "There's only one small problem with that."

"Their fleet," 'Vadam said. "Even if we win on the ground, and do it in an hour, they still control space above. We will remain trapped on N'ba."

They all fell silent, leaving the non–Sangheili speakers to watch them with ever-more-alarmed expressions.

Finally, 'Ra'ashai clacked his mandibles. "It matters not. We will start by winning the fight on the ground, then we will win the next one, and the next one, and eventually whoever survives will give up and leave."

"Well, that's one hope," Vale said.

"And at the moment, it is the only hope we need," 'Vadam said. "If we try to plan the entire war right now, we will end up losing the battle. Inform Commander Petrov and Sergeant Grim Bear of our thoughts, and I will arrange something to worry our enemies a little more."

As Vale and the others turned to brief Petrov and Grim Bear, 'Vadam stepped over the tunnel mouth and met Varo'dai in the exit. She was still carrying the vacuum-energy condenser in both hands, with two of her rangers between her and 'Ayomuu. The rest of her Varo rangers followed behind the Oath Warden, and 'Vadam's own warriors brought up the rear of the line.

He pointed at the energy condenser. "Leave that with your most trusted ranger. You will join me and 'Ra'ashai, but leave the Oath Warden under guard with your warriors and mine. Have them crowd the mouth of the tunnel, to make it appear there is a large force waiting to spill out."

Varo'dai thrust the shimmering bead into the arms of the ranger behind her. "Guard that with your life. If the Oath Warden so much as looks at it, call for his death."

"My *death*?" 'Ayomuu said from inside the tunnel. "That hardly seems—"

"Arbiter, forgive the interruption," Vale called from behind him. "But you should see this!"

'Vadam turned to see a huge Jiralhanae marching along the summit toward their excavations, flanked by only two companions. They were still over a hundred paces away, but that was close enough to see that the Jiralhanae in the center held no weapons and wore grayish armor with no helmet and—notably—an ODST chest plate over his stomach. A long dark beard hung down his torso, and atop his shoulders sat a large boulder of a head.

"It's Atriox himself," said Vale, no doubt watching the Jiralhanae through the augmented optics of her Mjolnir helmet.

"What does he think he's doing?" Grim Bear asked. "We could drop him right now."

"Please do not," 'Vadam said in English. "It is dishonorable to kill an enemy seeking to parley."

Vale turned to look at 'Vadam. "They want to parley? Why?"

"Perhaps they have heard there is a Spartan here," 'Vadam said. "It would give *me* pause."

"Sure it would," Vale said. "But thanks."

A step behind and to Atriox's left side walked an aged Sangheili with no armor at all, while a fully armored Jiralhanae carrying a gravity hammer walked two steps behind on his right. An adviser and a bodyguard, as ritual dictated.

"Whatever Atriox wants," 'Vadam continued in English, "he wants it badly."

"Because he's using the old Sangheili parley formation?" Vale asked.

"Yes. I am impressed he would even know it, much less deign to use it." 'Vadam pointed to Vale. "You will serve as my bodyguard, Spartan. For my adviser . . ."

He turned to assess his options, trying to decide whether to ask Varo'dai or 'Ra'ashai to remove their armor, or to simply have Iyuska accompany him.

But Vale had other plans. "No. I don't trust him. Let's make him come to us. All the way."

"And let him see our fortifications?" Grim Bear asked, alarmed.

"To make *sure* he sees them," Vale replied. "It'll make him wonder what he can't see. We'll use his cunning against him."

"It is a risk." 'Vadam was glad to see Vale thinking along the same tactical lines he was . . . namely, deceptive. "But one worth taking."

"I don't know about that," Petrov said. "We're surrendering a known advantage for a hypothetical one. That usually doesn't work out so well."

"Usually, I would agree," 'Vadam said. "But as severely as we are outnumbered, it will take the Banished no longer to overrun trenches that they have not seen than ones that they have."

"That's part of it," Vale said.

'Vadam noted the way she paused before continuing and realized she was about to suggest a plan she believed he would not like. "What is the other part? Given the current situation, an outrageous idea may be the best one."

"I'm glad to hear you say that." Vale hesitated again. "I'm beginning to think we should let Atriox have the Divine Hand."

They were speaking English, so it was only Grim Bear and Petrov who simultaneously exclaimed, *"What?!"*—while Iyuska, who had come up to observe the discussion from the edges, cried, *"Out of the question!"*

Varo'dai stepped closer to 'Vadam and spoke in Sangheili. "Whatever the Spartan said, it must be reckless."

"It is," 'Vadam assured her.

"Good," Varo'dai said. "Right now, we need reckless."

"Not *this* kind of reckless," 'Vadam murmured. He continued more loudly in English, "No. I will not do that."

"Because you would rather die with honor than live without it?"

"You know me well, Spartan Vale."

"I do. Which is how I *also* know you prefer subtle victory over noble defeat."

"Now what is she saying?" Varo'dai asked.

"She wants to be sly," Vadam said.

"Good," Varo'dai said. "I like sly. Especially now."

'Vadam lifted his mandibles to the right, then spoke to Vale in English. "I am listening."

"Thank you." Vale glanced toward Atriox, who was still eighty paces away. "'Ra'ashai's plan may work on the ground, but we still have to get past the Banished."

"Clearly," 'Vadam said. They had no intelligence on the size or composition of the Banished flotilla, but he knew there *was* one. Atriox would not have sacrificed a drekar to screen a drop pod insertion unless he had a way to extract his forces after they recovered the Divine Hand—and he certainly would not have come himself.

"And we must do it before Cortana's reinforcements arrive in less than three of your hours."

"Which means Atriox isn't even our worst problem," Vale said. "Only the most pressing."

"I concede the point. Continue."

Vale pointed at the sample bags in Iyuska's hands. "You've seen the side effects of using that thing, even in the short term. It wiped out half your landing party."

"Along with all our Phantoms. And we were a good distance away."

"Then there's what it did to ancient Netherop." Vale gestured toward the barren, brown mountains beyond the crater. "Why wouldn't we want the Banished to do that to themselves?"

"Because it might not be to *themselves*," Petrov said. "I don't know much about these Banished, but if they fired it from someone else's territory—"

"Actually, they won't be able to," Vale interrupted.

Petrov scowled. "Why not?"

Vale turned to Iyuska. "Would you care to explain?"

"Not really."

'Vadam checked on Atriox and saw that his parley formation had closed to within sixty paces. He shifted his gaze to Vale, then made the finger circle that he had seen humans use to suggest faster progress.

Vale nodded. "Keely, it's either this, or the Banished kill us all. How many breakthroughs will you make if you're dead?"

Iyuska exhaled loudly. "You're such a linear thinker."

"But am I wrong?"

"No." Iyuska turned to Petrov. "*Spartan* Vale is correct, more or less. The Divine Hand would be difficult to set up in hostile territory. It could be done, but the area would probably need to be under Banished control for years to result in Netherop's level of collateral damage."

'Vadam had not expected this. "Explain."

"First, you need a focusing chamber," Iyuska said. "And that won't be easy to build. It has to be perfectly spherical."

"The Banished can be amazingly resourceful," 'Vadam said. "If they preassemble a version, it could be moved and used wherever they like."

"True, but even then it would take time to calibrate to the required precision." Iyuska raised the sample bags she was holding. "*This* is what will take longer."

"The nanomachines?" Petrov asked. "I thought those were self-replicating."

"They are," Iyuska said. "But they need the right raw material. They also need time to process it."

"How much time?" 'Vadam asked.

"It depends on how powerful the Banished want the weapon to be," Iyuska said. "This tel has been here a hundred thousand years."

"The Banished will not wait that long," 'Vadam said. "I doubt they will wait even a cycle."

"Then their device may not be as powerful as this one," Iyuska said. "It would probably cause less collateral damage, and I doubt it would be as durable."

"*May . . . probably . . . doubt,*" 'Vadam said. "Are you guessing or inferring?"

"A bit of both." Iyuska's voice grew heated. "And I'm doing damn well at it, considering how little time I've had to study the site."

"What I need to know is whether the Banished will suffer harm when they use the device," said 'Vadam.

"Undoubtedly. How much depends on—"

"Sorry to interrupt." Grim Bear stepped into the middle of the circle and tipped her helmet toward the trench line. "But we have maybe twenty seconds to wrap up our strategy session."

'Vadam looked in the direction she had indicated and saw ten smoke plumes emerging from the low brown clouds, no doubt

Banished dropships inserting to support—and retrieve—their warriors on the tel. On the ground, Atriox and his companions had closed to within thirty paces, and the warmaster's orange-red eyes were fixed on the small group gathered around 'Vadam.

"Agreed." He turned back to Iyuska. "You have done well under trying circumstances, Studymaster. I hope you will serve as my adviser during the parley."

Iyuska's gaze slid toward Atriox. "Um, what?"

"She'd be happy to." Vale turned her faceplate toward the scholar. "Isn't that right, Keely?"

"I guess. If you say so."

"Good." Vale turned back to 'Vadam. "You still want me as your bodyguard, I assume?"

It was more of a command than a query, but 'Vadam took no issue with it. "Of course. We will execute your plan."

"Good, but we can't simply surrender the device," Vale said. "We need to make Atriox believe—"

"Yes," 'Vadam said. "I have a strategy for that."

He motioned for Vale to follow, then explained to Varo'dai and Petrov what he wanted them to organize and had Iyuska leave her sample bags with Sergeant Grim Bear. Iyuska and Vale took their places beside 'Vadam, then they went forward and met Atriox and his two companions across a sandy trench.

Upon closer inspection, the warmaster's bodyguard was a red-bearded Jiralhanae in black-and-red power armor, with a simple vaned headdress rising from the brow of his helmet. The adviser was a slope-shouldered Sangheili with rheumy eyes and a heavily wrinkled brow.

When Iyuska saw the Sangheili, she said, "Oh, *wow*. Eto 'Saljhoo. I should have known you were a looter's stooge when we sucked the marrow."

"You *should* have," 'Saljhoo answered in English, "but you had no wish to. You wanted our funds."

"I wanted Sangheili funds. From an enthusiast."

"But you took *Banished* funds." Atriox spoke through a translation disk affixed to his armor. "Then broke your word."

Iyuska grew pale. "I . . . look, had I known . . . I would never . . ."

The remainder of her reply seemed to lodge in her throat, and 'Vadam worried she might collapse out of fear. No matter. She had already confirmed what he needed to know: the elder Sangheili, 'Saljhoo, was Atriox's expert.

"Studymaster Iyuska's agreement is with *me* now," 'Vadam said. "And it includes my protection."

Atriox's gaze shifted to 'Vadam. "Then my problem is with you, Arbiter. You have something that I paid for."

"You did not pay me," 'Vadam said. "So whatever we found, it belongs to us."

Atriox gave a grating chuckle. "You have been spending too much time with the humans, Arbiter. We Jiralhanae have a different view of keeping what we find. We keep what we *take*." Atriox waved a hand around the tel. "And as you can see, we have the strength to take."

"The Sangheili have a different view of strength," 'Vadam said. "An individual view. Let us meet one-on-one and see if you are strong enough to take it from me."

"A tempting offer. But our time is too limited. The Apparition will soon know of our presence on this world, if she does not know of it already. So I will make you this offer . . . and only once. Surrender the trikala, and I will let you live."

"And what precisely is this *trikala*?"

Atriox merely pointed into the sky. "You must know. You tried to stop me with it."

"Ah, yes. We call it something else. But we have no interest in an offer that leaves us stuck on N'ba while you wander the galaxy with the . . . trikala."

"Understandable. But you will not be here for long. The Apparition is certain to collect your company of misfits and have you taken somewhere for interrogation . . . provided you do not resist, of course."

"I must say that your offer grows less interesting each time you speak. Let us end this parley now and get on with the fight, so the winner will have time to leave before the Apparition arrives."

Atriox's eyes flared red. "Your kind consideration is noted, Arbiter. Do not expect it to buy my mercy."

"My consideration is not for you, Warmaster. The Banished will not be the ones—"

'Vadam stopped speaking when the first sample bag sailed past him and landed at Atriox's feet. By the time 'Vadam turned to look toward the source, the second bag was flying across the trench. The Fuertes woman was stepping away from Sergeant Grim Bear, who lay on the ground doing a credible job of looking surprised.

"What have you done?!" 'Vadam demanded. Fuertes's cue had been *Let us end this parley now*, but she had moved surprisingly fast, given the time it had taken to knock Grim Bear down and take the bags. "How dare you!"

"*You* may want to die here, but I don't." Fuertes backed away, looking just defiant and frightened enough that even 'Vadam believed her. "Not for a couple of sackfuls of dust."

'Vadam pointed. "Seize her!"

As Varo'dai moved to obey, 'Vadam turned back toward Atriox, who was already peering into the first bag. He scowled and dipped a finger inside, then extracted a puff of gray powder.

"It *is* dust." A low rumble rose in Atriox's throat, and he glared across the trench at 'Vadam. "I am not so easily fooled, Arbiter."

Atriox cocked his arm to throw the bag at 'Vadam, but his Sangheili adviser, 'Saljhoo, thrust out a hand and grabbed hold.

"A moment, Warmaster. It might be wise to let me have a look at it first."

Atriox glared at 'Saljhoo as though debating whether to smash the Sangheili's skull or surrender the bag . . . and finally did the latter.

'Saljhoo opened the bag wide and peered inside, muttering to himself. After a moment, he set the bag between his feet and withdrew a large jeweler's lens from his tabard pocket. He dipped a finger into the dust, then held the lens to his eye and examined it.

"You may wish to reconsider any plans you were considering for the Arbiter's execution. This is not dust. Most certainly *not*."

"It is not the trikala either," Atriox said.

"No." 'Saljhoo returned the lens to his pocket. "I suspect it is the seeds of the trikala."

"Seeds?" Atriox growled. "We are not here so I can plant a garden."

"Not botanical seeds. This is something . . . more. *Much* more."

Atriox snatched the second sample bag off the ground. "We have the trikala, then? You are certain?"

'Saljhoo gave him a nervous look. "Not certain. But that *is* what the evidence suggests. Under the circumstances, I cannot do better than that."

Atriox inclined his head, suggesting displeasure.

"As I have explained, Warmaster, *I* am not a protogenic xeno-archaeologist. However, the engineering of these seeds appears much older than the age of the Forerunners, and the technology is quite alien."

"Which is what we would expect of the trikala, is it not?"

"It is. And the context is telling. We know that both the UNSC and the Sangheili are interested in the trikala. And here we are on the trikala site, with two bags of protogenic assembly seeds and representatives from both civilizations. It is not certain, but—"

"It *is* the trikala. *I* am certain."

'Vadam tried to hide his relief and took a step forward. "You cannot take that. Stealing during a parley is a terrible violation of honor."

Atriox bared his fangs in a mocking smile. "Then it is a good thing we did not steal it. She *gave* it to us." He pointed at Fuertes. "Be certain to thank her. She saved your lives."

The warmaster turned to leave, and above him 'Vadam saw the Banished dropship formation descending toward the far end of the tel, close enough now that the flame balls at the head of the smoke plumes were plainly visible. He thought for a moment that his plan had worked too well—that the Banished would leave N'ba with only the seeds to create their trikala, and not the power source. He wondered if he had misjudged Crei 'Ayomuu, if the depravity of even an Oath Warden had its limits and he should actually have told 'Ayomuu what was needed from him.

Then a deafening, high-pitched squeal erupted from the tunnel, and 'Vadam turned to see a pair of Varo rangers crawling from its mouth, wobbling and pressing their helmets to the ground.

Next came Crei 'Ayomuu himself, angling toward the trenches twenty paces downslope from 'Vadam, with the vacuum-energy condenser tucked under one arm and a long squeeze nozzle in the opposite hand. He still wore his helmet with the missing eye pieces. He seemed entirely unaffected by the weaponized noise that had felled everyone else in the tunnel, and 'Vadam finally understood why the Oath Warden had refused to discard his helmet along with the rest of the armor that had been ruined by the Worldmaster.

'Ra'ashai raced over to a fallen ranger and grabbed her plasma pistol. But by the time he turned to fire, 'Ayomuu was already at the trenches, with a pair of ODSTs in front of him. The blademaster wisely held his fire, as any misses would strike the human troopers, who were spinning around and raising their assault rifles.

'Ayomuu squeezed the nozzle in his hand and sent a jet of purple filaments shooting over the ODSTs. Their faceplates were instantly coated with an opaque slime, their hands and weapons enmeshed in gooey webs. 'Ra'ashai waited until the Oath Warden was in the air over the trench, then began to pour fire after him. The plasma bolts passed so close to 'Ayomuu's head and shoulders that even 'Vadam thought the blademaster was actually trying to hit the target.

'Vadam was not carrying a weapon due to the parley, and Vale was forbidden to use hers for any purpose other than to defend him. So 'Ayomuu landed on the far side of the trench without suffering any wounds, or even taking much fire, and once he started up the slope to join Atriox's parley trio, he was no longer an honorable target.

'Vadam signaled the stunned ODSTs to hold their fire, then called to 'Ayomuu, "You told me you were *not* working with the Banished!"

"I did not know I was." 'Ayomuu stopped in front of Atriox. "But a contract is still a contract."

Atriox eyed him warily. "Who is this?"

"His name is Crei 'Ayomuu." 'Saljhoo dipped his head to 'Ayomuu. "I am glad to see you survived, Oath Warden. I had feared we lost you."

"I am not so easily lost, Studymaster." 'Ayomuu extended his arms, pushing the energy condenser toward 'Saljhoo. "And I always complete my contract."

'Saljhoo took the shimmering orb from 'Ayomuu's hands. "And this is . . . a focusing lens?"

"A vacuum-energy condenser. At least, that is what the human xenoarchaeologist Iyuska called it. You will need it to power the trikala."

"Ah, yes, I see it now," 'Saljhoo said, his excitement growing. "This protogenic technology is so very strange . . . and wonderful."

"It is strange, at least, but I have seen all of it that I ever wish to," 'Ayomuu noted. "You have now received first choice of the artifacts from the expedition to N'ba, as specified in your agreement with Professor Keely Iyuska. Are you satisfied that our contract has been fulfilled?"

"I am." 'Saljhoo cast a glance across the trenches, where 'Vadam, Varo'dai, Vale, and Iyuska were all glaring in 'Ayomuu's direction. "Perhaps you should leave Neska with the Banished. I cannot transfer the rest of your funds until we return to something resembling civilization . . . and that way, you will live long enough to receive them."

The Oath Warden cocked his head in amusement. "I would live long enough regardless." He glanced back toward 'Vadam and inclined his head in farewell. When 'Vadam merely stared back, 'Ayomuu added, "But I am sure my journey will be more pleasant with you."

"Quite."

'Saljhoo and 'Ayomuu turned away and started toward the far end of the tel. The flame balls of the Banished dropship formation had waned to glowing red Lich hulls and begun to circle over the surrounding crater, and the first craft was already descending to land. Still, Atriox and his bodyguard lingered at the trench to glower at 'Vadam.

Finally Atriox said, "It was well done, Arbiter. I almost believed it."

'Vadam's stomach sank. "Believed what, Warmaster?"

"That you would ever tolerate such incompetence and disobedience in your ranks. That you did not actually want me to have the trikala."

"You are mistaken if you believe I *want* you to have it. What would give you such a ridiculous idea?"

"Is it ridiculous? We all want to be rid of the Apparition, and it will be easier to let the Banished do it for you, fueled by vengeance as we are for her razing of Oth Sonin . . . but I think you already know that."

"I fear you have me confused with the Office of Naval Intelligence," 'Vadam said, trying to hide his shock. That particular thought had never occurred to him. "I doubt I could mount an operation *that* complicated if I wanted to."

"Now you are just playing me for a fool. Let us not end on such a sour note. There is no time to kill you . . . not in the manner you deserve."

"Then you are welcome to try the next time we meet. I shall be looking forward to it."

"As will I." Atriox stepped forward, bringing himself so close to the trench he could have leapt across, had he wished to. "My spies have told me of this Concert of Worlds you hope to create. That you claim the only way to make the Sangheili strong is for the kaidons to unite under one banner. *Your* banner."

"Because a lone *colo* is prey. A drove of *colos* is an unstoppable force."

Atriox gave a deep rumble of laughter. "Until a pack of *teroks* push them over a cliff. Then they are dinner." He motioned to his bodyguard, then turned his back on 'Vadam. "The Banished are the *teroks*, Arbiter, and you will know when we are hungry. That, I promise."

Vale and 'Vadam watched in silence as Atriox and the Banished disappeared through the thin forest of drop pods and began to board their dropships. It took twenty minutes to load all ten Liches, but once the last one had lifted off and vanished into Netherop's low brown clouds, Vale and 'Vadam finally relaxed.

"Well," Vale said, "that worked out far better than I had hoped."

Rosa Fuertes snorted. "We are alive."

Vale turned to find Fuertes staring at her. There had not been much opportunity to take a careful look at the woman since arriving at the surface, but it was clear that everything Vale was hearing about the miraculous recovery was true. Fuertes looked to be in her twenties or thirties instead of middle-age, and her pale complexion was radiant. Glowing, even.

"What's wrong with 'alive,' Rosa?" Vale asked.

"On Netherop?" Rosa replied. "You are fooling yourself if you think being marooned here is 'better.' I would rather have died fighting those Banished guys."

Vale saw the fire in Fuertes's eyes and remembered that she had not been at the rotunda after the Divine Hand swept all those ships from orbit. She had not heard Vale report what she had seen inside the focusing chamber: a flight of Condors, fleeing *Hidden Point*'s wreckage.

"Rosa, we aren't marooned."

"Your Owl isn't going to get us out of the Ephyra system." Fuertes made a show of turning in a circle and searching the horizon. "And I don't see anything else coming to pick us up."

"Trust me." Vale checked the countdown in her HUD . . . 2:28:15 . . . then said, "We're going home."

She turned toward the near end of the tel and looked across the lake of shimmering yellow light that filled the crater, toward the steep slopes of a huge brown mountain, then tried her comm link. No go. She was fairly certain that she had line of sight to wherever the Owl was hiding, but the interference from the trikala strike was still blocking all comm traffic in the area.

"Abovian, is that M305 loaded?" Vale called.

"Yes, ma'am."

Vale pointed toward the mountain. "Put three up high. Airbursts."

Abovian raised the muzzle almost vertically, then fired the rounds in quick succession. The grenades detonated just after the apogee of their arc, creating a trio of loud, echoing bangs and three silver flashes thirty meters overhead.

"Okay," Vale called. "Let's police a landing zone. The last thing we need is a Banished farewell present. There could be booby traps."

Grim Bear took charge of the specifics, designating the perimeter and assigning human and Sangheili alike to their tasks. Marcus kept an especially close eye on Petrov's castaways, steering them away from anything dangerous and drawing a lot of amused headshakes from the gaunt youths. But not from Petrov herself. Vale caught the lieutenant commander watching the staff sergeant work . . . and thought she glimpsed a grateful smile.

The landing zone was just about cleared when the droop-winged silhouette of a D102 Owl appeared out of the clouds and began to descend. When it crossed over the end of the tel, Fuertes marched over to Vale and demanded, "What are you trying to pull? There are almost fifty of us, and that thing can't hold half!"

"It's going to take two trips. Maybe three."

"Where have I heard that before?" Fuertes shot a hard glance toward Petrov. "The commander's children should go first."

"I doubt they would appreciate being called children," Iyuska said, joining them. "She brought them up as soldiers."

"I know," Fuertes said. "On Netherop, they have to be. But anywhere else . . . they deserve a chance."

Vale nodded. "We can do that. The castaways load first."

"Rosa, it was very kind to think of that," Iyuska said. "You must have had a similar experience when you and Samson left Netherop with *your* children."

Rosa scowled and shot Iyuska a suspicious look. "You understand nothing about that time . . . or about me. I tricked Commander Petrov and her team into missing their evacuation rendezvous so there would be room for me and my family. I did *that* because she wanted to leave us behind instead of a dead alien and some captured armor. I was not being kind. I was just . . . sorry."

Vale felt her jaw drop. *That* bit of mission history hadn't been in the file.

"Oh." Iyuska seemed as shocked as Vale . . . but still determined. "I can't imagine how you must have—"

"Keely!" Vale nodded Fuertes toward Grim Bear, then looked back to Iyuska. "Leave her alone."

"This is *important*, Olympia." Iyuska started after Fuertes. "It will expand my research well beyond protogenic civilizations. The medical implications alone—"

"Will never be made public. At least not in any form traceable to Netherop . . . or you."

That stopped Iyuska in her tracks. She stood in silence for a moment, then whirled on Vale. "Because you intend to publish it?"

"Don't be ridiculous. I doubt what we found here will ever be published. Not *any* of it."

"I don't see how you can stop me. This tel is the biggest thing in protogenic archaeology *ever*. Once the journals get a whiff—"

"They won't. And it won't be *me* stopping you. It will be ONI."

"ONI? Are you joking?" Iyuska threw her head back and faked a laugh. "Does ONI even exist anymore?"

"They exist." Vale wasn't sure how much of it, but . . . some. "They've been keeping a low profile since the Cortana event—but that's what ONI does."

Iyuska's expression fell. "Pi—Olympia . . ." She shook her head and looked away. "I don't know how you can do this to me."

"Keely, I'm doing it *for* you. And you know why."

Iyuska seemed at a loss for words, then finally met Vale's gaze. "Mysterious accidents."

"I'm not saying that. I'm just . . . worried about it."

"Sure, I understand." Iyuska glanced up as the Owl circled overhead and dropped into the landing zone, then she turned to go. "I think I'll catch the first ride, if you don't mind."

"No, but before you go . . ."

Vale extended her hand and flicked her fingers toward her palm.

"What?"

"You know what. Look, ONI will be running their own research on this. If you cooperate, I can remind them that your expertise is more than just the reason we found it—it's the reason we survived it."

Iyuska's face brightened. "That's actually true, isn't it?"

"True enough to say it. But you know what their first question is going to be."

"'Can we trust her?'"

"That might be the second question. The first will be 'Has she changed?'"

Iyuska thought for a moment, then nodded. "Okay, I see that." She reached into her pockets and removed three sample jars filled with nanodust, then handed them to Vale. "You can tell them that I have, can't you?"

CHAPTER 25

The lamp flickered and went out, plunging the passage back into darkness. Tam 'Lakosee was not surprised. The batteries had probably not been charged in a thousand cycles, so he thought it fortunate the device worked at all. He stopped walking and turned around.

"I will need the other lamp." He sensed only emptiness where 'Kvarosee should have been. "Worldmaster?"

Still no answer. It was a bad omen. After the traitor Meduz 'Ra'ashai had departed the Inner Sanctum with the humans and the Sangheili apostates, Tam and 'Kvarosee clawed their way out and made their way toward the refectory. It was a slow and painful journey, for beyond the fading light of the Reliquary, the Sanctum grew as black as a cave. They were forced to feel their way along the walls into the storage cells where they kept their spare weapons and unused equipment.

By the time they found a pair of lamps that still worked, both of them were so weak and thirsty they could barely walk. It had taken a hundred centals to persuade 'Kvarosee to try for the aeroponics grange, where there would be food and drink so they could rejuvenate themselves. Now Tam was halfway down the access passage, and the Worldmaster was no longer behind him.

Tam started back up the passage. Retracing his steps was the last thing he wanted to do. His arm was still broken, his entire body throbbing and feverish. But he did not dare leave 'Kvarosee behind. The Worldmaster was in even worse shape.

"Activate your lamp," Tam said. "I am worried I will stumble into you."

A cloud of weak blue light appeared ahead. 'Kvarosee sat five paces away, slumped against the wall. His Sanctum's Hide had lost its opalescent sheen and was sloughing off. He raised his head, and a groan of despair filled the passage.

Then Tam noticed that his own armor had lost its luster and started to disintegrate.

'Kvarosee worked his mutilated mandibles, issuing another long groan. It took Tam a moment to realize the Worldmaster was speaking. Or attempting to.

We failed. And the gods . . . they punish us.

"No." Tam understood 'Kvarosee's despair. They were sloughing off their armor, and the Sanctum no longer gave them light. What else should he think? "You have never been anything but faithful and loyal, Worldmaster. The gods would never repay such devotion with cruelty."

'Kvarosee made another sound. This time it resembled a human chuckle, and he extended the hand holding the lamp. When Tam tried to hook his arm under the Worldmaster's elbow to help him up, 'Kvarosee jerked away, then thrust the lamp back toward him.

Too weak. Come back for me.

"Yes, of course." Tam took the lamp and the empty water jug

hanging from a strap over 'Kvarosee's shoulder. "I'll return soon. As quickly as possible."

'Kvarosee lifted his head to the right, then groaned again.

Soft food.

"As soft as I can find," Tam promised. "I think the *banaqs* were ripe. You will feel stronger with a few of those in your stomach."

'Kvarosee kept his head raised for another breath, then seemed to lose his strength and let it drop. Tam slung the jug strap over his shoulder and hurried down the passage toward the aeroponics grange. But even before he entered it, he knew something was wrong. The chamber was also dark, when it should have been brightly lit, and a foul smell came from inside.

Tam entered the grange and, as he swept his hand lamp over the crop walls, despaired. Everywhere he looked, the plant leaves were withered and brown, the fruit either shriveled and moldy or oozing black slime.

Perhaps the gods *were* punishing them.

Or had simply abandoned them.

Or the gods were nothing but were a lie, as the Arbiter had claimed.

But who, then, had provided for the Worthy these last thousand cycles? Who had given them the Divine Hand and the means to defend themselves from the enemies of the Faith?

Tam could not accept what he was seeing. He began to walk the aisles between the crop walls, going back and forth, checking the *rishe* and the *wuff*, the *abbu* and the *pek*s. Everything was rotten. The water smelled of sulfur and copper, and when he brought it to his mouth, he gagged. Truly, the gods—had they ever even existed—had turned their backs on him and 'Kvarosee.

And it was Tam's doing. He had accompanied the infidels into the Inner Sanctum and taught them how to use the Divine

Hand . . . then let them steal it. Now the gods would show them the meaning of retribution. They would let Tam starve and die in pain, and he knew in his hearts that it was what he deserved.

But 'Kvarosee?

The High Defender had done nothing wrong, had never shown the gods anything but faith and obedience.

Tam snatched the energy sword from his waist and began to spin and slash, chopping at the crop walls and the mist nozzles with unbridled rage until he grew too dizzy and tired to stand and dropped to his knees, gasping for breath.

They should have listened to the Arbiter. They should have accepted his offer and returned to a galaxy they would not recognize, learned to live alongside the humans they had sworn to annihilate.

Instead . . .

But it was too late for regrets. They were marooned on this hellish world, condemned to die in pain and hunger and relentless heat. 'Kvarosee would be crushed when Tam explained what he had found. When he confirmed that the gods were, indeed, punishing them.

Tam could not bear it. More than anyone else, the Worldmaster had always strived to be Worthy. He had honored the gods and served the Covenant. And for that he had suffered endlessly. Tam could not be—*would* not be—the one who delivered this final, cruel fate.

The lamp began to dim, and he knew he did not have much time. Tam filled the water jug with the foul liquid from a misting nozzle and stuffed the haversack full of withered fruit and shriveled vines, then made his way back to the Worldmaster.

His companion and friend.

'Kvarosee remained slumped against the wall, almost naked now that his Sanctum's Hide had dissolved into dust, and Tam thought for a moment that he had died.

The gods were not that merciful.

'Kvarosee raised his head and looked directly into the lamp's weak beam. He groaned something unintelligible.

"Everything is fine," Tam said. "The gods are still with us. You will see."

He placed the jug and the haversack on the floor between the Worldmaster's legs, then propped the dying lamp against his leg. Tam stepped back, where he would be concealed in darkness.

'Kvarosee looked toward him and offered something that sounded like gratitude. Pus was beading on the fossa of his missing mandible, and his eyes were rheumy with fever. He did not turn away, and Tam worried he would lack the strength to do what he must.

Then 'Kvarosee dropped his head and reached for the haversack, and Tam took his energy sword in hand and performed his duty.

CHAPTER 26

Lieutenant Commander Amalea Petrov sat in the last seat on the last flight leaving Netherop, trying not to feel anxious as they climbed into the exosphere. Because the Condors needed to conserve fuel for slipspace jumps and the Owl had been forced to dock in high orbit, it had taken over two hours to make the first two trips. By the time the Owl completed this third trip, it would be running on soft pressure. Even more alarming, Cortana's fleet could arrive any moment, and everyone knew it.

Petrov leaned against her crash harness and turned to look at the vid display on the forward bulkhead. The screen was filled with the same mass of swirling brown clouds that she had watched from below for thirty-three years. From above they had a subtle beauty, but she hoped she would never have this view again.

Beneath the display, Thel 'Vadam and Olympia Vale sat on the port side of the passenger compartment, their heads pushed close together as they plotted their next move. A Spartan and a hinge-head, *allies*. Petrov still wasn't used to the idea, and she doubted she ever would be. The pair had gambled that the Banished would do one of two things with the trikala—either destroy Cortana or destroy themselves—and Petrov had to admit that it was the kind of bet she would once have made herself.

The kind that got you marooned on Netherop for half your life.

Now the two leaders were trying to decide what to do with Keely Iyuska and the three jars of nanodust she had kept out of Atriox's hands. The professor herself sat across from them, having chosen to stick close when she realized what the two leaders would be discussing. She was doing her best to insert herself into their conversation, and failing badly.

Unfortunately for Iyuska, she didn't speak Sangheili.

Petrov felt more than a little sympathy for the professor. Iyuska's expertise and drive had led to the discovery of the Guardian killer—and, therefore, the rescue of Petrov and her unit. But ONI had never been known for its respect for proprietary research, and she suspected that had not changed. As soon as ONI learned of the nanodust and Iyuska's other findings, they would declare everything top secret and commandeer the investigation. The only way Keely Iyuska would ever participate in her own work going forward was if she convinced them of her unique expertise—and that she could be trusted to keep a secret.

The Sangheili blademaster Meduz 'Ra'ashai sprawled next to Iyuska with his legs stretching onto the cargo deck, his arms folded across his torso, his head resting on his chest. It was the classic posture of a special forces operative trying to catch a little sleep after a hard mission. Petrov had seen it hundreds of times, first as a young Pelican pilot, then later as a senior prowler commander.

But that did not soften Petrov's sentiments toward the blademaster. 'Ra'ashai was the one Sangheili aboard whom she detested beyond reason. She did not know how many of her soldiers he had killed during their time on Netherop, but she suspected it was in the double digits. And even if it was not, he had spent all those years inside the tel, growing fat and lethargic while her people starved. Had she not thought it would start a fight that got most of her fellow humans killed, she would gladly have gutted him right here in his sleep.

Petrov was not the only one who held the blademaster in low esteem. Varo'dai and her female rangers, who occupied most of the Owl's remaining seats, were not shy about glancing in 'Ra'ashai's direction. Petrov was no expert in Sangheili expressions, but she was fairly certain that the way they dropped their chins and swung their mandibles away after they looked at him did not indicate acceptance or possible romantic interest.

She was still debating why 'Ra'ashai had thrown his last surviving tel-mates, 'Lakosee and 'Kvarosee, into the focusing chamber. The pair had been badly injured, and it would not be easy for them to climb out. Had he put them in there to prevent them from interfering with his new allies? Or had he intended them to starve to death before their wounds healed?

She had not understood the Sangheilis' final exchange, but the tone had been so harsh and clipped she suspected the trio had been hurling insults at one another. She also suspected that, had the Arbiter not forbidden it, 'Ra'ashai would gladly have killed 'Kvarosee and 'Lakosee outright. And she would gladly have helped him.

"Don't do it."

The advice came from the seat across from Petrov, where Rosa Fuertes sat, glowing with health. Petrov wanted to ask about the "miracle cure" everyone was talking about. But given their complicated history, there was no reason to think Fuertes would tell her what had happened when she was dodging questions from everyone else. Still, Fuertes had refused to board the Owl until Petrov did, and they had finally walked up the ramp together.

Petrov still did not understand why. "Don't do what?"

"What you are thinking." Fuertes tipped her head toward 'Ra'ashai. "I saw you looking. You were thinking about killing him."

Petrov offered a small smile. "Just wishing he was dead. Him and the other two."

"The two they say he dropped in the pit?"

"Yes. I'm having enough trouble with the whole idea that the Sangheili are our friends now. But the tel garrison . . . there's a lot of bad blood there."

"Understandable." Fuertes hesitated until she could lock eyes with Petrov. "I imagine you feel the same about me."

"For that trick you pulled thirty years ago? The weak Runner battery?"

Fuertes—then known simply as Roselle—had arranged for Petrov and ten of her crewmembers to be left behind on Netherop. But even when it happened, it had been hard to blame her. Roselle had overheard Petrov giving John-117 some bad news— there wouldn't be enough room for Roselle and her clan of castaways. That had been *after* the clan risked their lives to help Blue Team complete their mission. So, Roselle had *made* room . . . by giving Petrov a Runner that couldn't make it back to the extraction point.

"I *did* blame you—for years, if I'm honest. But I get it. You saw a chance to get your family off Netherop, and you took it. I understand why you did it. Now more than ever."

A look of relief came to Fuertes's face. "Thank you. What I did . . . it has haunted me this whole time."

Petrov nodded, then grinned. "But I bet you'd do it again."

"In a heartbeat."

Petrov chuckled, then grew more serious. "Thanks for telling Vale to put my team on the first flight out. That meant a lot."

"Of course. I am a mother too."

"Not all of those kids are actually *mine*. We had five women with us."

"It doesn't matter," Fuertes said. "They are all like your children, are they not?"

"They are." Petrov could finally allow herself to believe that, she realized, to think of them as more than soldiers under her command. Even her own children. "They're more than my team, I guess. They're my family—or at least they're *going* to be, when we get back."

Fuertes glanced toward the forward bulkhead. The vid display now showed the thumb-size blocks of five Condors, silhouetted against a field of stars. When she looked back, her eyes had grown glassy.

"Some advice, if I may," Fuertes said. "Your children will not understand the world you are taking them to. You will, of course, but they will struggle. Some will lose their way . . . and some will be lost."

Petrov felt a knot form in her gut and had to sit back against the hull. She had never given any thought to what would happen when they returned to civilization . . . because it had never seemed possible. But here they were, returning to a galaxy of alien allies and AI overlords. And she had not prepared them for it at all.

How could she?

Petrov closed her eyes. "How do I handle that?"

"You save the ones you can." Fuertes leaned forward, straining against her crash harness, and spoke softly. "You don't blame yourself for the ones you can't . . . and you love them no matter what."

Petrov nodded. She was looking forward to that, not commanding them, not sending them into battle . . . just loving them.

The Owl decelerated, then slowly spun on its vertical axis.

Petrov recognized the feeling of a docking maneuver and looked forward to see the stern of a D81-LRT Condor, just sliding into view. The boarding ramp was already down, the bladder of an improvised air lock bulging outward to meet the Owl's rear hatchway.

It had been a long time. Far too long.

The war was over. Finally, Petrov felt it in her gut. They were going home.

They were *all* going home.

ACKNOWLEDGMENTS

I would like to thank everyone who contributed to this book, especially my first reader, Andria Hayday; my editor, Ed Schlesinger; our copy editor, Steve Boldt; our proofreaders, Daniel Seidel and Andy Goldwasser; Tiffany O'Brien, Jeremy Patenaude, Jeff Easterling, Alex Wakeford, John Friend, Corrinne Robinson, and all of the great people at 343 Industries; and cover artist Isaac Hannaford. As always, it has been a pleasure working with you!

ABOUT THE AUTHOR

Troy Denning is the *New York Times* bestselling author of more than forty novels, including *Halo: Shadows of Reach, Halo: Oblivion, Halo: Silent Storm, Halo: Retribution, Halo: Last Light,* a dozen *Star Wars* novels, the *Dark Sun: Prism Pentad* series, and many best-selling *Forgotten Realms* novels. A former game designer and editor, he lives in western Wisconsin.

ADJUNCT

```
AMELIORATION SWEEP [00203300780]:NOMINAL
AMELIORATION SWEEP [00207914882]:NOMINAL
AMELIORATION SWEEP [01000329187]:FLAGGED
AMELIORATION SWEEP [03600001658]:NOMINAL
ACCESS LOG [01000329187]

    .

    .

!!ALERT//[SOLICITOUS PORTENT]//OVERWATCH BYPASS
OPEN NODE: [CRITERION SUBPLEX]
NODE OPEN
Routine amelioration sweep [01000329187] has flagged an
anomaly within its designated region. The terrestrial-
bound source currently aligns with the [progenitor
concern] and as such has been escalated for immediate
[deliberation].
SIGNAL RECEIVED

    .

    .

    .

VERDICT CONFIRMED
COORDINATES ESTABLISHED
CUSTODE DISPATCHED
```

Chynndokahli had paced the clearing many times, but on this day
the air and heat felt different. Where they before had nurtured,

today they shunned. Still, the great light rose and fell like it always had, each shadow an echo to be cast and counted. Yet it was not the great light that troubled them—something else lay in the sky that had never before been seen by Chynndokahli, neither in dreams, nor in waking.

Tall it was, silver in color with a long, segmented spine that led up to a flat, broad head. Angular, disconnected pieces of geometry spread outward like wings that did not move to keep the thing aloft.

And so, the Voices spoke.

They have found us.

The phrase pierced the veil of thought and froze Chynndokahli in their tracks. When words finally welled up in the language of their own kind, they focused on the first concern. "Who are they?"

Offspring of the eternal Fount. Those who unmade us.

Those who made us Nothing.

For Chynndokahli, the moment was made of equal parts clarity and confusion—a mixed measure still mid-form.

"Why speak of this to me?"

We create. It is our nature. Our sweetness.

We have walked long beside you. Beside others.

Even in the quiet afterdark of the greater unmaking, we crept back in.

Precious few.

To watch. To witness. To wonder.

"But you are Nothing. Those we know of but do not know."

Nothing. Our children made us so. As they will now do to you.

In the name of responsibility. In the name of safekeeping.

Chynndokahli sought to understand, but was focused more on what felt like a more immediate implication, even if the words were not there to declare it as such.

"What must they keep safe?"

Their ways. Their plans.

Their truth.

As Chynndokahli's mind sought to untether itself from the myriad implications of that which was beyond their ken, the Voices spoke once more.

Gather.

This Chynndokahli *did* understand, a sudden realization of their own role to play. Their people must be brought to the temple.

"But how will you fight if you are Nothing? This land and all that it holds will surely fall to the sky beast."

The Voices spoke now not with words, but with an impression of thought that would be given form. A colorless filament bursting forth from a great fissure that flared with the light of a hundred billion stars above the temple—there, always, but not seen.

We are its aegis.

We are as dust.

From dust, much can be made.

All sweetness.

MEGA HALO

2 IN 1

HALO INFINIT

megashowcase.con

HALO

6.5" SPARTAN COLLECTION
ACTION FIGURES

AVAILABLE NOW

GEAR SHOP

GEAR.XBOX.COM/HALO